Books l

STAR FORCE SERIES
Swarm
Extinction
Rebellion
Conquest
Battle Station

IMPERIUM SERIES
Mech Zero: The Dominant
Mech 1: The Parent
Mech 2: The Savant
Mech 3: The Empress

Other Books by B. V. Larson
Technomancer
Velocity
Shifting

Visit BVLarson.com for more information.

CONQUEST

(Star Force Series #4)

by

B. V. Larson

STAR FORCE SERIES
Swarm
Extinction
Rebellion
Conquest
Battle Station

Copyright © 2011 by the author.

ISBN-13: 978-1477614983
ISBN-10: 1477614982
BISAC: Fiction / Science Fiction / Adventure

I woke up around midday under a flapping tarp. I was in a lean-to, something Sandra and I had put together on the southern shore of Andros Island. The tarp was orange vinyl, and one hundred percent free of nanites. Sandra had insisted we leave all alien technology behind. I found our shelter's ruffling sounds, caused by the endless ocean winds, to be peaceful rather than annoying.

Groaning aloud, I raised myself onto one elbow. Blearily, I surveyed the white sandy beach and the clear blue waters of the Caribbean beyond. Sandra and I had chosen this secluded spot for our brief vacation in part because none of the laser turrets that ringed the island were visible from here. You had to walk out into the surf and look east or west to see them. I had tried it and inevitably, they'd spotted me almost as quickly as I had spotted them. The nearest turrets were around a thousand yards away, but they'd swung around and studied me intently. Was I harmless, or an enemy to be burned down without compunction? It was an odd feeling to be judged by your own software. Each time they allowed me to live another day I was left aware of that moment of indecision in their alien minds.

Today was a sad day, as it was the end of our brief three-day vacation on the beach. I had stolen this time as it was. We marines had come home to Earth at last, but we were far from safe. If anything, our doom could be seen with perfect clarity as it advanced upon us.

I had spent six days in the hospital after we'd returned to Earth. For six long days my internal nanites had itched and tickled inside my body, repairing my bones, skin, organs and tissues. I'd spent those days worrying. I now understood how doomed men of the past must have felt while they awaited the inexorable approach of their final defeats.

Napoleon during his last three days at Waterloo, King Leonidas at Thermopylae...Hitler, squatting in his bunker—which one was I? Was I playing the part of the hero making his last stand, or the delusional villain on the verge of taking down all he had ever held dear with him? I wasn't entirely sure.

I hadn't started the original war with the Macros, no matter what the less flattering commentators said. The most insulting of the fake online vids showed me shaking hands with hundred foot tall metal monsters before they demolished buildings full of screaming kindergarteners. I wondered at the amount of effort these video pranksters had gone to in order to cast me as a demon in battle armor. I wanted to give them each a beam rifle, a gallon of silver nanites and a pet Macro of their own to play with. Let them try to make peace with the machines while I complained about their choices.

The vids angered me because I *hadn't* started the war—but I most certainly had rekindled it, that I could not deny. The criticism that hurts the worst should always be listened to, I told myself, because it was closest to the truth.

I'd left the hospital a week before any doctor approved the decision. Six days I'd lain there, reading budget reports and talking to people who were nervous in my presence. It was as if they thought they might catch something deceptively deadly. I was sick of my sick-bed and tired of my visitors. The parade seemed infinite: celebrity well-wishers who turned a simple handshake into an interview. Politicians who came for private meetings, but brought cameramen in tow. Military people wanting to debrief me until my brain felt drained of useful thought. I knew I had to get moving again, so I did.

Every day since I'd left the hospital had been something like today. First I'd shaken myself awake, causing a wave of fresh pain in my healing ribs. Then I'd sucked in that pain, reveling in it. How many times had I told my marines that pain was a good thing? As long as you felt it, you had unassailable proof that you were still alive.

Sandra had led me down here, to this vacation spot, soon after I'd marched out of the hospital. Today, when she returned from combing the beach for interesting shells, she met me at the lean-to. We kissed and smiled at one another.

"It's over," I said. "We have to go back."

"Yes, I feel it too," she said. "We've been here too long. I'm not able to enjoy it any longer. I can't stop thinking about what's going on back at the base."

Without any argument, we packed a waiting crawler vehicle and drove it northward through the crashing waves, back to Fort Pierre and Star Force headquarters.

As we drove over wet sand with waves licking at our tires, I kept thinking about the Macros, wondering if I should have done something differently. What was done was done, I told myself sternly. If I'd started a new war, then it was time to win it, not cry about it. Now was not the time to dwell on the mistakes of the past, but instead to press onward. I had to fix what I could and cheat to cover the rest until things went my way.

Sandra and I held hands, but we hardly spoke on the journey back to base. We were both lost in our own thoughts. As we drew closer to home, our thoughts and expressions became grimmer.

We reached the base without incident. Before I entered the gates, however, I contacted Major Barrera and First Sergeant Kwon. Sandra already knew my plans. No one argued with me. They all knew what had to be done.

I reflected as I crossed the base to Fleet's grandiose new headquarters building that I'd built Star Force almost from the sand up. In many ways, the entirety of Andros Island bore the mark of my hand. Strung along every beach was an army of robotic turrets, aiming their laser projectors at every passerby. When I was on base, I could see them beyond the concrete walls, tracking every gull, swimmer and passing aircraft. They classified, identified and passed judgment upon everything that crept within their range. I watched a company of my marines exercise between two of them, oblivious to the fact the turrets watched them and contemplated an instant incineration for any man who might trip a neural chain and become designated as hostile. How trusting they were of my software.

Crow had left his stamp upon this organization and this land as well. He'd done very little Nano design work, and he rarely worked on new weapons systems to combat the Macros. But he had lovingly shaped his own sprawling quarters and his office was reportedly huge. I had yet to set foot inside his new building since my return. The visit was long overdue.

I walked into Fleet headquarters at one p. m. on a Thursday afternoon. In my hand, I had a folder stuffed with budget reports. I didn't like what was printed on that blizzard of paper.

Mysteriously, Fleet's building had grown to be four stories tall in my absence. It was the largest building on base now, except for the hospital itself. The place hummed with staffers. Most of the staffers were clerks working on computers in their cubicles. I walked through rows of them, keeping my expression as blank as possible, but I imagined I was scowling somewhat. It was hard not to. Crow had stinted himself nothing. I could only imagine the bloated budget he rode herd upon, sucked out of every nation on Earth.

Crow held court in a palatial office on the fourth floor. There was plenty of room left over up there for his army of clerks. I noted as I walked down the center aisle that the clerks on the fourth floor were *different*. They were almost all female. Most of the women were startlingly attractive, and the majority were Asians.

There were guards here and there, armed with normal rifles rather than beamers. That was a new base regulation Crow had instituted, beamers were forbidden while in the presence of civilians who had no protection against blindness and radiation. I didn't approve of the rule, as regular ballistic weaponry wasn't particularly effective against Macros—or even our own marines.

I could tell right off these base troops were poorly disciplined. They hadn't been trained as shock-troops by veterans like First Sergeant Kwon. Most sat with their butts on the corner of a desk and relentlessly flirted with the half-interested clerks. The rest smoked near the windows while tapping at their smartphones.

By the time I reached Crow's door, I had been confronted by a half-dozen panicked staffers. There were a thousand reasons I

4

couldn't take another step. I ignored them all. I'd long ago learned that the key to bypassing bureaucrats was to maintain momentum and never stop walking. Eventually, these fluttering minions gave up on stalling me and switched to whispering warnings into their phones instead.

I reached for Crow's office door, which was a good twelve feet tall and built of fine island mahogany. The golden latches twisted before I could touch them, and the stately doors swung open to reveal a sumptuous interior. There was orange carpet underfoot, thick and soft. Fan blades shaped like palm fronds spun overhead. A massive desk built of rosewood filled the center of the room.

There, standing in the middle of it all, was Crow himself. His blue eyes were open wide, as were his grinning lips. He had a sunburn and his reddened face made the whiteness of his big square teeth all the more noticeable.

"Come on in, Colonel!" he greeted me, waving me forward with a sweep of his arm. "I hadn't expected you would be done with your holiday so soon, but I'm glad you're back."

I nodded, accepting his lie, and walked into the office. A few women with long dark hair and navy-blue business skirts swarmed quietly at the threshold behind me. Their eyes darted and they whispered to one another in hushed excitement. Crow shooed them back and closed the massive doors in their faces.

I stood with my hands on my hips, admiring his office. "Nice flat you've got yourself here, Jack," I said.

His face puckered just for a second, then smoothed back into a smile. I knew he didn't like it when I ignored his title of Admiral, but I didn't care.

"Glad you could drop by. You should build yourself a better building. I know a few architects. Everyone swears they're the best in the hemisphere."

"I noticed," I said, "and that brings me to the reason I've come."

I tossed a sheath of paper on his huge desk. The desk was so big the folder looked like a snowflake on a football field.

Crow picked through the printouts, frowning at them. "Spreadsheets?"

"Yes, budgets. Fleet is sucking up all the accounts. I don't know how that got started, but it's going to stop today."

Crow worked his mouth for a second, but nothing came out. Then he got his bearings again. I figured he was out of practice at the art of dealing with me. For months, everyone around here had been his frightened yes-man.

"I'll see what I can do about that, Kyle," he said. "I'm sure we can come to some arrangement. Possibly, a bump up is in order for the Marines. Your side of the house took a beating out there. You'll need to rebuild."

I nodded slowly, staring at him. He bent over the papers, took out a pencil and made some adjustments. The pencil scratched briefly.

"Yes…I'll cancel the officer's private stadium. That's a morale-building project, you know. Plenty of my mates will be disappointed, but we have to keep our priorities in order."

I shook my head slowly. "Fifty-fifty," I said.

He blinked at me, and cocked his head to one side. "I don't quite follow you there—"

"Oh yeah, you do. Fleet gets half of all incoming funds and the Marines get the other half. That's it. End of story."

Crow flashed then, as I knew he would eventually. The man had a temper, and I was surprised he'd managed to keep it under wraps for this long.

He sprang at me. It was sudden, almost thoughtless. His eyes were bulging in his head like boiled eggs. He didn't punch me, he extended a single finger and poked me with it. My chest muscles tightened, but that only made my ribs hurt more. I whipped up my hand, grabbed his wrist and twisted. He went down on his face.

He bounced back up. I stood there, staring at him. My eyes were slits and my mouth was a tight line. His nose was bleeding, probably from hitting that gaudy orange carpet with excessive force. I was bleeding too, from the hole his finger had punched into my chest muscles.

I crossed my arms. He took a deep breath and crossed his. He laughed suddenly.

"Same old shit between us," he said. "Two alpha dogs, only one pack."

"Right," I said, "but you're all done humping my leg."

Crow nodded. "Okay mate. You win. Seventy-thirty. I'll write it up today. There will be a lot of damage, a lot of good projects cancelled, but Fleet will survive."

"Fifty-fifty or we go for it right here," I said.

He took a step toward me and I thought he was going to punch me this time. I wasn't really in good enough shape for a brawl. My bones weren't completely reattached in places. But I was ready for it anyway.

Crow stopped with his bloody nose no more than six inches from mine. "You've got the biggest pair, mate. You know I've always admired that about you. But do you know where you are, my man? Do you know how many armed men I have in this building?"

Crow was escalating. I blinked in mild surprise. I hadn't been sure he'd go so far, not over a few percentage points on a budget. Maybe he thought this conflict between the two of us had been inevitable. I'd come to that conclusion myself, while laying in my hospital bed reading reports for days. Maybe he'd figured out he might as well go for broke right now, and determine who was going to run Star Force once and for all. He'd probably enjoyed ruling Andros single-handedly while I was gone. It was natural enough for a man like him.

"You just blinked, Kyle," Crow said, his mouth twitching. "Yeah, I saw it. You've overplayed your hand by coming here."

Over the years, I'd come to understand Crow's behavior patterns. The man was quite predictable. When he saw weakness, he lunged. When he saw strength, he pulled back and bided his time. It was time to show him strength.

I pointed calmly to his desk. "You've got security systems in this mahogany aircraft carrier of yours, don't you?"

"You bet I do."

"Use them. Check your cameras."

He walked around his desk warily, keeping his eye on me. We could both move very quickly with our nanite-enhanced bodies. In less than a second of distraction, either of us might be able to launch a preemptive strike against the other.

Crow tapped his desk, and the top of it lit up. I was impressed. I'd been fooled into thinking it was real mahogany, but the surface was essentially only a wood-grain screen-saver. A dozen views from every floor flashed up on the desk. I understood instantly why the desk was so big. It was actually his observation system.

Crow sucked his teeth. He didn't say anything for a moment. I glanced at the scenes displayed in a score of boxes on his desk. In most of them, one of my marines in combat gear stood in front of one of his lackadaisical guards. My men were wearing battle armor and goggles. They had beamers pressed up against the throats of his men, who hadn't bothered to fire a shot. There was no point in using bullets on my marines. It would only piss them off and possibly result in death for the shooter. A few of my boys waved at the camera pick-ups that were placed all over the building.

I pulled out my com-link. Sandra answered immediately.

"You need me inside?" she said.

"Come on in, but take it easy," I said.

Sandra had never been good at taking it easy. The roof above us tore itself apart. An explosion of white plaster dust, insulation and wires fell into the office. Fortunately, only sheetrock and a single rafter fell, and they didn't land on Crow's desk. It would have been a shame to ruin it.

Sandra was a strange combination of chief bodyguard and girlfriend. She'd been altered more than anyone else under my command. She had not only been nanotized, but upgraded by an intelligent race of microbiotic creatures as well. Unfortunately, the microbiotics had all died tragically. Otherwise, I might have been able to upgrade all my marines in a similar fashion.

She sprang out of the dusty mess and moved in a blur. An instant later she stood atop the desk. She had both her arms operating again, but I could tell the right one was still healing. After all, she'd had it torn off less than a month ago.

She carried twin knives in her hands instead of guns. Two combat knives with molecularly-aligned, carbon blades. She'd used the blades to claw her way through the ceiling. A shaft of sunlight came beaming down through the haze of plaster dust, turning the floating motes golden.

"Is today the day?" Sandra asked, staring at Crow as one might stare at a turkey in need of carving.

"I'm not sure," I said. I turned to Crow and raised my eyebrows expectantly.

8

Crow's eyes were bigger than usual. I waited for him to speak. He eyed me, then Sandra. Lastly, he eyed the helpless guards depicted all over his desktop.

"Fifty-Fifty," he said quietly.

"The Marines need a new headquarters," I said. "Now."

Crow's cheek twitched a fraction. "Take this building. I'll build a new center for Fleet."

Just like that, Crow had reversed himself. He had seen strength, and in the face of it, he'd backed off to bide his time. I knew this new truce wouldn't last forever, but with luck, it wouldn't have to.

"You drive a hard bargain Admiral," I said, "but I accept your terms."

2

Major Barrera was among the first of my staff to move into the new building. A swarthy, barrel-chested man with a mean look to him, he'd been my exec on Andros Island ever since we'd declared our independence from the governments of Earth. He was quiet, efficient and loyal—the polar opposite of Crow.

Barrera carried a box under each arm and wore a grin on his face. I ushered him to one of the prime corner offices on the top floor. He couldn't wait to move in. I'd seen the tin-roofed shack Crow had assigned him to previously, and I couldn't blame him for being happy about the upgrade.

"Good to have you back, sir," he said.

I nodded. "Good to be here, Major. Call a mandatory staff meeting for noon today in my office."

"Yes, sir," he said, putting the boxes down on his desk. He immediately left to work on the task I'd assigned him. His new office could wait until the job was done.

I nodded to myself, looking after him as he stabbed fingers at his com link. Classic Barrera. He hadn't asked what the meeting was about. He hadn't insisted on an agenda he could email around or post on some automated scheduler. He just took the order and ran with it. I knew he'd find everyone who wasn't available via their com-link and hassle them in person. Once again, I considered raising his rank. But then I would probably have to raise mine as well. Giving myself promotions always felt weird, so I'd avoided it for a long time now. I'd look into it later.

It was a shame to send Crow's attractive clerical people packing, but I only had enough actual work for a few of them. When I looked into what they'd been doing for him, most had spent their time buying stuff. They were titled: *purchasing agents.* They worked tirelessly online and over the phone to get rare items shipped to Andros Island. At first, there had been some reluctance to send so many specialized goods and services down to a half-deserted island in the Caribbean, but word soon got around that we were loaded with government funding. Our accounts were always paid on time, so the merchants of the world stepped up to make the deliveries happen.

It was jaw-dropping, the things Crow had been ordering on a daily basis. Sure, many of the budget items were understandable. Our Nano tech factories could duplicate almost anything, but required a lot of rare earths as raw materials to do it. Palladium, promethium and neodymium were used in the construction of our fusion generators. Holmium and erbium were required for our lasers. We needed shocking quantities of these unusual minerals, and as the market tightened up the prices had skyrocketed.

It was the luxury items that I objected to. Crow had ordered a slew of personal compression chambers, for instance. These egg-like machines reportedly used something called hyperbaric medicine to improve circulation. Ensconced inside, a user could read or listen to soft music during half-hour treatments. A legitimate use for these systems was decompression therapy for our troops injured in space. Many had suffered a loss of vacc suit pressure during our last battle with the Macros and had required atmospheric and oxygen regularity afterward to prevent embolisms. What I objected to was Crow's purchase of three hundred and eighty of these units at a cost of nearly half a million dollars apiece. When I questioned the purchasing agent in charge, she'd explained the systems had side benefits beyond basic medical purposes. Supposedly, they were capable of providing holistic health treatments, filling users with a sense of inner peace.

I stared at the purchasing agent, a woman named Ping. She blinked rapidly and attempted a shy smile, which I did not return. She was particularly young and freshly-hired. She was also younger and more attractive than the average—even among Crow's best. Her hair was perfectly coifed and she wore a business

11

suit that didn't show a single crease. Her black hair was as long and straight as her skirt was short. Crow had apparently insisted on a dress code.

"Do you think this is a valid expense?" I asked, keeping my voice neutral.

Ping stared at me, trying to ascertain what the correct answer was. I retained my poker face, not giving her a clue. At last, she tried to answer.

"No, sir," she said. "It's a waste of money."

I nodded slowly. Most of them had defended their work. Maybe word was getting around. No matter how pretty they were, every bureaucrat who told me buys like this were a good idea had been immediately escorted down the backstairs of the building and put on a ship to the mainland.

"Good answer," I said. "I don't want marines who are filled with inner peace. I want killers. Return to your desk and start returning these damned bullshit health-machines."

"Should I return them all, Colonel?"

"Keep five," I said, "for the hospital."

As I watched Ping leave, I wondered if I was being too hard on the girls. I told myself I probably wasn't being hard enough. I should have fired them all. Sandra certainly would have preferred it that way. She'd wandered by my office door on occasion as she prowled the building. I knew every time another female underling walked into my office it annoyed her, she'd always been the jealous type. But the steady stream of firings had kept her mollified thus far. Not even Sandra could accuse me of flirting after watching a parade of unhappy women exit the building.

First Sergeant Kwon walked in on me before I could bring in the next terrified clerk. Kwon had been with me for years through many campaigns. I'd found him reliable, if unimaginative. He was a huge man of Korean descent. Wearing full combat gear and full of nanites, I calculated he had to weigh nearly a ton, but I'd never asked him to step on a scale. I could tell Crow's office had quality flooring when it didn't creak under Kwon's heavy tread.

Kwon walked up to my debris-strewn desk and looked around at the destruction. He didn't ask any questions and he didn't look surprised. It took a lot to surprise one of my veterans.

"Colonel," he said, "Crow's guard unit has left the building. Fleet has not made any aggressive moves against us."

"No complaints from them at all?"

"I wouldn't say that, sir. I received what you would call a 'stink-eye', many times."

I nodded. "Good enough. What about the hovertanks?"

"Seven of them have been deployed around our new headquarters. The new laser turrets aren't set up yet, but will be positioned by tomorrow."

"Excellent. *Trust, but verify.* Remember that, First Sergeant."

Kwon stared at me. "What exactly does that mean, sir?"

"It means we'll pretend to believe Crow. We'll assume he'll honor his bargain. But at the same time we'll make damned sure he's doing as we agreed."

"Oh. I see, sir."

I wasn't sure if Kwon understood or not, but it really didn't matter. He'd do as I asked, and he'd make sure Crow did the same. I decided not to discuss the matter further with Kwon. It never helped a unit's morale to dwell on the fact their higher-ups were engaged in a power struggle.

Kwon left and I went back to my firings. It was only ten a. m. when I finished kicking the last desk-jockey out of my new building. Rather than sending her home, I'd reassigned her to Crow's building as he'd requested. I twisted my lips and shook my head as I watched her leave. She thanked me repeatedly. I nodded and waved, shooing her out. Hopefully, she would still feel like thanking me after spending a month enduring her new boss.

Major Barrera appeared at the entrance and knocked at the doors, which I'd left standing open all morning.

"Come on in, Major," I said.

He walked briskly inside and stood at attention in front of my massive desk. I saw his eyes wander, however. He took stock of my new office, looking around in concern. The hole in the ceiling was now letting in a drizzle of tropical rain, rather than plaster dust.

"At ease," I said. "Talk to me."

"Colonel, we have a situation," Barrera said. His voice was quiet, his tones as flat as always. He was the perfect straight man.

"I know, but it's only rain," I assured him, attempting a joke. I leaned back in Crow's big leather chair and pointed up at the hole Sandra had cut into the ceiling. "Haven't had a second to get it fixed yet. I hated the orange carpet, anyway."

"No, sir, I'm not talking about the carpet or the rain. We've received reports of unexplained shutdowns."

"Do you think Crow is up to something?"

"No, sir," Barrera said. His voice remained flat and unexcited.

"Well then, can it wait until the general staff meeting at noon?"

"No, sir."

I frowned. "What's shutting down?"

"The mines sir, the ones we set near the Venus ring."

I stood up and leaned on the desk. I tapped at it, but the computer didn't respond to my touches. I muttered curses. "Have Macro ships come through the ring? What have our probes detected?"

"No ships. Nothing yet, sir. The mines are just deactivating, apparently on their own."

"I don't know how to work this desk yet," I complained, still working my fingers on the giant computer. I managed to get a login box, but that was it. "Can you bring up the situation on this screen?"

"I don't know how to operate it, either."

I tapped at it angrily. The interface worked differently than the ones I'd used before, and Crow had put a password on everything. I wiped away a gray muddy coating of plaster dust and rainwater. It looked like paste and smeared the screen.

"Get some of those surviving clerks in here. Put them to work cleaning this thing and getting it operating. Call Major Sarin. Call everyone, we're having the meeting right now."

"Including Admiral Crow?"

I only hesitated a second. "Yeah. Get him in here too."

Barrera hurried out the doors, leaving them open. He had his com-link plugged into his ear and tapped out codes to contact my key staff. I knew he'd round them up and get them in here faster than I could.

I took what I suspected might be a final moment of calm to stand up and walk around my new office. I stepped to the big windows and stared outside. Crow had specially built these windows. They were more than a dozen feet high, cut at a slant at the top to meet the roof. They were made of inch-thick ballistic glass. He'd had them custom-made to order in Luxemburg and imported. I didn't even want to know what they'd cost Star Force. The windows went from his ugly carpet up to the rafters. They were absurd in a way, but they afforded a fantastic view.

Outside, the forest was verdant and every palm frond whipped in the brisk winds. A mild rainstorm was passing through, freshening up the air. Pacing, I crossed the office to the sea side and watched the surf pound the sands with whitecaps. Sandra and I had hoped to have a date out on the beach soon, but now it looked like that wasn't going to happen.

I stared at the base and the darkening sea. Many of the buildings were made of smart-metal now, alloys generated by constructive nanites. They had the look of brushed stainless steel, with a yellowy hint of bronze in the mix. After a year in space, I'd only just begun to enjoy the feeling of being home on Earth again. It had been less than two weeks. That was all the time the enemy had seen fit to give me.

I lifted my gaze up to the clouds. Silver rain fell in sheets from the heavens. I realized how beautiful real rain was. Unlike the worlds I'd visited over the last year, there was something magical about an earthly rainstorm. I still marveled every time I witnessed one.

I couldn't see the stars, but I knew they were up there beyond the rainclouds, cold white lights hanging in space. Those stars were timeless and immortal when compared to pathetic biotics like me, creatures who scrabbled and fought over these cast-off stellar pebbles which we called planets.

In my heart of hearts, I was sure the Macros were gathering out there in space. They had returned.

3

Twenty minutes after I'd sent Barrera out to round people up, I had a small tense group in my office. Major Sarin, Sandra, Kwon and Barrera himself were all there. The only important player that was still missing was Crow. He was probably at the officer's club, scheming over a pint.

The big desk was clean now, but not yet functional. I tasked Major Sarin with resetting the software and removing all the passwords.

"I want this thing in public, multi-user mode," I said. "We need to have an operational center and this is going to be it."

"Give me a few minutes, sir," Sarin said. She bent over the table, working with both hands intently. She had a virtual keyboard out on the screen and tapped at it. Occasionally, a speaker I couldn't see beeped or bonked.

"Kwon, give me the device," I said, extending my hand.

Everyone looked up at that, eyes widening in alarm. Kwon's right arm swung up. In his gloved fist he held one spike of a strange, star-shaped object. It looked like an old-fashioned caltrops, a set of spikes welded together that presented a sharp point aiming upward no matter how you threw it down. They'd used them to stop cavalry charges in the old days. But the spikes on this caltrop were over a foot long and at the center was a brainbox, attached to a micro-nuclear explosive charge.

Every eye in the place tracked the mine as Kwon handed it over to me. Even Major Sarin stopped tapping at the computer. I lifted the weapon and shook it experimentally.

"You know, if you threw one of these things at a man," I said, "the spikes might well kill him. It wouldn't even have to explode."

Major Sarin opened her mouth, then closed it again.

"What is it, Major?"

"That thing isn't armed, is it?"

"Sure it is. But it's not activated. You have to press this button right here." I demonstrated, letting my thumb hover over a blue oval stud on one of the spikes.

I smiled as they all watched nervously. I wasn't sure if I should feel insulted or not. "Stop worrying," I told them. "If it goes off, you won't feel a thing."

"Are we starting the meeting yet, sir?" Major Barrera asked. "I should close the doors."

I shook my head. "I'm waiting for Crow. Go get him."

Major Barrera turned around, but before he reached the door, I called him back. "On second thought, I need you here. Kwon, take a team of marines in gear and collect the Admiral, will you. Tell him we have an emergency. The Macros are back."

That last line got everyone to look at me rather than the mine in my fist.

"That's right," I said, "and that leads us to this bizarre object. This is the only thing we've got defending our borders right now."

"Colonel," Major Sarin said. "I think I've got the screen working now. At least, we can display Star Force data coming from the probes and ships."

The screen finally flickered into life. We all stared at a map of our solar system. A dozen green contacts popped up like stars. Tiny, illegible print followed each contact like a tail as they crept over the screen. Most of the contacts were around Earth. A few hugged the Moon, while two more sat on station near each of the rings that connected our star system to the rest of the universe.

"I assume these green contacts are our ships?"

"Yes, sir," Major Sarin confirmed. "And the large blue structures are the rings."

The rings were gigantic circular monoliths, miles in diameter. They were built of unknown solid materials. We suspected they were somehow sculpted from collapsed matter—stardust. Two of them had been discovered in our home system. One was embedded in the surface of Venus while the other was at the center of a maelstrom of comets out in the Oort cloud. Flying a ship through either of these rings transported the vessel to another star system. As far as we could determine, the travel time between these star systems was zero.

We didn't know who had built the rings, but we did know how to use them. That's how the story went with most of Earth's alien-adopted technology. We could use these devices, but had little idea how they actually functioned. I'd often thought we were like a pack of cavemen with Winchester rifles riding around on water-scooters. We had no clue what we were doing, but we were dangerous and having a lot of fun.

I switched the mine from my right hand to my left. I thought I heard someone gasp as I performed the maneuver, but I wasn't sure who it was. I ignored them and tapped on the blue circle representing the Venus ring on the glass surface of the big computer. As I'd hoped, the image expanded to fill the tabletop.

Much smaller contacts, these were yellow in color, sprang into existence. There were hundreds of them.

"Mines," I said. "Just like this one. We've been deploying them at both rings to stop enemy intrusions. Now, according to reports, they are deactivating themselves out near the Venus Ring."

Crow finally made an appearance. Kwon was right behind him, towering over his shoulder. Crow looked red-faced and bleary-eyed. I knew even before I caught a whiff of his breath he'd been drinking all morning.

"Admiral," I said, "we're facing an emergency. Looks like the Macros are invading our system again."

Crow glared at me. "Can't even leave it alone for a few months, can you Riggs?"

I waved him up to the computer table. "What's this then?" he muttered. "The resolution is all wrong."

"Fix it for me," I said, struggling not to lose my temper.

Crow twisted his lips and muttered about *wallies* and *diggers*— Aussie slang for idiots and foot-soldiers. To Crow, they were one and the same. He did tap up a dialog box on the big screen, however, and input a general unlock code. The system had essentially been in safe mode up until that moment. The screen shuddered then clicked as it turned itself off and on again. Very quickly, the system blazed into life.

I was immediately impressed. I'd never seen such a fast, responsive, gigantic computer before. "How much did this thing cost us?" I asked. "No, on second thought, don't tell me."

"Are we sure it's the Macros, Kyle?" Crow asked.

The screen had returned to its previous settings and now displayed the Venus situation in greater detail. Before I could respond, a tiny white spot grew and vanished on the screen.

"There," Major Sarin said. "I saw that one wink out. Something took that mine offline."

"Was it destroyed, or did it malfunction?" Crow asked.

"We aren't sure of anything," I told him. "But who else would it be, other than the Macros? The Worms and all the other races we've encountered are on the other side of our system, reachable via the Oort Cloud ring. The big Macro fleet, when it came calling the last time, came through the Venus ring."

Crow nodded. "I remember. We all almost shat our collective pants." He rubbed his face and eyes, as if trying to wake up.

"Get the Admiral some coffee. Black and strong," I ordered.

Major Barrera relayed my command to the staffers outside.

Crow flicked his eyes to me. I could tell he was happy to hear me use his rank. I figured it was the least I could do. Star Force couldn't afford more internal struggles now.

"Kwon," I said, "I need you to oversee the new building defenses. We're canceling all leaves, everything. We're canceling sleep too, for the foreseeable future. And close the door on the way out."

Kwon nodded and thumped away. He left behind five of us in my office. In case there was going to be any shouting or crying, I didn't want the staffers outside to spread it all around the base—or the world.

"What do you want me to do, Colonel Riggs?" Crow asked. "Fly my fleet into the teeth of those machines? If that's it, I'll give you two guesses as to my answer."

I didn't reply immediately, as I was uncertain what I wanted him to do. I scratched my cheek. I hadn't shaved since leaving for the beach. Several days of stubble rasped against the fingertips of my glove.

"If the Macros are about to come through in strength," I said, "they could destroy our small space-borne force. Fleet just isn't strong enough yet to do more than harass the Macro battle fleet."

"Right you are," Crow said. "Hold back and keep building, I say."

"On the other hand, we might be able to ambush them if they come through piecemeal. I'd hate to lose that opportunity by holding back now. If some of our mines survive this attack and score hits on their ships, we could finish off the damaged vessels."

"Look," Crow said, "that sounds good, but it isn't going to happen. They obviously know about our mines. They are sweeping them out of the way somehow. They aren't going to come through until they know the way is clear."

I nodded. "Okay, order your two ships stationed at Venus to move in closer. I want video of these lost mines."

Crow looked thoughtful. "Don't like losing two fighters. We have so few. They don't even have any mines left in their holds, you know. They are waiting for rotation back to Earth. I'll send out two new ships to relieve them immediately, with a hold full of fresh mines."

I shook my head. "We have to know what they are doing, Crow. Can't you see that?"

Everyone looked at him. He wore a stubborn look on his face. Barrera handed him a mug of coffee, and he sipped at it, not responding. I began to wish I'd waited to kick him out of his office a few days longer. We didn't need this squabble between the commanders doing us strategic harm.

Crow stared at the screen and sipped more coffee.

"Well?" I asked.

"I'm thinking."

I took a deep, slow breath. We were both hotheads. Crow gave me time to think about a lot of things, while he drank his coffee. I thought about apologizing. I thought about shooting him on the spot. I thought about unilaterally ordering the ships to press in at Venus—but I wasn't sure they would do it. Fleet was loyal to Crow. He'd always done his best to hold onto that trump card.

"Look," I growled at last, when I couldn't take it any longer, "I'll give you back this office and fix your ugly orange carpet."

Crow looked at me smugly. There was a hint of triumph in his eyes that made me want to punch him.

"Very generous of you. But I never liked this orange shade myself. Looked good in the catalog, you understand—I've been thinking avocado green, for next time. You yanks like that color, don't you?"

"We love it," I said through gritted teeth.

"All right then, Star Force will build me a new building, with a new office and a new avocado-green carpet. All of which will be billed to the Marine side of the budget. Agreed?"

My desire to punch him had expanded. Now, I wanted to kill him. I think Sandra and Barrera did too.

I nodded slowly. I held out my hand to shake. Crow took it warily and we shook.

"But Crow," I said as he relayed the orders to his ships. "Don't ever hold my world hostage over something petty again."

"Wouldn't think of it, mate."

He grinned.

-4-

The hours crept by and the mines kept winking out up there around Venus. No one had thought of a good reason for them to do so. Crow's ships had moved in closer to the field and investigated, but the vanishing mines were down inside the atmosphere of the planet. Venus wasn't an easy planet to investigate. The upper atmosphere was covered in mocha and cream-colored clouds of sulfuric acid. These clouds blew around the planet at about two hundred miles per hour like a continuously stirred pot. Beneath the killer cloud-cover things became nasty. The surface temperature was a cozy nine hundred degrees Fahrenheit and the pressure was enough to crush a submarine.

I put the entire base on alert and assigned Major Barrera to kicking everyone's butt into gear. He marched off and I soon heard sirens and pounding feet all around the base. At lunchtime, the group took a break. The truth was we didn't have much to do until we learned more. Alone in my office, I received a message from the receptionist.

"There's a young woman here to see you, Colonel," said the voice. The receptionist wasn't someone I knew yet, but she sounded reproachful.

I frowned at the intercom. "Who is it?"

"She says her name is Ping. She seems—upset."

I grimaced, remembering her. Had Crow managed to proposition her already? Sighing, I ordered that she be sent up. After I had done so, I reflexively looked to the window ledge

22

where Sandra had spent much of the morning. She was gone. I shrugged, at least I didn't have to worry about that kind of misunderstanding.

A few moments later, I heard a loud commotion outside my office door. With my hand on my sidearm, I walked to the twin mahogany leaves and threw them wide. Sandra stood there with an odd look on her face. In her arms she carried what looked at first to be a broken doll. I looked again, and recognized the body. I backed away, despite myself. Sandra advanced. She appeared distraught.

Behind her, the office staff that had survived the morning sweep of lay-offs were ducking under desks and whispering in every cubicle. I slammed the doors and turned to Sandra.

"What did you do?" I asked in a low voice.

"I had to, Kyle. It's terrible. She's so young."

I looked Ping over. Her neck had been snapped. Her long, black hair hung down, almost brushing the carpet. I eyed Sandra, who was looking at the limp form she held effortlessly in her arms. I was reminded of a housecat who has brought a dead blue jay into the house to show it off. At least in Sandra's eyes there was remorse, not the pride of a hunter.

"Sandra?" I asked, trying to sound gentle. Inside, I was a turmoil. "Did you...did you lose your temper?"

"No, nothing like that. See this?"

Sandra lifted the girl's shirt. Underneath, strapped around her thin midriff, the girl had hidden a belt of C4 and a blasting cap. I stared.

"Don't worry, I pulled out the mercury cap," Sandra said. "It was nothing complex."

I still stared at the body and the bomb wrapped around her. "What the hell *is* this?"

"I didn't mean to kill her, but couldn't let her get to you. I was watching the entrance. When I saw her come in, I moved on her. I didn't know if she was nanotized or not. My first blow killed her. I only meant to knock her out, Kyle."

I looked up at Sandra finally. Her eyes were full of tears.

"Ping was an assassin?" I asked, still trying to grasp the situation fully. "But I talked to her only this morning. Could Crow have ordered this so soon?"

"Who else?" Sandra asked.

I began to pace on the orange carpet, which was now showing many overlapping stains. "I don't know. It could have been Kerr and his Pentagon boys, making their next move. They tried to take Star Force out last year. Maybe this time, they are taking a new approach. Maybe they want to kill the snake by removing the head."

"You're right," Sandra said thoughtfully. "It could be a lot of people. How could Crow have known you were going to take over his building today? All the records show this girl was just hired. How could he have recruited her so quickly, then sent her after you?"

"He couldn't have," I said. "These things usually take significant planning. I think Ping was surprised to meet me in person today, and she wasn't ready to move. But then she put on her bomb and made the attempt. She had to have support to do this. She was an asset placed here by someone."

"Maybe she wasn't just after you, Kyle. Maybe was supposed to kill Crow, or whoever was in charge."

I nodded my head. Inside, I felt despair. This was just what we needed today. While the Macros knocked on our doorstep again, Earth had sent a fresh round of assassins after us. And one so young and seemingly innocent, too. For a selfish second, I was glad I hadn't been the one forced to kill her. I looked at Sandra, and I felt for her. I understood her pain. I'd gone through similar soul-searching when I'd killed Esmeralda, an assassin the Pentagon had sent for me a long time ago.

"How did you spot her?" I asked.

"I didn't," Sandra said. "I...I smelled the explosive on her."

I suppressed the urge to react with a look of alarm. I simply nodded. I knew her senses were heightened. In this case, it had allowed her to perform her prime function as my bodyguard. My girlfriend was a freak, but it was best not to think about that. After all, I was something of a freak as well. The differences between us were only a matter of degree.

I called for emergency personnel and found they were already waiting outside my office door. They checked the bomb and declared it defused. Then they took Ping's body away on a gurney with a sheet over the face. I let them spread the information that a spy had been dealt with. I knew the rest of the staff would be

24

horrified, and when they learned she was actually an assassin who had nearly bombed the building, their horror would turn to fear.

Lunchtime had come and gone. I ordered food brought in while we watched the emergency situation unfold out around Venus. I tried to put Ping out of my mind, but it was difficult. I kept seeing her dead, bloodless face.

I had the roof patched with a barrel of construction nanites, forming a shield which I'd ordered to plane out and form a metal barrier over the entire roof. At least I didn't have to worry about raindrops soaking the carpet anymore.

Only Crow, Major Sarin and I still circled the big table. Sandra had faded out again at some point. Her self-appointed task was to be my personal security team in addition to performing general snooping. As she had demonstrated with poor Ping, she was very good at both tasks. I knew she was out there somewhere, probably within a few hundred yards of my new office, ghosting around. I sincerely hope she didn't bring me any more bodies today.

"Admiral Crow," I said, "it's time to put the Fleet up into orbit. We need them ready to mass. Depending on how this plays out, a quick strike by our forces could be decisive."

"It could also be suicidal," he said.

"Just put up the ships. We can talk about whether we need to use them or not when the time comes."

Crow shook his head slowly. He stared intently at the table with me. "I don't know, Colonel. Let's say only one Macro pokes his nose up at Venus. If we fly all our ships after one scout, he can retreat and report back as to our precise strength."

I tried not to grind my teeth. "What do you suggest we do then?"

"I'll send up two squadrons. Enough to chase off a scout. I'll even start them flying in the direction of Venus. They can always turn around and run if need be."

I didn't like the idea of splitting our forces, but Crow had a point. We didn't have any room for mistakes. And the Macros had in the past made judgments concerning whether or not to attack based on perceived strength or weakness. If they calculated they had enough power to wipe us out, they would not hesitate to move. If, on the other hand, they were not sure they had enough strength, they would wait indefinitely. They didn't like unknowns, and they

25

didn't take half-measures. They waited for a sure thing, then they always bet the house.

Crow relayed his orders to Fleet and within minutes ships began to lift off from the island. Darkness gathered over the Caribbean. The rain clouds had thickened, making it nearly black outside. In the gloom, our ships were shadows with gleaming engines. Silver rain trailed out behind each of them as they rose up in single file. They were silent, deadly. But they were nowhere near enough to face the entire Macro battle fleet. I'd once sat in space, facing down that battle fleet with seven hundred smaller ships of my own at my back. I'd calculated their numbers then to be around a thousand. I had been off slightly, as later estimates put the number at somewhere closer to five hundred. But it hardly mattered, as each of their cruisers was worth a squadron of our smallest vessels in combat. We were no match for them. In terms of firepower, they outgunned us a hundred to one.

"Sir?" asked Major Sarin, staring out one of the big ballistic glass windows to the east. "Is that Sandra—outside on the ledge?"

I glanced in the direction Sarin had indicated. I saw my girl out there, crouching on a foot-wide strip of concrete four floors up. Rain dripped off her hair and the tip of her nose. She had the attitude of a listening predator. She watched our ships fly into the sky, then tilted her lovely face to stare downward four floors to the ground. From her vantage, I realized she could watch the sky, the base, and me inside my office. With her heightened senses, I knew she could probably hear our conversation despite the thick glass.

"She likes rooftops, especially during rainstorms," I said, as if that explained everything. "Since our return from the campaign, I haven't had time to ask her why yet."

Crow laughed quietly, shaking his head. "You sure can pick'em Kyle."

Sandra turned her head toward us then. I realized she had heard us, despite the ballistic glass, the rainstorm and everything. She lifted her hand and extended her middle finger toward Crow in slow motion. I chuckled. That was my girl. She was easily the scariest woman, if not the scariest person, on Earth.

We broke up the meeting at that point, as there wasn't much else we could do as a team. The office would work well as a battle management center, but at the moment, there wasn't any battle to

26

manage. I hoped it would be a long time until there would be, but it wasn't a strong hope.

I headed out of the building toward the mess hall. I'd grown tired of sandwiches and coffee. I wanted a real sit-down meal and a minute or two to think clearly.

Behind me on the sidewalk—we actually had sidewalks now, not just open sand and scrubby beach grasses—I heard a splash and a double-thump. I crouched and whirled. The first thought in my mind was that of assassination. I had plenty of enemies on Earth, not the least of which was Crow himself. Was this the moment? The first attempt on my life since returning to Earth?

It was only Sandra. She stood up quickly, naturally. Her legs weren't broken, nor even unsteady. She waved to me, smiled, and hurried to catch up.

I looked behind her and upward. I'd just passed by the big windows of my office. She must have jumped down here in a single bound. She'd been physically enhanced much further than the rest of us, due to the combination of nanites and the unknown efforts of the microbiotic aliens. I'd been impressed with her physique and skills in space, but here on Earth with much higher gravity, I hadn't been sure how she would perform. I could see now she was equally impressive under the pull of a planet's mass.

"Join me for dinner?" I asked.

"Just try to stop me."

I reached out my hand and she took it. I walked with her to the mess hall and ordered the best food ever served on a military base. I had turtle soup, followed by a plate of fresh venison. Sandra ordered escargot and a truffle soufflé. Every flavor was marvelous. Of all Crow's excesses, here was one I could at least enjoy. Sandra and I ate and chatted as lightly as possible. We had a long-standing agreement to try to keep the business of war out of our personal lives. Usually, we failed at this…but not tonight. Maybe it was the very seriousness of our situation that allowed us to suspend talk of weighty things. It was only after a shared dessert of raspberry flan that the subject of our impending doom finally came up.

"I know you have a plan, Kyle," she said to me finally as our spoons clinked against one another, competing for the last bites of dessert.

"I always do," I lied smoothly. Sandra knew me pretty well, but I could still pull the wool over her eyes on some things when I needed to. It was part of my theory of military leadership that the troops had to believe in the all-powerful nature of their leader. It gave them hope in the darkest of situations. Only I had to live with the truth.

"What I'm worried about is your self-sacrificing nature. You have a complex about it Kyle. You really do."

"Have you been reading magazines again?"

She flashed me an annoyed glance. "I don't read magazines. You know that."

"Online blogs then."

"Articles, I read articles. Do you want me to be a fluff?"

"I gave up on that hope long ago."

"All right then," she said leaning close. "You have a class A personality. Did you know that?"

"Alpha dog, that's me," I admitted. I felt like kissing her when she came close, but I figured this wasn't the time.

"That's not all of it. You are also a risk-taker. A daredevil. I've read all about it. Women are attracted to your type, because they feel protected—but then when they become involved, they don't like it anymore. They are upset by the very traits that drew them in the first place. Strange, isn't it?"

"Sounds unfair to me," I said. I was beginning to frown. I didn't like where this conversation might be headed. Was she trying to pull back?

She sensed my mood and reached out a hand, touching my wrist. "Don't worry. I'm not changing my mind about anything. I just wanted to read up on us, about our relationship."

I sighed and tried to calm down. As always, I didn't want to lose Sandra. Especially not to some bullshit she'd read in an article somewhere.

"What I'm trying to get to," she said, "is that I don't want you to take unnecessary personal risks. Not this time. You've given your entire life to this world. It has given you little back."

"I don't know," I said, waving to the swathe of empty plates between us. "The food is pretty good."

"Stop joking around," she snapped, "I don't want you to go out there again and die on me. You *can* die. You do know that, don't you?"

"Yeah, sure."

"Promise me then. Promise me you won't try to kill yourself, or—"

"Look," I said, then paused. How could I delicately tell her I was going to do whatever I damned well thought needed doing? "This isn't just about my ego or personality. I'm leading Earth through a war. Risks have to be taken. Look at my record. I've done some amazing things and here I am, still in one piece. I need you to trust me."

Sandra stared at me. I could tell by the way she had tightened her dark, lovely eyes she didn't trust me as far as she could throw me—which was quite a distance.

It was her turn to sigh and lean back. "I had to try," she said. "Let's get out of here. I want to make love before these aliens come and kill us all."

"Okay."

We headed for our on-base quarters, an unimpressive but private bungalow, and we did make love. I was glad no one shared a wall with us, they would have complained. This time, we broke the couch and the coffee table. We both had a few scratches when we were done, but we hardly noticed as the nanites knitted our skins back together.

Sandra broke out a bottle of whiskey, but I waved it away. "Nothing so strong," I said. "I have to stay reasonably sharp—in case the call comes."

She didn't ask what call I was talking about. We both knew. She put away the whiskey for a happier future night and brought out a giant bottle of beer. It was malted stuff, the kind they only seem to have at all-night convenience stores. We shared it and laughed, talking about happier times. It was a good evening.

I was lying on the broken couch at an odd angle when the call finally did come in. Sandra was draped over me. Despite all her strength and agility, she didn't seem to weigh much more than a housecat.

I picked up my headset and held it to my ear. I didn't even open my eyes.

"There's something down there, sir," Major Barrera buzzed in my ear.

Didn't the man ever sleep? It had to be four a. m.

"Down where?" I asked.

"Hugging the surface of Venus."

I lifted myself off the couch. Sandra's body was tossed up and out of the way. I knew she was too tough to be hurt. She sank back down on the couch, moaned in protest and buried her face in the cushions.

"A ship?" I said, hunting for my shoes with fumbling hands. "A Macro ship?"

"No, sir. I think it's one of ours."

-5-

I reached my new headquarters building less than three minutes later. In the hallways and stairwells, a few janitorial people scattered at my thundering approach. It was a good thing too, as I might have plowed right through them in my haste. Without nanites in their bodies to harden their flesh, they would have gone down hard.

I hit the doors of my office at a run. They opened with a cracking sound that sounded expensive. I didn't care. If the mahogany broke, I'd replace it with steel—or better yet a nanite wall.

Major Barrera stood over the table alone. He didn't look up as I charged in.

"The contact is right there," he said. "Very close to the ring."

I saw a yellow-gold collection of pixels on the screen. There was no identifying stream of letters behind it. Our two ships were in close now, they had come down into the upper clouds of sulfuric acid. I'd been in those clouds and it was no picnic, but they were determined to gather all the information they could. I was proud of the pilots. They knew the score, so they'd taken the risk.

"Any radio contact?"

"They haven't tried yet. They spotted it on their sensors and contacted us first."

I nodded. "Get me in touch with that unknown vessel," I ordered. "Patch me through relaying the signal through our ships.

We should be able to open a channel down to the surface from here."

Barrera worked the table. It took him longer than Major Sarin to do the task.

"Where's Major Sarin?" I asked.

"Getting out of bed. I contacted her second."

"How far is Venus right now? What kind of propagation delay are we going to have?"

"About a hundred million kilometers range from Earth," he said. "Any message will take five minutes to get there and five minutes back. Ten minutes round trip to hear the response."

"I'll send the message blind, then. Send this: Unknown contact on Venus, please respond and indicate your intent. You are not authorized to be in this region. If you are damaging Star Force equipment, you will be held accountable."

Major Barrera glanced up at me. "Do we want to start off with a threatening position, sir?"

"Just send it. If the ship is one of ours I'm definitely in a threatening mood."

The signal went out, and we waited for the response. Major Sarin trotted in as we waited and we briefed her on the situation. She took over communications and Major Barrera went back to whipping people out of bed. We soon had staffers wandering the top floor, looking bleary and worried at the same time. Donuts, coffee and bacon arrived just in time, and I dug in.

While sipping the coffee and chewing a piece of bacon, I continued to stare at the screen. Two more mines had gone off the board since I'd sent out the message. Out of roughly fifteen hundred mines, we were down to about six hundred now. We could rebuild them, but it would take time to get them out there.

I happened to glance back out on the ledge outside. There was Sandra, on the other side of that thick glass, watching us. For the first time since we'd returned from deep space, she looked worried.

Crow was the last man on deck as usual. By then, the response was due back from Venus, if they were going to respond. Finally, it came in.

"Hello? Colonel Riggs? Is that your voice? I'm authorized to be here. You gave me that authorization."

Everyone exchanged glances. We all knew the voice. It was Marvin.

On our fateful return journey from Helios and Eden, we'd rebelled against our machine masters, the Macros. We'd formed an informal alliance with other biotic races we met along the way, including the Centaurs, a herd people with an odd outlook on life. I'd asked for an exchange of information, and they'd sent me the neural contents of a grand old brainbox. It was so full of petabytes of information, we'd barely been able to build a brainbox big enough to hold the download. Unfortunately, we'd had to retreat from the Eden star system before we could complete the transmission.

What we'd gotten after that aborted download became known as Marvin. He was a genius—with gaps. His knowledge and personality weren't complete. He had set about helping us, however, with translation duties and the like. I'd given him a few robotic pieces to make him self-mobile, and he'd added more of his own design. After we'd returned to Earth, I'd honored my bargain with him, giving him a spacefaring body.

Apparently, keeping my bargain with him had come back to bite me in the ass. I gripped my headset and pressed it into my cheek. I wanted to apply enough pressure to destroy it, but I resisted the temptation.

"Marvin," I began as calmly as I could, "this is Colonel Riggs. We are monitoring your activities. You have disabled a large number of our mines on Venus. You do not have the authority to do so. You will cease and desist, immediately. In addition, you will begin reactivating the mines you turned off."

When I'd finished and transmitted the message, Crow let loose with a long, nasty laugh.

"I enjoy a good joke as much as the next bloke, but this is too much, Kyle!" he cackled. "Hoist by your own petard, eh mate? Such a perfect metaphor, only this time it seems the petards are being turned into duds by your pet robot."

I ignored him with difficulty. Major Sarin, sensing my mood, raised her hand slowly. I gestured impatiently for her to speak.

"I think we can stand down our full alert now, sir," she said.

"Why's that?" I asked.

"Well—because there isn't any threat. It's just Marvin, turning off the mines so he could go through the ring. Right?"

I shook my head. "Marvin has the same onboard codes as the rest of us. He doesn't need to deactivate the mines to go through the ring. He can sail right by the minefield just like any Star Force ship."

"What's he doing, then?"

"I have no idea."

"You've got that right!" Crow hooted at me. He walked over to the breakfast tray I'd had wheeled in and served himself some coffee. He continued muttering and chuckling to himself, stuffing croissants into his mouth. "I almost soiled myself when the call came in from Barrera. You lot really should verify your nonsense before you hit the panic button."

I gave him a dark glance, then returned my attention to the big screen. "Have the mines stopped being deactivated? How many do we have left?"

"Our sensors will take five minutes to update the count of mines, sir," Sarin said. "I can tell you the orbital field is intact. Eighty-five percent of the mines laid on the surface around the ring, however, have been deactivated."

I closed my eyes for a moment, letting the horror of the situation sink in. Not for the first time, I wondered if I should have destroyed Marvin upon our return to Earth. I'd felt some form of loyalty toward him, and had treated him like a person. Had that been a mistake? He was a machine, after all. No matter how sophisticated, he was not alive. Perhaps this had always been the error biotics had made in the past when they accidentally created their own replacements. I could imagine working for long decades to craft a human-like intelligence, then feeling attached to it— defending its mistakes exactly as one would a child. But what if this immortal, alien intelligence turned out to be a killer? Or in Marvin's case, it was just too smart, inquisitive and independent to be trusted in the same universe with the rest of us?

I looked at the digital clock over Crow's tall, mahogany doors. It wasn't even five a. m. yet. Much too early for philosophical introspection.

"It does appear I've made a mistake," I said. "We'll investigate this matter, but if it turns out Marvin is switching off mines without good cause, he'll have to be destroyed."

I saw Barrera give a tiny nod of approval. He probably thought I should have disposed of Marvin long ago. Crow shook his head, grinning into a fresh mug of coffee. He was clearly marveling at my stupidity and enjoying the moment. Only Sarin looked upset. She knew Marvin better than the others. She knew how useful he'd been as a translator and technician. He'd taught us how to handle Macro equipment. Without him, we'd never have made it back to Earth.

Sarin had set up a timer. We had just over two minutes left before the next response returned from Marvin. I used the time to think about what Marvin was doing out there. I was baffled.

"What I don't understand is why he's doing this," I said. "He's a very deliberate entity normally."

"Maybe he's curious about the mines," Sarin said. "He's always been that way, poking around with new equipment."

I frowned. "I could see that with a single mine. He might deactivate it, take it apart, poke at it—even set if off experimentally. But to methodically switch off hundreds of them? I just don't understand it."

"Times about up," Barrera said.

I glanced at the clock that measured the roundtrip of a message to Venus and back again. It went negative nine seconds before the response came in. Marvin was considering his reply carefully.

"Colonel Riggs," Marvin's voice began, "I'm sorry about any confusion I may have caused. I'm almost finished with my assignment. If you will simply allow me to complete the deactivation of the field, I'll be on my way and you can turn them all back on again, if you like."

I bared my teeth at the screen, staring at the yellow glowing oval that was Marvin. Two more mines had vanished since we'd started the conversation. The group around me stepped to the board, huddling around it. Even Crow had lost his sense of humor.

"What the devil is that robot doing?" Crow said. "Sounds to me he's gone rogue, Kyle. I'm going to order my ships to descend and engage."

I nodded. "Deploy your ships, Admiral," I said. "But don't tell them to fire yet. Give me one more round with Marvin first. This could all be a misunderstanding of some kind. Marvin has been a loose cannon since I put him together, but there's always been a good reason."

Crow twisted his lips unhappily. "We should do it now, Kyle. He could slip away through the ring."

"In that case you can send your two ships after him, if you think it's worth it."

Crow grunted unhappily. He stepped aside and relayed his orders to the two small ships. Marvin was essentially a self-guided ship, but I hadn't built him with any armament. He had sensors, a manipulation arm and an engine, but that was all. Clearly, he was using that arm to deactivate my mines one by one.

I keyed my headset again. "Marvin, this is your last chance. You will stop deactivating mines and begin putting them back. Answer me this: Why are you deactivating them in the first place? You will explain your actions thoroughly with your next transmission, to my satisfaction. If you either refuse to explain or continue deactivating mines, I will have no choice but to destroy you. Please Marvin, for the sake of our friendship, comply."

Major Sarin fired off the transmission and reset the timer. It was a very long ten minutes. At last, the response came in.

"Colonel Riggs, this is an unnecessary misunderstanding! My motivations are entirely innocent! I should have asked permission, I suppose, but I was afraid you would deny it, on the basis of some technicality. I've struck a bargain with the entities on the far side of this ring. They assure me if I deactivate the minefield, they will allow me to explore the star system on their side. Think of the possibilities! You don't have any cause to worry. They've assured me they are only interested in bringing an end to this conflict between themselves and Earth. They say the minefield must be removed so they can bring their fleet through the ring safely and end the war."

I rocked back on my heels, stunned.

"Entities?" Crow cried aloud. "He's talking about the bloody Macros! That little tin traitor!"

I leaned forward again, trying to think. All my nightmares were returning. Giant, titanium nightmares that stood a hundred feet tall.

I understood what had happened now, as incredible as it seemed. Marvin had explored, as inquisitively as ever. He'd gone too far, exploring outside the system. He'd gone past the Venus ring to the blue giant star system I'd once visited. That system was full of Macros who were mining the various rocks that floated nearby.

Understanding Marvin's psychology, I supposed the blue star system was a mystery that drove him to desperation with curiosity. We'd more or less quarantined the region, not bothering to send even an occasional scout through the ring to check out what was happening on the far side. Normally, when dealing with a human opponent, it was best to keep close tabs on the enemy activity. With the Macros, even scouting might well prove to be a trigger. We didn't have much of a fleet yet, and we'd figured it was best to lie low, building up as fast as we could for as long as we could. When the Macros finally came back to Earth, months or years from now, we hoped to have built a force that could withstand their assault.

The Macros had other ideas, however. They were building up on the far side of the ring even now and they knew about our minefield. When Marvin had talked to them, they had offered him a trade. If he turned off the minefield they'd allow him to explore their territory and they promised to end the conflict with Earth.

I knew what they'd really meant by that. They had no intentions of granting us peace. Ours would be the peace of the dead. The final peace all extinct species come to know.

-6-

Conversing with Marvin under the best of circumstances had always been difficult. He wasn't human, and his thought processes didn't follow patterns that seemed completely rational to our minds. Additionally, he was deceptive. Sometimes he seemed childish to me—at other moments he was more like an ancient, evil genius.

On this occasion, instead of having him within easy reach, I had to deal with the vast distance between Earth's orbit and that of Venus. With the fate of Earth's security hanging in the balance, I found the ten minute round trip for each exchange exasperating.

It was a full minute after digesting Marvin's last statement indicating he was cooperating with the Macros before I could put together a sane response. I waved the rest of my staff to silence and lowered my chin to my chest. I cleared my throat and keyed open the microphone.

"Marvin, we've been friends for a long time. I built the body you'd always wanted, allowing you to explore to your heart's content. I did not however, anticipate you exiting the system so soon. I know you can't have visited every planetary body near Earth so quickly. I urge you to focus your explorations here around our star for now. The Macros are not like humans, Marvin. They do not always keep their arrangements. We on the other hand have kept ours. If you will help us and do as we require today, I'll guarantee you access to other star systems to satisfy your curiosity to the fullest in the future."

I sent the message. Crow stared at me with narrowed eyes.

"Yeah…good talking, mate," he said. "I get it now. Make the little bugger think we're his best friends, still. With the next message, try to get him to move up higher, away from the surface of Venus. Our lasers can't penetrate those upper clouds. Even if I send the ships down closer, it'll be hard to get a lock on him down in that high-pressure soup. Talk him up out of that thick atmosphere and my boys will burn him to atoms."

I looked at Crow thoughtfully for a second.

"What you describe may well happen," I said. "But I still hold out hope we can work with Marvin, that he can reverse this situation."

Crow's jaw sagged. He closed it again with an audible smacking sound. "What the hell are you talking about, Kyle? We've got to kill him while we can. He'll dump everything he's got to the Macros, if he hasn't already. Our codes, everything."

I shook my head slowly. "He could have done that already. He clearly hasn't as he's out there turning off mines rather than just inviting the Macros in."

Major Barrera rumbled, clearing his throat. I looked at him expectantly.

"With all due respect, sir," he said to me. "Admiral Crow is correct. Marvin has gone rogue and has had contact with the enemy. We can no longer do anything other than destroy him at the earliest opportunity."

I glanced at Major Sarin, thinking she might offer an opinion. She frowned down at the screen, not meeting my eyes. I knew her well enough to read her thoughts. She didn't know what to do. She knew Marvin better than the others and was as conflicted as I was.

"We haven't seen the nose of a single Macro ship yet," I said. "Let's see what Marvin says, first."

The clock ticked down. We all watched it, and the yellow blip that was Marvin. It seemed to me that it had shifted slightly closer to the ring.

"Is he moving toward the ring?" I asked.

Major Sarin nodded. Everyone stared quietly, except for Crow, who muttered a steady stream of curses in Aussie slang. I understood the sentiment. It appeared Marvin was going toward the ring, which could only mean one thing. He had thought it through and decided to act before we could carry out our threats.

"He's going to run back to his new Macro friends," Crow said. "I'm giving the order to my ships to fire Kyle, whether you agree or not."

Reluctantly, I nodded. Crow ordered his ships to move. It would take them time to receive the order then time to travel down through the atmosphere and to reach effective firing range. In any case, time was definitely running out for Marvin. It was running out for all of us.

At long last, the timer went negative. The response came in quickly. "What do you want me to do, Colonel Riggs?" Marvin asked. "As you can see, I've reset one of the devices."

I could see it now, a new tiny contact lit up on the board. It hardly mattered, however. It would take him hours to turn them all back on. At least as long as it had to turn them all off. He was hovering very close to the ring now. Our ships were descending. They'd entered those turbulent clouds. They already had orders to fire.

"Put up another timer," I ordered Sarin. "Estimate how long we have until our ships are within range. Subtract five minutes from it for the propagation delay."

Major Sarin worked the screen with her fingers. A timer swam up with light blue digits displaying twenty-two minutes. That was how long Marvin had to convince me I should let him live.

I tilted my head up and reviewed the worried faces. Everyone was staring at me. "I want to hear opinions. You each have ten seconds to give them."

"You know what I think," Crow said. "No choice. No choice at all. Talk him into standing still long enough for us to blast him."

I shifted my eyes to Major Barrera.

"The Admiral is correct, sir," he said. "The risk is too high. I have to vote with him."

I turned to Major Sarin next.

She sighed, shaking her head. "I'll miss Marvin, but I can't see any other path. We can't trust him. The stakes are too high."

My eyes lingered on her face. Of all of them, her opinion meant the most to me. She'd worked with Marvin, and she wasn't quick to pull a trigger on anyone.

Something caught my eye then, out the window. It was Sandra, still outside clinging to the ledge. I reflected that she never seemed to get cold or hot anymore. She rarely reported discomfort of any kind. Crouching on ledges out in the elements seemed to agree with her, in fact. When she saw that she'd caught my eye, she gave me a thumbs-down gesture. I nodded, accepting her vote along with the others.

I rubbed my face with my palm for a moment, thinking hard. Finally, I keyed open the channel and spoke to Marvin.

"All right Marvin," I said. "Here's what I want you do to, if you want to live another hour. Fly through to the other side. Tell the Macros you've cleared all the mines you can. Tell them they can come through the ring safely, right now. After that, I would run away and hide, if I were you."

I tapped the send box on the screen. All the officers standing around me stared in disbelief.

"You tremendous bastard," Crow said, breathing hard. "You're going to trust him? On the basis of some kind of Yankee intuition? Do you realize you may have just killed us all?"

I avoided their gazes and stared down at the screen, nodding.

"Possibly," I admitted.

Long minutes went by. Another tiny contact went gold on the screen during that span. Marvin had dutifully used the time to activate another mine. At least this one was close to the ring and might actually do some good.

Suddenly, we saw Marvin moving toward the ring. Almost simultaneously, his last message returned to us.

"Command accepted," the message said.

A moment later, Marvin's golden oval was gone. He'd vanished on his way to another star system.

If I'd found the waiting tough before, now it was excruciating. Crow spent the next half-hour pacing and cursing at me. I didn't argue with him. Quite possibly, he was right. Finally, however, I'd had enough. I'd expected Marvin to pop back out of the ring by now, or a Macro to show its nose. Neither had happened. That wasn't good from our point of view. I decided to attempt to explain my reasoning to the others.

"Look," I said. "If the Macros come through now, they will find a small minefield at the ring, but when they come up out of the atmosphere, they will hit lot more of them. Our orbital field is still in place and we put it right where they gathered the last time they brought their fleet through."

"Okay," Crow said, furious. "I'll give you that. We'll destroy a ship or two."

"More than that. We've run simulations. Barrera, have you run new numbers given our current distribution and past Macro performance?"

"These are only estimates," Barrera said, "But they should lose fifty ships, more or less."

Fifty ships. I knew that wasn't enough. Unfortunately, Crow knew it too.

"That's a joke, that is," he said. "Right—well, right. At least we know what to put on our planet's tombstone. I can see it now: *We invited the Macros in, and managed to kill nearly ten percent of their battle fleet. Please urinate on our fool graves, it makes the grass grow."*

I ignored Crow. "Major Barrera, let's factor in their knowledge of the minefield at the ring. If they decided to come in hot, how could they do it?"

"Their probable approach would be a barrage of nuclear missiles fired through ring to clear the mines."

"If they are ready to come through now, why haven't they done so already?"

"Do you want speculation, sir?"

"Yes."

"They must want to achieve some level of surprise. Perhaps they thought they could slip in and gather their strength behind Venus as they did last time. We made no move against them on that occasion because we had no fleet strength."

"I agree," I said. "They were trying to sneak in. But they were going to come in any case."

"You still haven't given me a good reason to invite them in now," Crow complained.

"These machines—*especially* these machines—are quite capable of learning. But they tend to be predictable. If something works for them once, they like to repeat the same move until thoroughly convinced it is no longer working."

I cited cases for them, such as the sequential suicidal approach of invasion ships when we'd first met the Macros. They'd lost several before changing tactics to a larger force. Then there was the lining up of ships when entering the Worm system. They'd allowed two thirds of their task force to be destroyed in that instance before achieving bombardment superiority and suppressing the Worm counter fire. The list went on. They were more than willing to allow a large portion of their forces to be destroyed, once committed to an action. But they would then weigh the results afterward and alter their tactics deliberately.

I thought the crucial difference in their behavioral patterns was an absence of factors such as morale. This enemy didn't feel fear, or regret. They calculated odds. If they lost a hundred ships, they analyzed why and built a hundred more. They didn't run screaming from a battlefield, hang their failed generals or fall prey to combat stress disorder. In short, they tended to make big sweeping moves

43

and once they'd decided to make those moves they stuck with them until they won or were wiped out. Retreats were rare, but once they'd decided to pull back, they did so with as much certainty and determination as they exhibited when attacking.

"Okay," Crow said, with a tone of weariness. "We know they are alien machines that don't think the way we do. Now, tell us why you invited them to visit here today."

"Because I think they might accept the invitation. Please understand, they are going to come soon, one way or another. I'm hoping they haven't gathered all their strength yet. I'm hoping to face them before they are ready. What if they only have fifty ships? We will probably destroy them all with little loss and rebuild our minefield for the next wave. We have to hurt them at every opportunity."

"But the risk, man…"

"Yes," I said, "there is always a great deal of risk in war. We are on the losing side in this conflict and we must take risks in order to win. We have to roll the dice. If we simply throw all our ships up against theirs, we lose. But maybe, if we can pull a rabbit or two out of our hats, we can hold on. The Macros don't like losing in a strategic sense. If we kill enough of them, they will mark us down on their ledgers as more dangerous than previously estimated. That will translate to more time for us to prepare before they come again."

"If they have the kind of strength you're talking about, Colonel," Major Sarin said, "then they could fly here today, suffering all the losses we can inflict, and still annihilate Earth."

"Now you've got the picture, Major."

Sarin's face fell. Maybe she didn't like the picture, now that she had gotten it. She became quiet, studying the vivid, high definition image of Venus that lay between us. Venus itself was a swirling, light creamy-brown, but it had so many contacts floating around with it the planet reminded me of a Christmas ornament. If new red contacts began pouring out of the ring and spiraling upward, the Christmas ornament look would be complete.

"Do you trust Marvin to deliver the message you gave him?" Crow asked.

I thought about it. "Not entirely. But he's not an idiot, Crow. He was already approaching the ring. He wasn't going to let your ships get within range anyway. He would have run. This way, he might do us some good."

"I hope you're right, mate."

More waiting. It was difficult, but after some thirty minutes, new contacts appeared.

"Something's coming through sir. Lots of somethings."

"Order your ships to pull back, Admiral," I said.

Crow relayed the command, but it was too late. They were too close to the ring. They got off a few shots as the Macro cruisers began to wriggle through the ring, one after another. Then one of them vanished.

"Dammit," Crow whispered as the second of his two ships winked out.

"Give me a count, Barrera."

"Thirty-five ships, sir. Single file, all cruisers. They've only lost two so far due to the mines we had left waiting for them at the ring."

I ground my teeth, and felt the muscles in my cheek jumping of their own accord. "How long before they can reach Earth?"

"Two days—maybe less."

We all watched as the parade continued. When the first cruisers nosed up into orbit over Venus' cloud layer, we had our moment of revenge.

"They've run into the orbital minefield, Colonel. Looks like the first nine ships are going down."

We all cheered, we couldn't help it. The heavy mahogany doors opened with a bang then. We all looked up, startled. Sandra stood there, dripping wet. She had a long black raincoat and a black fedora on her head, but she was still soaking.

"Everybody knows," she said.

I could hear some cheering behind her. I walked out into the open floor with its ranks of cubicles. Every screen was watching some version of our visual.

Sandra was right behind me, whispering over my shoulder. "I thought you should know," she said. "If this is supposed to be a secret, the whole world is watching with you."

"Great," I said, feeling slightly more tense, if such a thing were possible.

"Sir?" Major Sarin called to me from my office. "It's General Kerr, sir. He's on the line—conference-calling with the President of the United States."

I turned around and slammed the big doors. I made a dismissive gesture toward Major Sarin, the President and Kerr. They could all wait. I had a war to run.

I heard Sarin speaking quietly into the headset. "Colonel Riggs is unavoidably detained by the situation, sirs. He apologizes and will get back to you at the earliest opportunity."

"Kyle," Sandra whispered at my shoulder.

I glanced back at her. She had a wild, suspicious look on her face. "Don't you get in a ship and go out there. Not this time. I don't even want you thinking about it."

I looked at her. "Honestly, I hadn't even thought of that one yet. We have many hours before we scramble the Fleet."

"Just don't scramble with them."

I shook my head. "No promises."

She crossed her arms and glared at the image of Venus. The rest of the command staff stood around, operating different sections of the big table, talking to others on headsets. Crow was counting his ships and ordering pilots to report in. Major Barrera had called out the hovertank reserves and ordered them to take up stations around the island.

"It's not fair," Sandra said. "We just got home. We deserved a longer break than this."

"I'll file a complaint with Macro Command tomorrow, my dear," I said.

"Don't be a smart ass. We're all about to die."

I thought about denying it, but there didn't seem to be any basis on which I could blow any happiness into her ears. Things were bad, and getting worse with each Macro ship that flowed out of the ring and sailed gracefully up to orbit Venus.

We were aided somewhat by the vicious clouds and pressure of Venus in the end. Normally, it took as many as ten mines to take out a cruiser. But when you added in high winds, sulfuric acid and intense pressure, the ships we damaged even lightly were often disabled.

"Forty-six ships have been disabled or destroyed, sir," Barrera reported after another twenty minutes.

"How many have survived?"

"Ninety-two," he said.

"All cruisers?" I asked.

"Yes, sir. They stopped coming through a moment ago."

I strode to the table and stared at it, fixated. "You didn't tell me they were all through."

"I'm not sure they are, sir. They could have another wave coming."

I shook my head and a slow, grim smile spread over my face. "No, Major. The Macros don't work that way. If there are more ships coming, they are days away at least. They are gamblers who push their whole pile of chips into the pot when they make a bet. This is all they have at the moment."

We watched closely for another hour, but ninety-two ships remained the total. About a quarter of what I'd faced years ago when their battle fleet had last come to our system.

"They are forming up ranks behind Venus, sir," Major Barrera said.

I didn't bother to respond. I watched the Macros morph into a long crescent of glittering red contacts.

"Why are they waiting?" Sandra asked.

"Repairs," I said, shrugging. "Or maybe they are on hold until reinforcements arrive."

"Reinforcements? There are more of them? Where are they now?" Sandra asked, voicing the questions in everyone's mind.

"We don't know," I said. "But I'm damned glad they aren't here at the moment."

"So many... Can Fleet destroy them all, Kyle?"

I eyed the screen. "No," I said. "But we might not have to."

-8-

After the Macros did nothing for a full hour, I broke up the meeting. We didn't know how much time we had, but I figured we didn't have any extra hours to waste getting ready.

I left Major Barrera in my office, with orders to monitor everything and call me back in if anything changed. He nodded without looking away from the big screen. I left him there, confident the situation was in good hands for now.

Crow hurried to catch up with me out on the sidewalk. I was thinking hard and heading toward *Socorro*. I hadn't flown my personal ship since I'd been back, and it was about time I got into this game personally.

"Kyle," Crow said at my shoulder.

I glanced at him, expecting another hail of jokes at my expense. I was surprised to see a worried, haggard expression on his face.

"Look," he said, "we have to pull it together. I'm serious. We're all in this together, and we're all going to die this time if we cock it up."

"Agreed."

We were walking side-by-side now. I'd slowed down a bit, but kept moving toward the collection of circular pits we used as a landing field at the southern edge of the base. They looked like blast-pans from an aerial perspective, but since our ships usually used gravitational repellers to lift off and land, they weren't used that way. The low walls of concrete around each landing pit mostly

48

served to shelter crews and cargo from the weather. They also helped manage traffic. If a ship was told to land in pit eighteen, everyone knew where they were headed.

I heard a sound behind us. A thump and a splash. I glanced back, not really surprised. Crow's reaction was much more dramatic. He stopped and whirled, eyeing Sandra who now walked behind us. She nodded to him coolly, and he nodded back. She wore her raincoat and a black fedora. Maybe she'd grown tired of having rain running down her face.

Crow started walking with me again. Sandra shadowed us about five paces behind. She reminded me of a Secret Service agent, trailing dignitaries while they had a private conversation. I knew Sandra could hear everything we were saying, but by staying behind she gave people the illusion they were speaking with me privately.

Many powerful men had bodyguards, that was nothing new. In my case, I only had one lovely agent, but that was all I needed. Now and then, Crow gave Sandra a quick, worried glance over his shoulder. No one liked to have her behind them. Everyone knew she could probably kill them before they could move. That was the beauty of the arrangement.

"I've got something I need to show you, mate," Crow said, keeping his voice low.

"Can it wait? I'm going to set my factories to produce defensive materials."

"*Your* factories? Don't you mean Star Force's factories?"

"Excuse me."

Crow threw up his hands. "There I go again. Sorry. Let's start over on the subject of factories. I've got more of them."

For the first moment of the entire conversation, he had my full attention. Crow smiled. Some of his natural smugness began to shine through again.

"Yeah, you heard me right," he said. "Did you think you were the only one with a secret base on this island? The only difference is I've managed to keep my base an actual secret."

I heard a muttered curse behind us. Neither of us glanced toward Sandra, who was obviously listening in.

Like Sandra, my first reaction was anger. But I quickly realized that was a foolish response. After all, hadn't I built my own base of

Nanotech power? More importantly, if Crow had factories he could commit to the defensive effort, that would strengthen our position against the Macros. We could shout about who should have told what to whom later on.

Crow watched all these thoughts and emotions play out over my face with amusement.

"How many do you have?" I asked.

"Do you want to come see it? My holiest of holies? My inner sanctum?"

"I didn't say I wanted to get married."

Crow produced a harsh laugh. "Don't worry. You aren't my type, mate. Come on, let's take your ship."

We'd reached pit eighteen. I hopped over the low concrete wall and walked up to the ship. Crow and Sandra trailed behind. I told *Socorro* to open her hatch and Crow followed me up a short ramp. Sandra hurried quietly after us.

I ordered the ship to create a third chair inside the bridge. Crow climbed onto the raised gleaming shell that had contoured itself into the shape of a crash seat. To normal people it would have been uncomfortable. But nanotized Star Force personnel didn't care about hard surfaces against their backsides.

"No safety harness?" Crow asked, half-joking.

His seat, being a makeshift facsimile created by the ship, looked more like a steel bathtub than a real padded seat. There were no belts or buckles. Before I could answer, Sandra spoke up.

"Socorro," she said, "restrain Admiral Crow. Secure him to his seat."

Six thin black arms rose up, whipping like steel tentacles. They grabbed each limb and the last two crossed his chest. He was held firmly to his seat.

"Happy?" she asked.

"Not at all," Crow said. "This reminds me of a dentist I once knew in Sydney." Turning back to me, he said: "Shouldn't give your girlfriend the keys, mate. Bad policy, that."

Crow was referring to the *Socorro's* command permissions. Sandra was able to order the ship to do things, including flying it in my absence. Sandra opened her mouth to make another snappy reply, but I raised my hand. "I'm the commander on this ship. Socorro, loosen Crow's restraints. Allow him to adjust or remove them by touch or command. They should function as automated support systems, not shackles."

"Options set," said the ship.

"Now, Jack," I said. "Tell me where to fly."

Crow gave me the coordinates. We took off and within a few minutes were hovering over the northern edge of the island. We'd never done much with the land up here, it was mostly undeveloped swamp and forestland. Bahaman pines ruled the area, standing out among sprays of tall grass and expanses of sand. Gliding down over a wetland area Crow had us set down in a small body of water.

I went with it, only mildly surprised to be coming down in a pond. In order to have hidden a base for this long, Crow had to have put it underwater or underground. There were simply too many flyovers on Andros Island to hide it for any length of time in any other way.

To my surprise, the pond we descended into opened up and turned black as we came down into it. I had the external cameras on and was able to watch visually during our descent.

"Ah," as I said, nodding to myself. "There is no pond, is there?"

"Give the man a prize!" Crow said, chuckling.

We continued to descend. Lights glimmered below. I saw concrete and fluorescent lamps that automatically sensed our approach and flickered into life.

"What the hell is going on?" Sandra demanded.

"Nanites," I explained. "Crow made a false pond with a surface of nanites. As we approached, it opened. Like a giant version of our melting walls aboard any ship."

"It looked so real."

Crow leaned forward, plucking away the tiny black arms that attempted to restrain him. He slapped at them and they reluctantly retreated, as per my instructions. "That's the genius of it," he said proudly. "There is some water involved. I have the nanites pool up about an inch on the surface of the roof. When a ship comes down, they bud up in the center and push it away automatically. You're not the only one who can program a mass of nanites, Kyle."

I nodded. I had to admit, Crow had me beat in the area of deception. "When did you build this place?"

"Quite a while back," he said. "Remember when you first announced war on the mainland?"

"As I recall, they announced war on Star Force."

"Well, in any case, I was worried they would get all our factories. I'd already stashed one by then. Since that time, I've built more with the first one."

I craned my neck around to look at the sneaky bastard appreciatively. "How did I lose count of a factory?"

Crow shrugged. "Remember all those ships we lost fighting the Macros? Our original ships? They all had factories of their own you know, every one of them. Now, what if the Macros knocked out a few of those craft without destroying them utterly. Without ruining the factory component...."

"You found one of our downed ships and recovered the factory without telling me about it?"

"Salvage-rights mate. One of the oldest laws of sea, you should look into it."

"Okay," I said, shedding complaints and arguments as quickly as they popped into my mind. They didn't matter now, I kept reminding myself. "What the hell have you been doing with these factories all this time—what's it been, two years?"

"Nearly that long," Crow said. "Well, for the most part, I've been building *more* factories."

I got up out of my seat and put my hands on my hips. I smiled at him, and he slowly grinned back.

"You magnificent bastard," I said. "I've never felt like hugging you before."

"I'm hoping you never do again," Sandra said. "What are you two so happy about?"

"I'll show you," Crow said. "Open up your ship, Kyle."

I touched a section of *Socorro's* inner hull. The wall and part of the floor melted away. A moment later, a dulling gleaming metal ramp formed leading down to the concrete floor.

"This is where the budget and materials have been going, isn't it?" I asked. I thought about the extra materials Star Force had been swallowing. All the double-accounting and extravagant prices were suddenly making sense to me. Crow had been hiding massive shipments of materials for his pet project. Building factories didn't take a lot of bulk, but they took more precious metals and time than anything else we could produce.

"Exactly," Crow said. "I didn't hire a hundred extra purchasing clerks to feather my nest with trinkets."

"Just factories?" I asked. "Is that all you've been building?"

"At first, yes," Crow said, "but—well, let me show you."

We all stood on a dark section of stained concrete. A single factory was in evidence. The maw at the top of it was aimed upward, clearly waiting to be fed materials through the opening that mimicked a pond overhead. Like every one of these strange systems we called 'factories', it was a spheroid about twelve feet in diameter that sat in the center of the structure. It resembled an old-fashioned steel kettle, but the surface was uneven, full of ripples and bulges that hinted the machine was loaded with unimaginable components. The strangely twisting internals made me think of a man's guts pressing out against a thin, metal skin.

In every direction around us shadows hung. The pool of bright light we stood within made the darker regions impossibly dense. I couldn't see a thing beyond the single factory in the lit region.

Sandra gasped, however. "Kyle? Do you see them all? They are *fantastic*!"

Crow looked at her and smiled. He made a slow waving motion with his left arm. The lights came up then, revealing a vast area. I turned around, taking it all in. The area resembled a parking garage with a triply-high ceiling. Round metallic columns of what looked like construction nanites stood, holding up the roof. The columns undulated in shape, reminding me of three-foot thick termite mounds. The floor was concrete, but roof was all metal—all dully gleaming masses of constructive nanites.

What I saw between those columns wasn't more factories, as I had expected. Instead, my eyes feasted upon ships. Nine sleek, beautiful ships. They looked like birds of prey nesting here in the dark.

"They are my design," I said. "My destroyers."

"Indeed they are, mate," Crow said. "Fully-armed, this lot. Not like the ragtag force we threw together to face the Macros the last time they came into orbit. Every ship in the squadron has three heavy guns. I'd say any three of them can take down an enemy cruiser easily."

Getting over my wonderment, I whirled on him and grabbed up a wad of his shirt. "You could have deployed them," I yelled in his face. "You could have put them into the sky when the four cruisers came down and went on their bombardment run over Earth. Instead, you sat back and put up a token force for show. You let my men die up there fighting ship-to-ship!"

Sandra moved in a blur. It was as if she had waited for this instant all her life—perhaps she had. She moved behind Crow, grabbed up his arms with her small, steel-like hands. Crow reacted violently. He twisted away and whirled to face her. He was strong and fast, but not fast enough.

Crow froze when he realized Sandra had placed one of her incredibly sharp blades at his throat.

"Nanites can't save you if your head is on the floor, Jack," she whispered into his face.

They were both panting. I decided it was time to intervene. "Let's stand down, you two."

"Let me do it, Kyle," Sandra said. The two had locked stares. "He let Gorski die up there on the *Jolly Rodger*. Gorski, and a hundred others like him. I want to cut the good admiral."

I knew Sandra was firmly in the grip of one of her blood-lusting moods. I'd seen it before while fighting Macros. I had to move carefully to talk her down.

"You are by no means the first who's had that wish, Sandra," I said, keeping my voice calm in the hopes it would calm them both.

"You'll have to take a number for the privilege," Crow said.

I eyed him. He didn't sound as if he were as worried as he should be. Then I saw it.

"Sandra, behind you," I said.

She bound forward, spinning around in the air before she came down. Something long and dark snaked forward from the nearest of the destroyers. In the excitement of the combat, it had reached for her. Three thick fingers clicked together where her body had been a moment before. The arm itself was as thick as a tree trunk while the fingers were like black metal fire hoses with minds of their own. The arm rose up like a rearing cobra and darted forward to catch Sandra. She slashed at it and sprang out of the way. A spray of white sparks lit up our faces. One of the fingers was now about a foot shorter than it had been.

"All right, all right," I said. "That's enough you two. Stand down! We've got billions of people to worry about. Get your heads on straight, that's an order."

Crow waved back the arm. Sandra stood behind me with both of her knives in her hands. Crow and Sandra were breathing hard. Their eyes were wide and possessed by a wild light. I reflected that I'd been foolish to bring these two into close proximity. Neither was the best at self-control.

"I'm an Admiral," Crow reminded me. He rubbed at his throat, where he was indeed bleeding from a thread-like cut. "A Colonel doesn't command an Admiral."

"I told you I would cut you," Sandra said over my shoulder to Crow. She dipped her head close to my ear then and whispered: "You don't order me around, either, Kyle. You know that."

I sighed. Normally, I would tell them to shake hands, but I figured someone would be minus some fingers afterward.

"Okay," I said to Crow. "Tell us how long you've been hiding these ships. And how many do you have?"

"He's got nine," Sandra said. "Can't you see them all?"

I shook my head. "I only see one factory. You said you built more. I have to know what assets I have if I'm going to win this fight, Crow."

Admiral Jack Crow looked irritable, but resigned. "Yeah. That's why I brought you and you're delicate flower of a girlfriend out here. So much for gratitude."

I felt Sandra bristle behind me. I held up a hand again to prevent another outburst. "Just give me the numbers."

"You have to understand, Kyle. When you came down in those Macro ships I wasn't ready. I didn't have these ships manned. I had no trained crews for the destroyers yet. I didn't know if we could take them down, especially with green crews. Just getting pilots out here would have taken longer than the battle did in the end. I—"

"Cut the excuses and give me some numbers," I said.

"All right. On the top floor, we have nine ships here. All the ships are on the first floor. Easier to fly out, you understand. The factories are building another squadron like this one."

"Makes sense. What about the factories you spoke of?"

"On the floor below, we have twenty-one more factories. This one is special," he said, walking over to the unit I'd seen first. "It's the first one, but that's not why it's special. It's my preprocessor. It takes in raw materials, refines them a bit, then distributes the partly digested product down these tubes to the factories below. That speeds up overall production, you see."

I walked around the unit, inspecting his setup. In spite of myself, I was very impressed. "You aren't a computer architecture expert, Crow," I said. "Who helped you with this design?"

He cleared his throat. "I had a little help. Yeah, sure. I worked with General Kerr. He has a thousand computer geeks like you to back him up."

I looked at him sharply. "Pentagon people?"

"Further out than that."

"Langley?"

Crow shrugged. "Spooks come in many flavors."

"Do they know about this installation?"

Crow smiled. "No. But they know something like it must exist."

"How the hell did you get them to help you? Without them knowing what was really up?"

Crow looked modest. It was an odd look for him. "It was nothing, really. Just a bit of deception. They think I'm programming your machines at your base. I traded them some components for weapons and guidance systems. Brainboxes, sensors. But never a factory of their own. They are still dependent on us for any real production of Nanotech."

I frowned, disturbed. Crow had been busy. But I supposed I should have expected that. He was a proactive person with ambitions that bordered on the delusional. In my long absence, I should have realized he'd try something like this.

"What were you doing with all these ships?" I asked. "Building them up in secret? Why?"

"I wanted Fleet to be strong. I've always said that."

"Yes, you have."

"I know him," Sandra said. "He intended to take over the world when no one was looking."

I glanced quickly at Crow. He appeared slightly embarrassed. If I had to guess, I'd say that Sandra had hit the nail on the head. I shook my head and walked back toward *Socorro*. Crow and Sandra followed, keeping a wary distance apart.

"Admiral, I demand that you put these nine destroyers under regular Fleet command," I said, standing on the ramp. "Move them to Fort Pierre and get them crewed up and ready to fight. In addition, bring home any other ships you might be hiding and not telling me about.

"There may be a few more..." Crow admitted. "But once I show my hand, the eyes in the sky will know about this base. The secret will be out forever."

I nodded. The governments of the world had slowly built up dozens of satellites that just happened to pass by our latitude on a regular basis. Supposedly, they were for communications and the like. But we knew better. They were spying eyes, and they were tolerated for now. One thing was for certain, there was no way we could field nine new, large ships out of a pond without someone noticing. The reason why all that mattered is they had once tried to take our island away from us, to gain control of Star Force and our Nano technology. I didn't think we could afford to worry about that now, however.

"We have to commit now, Jack," I told him. "All the chips are on the table this time. If the Macros get to Earth, you'll be as dead as the rest of us and your glory days will never come."

"Agreed," Crow said. "What do you think we should do with the rest of the factories while we wait for the Macros to make their next move?"

"Keep building destroyers," I said. "As fast as you can."

-9-

I flew *Socorro* to my own secret base full of factories. Like Crow's base, it wasn't such a secret anymore. Before I got out of my ship, I dressed myself in one of the surviving battle suits I'd designed and utilized to great effect during our recent return journey to Earth.

We put down in one of three circular landing pits set up outside the base. There were thirty laser turrets ringing the base perimeter now, many of them squatting atop a shed with a factory inside. Every one of those thirty projectors tracked *Socorro* as we made our final approach. I'd set these turrets to 'extra-paranoid' due to the strategic importance of the factories they were protecting. It was unnerving to have them aim at me, but I felt it was necessary. Even though they recognized my ship and who was in it, I knew they were thinking hard, trying to determine any excuse they could to burn me out of the sky.

We walked from the landing pits to the base gates. We were challenged at the gates by my marines. Most were American, but there was a number of Indian *Ghatak* troops mixed in. I'd hand-picked these men for loyalty and their suspicious natures. The guards at the gate opened a dissolving curtain of nanites and waved us inside after a few terse questions.

"We aren't going to fight someone today, are we Kyle?" Sandra asked warily. She watched the marines who stared back in stony silence.

"Not today," I said. "Unless the Macros make a move, I'm going to spend the day programming."

58

"Oh," she said, sounding disappointed. "Will there be any time for a break, later?"

I smiled at her. "We'll meet up for dinner, I promise. In the meantime, you don't have to sit around with me while I talk to the factories."

Sandra twisted her lips. "I know you too well. You don't want me distracting you while you are trying to program."

I shrugged. "Sadly, programming is best done in solitary confinement."

"If we weren't all about to die, I would complain—but instead I'm going to let you work in peace."

"Great. I'm sure you'll find something to do."

"Yeah, maybe I'll take up bird-watching."

I could tell she would be boredly twitching her tail all day. Like all commanders, I hated to see talent sit around idle. I had a sudden thought.

"How about I have you work the com-links and monitor communications for me? Tell me what's happening. Relay to Major Barrera a report about Crow's stash of ships. Tell him he's bringing them in to Fort Pierre. Let him know what to expect."

She agreed and walked away happily toward the communications shed. I watched her go, my eyes lingering on her shapely form. Had the microbiotics somehow perfected the musculature of her body? I wasn't sure, but I thought she might have lost five pounds of fluff and had it turned into muscle. It didn't seem to matter anymore what she ate, her metabolism had been heavily redesigned. If I ever ran into that race of microbes again, I figured I owed them one.

At the base of every laser turret was a shed, and inside every shed was a factory. These were identical in size and function to the ones Crow had built and secreted away on his own. I looked at the laser turret with my hands on my hips, reflecting on the two very different approaches Crow and I had taken concerning the protection of our most precious commodity. Overall, I had to give Crow the blue ribbon. Deception provided better security than armed defense—as long as one kept the secret.

There was no one in Shed Six when I entered. I looked around the room. There were pallets of supplies. I'd always insisted we maintain a stockpile of raw materials to keep the machines busy.

These days with Fleet being strong again, Nano ships made regular deliveries, pouring the raw materials into the maws up on the roof. Tubes ran upward from the top of the factories central spheroid to the roof of the shed where the materials intakes were. An output port was on the side of every laser turret, built to yawn open or squeeze closed like a metal orifice. Right now, they were closed up tightly.

I sat down on the programmers stool and began conversing with Unit Six. I ordered them all to link-up and shut down any production that wasn't immediately useful to defense. It was a shame, really. They were engaged in the production of a dozen useful goods—useful in peacetime, that was. Medical equipment was the primary export we had on the island when we weren't building up weaponry. The Nanos had quite an extensive knowledge of the human body after having spent nearly a century dissecting specimens of our species. A brainbox, sensor kit and a set of three whipping arms were enough to do pretty much any surgery people cared to attempt. Combined with a generous helping of medical nanites, they could save a lot of lives normal human medicine couldn't cope with. But programs like that would have to go on hold now. With the Macros entering our skies again, everything had to be thrown into defense. Everything.

Over the past few weeks, I'd reviewed our tactics against the Macros. One element that had been surprisingly effective was boarding efforts by our troops. In effect, my Marines had operated like independent spaceships in the final battles. The Macro cruisers as currently designed were not well-suited to stopping a mass attack by extremely small opponents. They usually only had one big gun on a belly turret. They also possessed a large number of missile launchers, but individual flying men weren't the best targets for missile weapons. The best defense they'd had against my marines had been their own onboard marines, which had been larger and more effective than humans.

I recalled the boarding parties of the enemy. They had been very sophisticated. Flying on racks that resembled carrier trailers with a dozen automobiles chained into place, the enemy machines had been able to ride their delivery systems to my ship like troops aboard a missile, then deployed as individual fighters. They'd very nearly taken my ship with those tactics.

60

In comparison, our systems were primitive and unreliable. I had placed my own marines in a lightly-armored spacesuit and stood them atop a propulsion system my men affectionately called 'skateboards'. In truth, they looked more like the pizza dishes kids went sledding on than skateboards, but they did require balance and skill to fly properly.

I needed a redesign. I wanted a system that could more safely and effectively deliver one of my marines to the enemy. Heavier armor would likely be required as well. The system designed would work best if it was able to function in multiple varied environments. Open space, certainly. But there were plenty of other conditions my marines might be required to operate under. They might need to fight on land, under the sea, on a high gravity world or even flying around in a planetary atmosphere—Earth's atmosphere, specifically.

After doing some sketches, checking on weight allowances and gross materials, I was ready to build a prototype.

"Unit Six," I said. "Respond."

"Unit Six responding."

"We are going to create a new program. Make space for it now without deleting existing programs."

"Done."

"Load battle suit configuration from my suit's repository," I ordered.

Unit Six paused for a moment. I knew it was transferring data wirelessly from the recording brainbox on my own battle suit. My current design of such suits was naturally stored in the suit's brainbox, along with a lot of other useful information. I'd just finished my long series of alterations when Sandra contacted me.

"What's up?" I asked.

"General Kerr. He knows about the Macros and others things. He's demanding to talk to you."

About a hundred and fifty times a day some foreign dignitary demanded to talk to me. I dodged ninety-nine percent of them. General Kerr, however, had to my knowledge never wasted my valuable time.

"Just a second," I told Sandra.

"Unit Six," I said. "Build me that prototype as currently designed."

"Working."

"Give me a time estimate to completion."

"One hour, nine minutes."

"Good," I said. "Run program."

"Executing."

The machine near me began digesting metals and gently heating up. A quiet, thrumming filled the room. For the hundredth time, I wondered what the hell these things were doing inside. I felt like a monkey running a microwave.

"Sandra? Could you come in here and babysit this machine while I walk over to base headquarters and to General Kerr? I want to have the big screen in front of me, as I'm sure he'll want a tactical update. After I get off the phone with Kerr, we can eat."

"Eat?" she asked. "I know you, this will not be a real date. You mean you'll bring some food to Shed Six, don't you?"

"Yeah," I said. "No time to fly Socorro to Miami tonight."

She sighed. "All right. I'll be right there to babysit your machine. I'm only going to do it for ten minutes, however. I want you to hang up on him after that."

I chuckled.

I walked over to headquarters. Once inside, I adjusted my headset and opened up a channel to General Kerr.

"Kyle? Is this damned thing on? Are we connected? Talk to me, Colonel Riggs."

"What can I do for you General?" I asked, trying to sound positive.

"You just had to do it, didn't you son? You just had to play tag with the aliens again, piss them off and bring them straight home to eat my planet."

"You were happy enough when I destroyed the four cruisers bombarding Europe."

"Four cruisers? I'd trade my wife and kids in a straight-up swap right this second, to be facing only four cruisers. Can you see your screen? Can you see the red triangles floating around Venus? They tell me those are hot death for Earth."

"Yes, General. I'm looking at the same data you are."

"Self-sacrifice, if that will help," General Kerr went on in my earpiece. "I'll face them alone out there in my undies, if that's how you want it. No suit, no nanites. Just give me a pistol, that's all I ask. Pistols will fire in space, won't they?"

"Um, yes they will, sir," I said, frowning. The general was often excitable during stressful moments, but I couldn't recall having heard him in a mood like this. "Have you been drinking, General?" I asked gently.

"Damn straight I have. And I'll tell you why. You want to hear why, mister-professor-colonel Riggs?"

I had a feeling I was going to hear why no matter what I said, so I kept quiet.

"Because you brought home one hundred Macro cruisers to kill us all, that's why! And they rolled right through your little minefield. I bet you thought we didn't know about all that, but we primitives hiding in caves at NORAD have a few cameras of our own left in the sky."

"I'm sure you do," I said. "But there are only ninety-two enemy ships, sir."

"What?"

"There are only ninety-two surviving vessels, and many of them are damaged."

"I don't give a rat's dick about that. Ten would be more than enough. We saw it all. We saw your mines fail to stop them, and we saw them form up behind Venus, just like last time."

"Um, you have described the situation fairly well. Now, if you don't mind—"

"What I want to know is: What the hell you are going to do about it?"

I thought quietly for a second.

"Hello? Riggs? Don't get prissy with me—"

"Perhaps you can help, General," I said.

"How so?"

"You can sober up, then talk to every military worth a damn on Earth. Tell them not to fire if the Macros come close. Tell them to wait until they are fired upon, or I request their aid."

"We have to fire first! It's use-it-or-lose-it when you're talking about nuclear weapons, son."

"Normally, yes. But I want you to hold back. I know the U. S. and several other nations have built up a stockpile of surface-to-space missiles. But I don't want you to fire them off until I ask for your help."

"That's it?" he asked. "That's all you want from us? We're supposed to sit on our hands and *not* use the only effective weapons we have? Do you understand the concept of a preemptive strike? If not, I will explain it to you: The basic idea is to *fire first*."

"I understand that, sir. I'm just asking you to convince all the players to stand down until the time is right."

Kerr was silent for several seconds. "Are you concocting some kind of new deal with the Macros, Kyle? I don't like the smell of this. Not one bit. Don't be giving them any of our real estate or our first born sons. Not this time."

"Wouldn't dream of it, sir," I said. "Do I have your government's cooperation?"

Kerr laughed. "Hell no. But you might in forty-eight hours. Kerr out."

The signal did not disconnect, however. I heard rustling and a small crash through my headset. I thought maybe the general had tripped over a cord. "Get that off me and find some coffee!" I heard him shout. Moments later the signal finally cut out.

I sat still, rubbing my face and thinking for five full minutes before Sandra showed up and barged in. I turned to her, shaking my head.

"I don't have time to eat," I told her.

"I figured you'd say that," she said. I noticed she was carrying a tray of sandwiches and a bottle of water.

We ate together quietly. She watched me while I brooded.

"Anything I can do?" she asked.

"Can you think of a way to take out ninety-two angry Macros?"

She shook her head.

I forced a smile and kept chewing.

-10-

I fell asleep late that night inside Shed Six. My com-link beeped and woke me up. I had no idea what time it was, as the interior of the shed had no windows. Even if it had possessed a window, the view would have consisted of the interior metal walls of the laser turret.

Sitting up, I noticed that Sandra was gone, and that the prototype of my new battle suit was lying in the output tray. The last thing I noticed was my com-link light, which was blinking red. I reached for it, and it beeped again.

"Riggs here."

"Colonel, we have new contacts," Major Barrera said. He sounded as solid as always. I wondered what time it was. I wondered what *day* it was.

"Contacts?" I asked. "At the Venus ring? Give me the count and configuration."

"They are at the Venus ring. The new contacts are invasion ships. Cylindrical shape and size match our recognition patterns perfectly. There are six of them, sir."

"Did they all make it through the minefield?"

"The minefield had been completely eradicated, sir. The Macros spent all night shooting down every mine we had out there."

I lifted my helmet and checked the chronometer inside. It was four-thirty a. m. Barrera was still on station at my desk computer where I'd left him yesterday. Apparently, he'd never slept. Despite all that, he sounded calm and competent.

I found some cold coffee in a plastic container Sandra had brought yesterday with the sandwiches. I sipped it and grimaced. It was awful.

"Are they moving yet?" I said.

"No, sir. Not yet."

"Good. Keep me updated."

"Will do."

I disconnected and stretched. The enemy fleet had been waiting for reinforcements after all. Logically, since they hadn't moved on, there were more ships still to come. I hoped they wouldn't show up for months and when they did, that the additional forces were insignificant. It was a faint hope.

Sandra showed up around six with breakfast. By that time, I had most of my new suit on and had her help me with the helmet. The problem was with the design, I could see right away. I needed to alter the helmet so it was self-sealing with trained nanites. With the gloves so thick and unwieldy, I couldn't fasten the catches on the helmet by myself. That was unacceptable design. I didn't want to put my troops in vacc suits that couldn't be put on solo. If they were caught in an emergency situation alone, that could mean a dead marine.

"You look like some kind of freak," Sandra told me when I was all suited-up.

"Thanks," I said. My voice echoed and was somewhat muffled inside the suit. I sounded like I had a garbage can pulled over my head.

I didn't have a mirror handy, but I knew I must look rather daunting. This new battle suit wasn't like the old ones, which were basically nano-fiber with a series of solid form-fitting plates over vital areas. Instead, it was all solid plates of dull, black metal. The plates interlocked and slid over one another to allow reasonably freeform movement. The nano-fiber interior was still there, underneath this heavier exterior of inch-thick plating.

"Why the heavy armor?" Sandra asked. "Other than to stop incoming fire?"

"The new equipment was too heavy otherwise," I said. "It would work okay in zero-gee, but under acceleration or a high gravity planet it would be hard to move. So, this suit is different. It's an exoskeleton."

"It makes you stronger?"

"Much stronger."

Sandra stood back, cocking her head and smiling. "Arm-wrestle me," she said.

I snorted. "We don't have time for—"

"Come on, you said you wanted to test the suit."

"Okay, here," I said, squatting down on a stool beside a steel table. We'd finally upgraded our furniture to withstand our gross body-weights. The stool sagged under me all the same. I wondered if we would have to upgrade everything again.

"If you pull my arm off, you have to take me to the infirmary to put it back on again," Sandra said, looking worriedly at the claw I put up in front of her.

"I'll be careful," I said. "No squeezing your hand. I'll just use lateral force."

"Okay."

We must have been a strange sight, this hulking robotic monster sitting across from a girl that couldn't have been more than a tenth my weight—if that much. She reached up and took my humming arm.

"Your suit vibrates in my hand," she complained. "It feels funny."

"That's the exoskeleton. Ready?"

"Why not?"

I locked my arm, but didn't move it. She pushed. I felt the feedback, but it was nothing like the force she was applying. I let her cheat, standing up half-way for leverage and using her legs.

"Ready?" I said, pretending I couldn't feel her shoving and grunting.

"You bastard. I can't move that arm. I don't think I weigh enough."

Sandra had fantastic strength for her weight, but she wasn't really stronger than the average nanotized marine. What made her deadly was her speed and accuracy. The microbes had rebuilt her with high-performance in mind.

I suddenly made a sweeping, lateral motion with my arm, twisting at the waist. Sandra made a whooping sound and flew across the room. She caught herself, tumbled and came back up.

"It's not fair," she said. "You're a machine now. I might as well wrestle a tank."

I stood up, bumping the steel table. A heavy crease appeared at one corner. "Damn," I said. "I'm going to have to be careful in this outfit."

"What else can it do?"

"Come outside."

She followed me into the sunlight. Passing marines stared at me, and half the laser turrets swiveled to study me. I sweated for a moment. I was a new classification of contact to them—and possibly hostile. More turrets swung to cover me. I froze in place.

"Unit Six," I radioed back to the shed behind me. "Transfer the configuration and recognition patterns for the new prototype battle suit to all laser turrets. Mark as friendly. Do it now."

"Done."

After a few more seconds, the lasers relaxed and went back to scanning the skies and tracking birds in the trees.

"That was close, Kyle," Sandra said at my side.

"Yeah. I forgot."

Inside the suit, I stood motionless for a moment. I was trying to figure out how to control the new system for my next test. I'd built this prototype unit with the same Heads Up Display we used in our regular battle armor, but for some reason it wasn't responding.

"What are all these lights and lines for?" Sandra asked, walking around me in a circle. She traced various LEDs on the exoskeleton with her fingers.

"You need light in space," I explained. "Both for identification and just to see. I can change the colors too, like this...."

The lights running over the suit changed from a soft blue to a soft green.

"Oh no," she said, "change it back. I like blue better."

I tapped through the color palette back to blue.

"How will you tell one another apart in these things?" she asked. "I think the colors should mean something. How about rank?"

"Good idea."

68

"Blue for officers," she said. "I only want to see you in blue."

I laughed. "And the other ranks?"

"Red for most marines. Green for non-coms."

"All right," I said, liking her ideas. It would make the identification of my people easier in combat. I hoped the Macros wouldn't figure out they should shoot the guys who were lit up in blue—but I didn't worry too much. They didn't seem like they were overly interested in colors and insignia. I didn't think they really understood or cared about our command structure, which was very different from their own. Macro Command was a parallel-processing wireless network that consisted of every Macro in the region. They probably had no idea some of us were giving the orders while others followed them. In their social systems, everyone participated and instantly came to the same conclusion as to their next tactical move. In a sense, they were the ultimate egalitarians.

Sandra stepped back suddenly, looking up at me and smiling. "Okay," she said. "Enough fooling around. Let's see what this thing can do. Impress me—but don't get yourself killed."

I'd planned to work up to flight, but thought that now was as good a time as any to try it out. One of the major design goals for these suits was improved movement. Using the exoskeleton for dramatic leaps was only part of it. This battle suit had its own propulsion system. I'd placed propulsion disks in the feet and arms. The disks were miniature versions of the flying dishes my marines had rode into combat while boarding ships during the long flight home. With four smaller units, I hope to provide greater stability and more fluid maneuvering.

"Here it goes," I said, and applied thrust. It took a bit more than I thought it would, but after a moment of trembling, I was airborne. I rose up over the base, slowly applying more thrust.

Again, I caught the attention of the laser turrets. They snapped their projectors around to sight on me like a flock of suspicious cranes. They slowly turned away, however, as I hovered there in the middle of the base. I was only using the two bottom propulsion units, the ones on my feet. I could feel them vibrate there, tickling my toes slightly.

"Wow!" Sandra called, clapping her hands. "I didn't expect that. Go higher. How high can you go? Can you reach space?"

"No," I radioed down. "In zero-gee, I doubt I could reach escape velocity, but I could maneuver freely in orbit. In an atmosphere with Earth-level gravity, I suppose I could fly around above treetop level indefinitely."

"You should come down here and carry me. Like Superman."

"Yeah," I said. "Maybe later, after a bit more testing."

"We'll be dead by then," she said, pouting.

"Maybe."

I landed then, and tried running in the suit. Oddly, that was harder to manage than flying. Getting the rhythm right, pumping my legs up and down in the correct pattern at the correct time was difficult. I headed out to the forest and immediately ran into a tree. Bark chipped off showing the orange-white flesh of the tree. Soon after I stepped into holes and went tumbling. The test was a general failure. I could see the suit was going to take some getting used to. The problem was my natural body movements weren't quite in tune with the weight and mass I was trying to move now. I had the strength, but it was as if I'd gained a thousand pounds and a lot of muscle. It was all about the timing.

Another major issue was the isolation and lack of tactile feedback. When running, the human body gives the brain input from our feet and limbs as to where they are in relationship to the ground. With this suit on—well, it was like trying to cut your toenails with oven mitts on. There were lots of accidents.

Sandra glided after me as I trotted around among the trees. When I fell, she helped me back up. After an hour or so, I was doing better. At least I wasn't falling on my face and bumping into things all the time.

Sandra banged her fist on my metal-coated shoulder blade. I didn't really feel it, but I heard it.

I turned smoothly to face her. "What?"

"Let's shoot something," she said. "I know you would never build a monstrosity like this if it couldn't kill a Macro."

"Have you got autoshades?" I asked.

She smiled and I watched as her eyes darkened. I'd forgotten about that. She'd had them built in. A nice trick. Maybe I could train my nanites to do that.

I turned back and aimed forward. I extended a gloved fist. Inside the arms, I'd build laser projectors. I burned down a tall palm with a single blazing emission and a slashing motion. The palm toppled over, the fronds at the top fluttering wildly as it fell. Birds screamed protests at us.

"You have two lasers?" she asked. "One in each arm?"

"Right."

"You're twice the man I thought you were."

"So are you."

Sandra gave me an odd look, not sure if she had been insulted or not. Fortunately, she couldn't see my grin due to the glare on my faceplate.

-11-

A few days later I had all thirty one of my factories producing improved models of my new battle suit. The suits took about three hours to produce, but they didn't take much in the way of specialized materials. After two steady days of production, I had about five hundred of these specialized suits. I'd already taken volunteer marines and set up specialized crash-training courses.

Crow came to watch me lead a company out on the beach a mile or so south of Fort Pierre. He stood on the beach with his arms crossed as we flew over the waves, shot hot lasers into the ocean and practiced diving through the resulting plumes of steam.

Finally, Crow signaled me impatiently. I ordered Kwon, who was assisting me in the training, to continue to lead the troops through maneuver and fire exercises. After that, they were to run ten miles through hip deep water and back again through the forest.

I landed near Crow with a spray of sand. He wore black-out goggles that clashed with his sunburned skin.

"What's up, Jack?" I asked him. "News from Venus?"

"Nothing, I'm glad to report. But I'm here to find out what the hell you are up to."

I waved back with one clanking arm toward the company flying over the ocean. As I did so, two of my men slammed together and went into spins. One shot down into the ocean, causing a fountain of steaming water to shoot upward. The second caught himself and managed to keep flying.

"Good work, marine!" I roared the winner over the com-link. "Now, pull your buddy out of the surf. Tell him he owes you a beer."

I turned back to Crow. "I'm training these men to use their new suits. They are tricky to control, especially while in flight, as you can see. The key is to get a feel for the suit as an extension of your own body. To *be* the suit, so to speak. It's rather like learning exactly where the bumper of your car is even when you can't see it."

"Are you expecting to go up there and parallel park with the Macros?"

"No, sir. I'm expecting to destroy the enemy."

"With this lot? With a pack of marines in medieval armor? Have you gone mad, Kyle? I expected you to use our destroyer design to manufacture a dozen new destroyers for me."

I removed my helmet and shook my head. Sweat flew in a spiraling spray. The heat-dissipation units inside these things needed a little work. I hadn't turned on my air-conditioners yet, I didn't think I should have to given that we were only working in the tropics. Space—especially any region of space closer to the sun than Earth—was going to be a lot hotter than this beach. But I'd thought wrong. The exoskeletons created excess heat as they moved, probably due to unforeseen friction and the use of servos.

"I forget you weren't out there on our campaign," I told Crow.

He stiffened his expression immediately. I knew he took any reference to his absence on my last big mission as some kind of suggestion of cowardice on his part. That didn't bother me, so I kept on making the references.

"Just tell me why this isn't a gross waste of time and resources."

"Don't think about them as marines, Jack," I said. "Think of them as one-man fighters. And think of your destroyers as carriers for these fighters."

He tilted his head, looking at me. "You plan to attack the Macros with infantry?"

"You saw me do it when that diamond of four Macros hit Earth a few weeks ago."

"I'd thought that was a wild act of desperation."

"No…it was a tactic. And a damned effective one, too. These Macro cruisers aren't well designed to stop boarders. They have only one single large cannon and a number of missile ports with a limited supply of missile salvoes. They can't easily deal with large numbers of small attackers."

Crow nodded. I could tell I had him thinking, but he still doubted me. "Still sounds to me like an excuse to build up your marine forces when it's obvious we need every ship I can get."

"Every one of these suits is a ship. A very small one, but I already have five hundred of them. I'm training the pilots right now, as you can see."

I gestured with a sweeping arm out to the frolicking marines. They were doing stabilization maneuvers now. These consisted of one marine flying laterally, then being struck or spun around by other marines. He was to steady himself and get to his goal point as quickly as possible without touching the waves. The mission of the rest of each squad was to dunk the man running the gauntlet. There was surge of hooting and roaring laughter each time a man spun out of control and slammed into the ocean.

"You are putting these clowns on my destroyers?" Crow asked. "I've got them set up for a crew of six, just as our design required originally. One helmsman working with the brainbox to maneuver the ship. One communications officer to coordinate with the rest of the fleet and a squad of supporting frigate-class vessels. Add three gunners and a commander, and you have all the crewmembers the ship is built to hold."

"Nonsense," I said. "You forget I helped come up with the design, Jack. We don't need three gunners, first of all. The original design was to allow each of the three guns to target three different enemies and engage them at once. I now reject that operational theory. These enemy ships are all larger than our vessels. We will have to put dozens of lasers on one cruiser to bring it down. We only need one gunner per ship."

Crow shrugged, conceding my point. "All right, a crew of four then."

"Three," I said. The commander and the communications officer are redundant. The small ships get by with two men each now, we only need three to run one of the bigger destroyers. In truth, we'll probably have them all link up under a single commander to combine their firepower without any operational delay relaying orders from ship-to-ship."

He glanced at me unhappily. "You'll make a lot of Fleet people unhappy if you don't let them fly."

"Too bad. When we have a large enough number of ships, they'll get their chance."

"So, I gather you want to fill the other spots aboard with your trapeze artists, here?"

"Yes. More than that, I plan to put troop pods with small platoons on every vessel. Sixteen total marines in battle armor. They'll greatly increase the firepower of your destroyers."

Crow sniggered at that. "How the hell do you get around to believing that?"

I keyed my headset. "First Sergeant Kwon."

One of the marines out blazing over the waves slowed and lifted himself above the rest. His suit ran with green lights and glowing LED lines. His suit was easily the largest one out there.

"Here, sir," Kwon said.

"I want a live-fire exercise. Drop a grenade on its lowest yield setting one mile east. Put it down in the water, set to go off on contact with the bottom. Move like its real, First Sergeant. 'Cause it is."

"This is a live-fire exercise!" Kwon roared without a moment's hesitation. "Code November! I repeat, code November!"

My helmet suddenly buzzed with a cacophony of voices. Everyone was shouting at once. Most of the marines whirled around and headed for the shore. Most of the company wore suits with red streaming lights, designating them as grunts. The green-lit non-coms and the few blue-lit officers hung back, plucking floundering men out of the waves. Some were airlifted by two or more others, dragged out of the water and up onto the beach.

"What the hell are you up to, Kyle?"

"Just watch," I said.

About a minute after the last man was out of the water, the flash came. The black outline of a single marine battle suit came tumbling through the air back toward us. The flash loomed and grew behind him. It was brilliant even by the standards of men accustomed to high-powered laser fire.

When Kwon returned to the beach, there was a lot of cheering and back-slapping. After a blast of wind howled by, Crow walked down to the waves and stared at the swelling mushroom cloud. A fountain of steam a thousand feet high ballooned out at the bottom ocean.

When we could talk again, Crow turned to me. "You really are a crazy son-of-a-bitch, Riggs. Isn't there some kind of international law about tests like that in water? What have you got against fish, mate?"

"Not really keen on the taste," I said. "But I had to test the new grenades at some point. They are like our mines, but designed for the purpose of rupturing a cruiser hull with a single strike. We learned a lot aboard those cruisers, and one thing I've got down to a science is the amount of force it takes to dig through one of those hulls. Every one of my shipboard assault troops will carry one of these specialized grenades. If even one of them gets close to a cruiser—boom."

Crow took off his goggles and squinted at me a new air of respect. Either that, or he thought I was insane.

-12-

The Macros played statue out there in orbit over Venus for seventeen long days and nights. Then one hot, sunny afternoon everything changed. By that time, we'd begun to relax a fraction. I think it's only human nature to do so. How long can a person keep their bloodstreams full of heart-accelerating adrenalin? How long can one remain sleepless and worried? At some point, I believe the mind and the body naturally become immune to a threat that sits and waits. I imagined that if a tiger sat beside a watering hole, motionless for days, the animals would eventually come to ignore it. Perhaps the monkeys would even sit upon its back and preen. That was the moment a wise predator would make its move.

We'd stopped worrying every minute about the crouching Macro fleet. We all knew they were out there. We knew they were waiting for something. A signal, a mistake, or perhaps an aggressive move on our part. Speculation on what would make them act ran rampant through the base and the media outlets of the world. Nightly news and talk-shows discussed little else. In the end, it was the arrival of a single, final ship that changed the game.

"Colonel Riggs, sir," Major Barrera buzzed in my helmet. "We have a problem."

I was down at the landing pits and it was midday. The sun rode high overhead and blazed upon my back, as it tended to do in the tropics. I'd handed over the job of training assault troops to Kwon and others who were already more talented than I with the new battle suits. I had achieved a passable level of skill, and decided to

77

leave it at that. There were simply too many other duties to perform.

Today, my duty was a happy one. Crow had managed to complete construction of a second full wing of nine destroyers. He brought them in and put them down in nine landing pits at the edge of Fort Pierre. Eager crews rushed to the new vehicles and boarded them excitedly. They held scripts in their hands and went through the rote routine of ordering their ships to take new names and accept their new masters.

It was a relatively happy moment, and I watched the elated crews with a smile floating on my face. When Major Barrera's call came in, that smile faded to a memory.

"Talk to me, Major," I snapped.

"The Macros have a new arrival, sir."

"Cruiser or transport?"

"Neither, sir."

I paused for a second, and if I hadn't known the Nanos in my chest wouldn't allow such a thing, I'd say my heart skipped a beat as well. "What is it then?"

"Configuration unknown. It is extremely large, however."

"Just one ship?"

"Yes, sir."

"I'm coming to the command center. Order a full alert."

I wasn't wearing my battle suit, but I wished I was. I vaulted the wall of the landing pit I was in and ran toward the big headquarters building in the center of the base. I could see the sun glinting from the tall windows of my office even at this distance.

Almost before I knew it, a second figure was running along beside me. My shadow was smaller, lighter and much prettier than I was.

"What's wrong?" Sandra asked.

"You're never far from me, are you?" I asked. "Psychologists would call you obsessive."

"They can kiss my butt."

"Not without my permission."

"Why are we running?"

At that moment, the entire base underwent a transformation. A dozen sirens went off. A thousand lights whirled and flashed. A loudspeaker began making echoing statements that no one could understand. It didn't matter, because they all knew what to do.

Men and women darted by at angles past us, dressing themselves as they ran. Sometimes they slammed into one another or leapt clear of accidents about to happen. One problem with unnaturally fast, excited people is we tended to have more accidents. Fortunately, most of the base personnel were full of nanites and therefore too tough to care. They picked themselves up and ran on. Tucking in shirts, pulling on flight jackets and buckling goggles to their faces, everyone was grim-faced. There wasn't any doubt in any marine's mind why we were scrambling to battle stations. There could only be one answer: The enemy was finally moving again.

Marines with full combat lasers appeared here and there at the door of every major building. Even the automated laser turrets lining the base walls and the sea itself seemed agitated. They jerked and tracked racing troops with nervous twitches rather than smooth oscillations.

"The Macros," I shouted to Sandra.

She nodded back. She'd figured it out by now.

I ignored the elevator and bounded up the emergency stairwell, taking five or six steps at a time. If I'd been wearing the battle suit, I would have just flown up to the top floor. Occasionally, lieutenants recognized me and hailed me, asking me for directions. Sandra and I wordlessly passed them by in a blur. I didn't have time to hold anyone's hand today.

When I reached the fourth floor, the bevy of purchasing agents scattered, having learned by now to keep out of the central aisle that led to my office door. Today, with the sirens and loudspeakers blaring, it was doubly wise on their part. I thought I heard the mahogany door crack as I threw it open. I felt a pang about that. The wood was beautiful. I slammed it behind me and walked to the big desk computer, breathing hard.

I opened my mouth to tell Barrera to zoom in on this new ship, but the words died in my throat. He'd already done so. The image swam even closer as Major Sarin made spreading motions with her hands on the central screen area.

It was huge. It dwarfed the cruisers and invasion ships that lined up around it, even as they dwarfed our smallest Nano ship.

"It must have ten times the mass of a cruiser," Sandra said, staring at it with me.

"We estimate a displacement of a quarter million tons, sir," Major Barrera said. "That's a very loose estimate, of course. It largely depends on interior structure, materials used, hull thickness and the like. Roughly, it's the size of several supertankers, Earth's largest vessels."

"What was your basis for the calculation?"

"Due to measurements of wreckage, we have good numbers for the cruisers. They weigh in at about twenty thousand tons. This ship has the volume of approximately a dozen cruisers."

I touched the screen, rotating our point of view. The thing was shaped differently than a cruiser, which was more or less like an arrowhead in shape. This ship was bulbous. It had a forward section that resembled the head of an insect, with two humps to either side. The bottom was more or less flat, however.

Crow had finally arrived. He stepped up to the desk to join us. He whistled as he eyed the monstrous enemy vessel. The Macro fleet was now leaving orbit in a grand arc of glinting ships. The big new ship was leading the rest. The computer had plotted their course. They would circle around Venus once, then escape the planet's gravity and begin the long journey toward Earth. Their projected path was visible as a single yellow line that curved off the screen.

"What do we call this monster, a battleship?" Sandra asked.

"Too big for a battleship," Crow said. "Earth battleships are only about two or three times the size of a heavy cruiser. Let's call it a dreadnaught. That sounds more ominous."

"Dreadnaught it is," I said. I kept my voice neutral. I didn't look around at my officers' faces. They were all glum—except for Barrera of course. That man would go to his grave maintaining a professional demeanor.

"Give me a rundown on its armament," I said.

Barrera reached out to touch various points on the dreadnaught. They glowed blue after his fingertips left the glass. "On the flat belly-side, we've counted a series of six rotating cannon emplacements. These appear to be more or less equivalent to the bombardment units on the bottom of enemy cruisers. There is another serious problem, however. These bumps are lighter weapons clusters on the shoulders, here and here. There is another of these bristling pods on the fantail of the ship. They appear to be point-defense systems, sir."

I nodded, feeling deflated. "How many guns and what kind of range do they have?"

"We've counted eight beam-type weapons on each pod. That's a total of twenty-four light guns. They aren't powerful—less range and hitting power than the gun on any of our small Nano ships."

I swallowed. "They don't have to be big. They are for taking out small targets. It's as if they knew about my plans."

Major Barrera looked at me with raised eyebrows. "Impossible, sir. But they might have gotten a report concerning our recent tactics and brought this vessel to correct a perceived weakness."

"It was more than *perceived*!" I said, almost shouting. I took a deep breath and forced my mind to cool down. "Do these defensive pods give the dreadnaught complete coverage from every angle?"

"We've been working on that for the last minute or two," Major Barrera said. He brought up another screen with a wire-frame analysis of the giant ship. A series of domed regions grew outward from the ship forming reddish shells around it.

"See these regions?" Barrera asked, touching the three dome-like shells in turn. "They are our projected areas of enemy defensive fire. It appears that the pods do cover the ship from every angle, but it is most vulnerable from the flat underside. Anything approaching from that direction would have to face the six cannons, but the light defensive pods would be relatively ineffective."

"Six of those big cannons firing at you? That's suicide," Sandra said.

No one argued with her.

"Missile ports?" I asked. I was a glutton for punishment.

"There is one accompanying each of the defensive pods," Barrera said. "I'm not sure how many tubes they have in each grouping. I would assume this ship can fire a large number of missiles, given the enemy's fixation on them as their primary armament."

I straightened my back and clapped my hands together, making a loud popping noise. Everyone except for Barrera winced in response.

"Well," I said, "the enemy intentions are clear. They'll fly here behind that big bastard. If we throw missiles or flying marines at them, the defensive guns will take them out before we can reach the core of their fleet. When they get to Earth, the dreadnaught will roll over and use the cannons to bombard us—along with their missile salvoes."

"Here's the part where you demand I fly my Fleet out there to die gloriously, right mate?" Crow asked.

I shook my head slowly. "A head-on assault would be suicide. We've got about thirty destroyers now, but only the new ones you built are fully armed. The older ones were decoys as much as anything else. We have time to improve their weaponry, but that's it. Gathering every additional ship we could, I doubt we could put up more than another sixty small ships. Less than a hundred vessels all told. Even without the dreadnaught, they would have three times our firepower."

"What are we going to do then?" Crow demanded.

"We're going to have to let them get in close. Real close. That way, the dreadnaught can't protect the rest of their fleet."

They were silent for a second as they digested that idea.

"But," Major Sarin said, speaking for the first time in a long while. "If we did that, won't they be able to fire on Earth, Colonel?"

"They'd have that opportunity, yes," I said.

"They have invasion ships too. Six of them."

"I can count. If anyone else has a better plan, I want to hear it right now."

Everyone fell silent. No one looked happy. Even the unflappable Major Barrera was glowering at the screen. All of them knew the score. We were charged with the defense of Earth. Except for a few thousand modified ICBMs the Earthers could fire into the mix, we were the only thing standing between humanity and annihilation. Unfortunately, we were going to have to let this enemy come in close before engaging them. Very close.

"Hey!" Sandra said, pointing and tapping at the screen. "See that? That little yellow contact lifting off Venus behind the Macro fleet? Is that…?"

"Yeah," I said, unable to keep a hint of bitterness out of my voice. "That's Marvin. My guess is he's been hiding in the blue giant system on the other side of the ring. Now that the Macros are out of the way, he's finally come back here to watch the show."

-13-

They'd turned off the sirens, but everyone was tense, watching the skies. At their current acceleration rate, we had several days before the Macros reached Earth. We were going to use every second we had to dig in.

I managed to slip out a couple of hours after the Macros left Venus' orbit. I had the entire staff busy by then. I exited the headquarters building and made it all the way to my bungalow unnoticed.

This suit was one of the newer models. I'd made many refinements over the last few weeks and had come up with a superior design. Sandra had even put in a few additions of her own when I'd been too busy to work on them. In some cases, just trimming back the overlap of the armor plates increased my freedom of movement. I'd also beefed the fusion generator somewhat. The initial system didn't really provide enough power to keep both beam projectors embedded in the suit's arms going while the system was in flight. That was a critical drawback. If my marines were going into battle as swarms of tiny fighters in space, they had to be able to fly and shoot at the same time.

I had my battle suit half on by the time Sandra found me. When the door slammed, I played it cool.

"Ah, there you are," I called out. "Could you help me with my helmet? This thing is still hard to put on solo."

Sandra stalked over to me and crossed her arms under her breasts. She gave me a withering stare. "Just where do you think you're going?"

"Um...to war," I said. "Helmet?"

She took the helmet away from me and bounced it around in her hands as if it was a basketball. I knew it weighed about as much as she did. Her strength still surprised me sometimes.

"You were going to ditch me. *Again*. Don't even try to deny it. You are a serial-ditcher."

"Uh, I have a war to run, Sandra. At times, that is bound to put me in harm's way."

She shook her head, ducking as I reached for my helmet. "No, I don't think so. You don't need to be in a battle suit days before the Macros get here. There's only one reason you would be dressing up like this."

I sighed. "Yes, you're right. I'm going up. I have to."

"Why, Kyle?" she asked. Her voice shifted to a high, almost tearful note.

"I've got a plan. I really do. If it works, it might save this world another bloodbath."

"Let somebody else do it."

"I would if I could. But truthfully, no one else can."

Deflated, she lifted up my helmet and slid it down on my head. I winced as it went over my face. Sometimes, if put on roughly, these things could rip your nose half-off. But she did it gently.

"You know," she said as she adjusted my suit here and there. "I read in school that Samurai wives would sometimes help put on their husband's *Yoroi* armor before battle. They would line his body with a layer of silk, then the armor. They would make sure it was done right to ensure he would return from battle."

"I can't take you with me," I said. "Not this time."

"That means you're not coming back," she said.

"I'm—I'm really not sure if I am or not."

She hauled off then and kicked me in my heavily-armored butt. The kick was so hard I actually felt some sensation and rocked forward a bit. Inside my helmet, I grinned.

"What happened to all that business about understanding?" I demanded.

"I have my limits."

Sandra left me then, but turned around in the doorway.

"Come back," she said, "or I'll kill you myself."

With that stunning display of logic, she walked out of the bungalow into the afternoon sun. She left the door standing open behind her. A fresh breeze stirred the paper plates on the kitchen table and ruffled our blinds, but I couldn't feel it through the suit. After a minute or so of checking my readouts, I clanked out of the house and headed for the landing pits.

I'd always wanted to fly one of the new destroyers. I could have gone up in *Socorro*, but I didn't feel like it. After all, I'd designed these destroyers, and by damn if I was going to die today, then I was at least going to have the pleasure of flying one first.

I marched to the first of the destroyers. It was sleek and vaguely boomerang-shaped. I took a slow moment to admire her lines, then commed to the pilot to open the hatch. After identifying me, he did so hastily. I walked heavily up the ramp and found the bridge. It was relatively roomy compared to the smaller ships I was used to.

I'd chosen this particular destroyer at random. It happened to be resting in the closest land pit to my bungalow. I looked around at the lucky crew.

"Gentlemen," I said. "I'm commandeering this ship. Kindly get the hell out—now."

The crew stared at me. They were Fleet people, and wore blue nanite-cloth flight suits. They'd been training, preparing for the big day when this ship was needed in battle. I was still hoping that day wouldn't come. It was a faint hope.

One of the men got up out of his crash seat and frowned at me. He was a tall fellow with a dark, bristling beard.

"Colonel Riggs?" he said with a mild east European accent. "I'm Captain Miklos. We have only just been assigned this vessel. Why do you ask us to leave our new ship?"

Inwardly, I sighed. I had sympathy for Miklos. Getting your own new ship to command, especially one of these amazing new destroyers, was exhilarating. I knew I was seriously raining on his parade.

"I'm sorry, Captain," I said. "I need to take her up. With luck, I'll bring her back in a day or so."

"And if you have no luck, sir?"

"Then I won't be coming back at all."

Captain Miklos stared at me, nodding slowly as he gained an inkling of what I intended to do.

"Does our Admiral Crow approve of this expedition?"

"I haven't asked him. But if I did, he would most definitely approve."

Captain Miklos laughed briefly, catching my joke. It was no secret that Crow and I were frequently at each other's throats. Any risky action I took that removed me from the home front—especially a mission that might be fatal—was a winner in Crow's book.

"Will you not need a crew to go with you, Colonel?" Miklos asked suddenly. He lifted his chin and looked over his nose at me.

I reached up and removed my helmet. I could tell now I wasn't going to need the battle suit to take the ship by force. Hell, they were volunteering to go out there with me.

"Captain," I said, looking him eye-to-eye, "I can't ask you to make that kind of sacrifice. I'm only taking a destroyer because they are faster than the smaller ships. I don't need to kill a good crew along with it."

Miklos nodded. "I understand, sir. But do you have the right to order me off my own vessel?"

I sighed. Star Force was different than traditional national navies. We had slowly developed our own rules of conduct. We had started as a group of pirate captains in a loose association. In many ways, we still thought that way, especially among the members of the Fleet. A captain was still something of a king aboard his own vessel.

"No," I said. "I do not have that right."

Miklos seemed pleased. He knew I'd once been on the Fleet side of Star Force, and I understood their code of honor. "Colonel," he said. "I believe I know something of what you intend. But this ship is designed to be flown by a full crew. I ask if I can volunteer to accompany you—along with any of my crew who agree to join us."

Surprised by his adventurism, I agreed. "All right," I said. "She's your command. I'm visiting brass. If you agree to accept my missions as Fleet orders, you can fly this vessel for me."

He swept his eyes over his crew. During our discussion, the group had gathered on the bridge. All told, there were three. The complement of marines I'd planned for each of these ships weren't yet deployed. I was the only marine, and the only man in a battle suit.

In the end, all three agreed to come. None of them could bear to be the coward, to turn away while their captain and I watched them. Star Force did not recruit cowards. I was proud of them all, even if the gunner did look a little green.

"When do we take off, sir?" Captain Miklos asked.

"Immediately. I've already cleared it with traffic control. Give them my priority code."

I listed a series of letters and digits. I'd long since arranged codes to allow immediate access to the skies over Andros. Every day it seemed Crow added fresh red tape and I had to work to drive a knife through it. Today, that preparation helped. The destroyer lifted off without being challenged or even causing a stir on the base. As far as I knew, Crow thought I'd gone to eat dinner.

Even though I figured that Crow wouldn't try to stop me if he knew what I was doing, I didn't feel like explaining it to him. He would have objections if he suspected some of my contingency plans. He would also most likely insist I take *Socorro* instead of one of his precious new destroyers. He might be right in that regard, but I didn't care. If this went well, we wouldn't need the destroyer today. If it went badly, one ship more or less wasn't going to save Earth from the Macro fleet.

"What's the name of your ship, Captain?" I asked as I felt the deck heave and swell under my armored feet.

"The *Barbarossa*, sir," he said.

I nodded, my face registering some level of surprise. The name meant 'red beard' in Italian, but had been used in many other historical contexts. I was immediately curious as to how Captain Miklos had struck upon the name. Unlike traditional naval forces, Star Force had a long-standing tradition of allowing commanders to name their own ships. This stemmed from our roots, where each commander had to fight to the death to win the right to command each Nano ship. Captains usually thought long and hard before they assigned their first ship a name.

"Barbarossa..." I said thoughtfully. "That name means different things to different people, captain. Such as the German campaign to take out Russia in World War Two."

"That's not the meaning I was thinking of," Captain Miklos said quickly. "I reached back to the oldest meaning. Fredrick Barbarossa was the Holy Roman Emperor of a thousand years past, a great military leader. It has been whispered for centuries that he would return some day to save Europe from evil."

"Ah, I see," I said, getting the reference at last. "In that case, rest assured. This ship will get the chance to live up to its name very soon."

Captain Miklos looked pleased. I could tell this man had guts and dreams of glory. I liked him already. The other crewmembers exchanged worried glances. I didn't blame them—they were in for quite a ride.

-14-

We reached low orbit within minutes. We slid around the world near the equator once, then flung ourselves up and away sunward. About then, Crow had finally figured out I wasn't coming back from dinner.

"Riggs? Where are you taking my brand new destroyer?"

I grunted, unhappy to hear Crow's voice reverberate from the dull metal walls of the bridge. The volume seemed deeper and the chamber echoed somewhat. The size of the ship made everything feel a little different aboard the destroyer. I'd had a vague hope I would get away from Earth without having to explain myself to anyone other than Sandra. Those hopes had been firmly trashed.

"Greetings Admiral Crow," I said. "I'm taking the ship out for a shake-down cruise. You know I plan to put my marines on these vessels. I need to plan a release hatch and a launch and retrieval mechanism."

"Smooth bullshit," Crow marveled. "But it still smells. You are the only marine aboard, and there is no reason to fly right into the teeth of the approaching Macro fleet. Now, tell me what the bloody hell you are doing up there in my ship?"

I sighed. Crow was many things, but he wasn't dumb. I looked around at Captain Miklos and his crew. They appeared uncomfortable. I'm sure their loyalties were divided. If Admiral Crow ordered them to return to base, what would they do? I wasn't sure. I didn't feel right putting them on the spot, either. I decided to try to explain myself to Crow, at least partly—if only for the sake of the crew. But I was going to do what I had to.

I was still wearing my battle suit. I picked up my helmet, the one missing piece. Every one of the crew members watched me closely. The gunner looked baffled. The helmsman's face was blank. But Captain Miklos knew what the move signified. He eyed me worriedly. We exchanged glances, and he read the truth in my eyes. I didn't try to hide it. If Crow ordered us back, I was going to use the battle suit to take over *Barbarossa*. The crewmen had hand-beamers, but they were useless against heavy armor. They could only draw a few smoking scars on the outer plates. I didn't want to do something so monumentally unfair, but in war unpleasantness was often necessary.

"Jack," I said, taking in a deep breath, "you know I've had many dealings with the Macros. More than any other human we know of."

"Right," he said cautiously.

"Well, I've got some ideas. Things I want to try out. I want to talk to them, and see if I can redirect their rage."

Crow gave one of his dirty laughs. "No chance there, mate. If anything, you'll prod their backsides until they're even more pissed off."

"How can we be any worse off than we are right now?"

"Well, you have a point there. But I don't want you losing our best ground officer in space, as well as a perfectly good destroyer. *Barbarossa* is one of the best vessels in the fleet. And you didn't bother to even ask if you could take her up."

I knew that his last point was the element that irritated him the most. He hated it when I usurped his authority over any part of Fleet ops. I didn't blame him, but this had to be done. I decided to back down and throw him a bone. I was a firm believer in asking for forgiveness rather than permission.

"I apologize for that, Jack," I said. "I should have talked it over with you first."

"Oh right, I buy that, mate," Crow said sarcastically. "Well then…I suppose you can try out your plan, whatever the hell it is. I know you won't tell me the details, so I'm not even going to ask. But I do want to know if you plan to return *Barbarossa*."

"I absolutely do," I said.

"What about your own person?"

I hesitated. "I'm not so sure about that."

"Crazy bastard. I knew when you took off like a robber's dog you were a danger to yourself and the rest of us."

"The Macros are coming to stomp humanity into dust. The fleet outnumbers us four to one. I might as well try to talk to them."

"I know that. Everyone knows that. But why can't you just wait it out until they get closer to Earth? Why fly out there into their faces?"

"Have they fired any missiles yet, Admiral?" I asked.

"No, they haven't—" Crow broke off and fell silent for a second. "Oh. I get it."

"That's right. Once they launch a few thousand nukes at us, the time for negotiation will be long past. I need to talk to them before they decide to do that, sir."

"Bloody hell. Right…well, right. Just get on with it, then. Crow out."

I relaxed in my crash seat and put my helmet back down on the floor. Captain Miklos gave me a tiny nod of thanks. A chain-of-command crisis had been averted. The captain's face was white, but relieved. Around me, I saw the crewmen go back to their duties calmly. I think only the Captain understood that disaster had just been averted. He had kept command of his ship by a thread.

"How far out are we going, Colonel?" he asked me.

"Far enough to allow them to pick out our signal. Let's not fly directly toward them. I want to shift our course thirty degrees below the ecliptic for the next hour. At that point, our position should be clearly distinguishable from Earth's in the background."

Miklos blinked at me, trying to figure out my plan. At last, he nodded. "You want them to be certain it is *you* in this ship talking to them, not a signal relayed from Earth."

"Exactly."

"You want them to be certain of your location—in the *Barbarossa?*"

"Yes."

He thought about that. He didn't seem to like his conclusions. "Are you going to exit the ship, sir?"

"I don't know," I said. "It depends on what the Macros say."

"Colonel, self-sacrifice is a noble attribute, but there are limits to the logic of it."

I eyed him for a moment. His concern seemed genuine. "Have a little faith, Captain," I said, giving him my best, most reassuring smile. "I've always got a plan."

That line worked, as it usually did. Captain Miklos turned back to his screens and readouts with a more confident expression. Some of the color even returned to his cheeks above his bristling beard.

I *did* have a plan, of course. I even had a few back-up plans. But I wasn't sure if anyone aboard would like my ideas, so I kept them to myself.

We flew on into the face of the Macro fleet for the next hour. It was hard not to feel a growing sense of tension in my shoulders and neck as the enemy contacts swelled ever so slightly on our long range sensors. The Macro fleet was bunched up behind their big dreadnaught. They looked like a dripping snowball seen from head-on, with one big central mass and dozens of smaller contacts slipping out from behind the protective skirts of their mother from time to time. Things looked even worse as we slid below the plane of the ecliptic. The enemy fleet began to stretch out and lengthen as our viewpoint shifted. From this new perspective, the snowball had grown a short tail of specks like a comet. If we kept flying away at an angle, they would stretch out and out into a long mass. The thought that each of those specks was a Macro cruiser with greater firepower and much greater mass than our ship possessed was terrifying if one let your mind dwell upon it. I didn't bother.

After we were about two hours out from Earth, the Macros finally reacted to our presence.

"The enemy fleet is shifting formation, sir," the helmsman said.

I nodded, unsurprised. I glanced at the helmsman, a young, obviously inexperienced ensign. He had the look of a bookish fellow from a good college. I wondered why he'd joined Star Force, but there wasn't time to ask him.

"Describe the new formation," I said. I could, of course, figure that out for myself by looking at the forward wall of the bridge or checking on the linked-in sensor data. But I wanted to hear how he analyzed the input.

"Sir, the enemy seems to be shifting some of their ships away from us. The—the tail sir. The ships hiding behind their dreadnaught are moving to where we can't target them. Even though we are clearly out of range."

"That's a good sign. They don't like us being out here by ourselves. We're making them nervous. The fact they reacted to us at all shows an unusual lack of certainty on their part. Macros do not usually bother with reactive defensive postures."

"Could their change in tactics be due to the leadership of this new, larger vessel?" Captain Miklos asked.

I looked at him and nodded. "Yes, that's very possible. I've seen evidence before that the Macros get smarter with increasing numbers of them on the scene. Maybe their shared processing systems increase in capacity with the presence of more individuals."

"So Macro Command becomes more capable with larger fleets?"

"My guess is that it does."

"Sirs?" the helmsman interrupted, "they are shifting again. A sub-formation has broken away."

"Let me guess," I said. "Four ships in a diamond pattern?"

"Exactly sir."

"And, they're headed toward us?"

"Yes."

"Okay then," I said, sitting up perfectly straight. It was hard to do anything else in my battle suit, but I'd managed to slouch fractionally inside it. "They've noticed us, so it's time to talk to them. *Barbarossa*, open a directed channel to the Macro fleet."

There was no response for a second. I glanced at Miklos.

"Oh, sorry," he said. "Barbarossa, take all orders from Colonel Riggs as if I'd given them to you. Colonel Riggs is to be accepted as command personnel with full authority."

"Permissions set," said the ship.

I repeated my request.

"Channel open. Propagation delay due to distance is three minutes each way."

We waited the three long minutes before the ship spoke again. "No response has been received," the ship said.

94

"Barbarossa, relay the following," I ordered. "Macro Command, this is Colonel Kyle Riggs, commander of Star Force. I wish to negotiate the terms of my surrender."

Every eye on the bridge widened and every head swiveled to aim at me. The gunner's mouth hung open.

I ignored them all. I stared at the chronometer. I had six minutes to wait to hear Macro Command's response.

-15-

Macros generally ignored pleas and threats. They especially hated questions. But they were suckers for offers of surrender. If Star Force surrendered to them, that meant less loss to their fleets. That made a material difference to them.

In the end, the Macros were accountants at heart. They were like giant metal spreadsheets. To get their undivided attention, there had to be something sweet in the equation for them. Something that would significantly alter the bottom line. If they could talk me into giving up without a fight, their goals could be met with greater efficiency. That made it worth their time to acknowledge me.

"Incoming message: *Surrender offer accepted. Disarm your ship and alter speed and course to match that of the approaching fleet.*"

I chuckled. "They aren't giving us much of an opening offer, eh?" I asked Miklos.

He didn't respond. He didn't seem to know what to say, he just gave me a horrified look. I waved an armored hand toward the screen.

"Just listen," I told him. "Barbarossa, transmit messages from me beginning with the words 'Macro Command'."

"Ready."

"Macro Command, I am offering my own personal surrender. Not the surrender of Earth, my ship or any other Star Force assets. Before I agree to surrender, I must have assurances that all Earth will be spared from any attacks and that your fleet will leave this system peacefully. A state of peace shall then exist between our two peoples."

We had a long wait after that, so I got up and prepared myself a cool drink in the galley. I avoided alcohol, instead finding some stuff that looked like orange juice, but tasted like sweet plastic. I took a swig and grimaced. I threw the remaining half of the disgusting liquid on the ship's deck, along with squeeze bottle it came in. The bottle dribbled for a few seconds, then the nanite decking detected it, correctly classified it as trash, and swallowed it. A hump of silvery liquid metal indented, allowing the squeeze bottle to sink into the indentation. Then the deck flowed over the surface of it. I knew that the nanites would release the discarded item into space. You had to be careful what you tossed onto the decks in these ships.

Captain Miklos joined me in the galley. "We've got to get better supplies aboard these ships," I commented to him.

"Sir, I understand your plan, but I don't agree with it."

"You don't, huh?" I asked with vague interest. I glanced at him, my eyebrows raised. "You want to split one of these doughnuts with me? I'm not sure they're any good, either. With the amount of money Crow wastes, I figured we'd have lobster soufflé on every journey."

"Sir," Miklos said insistently. "You don't have to give yourself up to the enemy. They might well change their minds and destroy Earth anyway. You don't understand how valuable you are to our world."

"Very kind words, captain," I said, handing him half my doughnut. It was glazed with chocolate sprinkles. I preferred plain, but decided it would be too much work with armored gloves to pick off the sprinkles.

"They aren't just words, Colonel. They are the truth. You provide such a morale boost to the men. They aren't afraid to fight when you are with them. That is not because they feel safe—"

"Hell no," I laughed.

"—they know that they will die well in your service, and they feel confident of victory. That confidence you provide them—that is the key. Normally, that would not be enough for the troops to risk their lives, but the stakes here are so much different now. We aren't fighting over lines on a map, or for a family of monarchs. We are fighting for the existence of our species. The men will therefore die gladly if they know it is not in vain."

I frowned at Miklos. He was earnest and intense. I had no doubt he absolutely believed what he was saying. Maybe, he was right in a way. But I figured the equation was simpler than that. I was a leader who had learned how to instill confidence through bold action and impenetrable self-assuredness. I had as many doubts as anyone—perhaps more, since I knew the real score—but I didn't let those feelings bleed through and reach my marines.

"Don't worry so much," I told him. "I have a plan. I've always got a plan."

He followed me back out to the main deck, clearly still troubled. "You say that quite often, Colonel."

I would have shrugged, but my shoulders were encased in about a foot of armor. I noticed I only had a few seconds before the next response was due back from Macro Command. I took my seat and swallowed the last of my doughnut. At least it was fresh.

"Incoming Message: *Colonel Kyle Riggs is not the only enemy force in this star system. Your terms are unacceptable.*"

"The machines aren't buying it," I said. I hadn't thought it likely they would accept me as the sacrificial lamb and give us an easy out, but figured I had to try. Unfortunately, they had reasoned it through. Clearly, a lot more than one single human had been involved in destroying their cruisers recently. They wanted to eradicate all the cancer and kill everyone who had rebelled against them. It was only reasonable, from their point of view.

"That's why you brought the battle suit?" the gunner asked me in amazement. "You planned to fly out there to them and give yourself up?"

I nodded. "If they would go for it, sure. Why not? One commander traded for our entire species? A bargain. But unfortunately, they aren't buying today. They want a bigger pound of flesh than just me. I'm not surprised, but I have to admit, I'm slightly relieved."

No one looked like they blamed me.

"What are you going to tell them now, sir?" Captain Miklos asked.

"Now, it's time for plan B. And don't even ask about plan C. You don't want to hear about that."

I raised my voice to gain *Barbarossa's* attention. "Macro Command," I said, "if you agree to accept peace with Earth and leave our star system now, Star Force will agree to the following terms: We will surrender all our ships, equipment and personnel."

At this point, the crew of the *Barbarossa* were freaking out. Miklos had stood up from his chair. The gunner was reaching for his sidearm and the helmsman had his eyes closed. He looked like he was praying—or maybe he was passing out, I couldn't tell which.

"Colonel Riggs!" Miklos shouted.

I put my armored hand in his face. My second hand raised to point at the gunner. At first, the gunner lifted his lip to snarl at me, and then he began to lift his weapon.

"Don't," Miklos said. He pointed toward my battle suit arms. Both arms ended in beam weapons equivalent to a heavy beamer. The gunner was unaccustomed to them and had not understood the threat, but at this moment my twin projectors were activated and aiming at the crewmen. If I fired them at this close range, the crewmen would have the upper half of their torsos burned and blasted away within a second by the fantastic release of energy. The gunner lowered his weapon slowly.

I hadn't figured they would draw on me. I should have put my helmet on first. I was impressed that they had the guts to take such an action, but it didn't really matter, as the situation would be set in stone very soon.

"Furthermore," I continued, keeping both men under scrutiny. "Star Force will surrender Andros Island, our base on planet Earth. We will lay down our arms and obey Macro Command. End transmission."

"You can't do this, sir!" Captain Miklos hissed at me.

I lowered my arms. The moment my laser guns weren't aimed into their faces, the gunner brought up his weapon again.

"I won't let you surrender this ship, sir," the gunner told me, shaking with emotion. "I didn't join Star Force to serve the machines again. I understand you made that deal the first time without knowing the full consequences. But we can't lie down and do it all over again."

I tried futilely to shush him. He didn't calm down.

"He is your superior officer," Captain Miklos said.

"He can't just unilaterally consign our entire species to slavery," the gunner answered. "My entire family was killed by Macros. I won't serve them."

I looked from one man to the next, then glanced to the helmsman. He was still praying.

"Ensign," I said, addressing the gunner. "I like you. If we live long enough to return to Earth, I'm going to give you a promotion. Possibly, a command of your own. Captain, I'm impressed with you and your crew. Even your helmsman, because at least he's still manning his post and following orders."

They all looked confused. "Is this some kind of joke, sir?" Miklos asked.

"In a way, yes. But we won't know who has the last laugh for another two minutes."

They gave me blank looks, so I pointed to the chronometer. The next Macro reply was due in very soon.

Not knowing what to say, the men returned to their stations. Miklos looked like his cat had just died, while the gunner glared at me off and on. I didn't care. I was beyond caring. It was all up to the Macros now. Would they accept my terms or not?

It was a very long two minutes. Finally, the response came in.

"Terms accepted."

I whooped and laughed. I clapped my armored hands together, and the metal made a booming report in the enclosed space. The other men winced.

"I don't understand what there is to be happy about, Colonel," Miklos said.

I grinned at him. "Macro Command," I shouted, unable to contain my exuberance, "Star Force has changed its mind. Star Force has gone rogue. Star Force is entirely contained on the land mass known as Andros Island, plus a few Fleet elements in space such as this ship. Riggs out. Barbarossa, send that and close the channel."

If I'd thought the crew were surprised before, now they were positively baffled. Even the helmsman's eyes were open again. He stared at me with the wary certainty of a one who knows he's looking at a madman.

100

"Colonel Riggs?" the gunner asked me. "So that's it? All of this was a big joke? Just to have some fun with the Macros?"

"Reason it through, ensign," I said.

Captain Miklos nodded slowly, thinking it over. But the helmsman, who'd kept quiet up until now, spoke first.

"I get it," he said. "When the Macros agreed to your terms, they agreed to classify all of Earth as peaceful. When you said Star Force has broken the deal, only we became possible hostiles."

"Correct," I said. "We entered into an agreement with them. They marked all humanity as peaceful slaves in their database somewhere. The next moment Star Force went rogue—"

"Which means when they get to Earth," Captain Miklos said, a new light dawning in his eyes, "they will only attack Star Force."

"You tricked them?" the gunner asked incredulously.

"Sort of," I said. "I'd call it a work-around. Like getting a computer to delete a file it doesn't want to by doing it in a manner that isn't blocked. The machine doesn't become angry, or *feel* tricked. All I did was talk them into classifying all Earth as peaceful. Once they accepted that, I reassigned this ship and all of Star Force as hostile. In a way, I reprogrammed the Macros."

"But won't they simply ignore everything we've said?"

I shook my head. "I've dealt with them before. Using a similar trick, I managed to get them to leave the annihilation of China to Star Force. Remember that? To work with them, you have to think like a hacker. These shenanigans would never work with a human being. But the Macros don't get emotional about it the way we do."

"Do you think they'll learn to stop falling for such deceptions someday?" Miklos asked me.

"Possibly, but I don't care right now, I—"

"Sirs," the helmsman broke in. "We've got missiles incoming. The Macros have fired upon us."

"There, you see?" I asked them. "They made a follow-up decision I should have seen coming. Well, don't look so pale, the missiles are about fifty million miles off. They won't get to us for a long time. Barbarossa, attention."

"Ready."

"Reverse course. Take us back to Earth at flank speed. Hold on, everyone."

Skinny black arms spit up out of the floor and grabbed us, acting as emergency harnesses. The ship heaved under our feet. The engines on this ship were very powerful, and even with stabilizers, we felt at least three Gs of force tossing us about as the ship flipped over and applied all the thrust she had.

"Course laid," said the ship.

"Barbarossa," Captain Miklos said, picking himself up off the deck and crawling into his command chair, "remove Colonel Riggs from the command personnel list unless I'm incapacitated."

"Options set."

I nodded to him, deciding it wasn't worth arguing about. I had boarded this vessel with the understanding I was visiting brass, not the operational commander. I'd taken liberties. Lots of them.

"I'm sorry, Colonel Riggs," he said.

He didn't look very sorry. I nodded and smiled.

"I understand," I said. "This is your ship…just one more thing."

"What's that, Colonel?"

"Have you got any beer?"

-16-

The ride home was relatively uneventful. The crew didn't seem to think so, however. I could tell they were green. They'd never had a swarm of sixteen semi-intelligent nuclear missiles trailing them and getting closer every minute. That sort of thing took some getting used to.

There wasn't anything to worry about, really. Even with the about-face and a long glide back to Earth—which was orbiting away from our position, making us chase after her—the math was in our favor.

"Stop worrying, Miklos," I said, "we'll be back at least an hour before the missiles slam into the ship."

"But we have to slow down to get home, and they keep accelerating," he said, tapping nervously at a spreadsheet on his tablet. "The kinetic energy alone, even discounting the warheads...."

"All right, I'll talk to Crow about it."

It took me a few minutes to get the good admiral on the com-link. Just thinking about talking to Crow made my three-beer buzz transform into an instant headache. I'd been in a celebratory mood. I'd managed to talk the Macros into targeting Star Force alone. It'd been such a coup I wanted to savor it. Now, as the disk of Earth grew huge on the forward wall of the bridge, I realized it was time to get back to work.

"So," Crow said, his voice replicated by the vibrating of the countless nanites that made up the walls of the bridge, "still alive, but running home to hide behind papa is that it? We've been watching your efforts at talking the Macros into a good mood. How'd that work out for you then, mate?"

"Just fine," I said expansively. "I talked them out of destroying our planet."

"You what? How is it then, might I ask, that I see a veritable horde of enemy ships on your ass? Not to mention the missile swarm, which they no doubt sent as a diplomatic gift?"

"I said I talked them out of destroying Earth," I said. "They still have grim plans for me. And for the rest of Star Force. I gave them your address as a reference."

I grinned at the crew, but none of them seemed to find my little joke as amusing as I did.

"Let me get this straight," Crow said. "They are coming straight here? To Andros Island?"

"Now you're catching on. If you want to keep this destroyer alive, I need you to make sure the laser turrets are on high alert. I'm going to fly over the island in low orbit. I need the turrets to shoot down those missiles."

"We've calculated the velocities. They'll only be in range for about two microseconds, do you realize that Riggs?"

"Yeah. Group them up on individual missiles so they don't all fire at the same ones. Also, I figure I might have to do a second full speed orbit just to give the turrets another shot."

"Hmm," Crow said. "I don't like it, Riggs. The Macros will be counting our guns. They've never seen how much firepower this island has. I don't want to tip my hand just yet."

"Then what do you suggest?"

"I could loft the fleet," Crow said doubtfully.

"Might help," I admitted, "if you want to keep this new destroyer of yours intact." I hadn't asked him to do it, so he could make the offer. I needed the support, but when dealing with Crow, one never wanted to seem weak. When Crow sensed weakness, he got ideas. For instance, he might get the idea that getting rid of the irritating Colonel Kyle Riggs was worth the loss of a single destroyer.

In the end Crow agreed to my plan. We streaked toward Earth, moving too fast to get into a real orbital pattern. We were beyond escape velocity the entire time. Using full engine power, I would be able to swing around the planet in a wide oval, bringing us back around the world for a second pass over Andros about thirty minutes later. Hopefully by that time the missiles trailing us would run out of maneuvering fuel or they would all be shot down.

While we waited, I popped a fourth beer and sipped it. The flavor was harsh. I looked at the can and saw a picture of a bear on it. Squinting at the label, I saw it was from Romania. I smiled at Miklos, who was still sweating in his command chair.

"You must like beer as well," I said, "have one with me."

He hesitated, then got up and opened a fresh one. He tipped it to me and took a swig. "How did you know it was mine?" he asked.

"The Romanian bear on the label. I just figured."

He smiled. I thought it might have been the first real smile I'd ever seen on his face.

"You know, Colonel," he said, taking a large swallow, "you are just as crazy as everyone says you are."

"Crazier," I told him confidently.

"What if we lose, sir?" he asked.

"You mean the war?"

"Yes. What if Star Force is destroyed, but the rest of Earth stays quiet and peaceful in order to survive."

I thought about it. "Then I suppose we will be like the Centaurs in their star system. Fantasizing we are at peace with the Macros, while they circle around trying to figure out how to eat us."

"Like Romania bears, eh?"

"Exactly."

His words cause me to remember something. I needed to talk to Earth. They couldn't fire on the Macros in any way, not even at their missiles, or they would be marked down as hostile again and everything I'd done out here today would be for nothing. I didn't think they had any armament capable of shooting down a Macro missile at this range, but I wasn't sure. They'd been building up as fast as possible, stealing bits of tech from Star Force wherever they could. Maybe they had a few surprises in store by now.

It took about seven minutes to get General Kerr on the com-link. I was surprised he wasn't sitting on the phone. He had to be aware of everything that was going on up here. Kerr and I had an odd relationship. We'd often been in antagonistic roles. But we needed each other often, too. Sometimes there wasn't any room for bullshit, and we both needed to communicate plainly. Many others had tried to establish themselves as intermediaries between various Earth governments and Star Force. I'd always rejected them and insisted on Kerr. It wasn't because I loved the guy—far from it. But I understood him fairly well and he understood me, too. Sometimes, when life or death decisions are being made on the fly, having a tight relationship with the guy on the other end of the line was very valuable.

"Riggs? Are you the one flying that batmobile?"

"General Kerr," I said, "this isn't a social call. Listen closely, please."

"Go ahead."

"There is a tight grouping of missiles following my ship back to Earth. It is imperative that Earth forces *do not* fire on those missiles. You must relay this to every military on the planet. When we cruise by, do not attempt to jam them. Do not attempt to obstruct them. Do not shoot them down. Preferably, you will not even actively ping them with radar or let one of your satellites drift close by. But I'm pretty sure that's too much to ask."

"It is too much to ask. I'm not even sure I can convince every nation on Earth to stand by and hope for the best."

"You don't have to. Just talk to the ten or so who actually have the capability to do anything effective. They must not provoke the coming Macro fleet. I have managed to convince them their only enemies on Earth consist of Star Force on Andros Island. All that diplomatic work will be for nothing if people get trigger happy down there."

General Kerr laughed. "That's what you call diplomacy? Looks to me like you got them royally pissed off. Classic Kyle Riggs. I've always said you had a silver tongue in your head."

I smiled grimly. "Right sir, I take after you. But in any case, any assets that fire on the aliens must be Star Force units."

Kerr paused. "Are you asking for operational control of some of my systems, Kyle?"

"No, sir," I said. "I'm asking for you to appear to be under my command if you get involved."

"Humph," he said. "I don't want to make promises, but I'll do my best."

"Remember what happened to China, sir. Remind them about that."

"Good point. Kerr out."

The first pass over Andros happened some thirty minutes later. We sailed by, scudding at the outer fringe of the atmosphere. Daringly, we brought our ship down to an attitude of around sixty-five miles. At our speed, there was good amount of friction and bumping even though the 'air' outside the ship consisted primarily of occasional hydrogen atoms.

The missiles passed by the same spot some ten minutes later. We watched on our nanite screens of metallic relief, but the more comprehensible data was available on normal LED screens at our stations. Crow's fleet hung up above us at that point, nearly a hundred vessels in low orbit. They all fired the moment we passed by and the missiles were in range. They only had a chance to fire once, but there were about a hundred and fifty shots.

Beams stabbed out invisibly in space. Without anything to burn, the light emissions weren't anything that would register on the human eye other than to blind and burn any retina in their path. Our sensors helped out, drawing bright green rays of pixels on our screens to show where the laser fire flickered and licked like momentary flames.

Eleven of the missiles vanished. I smiled, happy to see the success of my plans. Fleet had taken them out nicely. With any luck at all, the missiles would be running out of power to bank around the Earth. Even if they did make the turn, we had time to complete the maneuver again and shoot the rest of them down. If we hit eleven the first time, hitting five on the second pass should be done easily. Both my ship and the missiles were going to have to slow down somewhat further on the second pass to keep close to Earth.

The orbit took less than ten minutes. I let the missiles get closer this time, to keep them interested.

"Sir..." said the helmsman, "the missiles are changing course."

"Where...?" Miklos began.

I cut him off, shouting for a com-link to Crow. "Barbarossa, relay to Star Force control, move your ships. Repeat, scatter all vessels."

"Colonel Riggs is not command personnel."

"Send the message, Barbarossa!" Captain Miklos shouted. He had figured out what was happening.

We were too late. The missiles, moving at tremendous speed toward unsuspecting stationary targets, were nearly impossible to stop. The formation of the Star Force ships was thoughtless. They were in a flat formation over Earth, spread out at approximately the same altitude. The problem was they didn't have a free field of fire laterally toward something approaching at the same altitude they were. When the missiles swerved up to their altitude during the last seconds, half the ships could not fire on them without risking hitting their sisters.

Confusion caused the fleet to shift slightly as the last five missiles zoomed up toward them. It wasn't a scatter order, or an organized retreat. It was just confusion.

"They knocked out one missile—no, two," said the helmsman.

We were all glued to our screens. I'm not sure anyone was even breathing. Three clouds puffed into existence less than a second later. The clouds were a brilliant white release of energy. They expanded into bumpy spheres, then dissipated rapidly, turning into tiny pin pricks of light and finally nothing.

I wanted to put a hand to my face, but the big armored glove loomed close and I stopped myself before I pulled skin off.

"Losses?" I asked.

"Three hits, three ships. Two frigates and a destroyer—the *Valiant*, sir. It was her maiden voyage."

I nodded. No one said anything for a while as we decelerated and made our approach over Andros on our next orbit. Crow had played it badly, putting his ships too close to the kill zone and lining them all up at the same altitude. But I'd underestimated the intelligence of the enemy and hadn't warned him about the possibility. I was supposed to be the resident expert on Macro behavior. It was my guess Crow would blame me for the losses.

I reflected on the trick they'd played upon us. In my experience, Macros tended to choose a path and follow it doggedly, even if it was disastrous, like a line of mindless ants marching into a flame. But twice now they'd varied their behavior and shifted tactics when something didn't work the first time. Could it be the new dreadnaught had altered their behavioral patterns? Could it be a command ship of sorts? Maybe it made them more intelligent, more adaptable. It was a chilling thought, but the evidence was there.

"Admiral Crow is attempting to connect to you on a private channel, sir," said the helmsman.

I nodded slowly. I knew my helmet was beeping at me. Without looking, I knew who was making that little green light blink. But didn't answer the call.

"Ignore it," I said.

I didn't feel like listening to a tirade right now. I was doing a good enough job yelling at myself inside my own head. I should have just used all of Andros' guns and knocked out the missiles on the first pass. It didn't pay to be cagey when facing a swarm of nuke

-17-

Sandra had greeted me with subdued enthusiasm when I clanked out of the landing pit. I'd come back to her, as promised. She took me home and promptly removed my armor. It needed a good spraying out. I'd sweated a lot over the last dozen hours.

She joined me in the shower without a word. I really wasn't in the mood. My mind was whirling with tactics and should-have scenarios. But she was insistent and impossible to deny. We ended up on the bed, wet and dripping. There was still soap in my hair, one eye was closed from burning shampoo. I didn't care, and neither did she. Our homecoming celebration lasted for quite a while.

The Macro battle fleet arrived the next day. Somehow, I managed to get a solid night's sleep. At five a. m. we dressed and headed for headquarters. We reached the top floor, but no one called out a greeting. There was worry, if not outright fear, in every eye that met mine. I paused before opening the big doors at the end of the line of cubicles.

"I'm giving a new order," I said. "All non-combatant personnel are to evacuate the island. That doesn't include essential services like medical staff and repair people. But all you keyboard jockeys are to head down to the docks and float your butts north to the mainland."

You would have thought I had announced a Christmas bonus. They were grabbing their stuff and packing their purses as fast as they could.

I was still calling it my office, but since Crow had had no time to build himself a new one, we were really sharing it. He was there when I walked in and he was in a predictably sour mood.

I stepped up to the desk without a word. The Macro fleet was at the north the edge of the screen, looking like a short-tailed comet. The Earth was on the south end of the table, with Andros island represented at a mass of green contacts. Crow had withdrawn everything to one central point—Fort Pierre.

"Tell me how you do these things, Kyle?" he asked.

I didn't bother to look at him.

"Tell me how you take one ship on a suicide mission, but somehow end up surviving while killing three perfectly good crews."

"Next time, don't tell me we shouldn't use the laser turrets."

"Oh, so that's it, eh?" Crow asked, crossing his arms and glaring at me. "I'm the asshole here again, right? Somehow, I'm always the one cleaning up your messes and doing it wrong. Terribly wrong. So wrong, in fact, that millions of innocents are liable to be—"

"Shut up, Jack," Sandra said.

Crow heaved a sigh. But he did shut up. It was a blessing.

"On the upside," I said, "we've bought something with the blood of those three crews. We've got a surprise in our pockets."

"All right," Crow said. "How are we going to capitalize on it?"

"How long have we got?" I asked.

"About seven hours, sir," Major Sarin said.

"Long enough," I said. "First, let's move to our emergency facilities."

"Underground?" Crow asked. "Already?"

I looked at him. "You can stay up here if you like. I don't want to learn about any more enemy surprises the hard way."

Crow nodded and when we packed up to move eight stories down, he was the first one poking at the coffee and doughnuts. Normally the last man to show up for work, he was always first in line when food or personal safety was involved.

The headquarters building, like most of the major building at Fort Pierre, had a deep bunker underneath it. We'd built bunkers under Andros long ago. It wasn't easy. Underground facilities on this island tended to fill up with water. Even with pumps going

111

night and day to draw air down and pump water out, the bunkers were always dank. The older bunkers were built of concrete, and in those upper chambers the walls sweated and smelled faintly of mildew. Digging down deeper still we'd gotten smarter and used a nanite bubble inside the concrete. They were like a liner in a bucket. We shaped them the way we wanted and kept the bilge water and rot out.

The operational computer table down here wasn't as big and luxurious as the one up in my office, but it was a lot less exposed and fully functional. Standing around it were Crow, Major Sarin and Sandra. I'd put everyone else upstairs into the effort of organizing the resistance on the ground. Kwon was a few floors above in this same command bunker with a platoon of marines in full battle suits. Major Barrera was at a remote location on the island, with orders to direct tactical fire. If this command post was knocked out, he was to take over operational command of the defense.

I looked at Crow. He appeared far too comfortable to me with his coffee and doughnut. Chocolate sprinkles again. I wrinkled my nose.

"What's on your overly-fertile mind now, mate?" he asked.

"You," I said. "You are Fleet, and I think you need to take your ships out of here."

Crow looked a trifle more pale. "You want me to fly right into their teeth, do you?"

"No, not that. I think you should pull the fleet back. If you hover over the island, you will be priority targets. Lift off and go somewhere else. Hide behind the Moon if you like. They'll have a hard time hitting you there."

Crow appeared thoughtful. "Not a bad idea."

"But be ready to come back and hit the Macros in the butt when I call you. I've placed a platoon of battle suits on every destroyer. Remember to get them in close, then release them. With their grenades, they can do tremendous damage if you can get them in close enough."

Crow narrowed his eyes at me. "This isn't just a way to get me out of your hair, is it, Kyle? Maybe you don't want me spoiling your glory, eh?"

I smiled. "Don't worry, if any of us live to see another day, there will be plenty of glory to go around. The cavalry always comes in to save the day at the end. That's you."

We talked and planned for another hour. Finally, he agreed and headed for the landing pits. I'd figured he would. He didn't want to be at ground zero with a hundred Macro ships on the way anymore than I did.

"You should go with him, Kyle," Sandra told me. "Leave Jasmine and I here to man this command post. I don't trust Crow to bring the fleet home at the right moment. He'll hold back and screw us somehow."

I looked at the two women. Major Sarin and Sandra both looked at me with dark, pretty eyes.

"Objections noted," I said. "But I don't think this is the end of the game yet. I've got a few tricks in store for the Macros."

"I don't see any tricks," Sandra said, studying the map suspiciously.

"If you don't, then they won't either."

She made a face at me and I pretended not to notice. Major Sarin made a snuffling noise, it was almost a laugh. I wondered if Star Force was ever going to become as professional as a real military organization. Or if maybe we'd redefined how militaries operated. I figured that in time, we'd become tightly disciplined and bureaucratic. It seemed to happen that way in fledgling militaries throughout history. General George Washington's army had been little more than ragged band of militia. Over the course of a few centuries, they'd transformed from the minutemen of Lexington and Concord into the most powerful, professional military force on Earth. It took time to develop a military tradition.

Before I knew it, we were down to four hours. The Macros could fire missiles at us at any time, of course, but so far they'd held back. I suspected they wanted to get in close and make their salvos count. Maybe they believed they could take us out with their belly turrets alone and salvage more of the planet that way without worrying about fallout and the like. Or maybe they wanted to run their sensors over us carefully and pick the best targets.

By the time the shooting started, Crow was in position with his fleet of ninety-odd ships behind the Moon. They could return in less than an hour if need be. I'd asked him to come back out into near Earth orbit once the fighting began to shorten that time span, but still remain safely outside of laser range. If the Macros decided to attack them, they should run. If nothing else, they would be drawing off forces from the main fight back at Andros.

So far, the Macros had ignored our fleet maneuvering. They were on course for Andros and had never wavered from that trajectory. Their intent was clear. If they came here and obliterated our base of operations, our factories, command centers and troops, they could deal with the surviving fleet later. Or our fleet would have to come and commit to attacking their rear to save Andros. Either way, their move was the smart one. Andros Island couldn't run away, so it was an easy choice as first target.

When they were about three hours out and decelerating hard, they fired a salvo of missiles. This was much more terrifying than the first sixteen they'd sent after my ship. Each cruiser had sixteen missiles according to our estimates. They sent about half their total arsenal at us—over eight hundred missiles.

It was hard not to feel sick as the red contacts swelled on the screen. Dotted lines flickered into life all over the screen. Each of them led directly to Andros, representing the computer's estimate of every missile's trajectory. As they accelerated toward us, they left a solid line behind them, showing their path back to the firing ship. As we watched in stunned quiet, the trails began to curve and form gentle arcs.

"It's too many, Kyle," Sandra said. "We couldn't even stop sixteen before—how can we stop this? Nothing will live on the entire island."

"Not if they get here," I said. "But we've got better than a thousand automated guns aimed at the sky right now. And we've got some other moves to make. ETA on those missiles, Major Sarin?"

"They are still accelerating. The computer says…forty-nine minutes, Colonel."

I glanced at Major Sarin. Sandra was biting her lip, but Sarin was still cool. I wasn't sure if that was due to a greater trust in my abilities as a commander or a natural personality flaw that kept fear at bay.

"Major Sarin," I said, "we need some help. Get General Kerr on the line."

This time, there was no delay. Kerr was indeed sitting on his phone.

"Looks like you're toast, Riggs," he said. "Sorry to see it happen. Can't say as I'm surprised, though."

"Thanks for that vote of confidence, General. I need your help. You know those twenty-odd subs you have floating around Andros, hugging my shores?"

Kerr hesitated. "That is on a need-to-know basis—"

"Screw all that," I said. "I think it is clear we both *need* to know. I know because we have better sensors than you might realize, and because you once invaded Andros with troops from those same submarines."

"If you are asking me to unload marines on your doomed island, Riggs, you had better think again."

"Not at all, sir. I want you to unload something else. According to my intel, six of those subs are Ohio-class boomers, sir."

Kerr made a strangled sound.

"Don't bother to deny it," I told him. "Like I said—we have nanotech, better sensors, etc. I need those six subs to surface and fire their nuclear missiles. I need atmospheric bursts in the path of the Macro barrage. Lots of them. All at more or less the same time, with interlocking blast patterns. The concentric shockwaves will knock out the enemy missiles."

"Riggs, I don't have the authority—"

"You are sitting in NORAD. Get the authority. Talk to the President. Talk to God, I don't care. Just get those missiles armed and fire them. If you don't stop that barrage, you'll lose the subs anyway from concussion."

"What?"

"You heard me. We've plotted out every impact point. You'd better believe I'm not going to fire on anything that's coming down over the water."

"It'll take time, Riggs. I don't guarantee anything."

"Those are Ohio-class subs. I'm not sure what mix of tridents and tomahawks they have aboard. I'm hoping for tridents so they can reach up to a sub-orbital altitude and stop the missiles, but even low-flying tomahawks should be able to put up a concussive barrier. I'll feed you all the target coordinates and recommended timing from our brainboxes."

Kerr fell quiet for a time. I knew there were a lot of people around him, listening in. For all I knew the entire war room had circled around the phone in the background.

"General Kerr...?" I said after nearly a minute had gone by. Major Sarin had helpfully put a clock up on the screen. I was down to forty-four minutes. "Are you there, sir?"

"The President has given his approval, over the objections of several others."

"He's there in the war room with you?"

"Yes."

"Tell him he has my vote next fall, if I'm still technically a citizen, and I'm still alive."

"He says thanks. We've got a lot of work to do. Feed us those numbers."

I signaled Major Sarin urgently. I put the General on hold and opened the command channel so Major Barrera and his team could hear me, as could Crow in his ship, which had already lifted off.

"That's it, people," I said, standing up straight. "We're all set up."

"We're ready, sir," Barrera said evenly.

"Best of luck to you, Colonel Riggs," Crow said. "It's been a pleasure."

I keyed off the general command channel and eyed the clock. We had half an hour to wait.

"Put the U. S. subs on the board, will you Major?" I asked.

Sarin tapped at it expertly. Yellow contacts appeared. There was a loose ring of subs surrounding Andros as well as two tight groups of three subs further out in the deep ocean. The ring was made up of attack subs, while the two tight groupings were the boomers. We'd long ago read their small, but traceable, sonar signatures to identify them. Once you put a brainbox on the job with fast-learning neural net and good sensory input, they never forgot a given sub's signature. The subs weren't moving yet, but I kept hoping.

"What's going to happen, Kyle?" Sandra asked a few minutes later. "Is this crazy plan going to work?

I shrugged. "The fans are on—let's see which way the shit blows."

116

Watching the action helplessly from my bunker was nerve-wracking. I found the situation almost intolerable. It gave me some perspective on why the Pentagon types hated me so much. My survival, in fact the survival of the entity known as Star Force, was now in the hands of faceless individuals that were so far out of reach I couldn't even shout at them—not that it would do any good if they could hear me.

Around me, Sandra and Major Sarin stood tensely. All of us muttered things like "Come on, come on," and "Aren't they firing late?"

When the first round of tridents did finally launch from the western set of subs, I actually thought they were firing too early. But as I watched the missiles streak over my island, I realized they had to get up there and get that barrier of shockwaves going. Early was better than too late.

Trident missiles are equipped with mirved warheads. As far as I knew this was the first time the weapons had ever been fired in combat. Each trident carried no less than eight independent warheads. The sub crews didn't have time to be fancy with the targeting, they simply launched them into the path of the oncoming barrage in a somewhat scattered pattern.

I had a panicky thought as I watched six yellow lines pop onto the screen, tracking the launched missiles. What if my laser turrets shot down the tridents? They weren't targeting our island, but I knew the turrets were set to be highly paranoid.

I keyed open the command channel. "Major Barrera?"

"Sir?"

"Make sure our turrets are set to allow those tridents to pass overhead. Don't let them engage under—"

"I already thought of that one, sir," Barrera interrupted. "They've been configured to allow the subs to fire unmolested."

I heaved a sigh of relief. "Barrera," I said, "right here, right now, I'm promoting you to lieutenant colonel. You are officially second in command of the Star Force Marines. Congratulations."

"Thank you, sir."

I caught Major Sarin eyeing me. Had she expected to get promoted first? I had to admit, she had been key in our return to Earth. But I didn't want that proximity to color my judgment. Arguably, Barrera's feat of keeping a calm hand on the rudder back here on Andros while Crow ran wild for months was as big an achievement. I looked back down at the screen. I could still feel her dark eyes on me.

I didn't glance at her again. Competence wasn't enough for commanding officers in my book. What Sarin lacked was personal initiative. If she wanted a promotion, all she had to do was save the world from destruction a few times. Barrera had just proven it could be done.

I was vaguely surprised Sandra didn't object to the fact Sarin was staring at me. There had been a time in the recent past where I'd been less than professional with Major Sarin—with Jasmine. That was in the past now, but I knew Sandra maintained a vigilant eye over the two of us and the nature of our relationship. She wanted to make sure it stayed cordial, but distant. I half expected a pinch or something from Sandra, but it didn't come. She couldn't have missed the pain on Jasmine's face, so I calculated she knew it was all about the promotion and nothing further. Maybe Sandra approved of my passing over Major Sarin. I didn't care. I'd promoted Barrera for performance, not emotional reasons.

I looked at the clock again. There were two of them now, one in green digits that read 4:02 the second was in red and displayed 8:47.

"And the new green timer is?" I asked.

"Projected time until our missiles meet theirs," Major Sarin said.

I nodded. Sarin was very competent—she always provided quick, helpful operational support. But support wasn't command. She was doing her job, but she'd never really run anything independently. I decided if we survived the next few months I'd worry about it then. Maybe I'd give her a command of her own.

Still, I sensed her staring at me. Unbidden, the sensation of kissing Jasmine came into my head. I'd only kissed her once, but the tingle of it was sharp in my memory. I pushed the thought away. It had been a pleasant, brief moment, but now wasn't the time to relive it, even if she was watching me with hurt eyes. Maybe she thought I should have given her a promotion as a final gift before we all died.

I shook my head slightly, trying to clear it. Why was I dwelling on Jasmine? I was glad Sandra couldn't read my thoughts. She'd want to murder me herself.

I glanced at the green clock. We had two minutes to go until the opposing waves of missiles met up in the upper troposphere. Damn, this waiting was killing me.

In the end, the sub commanders weren't able to get all the missiles up, mirving and exploding like fireworks at the same time. But they did pretty well. The missiles from further away got there first and burst into sets of smaller contacts.

"They're going off too early," Sandra said.

Her fingers gripped the edge of the computer table so tightly I saw tiny fractures in the glass radiating from each thumb.

"Relax," I said. "They just released their eight warheads in a sprayed pattern. In a moment, the warheads will go off individually."

Then, as I spoke, they did blossom into white globes. Twenty-four airbursts. I hoped nobody was looking that way, as these bombs were high-yield. Each warhead had a potential yield of up to three point eight megatons. They were city-busters, not tactical warheads designed to destroy enemy forces.

They'd gone off a trifle early, I thought. The green clock still said there was sixteen seconds until the enemy barrage arrived. Better early than late, I told myself.

Seconds later, the next wave of missiles came in behind the first. These went off closer to our eastern shore. They were the backup wall, I realized, meant to stop the stragglers that got through the first wall of fire and turbulence. They lit up the sky with twenty-one bursts. Possibly, a few of the warheads had malfunctioned, or they had been knocked out by the blast waves from the first explosions.

All over the map interlocking mass explosions blossomed white. We felt these last twenty-one strikes. They rocked the bunker. The ceiling was made of nanites, so no concrete showered dust and chunks down on our heads. But the roof did shift, bubble and sag ominously.

"Is it going to cave in?" Sandra asked.

"Not a chance," I said confidently, although I had no way of knowing the truth. It either would or it wouldn't.

I stared at the screen. The front explosions were just beginning to fade when swarms of red contacts slammed into the barrier we'd created. They couldn't change course now. They were going too fast, and were too close to their goal. As the red streaks met the white spheres, I found myself turning the point of view, spinning it around so we could see the cloud from every angle. Was there a hole?

"Some of them must get through," Sandra said.

I sincerely hoped not, but I couldn't argue with her logic. The green clock read 0:00 while the red clock still had thirty-three seconds to go. I wanted to gnaw on my lip, but resisted the urge. If we took a real hit, I'd have a mouth full of blood and torn flesh. We all squinted our eyes and gritted our teeth, bracing our legs under the table.

The sirens were going off, air-raid sirens that warbled high and then low again. They had time for about three undulations before it was all over.

A red streak came down right on top of us. It was decelerating, but still coming in very fast. I saw lasers streak up, meeting it, burning it. But they were too late.

We were going to take a hit.

"Brace yourselves," I said unnecessarily. We were about to die. Bracing wasn't going to stop a direct hit from a thermonuclear device. Neither was a hundred feet of sandy, wet earth. If anything, the soil here would transmit the shock of the explosion straight down to our bunker. If we lived, we'd be digging ourselves out.

My last thought was for Kwon and his sixteen battle suited marines on the floors above us. I should have ordered them down deeper into the command post with us. But there simply wasn't time now.

-19-

When the impact came, it barely shook the room. All of us looked at the walls and ceiling with wide eyes.

"Was that it?" Sandra asked.

"I heard it strike sir," Major Sarin said. "It has to be down."

I nodded. "A dud. Or it was knocked out by all our counter fire and unable to detonate."

I thought fast for a few seconds. I watched the screen. A few more red streaks had made it through the barrier, but I saw less than a dozen. Those that went further over the island were shot at by more and more of my laser turrets as they came. They blinked and went out. Only two of the Macro missiles actually went off, and in both cases they were too high to do much damage. I figured the missiles knew they weren't going to reach their targets and had self-destructed. Either that, or they were damaged somehow and misfired. In either case, the overall results were excellent.

I began to smile. "We did it," I said.

"It actually worked," Sandra said. Her voice was that of someone who could not believe they were still alive.

"I thought we were dead, too," Major Sarin said quietly.

I glanced at her, feeling a pang of sympathy. Maybe that's why she'd been hurt in those final moments when I promoted Barrera. To be passed up for promotion was never pleasant, but it had to be more poignant when you were convinced you were in your final moments of life.

I felt a sharp jab in the ribs. Sandra smiled at me tightly when I looked down at her. She'd poked me with a pair of stiff fingers. I wasn't sure, but she might have cracked a rib.

I took in a sharp breath of air and looked away from Jasmine's lost face. My side ached, but I managed to speak in a natural-sounding voice. "Connect me to First Sergeant Kwon."

Major Sarin came alive and did as I asked.

I heard whooping and cheers. They came in a deafening chorus. I smiled slightly, it was hard not to.

"Kwon?"

"Yes, sir! The men here are celebrating. Can we go up yet?"

"That's why I'm calling. Get your helmets on. I'm going to suit-up as well. We have a piece of unexploded ordinance that came down in the base somewhere. You're team is to seek and dismantle that weapon."

The joyful chorus died down. A babble of low voices erupted as Kwon relayed my orders. Once the helmets were on, I could only hear Kwon's voice.

"We're on it, sir. I should have thought of that one. Please order the rest of the base personnel to stay underground."

I waved to Major Sarin, who put her hand to her headset and began contacting the other bunkers, emphasizing that the all-clear had not yet been sounded.

As Kwon's unit was the only team of marines on the base who had battle suits, I decided they were the logical ones to send up. If the warhead detonated, of course, their personal armor wouldn't make any difference. But fusion warheads used smaller explosions to get the reaction that caused the big bang. As well, the systems engine might ignite or the entire missile might be set to self-destruct upon sensing approaching enemies. We just didn't know how these missiles worked. We'd never been near an unexploded Macro missile before. I knew they had some level of machine intelligence. They were definitely smart weapons in every sense of the term.

"I don't want any surprises," I told Kwon. "Use the utmost caution. Don't let anyone play around with it."

"Right, sir."

"I'll be right there after I've suited up."

123

I walked quickly to my battle suit and climbed up into it. The easiest part of putting one of these things on was getting your legs inside. The suit expanded everywhere and split itself open across the chest. The legs however, remained standing by themselves. The suit's exoskeleton took care of balance and kept itself erect.

I jumped up on top of it, and slid my feet down into the two vertical tubes of the legs by pointing my toes. Once inside, the armor plates slid closer forming a tighter fit around my feet. I shoved my hands into the armholes and felt the suit clamp down on them. Now that I was inside, the chest area began closing over my torso. It was a disturbing process, and made one feel claustrophobic.

"A little help with the helmet, please," I said.

Sandra appeared in my face. "Are you crazy, Kyle? Why do you have to go up there?"

"I want to see what a Macro missile looks like."

"So have Kwon take a video and check it out later."

"Helmet?"

She made an exasperated sound and put the helmet on my head. I adjusted it and tapped the 'seal-ready' button with my chin. All the suit's systems went live and I heard oxygen begin to flow around my face. I clanked up the stairs. Sandra followed me. I had to order her to stay behind.

"When do I get one of these gorilla-suits so I can go with you?" she asked hotly.

I thought about it, not liking the idea. "Many of your special capacities would be blocked by a suit like this. It would greatly slow you down. Why don't you just stay here in the bunker and protect Jasmine for a while?"

"Because she isn't trying to play with a Macro bomb and get herself killed."

"I'll be right back," I said and clanked away. I could feel the two women staring after me.

When I reached the surface, I paused in shock. The forest was on fire in dozens of spots. All around the base, up and down the beach, the trees smoldered and billowed with white smoke. The trees nearest the water had taken the worst of it. I supposed I shouldn't have been surprised. You couldn't blow off forty-odd high-yield airbursts and not expect some damage. Fortunately, the blasts had been far enough offshore and high enough in the atmosphere they hadn't knocked the entire base and the forest around it flat. There was damage here and there. The base buildings looked like they'd been through a hurricane. Debris was strewn everywhere, but I didn't see any bodies.

I turned around to check out my new headquarters building. Every window appeared to be blown out, except for the large ballistic glass windows of my office on the top floor. Three of those showed impact stars, however. I wondered if I'd live long enough to repair them.

Tilting my helmeted head upward to the limits of the suit, I gazed at the blue-white sky. The wind was blowing westward, so I could see out over the water, despite the smoke from the burning trees. There were definitely some odd-looking clouds out there. A few of them looked like starfish, while others looked like puffy white doughnuts. I wasn't sure what the meteorological conditions were, but I was sure there were going to be some funny-looking turnips growing in Russia or wherever those radioactive clouds ended up coming down.

I goaded my suit into a trot and hopped over a barracks roof. I found Kwon's platoon out among the landing pits where the Macro missile had fallen. His men were standing outside of pit ten, encircling the concrete walls. They watched over the top of the barrier while someone in a suspiciously large suit clanked around inside a crater in the middle of the pit.

I engaged my gravity-repellers and sailed over their heads, landing in the pit with Kwon. I walked up and he turned awkwardly to meet me.

"Colonel? I didn't know you were coming to this party."

"What have we got, First Sergeant?"

"A hole sir. I can't see the missile at all."

"Hmm," I said, coming up to the smoking crater. I stood beside him and we both gazed down in a mass of molten, sandy soil. It was smoking and looked like a bullet wound in the surface of the island.

"Let's get a crawler out," I said. "We're going to have to dig it out."

A crawler was a new vehicle Crow had invented while I was away fighting for the Macros. It was similar to hovertank, but

125

wasn't designed for combat. They had no lasers, but instead had four nanite-arms and were equipped with a blade and a scoop they could use to mold the earth as desired. The crawlers had replaced vehicles such as bulldozers and backhoes on Andros. They were much more versatile. With their four incredibly powerful arms, they could lift cargo like giants. Working together, they could even move ships and small prefab buildings.

We summoned two of the automated vehicles to the spot. One looked lightly damaged from the blast waves that had rolled over the base. It had one mangled arm. But we poured a fresh barrel of constructive nanites into its maw and within a minute or two it had rebuilt itself.

"Now get in there and move the earth away from the metallic object in the center," I told the crawlers. "Do not touch it, or cause it to shift. When you get close, we'll go in and do the rest of the job by hand."

"Script written," said the master crawler. "Executing."

The second crawler followed the first and aped its actions. They were linked together in what was known as a master-slave relationship, meaning the brainbox of the first unit controlled the actions of both crawlers. It took less coordination that way. It was similar to the manner in which a nanite swarm operated. Somebody had to have a plan and be in charge.

The two crawlers worked their blades, scoops and arms impressively. They pushed back the circle of concrete walls in spots to get more room to work. Apparently, the Macro missile had sunk into the soil quite deeply. I wondered if we would find much more down there than a mass of twisted metal.

They bladed away a widening oval shape around the spot. The missile had partly disintegrated and left an area of debris that was, well…missile-shaped. Within twenty minutes, the crawlers had the landing pit torn apart and a race-track shaped hole around the object a dozen feet deep.

"This would make quite a swimming pool if we filled it in with gunite," I joked with Kwon.

The First Sergeant turned his suit laboriously to look at me. "A swimming pool, sir?"

His English had never improved much and he tended to take things literally. I waved away my words. "Never mind, First Sergeant. I think the crawlers are done."

The two machines had made themselves a pathway that led out of the hole like an earthen ramp. They raced out of it now, arms whipping around overhead carrying their final loads of earth in their scoops. Wet clumps of sand dribbled from the swaying scoops as they passed me.

"Mission accomplished," the master unit said as it whizzed past. It had many other missions to attend to today, given the state of the base, so I didn't ask any questions. The Crawler probably would have given unsatisfactory answers anyway.

"Break out the spades, men," I called to the waiting platoon. "This is the marines, so I know you guys know how to dig."

Indeed, they did know about digging. We headed down into that hole and circled the central mass that the crawlers had revealed. I almost regretted letting them get away. Perhaps they would have been more delicate with this next stage of the operation than my marines.

Spades flashed in the sun, biting deeply into sandy soil. I helped until I grew tired of it, then joined Kwon in walking around supervising the men. Here and there, they found a smoking piece of black metal. I ordered them to switch to another spot immediately, not to keep poking at it. We were here to reveal this wreck, not to stab it with shovel blades.

"The men want to know if they can open their suits, sir," Kwon asked me.

"No way," I said, I'm not having any acute radiation sickness today."

"How about just their helmets? They are sweating in their suits."

I pointed out toward the sea. Strange clouds were still visible on the horizon. "The wind is going the right way, but I'm not taking a chance. No one breathes outside a suit on Andros until I say so."

"Very good, sir," Kwon said. He didn't sound like he thought it was very good, but he'd stopped complaining.

It took us much longer than the crawlers took to dig out the rest of the wreckage. It would have taken us even longer if the mass hadn't become unstable and resulted in a minor avalanche of sand.

"Okay, pick yourselves up," I said. Many of the men were standing waist or even helmet deep in wet sand. "Use your repellers if you need to. Help each other."

All around me men were climbing out of holes and servos whined while nanite-impregnated materials flexed to lift marines back into the afternoon sunlight.

I think I was the one who saw it first, even though it didn't grab me. None of these men had seen a Macro up-close except for Kwon himself. He was bent over double, pulling a private out of a mound of sand at the time.

A familiar flash of bright metal. That was it, just bright metal and a sense of movement. It was more than enough to set off alarm bells in my head.

"There's something moving in there, men! Shoot long, steady beams. We have to disable it before it can set off the warhead."

Dirt flew. Flashing metal instruments—steel mandibles at the head of the Macro. They looked like a whirling mass of concentric lawnmower blades. I aimed my laser at the thorax and held down the firing button. A green glare filled the pit with brilliance. Everyone's autoshades engaged to keep them from being instantly blinded.

Men shouted, one screamed. The Macro had him and was tearing at his suit. He couldn't get his guns into line with it. The other men fired further back along the monster's metal body. Kwon joined me and we took the chance, firing deep into its guts, figuring if we didn't the marine would be dead anyway. Some of those flashing tools were drills that could dig through armor and bore into the meat of a marine very quickly.

Four concentrated beams did the job. The Macro crashed down, twitching and whining with straining servos. I stepped up, calling for a ceasefire.

"All right, that's it boys. Just make sure there aren't two of them inside this thing."

The marines dug much more gingerly after that. No one talked about removing their helmets anymore. I checked out the marine who'd been grabbed by the Macro. His armor was scratched and dented in spots, but the plates had held. The Macro hadn't been able to get to my man's flesh. Almost as significant, I found the private had managed to wrestle with and twist away two of those numerous flailing limbs. Employing his exoskeletal strength, he'd managed to damage the Macro as much as he was being damaged, even in hand-to-hand combat. I was impressed.

The single enemy Macro was the only one in the missile. I nodded to myself. It made a strange sort of sense. What better way to make a missile intelligent than to put one of your technicians aboard? Macro missiles were really kamikaze spaceships. They reminded me somewhat of my own men in battle suits. They just took it to the logical extreme, using their own troops like suicide bombers.

The warhead, when we found it, was inoperable. I wasn't surprised. If it had been repairable, the technician Macro would have set it off. There wasn't much to learn other than that. The missile had a single large warhead, an engine not unlike a small ship engine and a Macro technician as a pilot. A human pilot would never have survived the impact, but steel alloys were much tougher than flesh.

"There it is, Kwon," I said, kicking the smoking ruin of metal. The Macro was pitted with laser strikes. "Take a good, long look."

"Here's *what*, sir?"

"The first Macro to invade Andros Island. I have a feeling it won't be the last."

129

-20-

We'd survived their opening salvo, but the battle was far from over. We had about thirteen hours of breathing time before the next stage began. When I say 'breathing time' I mean a sweating, scrambling time during which we repaired our facilities and dug in as best we could.

I released about ten percent of our constructive nanite reserves to build more underground bunkers. I'd originally assumed our non-combatant personnel would be safe in villages located in more remote locations around the island, but I no longer believed that. Andros was about 2300 square miles of tropical paradise, mostly uninhabited even now that Star Force had taken it over. But the kind of toe-to-toe nuclear combat I'd seen today could easily devastate the entire landmass.

Accordingly, we spent a lot of our time letting crawlers dig holes and dumped barrels nanites into them with orders to form walls. When the nanites formed a roof of liquid metal and it had time to take solid form, we dumped the dirt back on top of the new structure. These new bunkers weren't very strong, really. They were like beer cans buried under a few inches of dirt. They couldn't take a direct strike, but they were much better than standing on the surface.

One area I was highly concerned about was my not-so-secret base on the western side of the island. I had a large number of my factories there, sitting inside sheds. Each of these sheds formed the basis for a laser turret. These were soon to become targets and might well be knocked out. The laser turrets had been intended to protect the duplication factories, but now I realized the turrets had become a danger to their existence by making them into targets.

We did the best we could with the time we had. I dragged the factories out into the forest, dug holes, filled them with nanites and buried them again. From an aerial viewpoint, it was highly dissatisfying. The factory locations were easily marked by fresh earth. Running out of time, I ordered the marine garrison there to put one man into every laser turret and one man into every sealed bunker with the factory. The rest went around the area spreading patches of earth to make *fake* bunkers. We ran out of time when the garrison had managed to dig about six simulated bunkers for every real one. I was less than pleased. If the enemy cruisers hung up above, freely bombarding the site from orbit, it wouldn't make any difference if there were three hundred bunkers for every factory. The Macros would keep firing until every interesting inch of the island was a blackened crater.

I kept these thoughts to myself and returned to our deep command post under the Fort Pierre headquarters building. Sandra was down there with Major Sarin, and I was glad to see neither of them had yet killed the other. Every time I left those two alone, I worried. Sandra was far more dangerous and impetuous, but Jasmine had a sidearm at all times and she was sneaky. She was the quiet kind, the sort of woman you didn't even know was in the room most of the time. I knew that if she decided to make a move some day, she would just draw and fire and that would be it. No speeches, no nothing.

Sandra was the opposite. She was all flash and fire. You always knew she was coming and what she was thinking—but you could never be sure if she was mad enough to really do something serious or not.

Kwon stumped down the metal steps after me. In his battle suit, even the nanites building the floors seemed to dent in and regret their existence under this heavy tread. We removed our helmets and joined the women. The four of us stood around the computer table, watching the Macro fleet decelerate overhead.

The enemy loomed over the Indian Ocean, slipping into Earth orbit. They bore down on us out of the east, and like burrowing

131

animals in the shadow of a hawk, we'd done our best to vanish underground.

"They are over Africa now," Kwon said, stating the obvious. "How long?"

Major Sarin tapped one of her clocks, and made a flicking motion with her fingertip. A new clock spawned and shot across the table, appearing to spin. It came to rest in front of Kwon. He chuckled at the cool graphical effect.

"Eleven minutes," he said, and stopped chuckling as meaning of that number sunk in.

I turned back to the big board. The dreadnaught was still in the lead, and if anything the train of cruisers behind it had hugged up closer to the big ship. Maybe they figured they would be protected in her wake. I hadn't done battle with a dreadnaught yet, so for all I knew they were right. We watched as the fleet passed Africa and began the long glide northwest over the Atlantic toward our island. They were clearly planning to halt over Andros and decelerated continuously as they came.

A signal beeped. "It's General Kerr, Colonel," Major Sarin said.

"Open the channel."

"Riggs?" Kerr's voice rang from the metal walls of the room.

"Here, sir."

"Not for long, by the look of it. Do you want our help? Is this when we launch our ship-killers?"

"I don't want you to do that, sir," I said. "Let Star Force handle this for now. If you launch from the states, they will know you are in this fight. Miami is a much softer target than my island. They don't see us all as a single, unified enemy at this point. Don't give them the opportunity to change their minds about that."

"I understand your plan, but do you really think they will let you guide them into your guns? To break themselves on your single fortified position?"

"That is my sincerest hope, General."

"Sounds loony to me. If I was their commander, I'd change my plans."

"Fortunately, you are not," I said with feeling. "The Macros are computers, sir. In most cases, computers do not reevaluate their

132

decisions once they've been made without new input. Don't give them that input."

"I'll await new input myself, then. Either from you, or the enemy."

"One more thing, General," I said before he disconnected. "I suggest you order your subs to submerge as deeply as you can. There's a trench to the east of Andros called the Tongue of the Ocean. Send them down there. They'll have a hard time burning that deeply into the ocean with a laser."

"What if they fire more missiles at you? The tridents worked so well last time, I figured you were going to be begging us for a repeat performance."

I shook my head and leaned against the computer. "Not this time, sir. They look like they're coming right down to sit on us. If they fire their smart missiles from directly above, we won't be able to stop them with a counter strike. We would have less than thirty seconds to react. Too short a time. I'd prefer you conserved the subs. We might well need every asset we have before this is over."

Kerr was quiet for a moment. I suspected he was calculating our odds of survival and not coming up with good numbers. I'd thought of this detail as well—the possibility the Macros would come in and unload the rest of their missiles on us at point-blank range. I didn't think they would do it—but I couldn't be sure. They'd lost badly the last time they'd fired a missile barrage, and Macros didn't like to repeat an error twice. They didn't know how slow and disjointed our command and control was. Macro Command could react quickly, so they tended to assume we could as well.

"We'll hold our fire then. Good luck down there, Riggs. Kerr out."

Major Sarin had put up a clock in the table area in front of each of us. The clock read seven minutes. I didn't want to stare at it, so I tapped the X in the corner and the clock vanished.

I looked up and saw everyone was looking at me. We didn't have anything to do for four long minutes. I lifted an armored finger and pointed to the line of spread-open suits along the far wall.

"I want you two suited up," I told the women. "We're all putting on full gear, helmets too. If they decide to unload on us, it might make the difference."

I thought for a second Sandra was going to object, but she didn't in the end. Kwon and I helped the women get into their suits and adjusted their helmets. By the time we were done, the Macros were sliding into low orbit overhead. They had decelerated a great deal. We clanked back to the computer.

"Be careful," I said, "set the suit gloves to delicate-equipment setting so you don't smash the tabletop. Remember to set them back if we get into a fight."

"Who are we going to fight down *here*?" Sandra asked.

"Macros like landings. There are six invasion ships in the rear of that formation. They aren't full of tourists. Remember the first time they came to Earth?"

Sandra didn't ask any more questions about it. We all stared as the last seconds ticked by.

"They are almost in range, sir," Major Sarin asked. "Any targeting changes?"

"No," I said. "We'll stick with the battle plan for now. We'll put a hundred or so beams on one cruiser at a time until it goes down."

There had been something of a spirited argument about that. Some of the commanders thought we should focus everything on that big bastard up front and burn it out of the sky. I didn't like that idea, as I didn't know how tough it was. If I spent several minutes of battle time shooting at it, even as they were taking my guns out one at a time, they might be able to retreat and keep the ship alive. Then I would be facing all the cruisers without having destroyed anything. On the other hand, I knew how much firepower it took to destroy one of their cruisers, having done so on several occasions in the past. Focusing on the smaller ships, we were guaranteed to destroy one about every ten seconds if we could get all thousand guns over the island on it at once. That would not be possible, however. If they were smart—and Macro Command *was* fairly smart—they would hang off one coast in a tight line and pound it, staying out of range of our guns on the other side.

Unfortunately, as they approached, I could see this was exactly their plan.

134

"They are down to a crawl, sir," Major Sarin said. "They are going to bombard the east coast of the island."

"That's why I had you put on these suits," I said. The clock read eight seconds. "Hang on. This is liable to be quite a ride."

-21-

The bombardment began about a minute after Major Sarin's clock ran out. That was a good thing, because they'd come in closer than I'd figured they would. That meant my laser turrets along the coastline were well within range.

"Targeting priorities, sir?" Lieutenant Colonel Barrera asked.

"Put a hundred on each cruiser, burn it until it goes down. Automatically retarget next available cruiser."

"Locked in sir. Are we ready to fire?"

I didn't answer right away. I wanted the Macros to come in as close as possible, allowing more of my turrets to be in effective range. Slowly, they glided near.

I felt small, rumbling impacts.

"The bombard had begun, sir," Major Sarin said.

"Any missile launches detected?"

"None, sir. So far, their missile ports are staying closed."

I grinned inside my helmet. "That's just how we want it," I said.

"Are we ready to fire, sir?" Barrera said.

"Hold fire. Let them inch in closer. They don't like to retreat, and I want as many guns in range as possible. Damage reports, Major Sarin?"

"Two turrets knocked out, one damaged. Update: three knocked out, one damaged."

"Put some kind of damage meter up for me," I said.

She deftly tapped at her screen, scripting a tiny app. She was the best at this type of thing.

"The ships appear to be down to a walking pace, sir," Barrera reported over the strategic command channel.

I thought I heard a tinge of worry in his voice. That was a rare thing, and it meant anyone else would be panicking at this point. I'd been holding back in hopes they would roll right over the center of the island allowing more of our guns to reach them. But if they were going to halt, we were taking hits now for nothing.

"How many guns can we get on them now?"

"About three hundred and sixty effectives, sir," Sarin said. "That number is dropping...."

"Commence firing. Bring them down!"

On the big screen, hundreds of thin green lines lanced out. They intersected on four points. At the center of each of those points, I knew, was an enemy cruiser under withering fire. If they would have just come in closer and lower, I could be certain of a win. But they were hanging back, wisely feeling their way. They would pound us while standing out over the ocean. From that position, they directed their more heavily armored snouts toward us.

Major Sarin had the counter up by now I glanced at it and my cheek twitched. We'd lost twelve turrets already. We hadn't taken out a single cruiser yet.

"Barrera," I shouted, "release the reserves. Send half the hovertanks to the east coast of the island. We need more firepower."

"Relaying that, sir," Barrera said. He sounded self-assured again, now that we were firing.

The laser turret count dipped down, they'd destroyed sixteen. Then suddenly, almost at the same moment, three of the enemy cruisers fell from the sky, burning. One exploded in a white flash.

A happy sound swept around the table. "Got a few of them, anyway," Kwon said expelling his breath as if he'd been holding it since the beginning. Maybe he had been.

I watched as the cruisers halted fully. It would be long minutes before the hovertanks could come out of their bunkers and fly to the east coast. I didn't like committing reserves so early, but I couldn't help but worry they'd demolish our defenses on one side of the island, then slowly swing around, cleaning off my ring of defenses. It was all a matter of attrition now, whichever side could take out the other faster would win.

The enemy fire was a shower of orange sparks that came down from each ship in continuous, pulsing streams from nearly a hundred cannons. In return, our fire was represented on the screen as green lances that drew thin lines from a spot on Andros up to the attacking ships. The green lines drew fans from many guns to each cruiser's belly. As soon as a ship went down, the beams cut out and moments later retargeted another ship and fired again. The cruisers came in a fraction closer, and I saw a new set of beams leap up to greet them. These were from the defensive grid around Fort Pierre itself. The laser turret count leapt upward by forty-one guns.

"They are in our range now," Sandra said happily.

"Yeah," Kwon said, "but that means they will begin pounding this base in return."

As if he were a prophet of doom, the impacts began seconds later. I'd been under fire many times, all of us had. But this was the worst bombardment I'd ever experienced. The walls shook and buckled. The computer table flickered as base power was cut out and the system automatically switched to backup fusion generators located in the bunker itself. I hoped our nanite lines which had dug themselves through the soil to sensor systems on the surface wouldn't be cut. The sensors themselves were unlikely to be knocked out as they were placed a half-mile out in the empty forest that surrounded the base.

The battle raged on, and I was pretty much helpless to do much about it. The enemy had lost twenty-one cruisers, but our count of active turrets had dropped to about one hundred forty. I calculated our odds, and didn't like them. They were at eight percent, while we were down to fifty. Once they broke the coastal defenses, they could cruise up or down the beach, outgunning us over every mile of beach. I began to sweat and to wish I'd had the foresight to place a massive central fortification in the middle of the island that could not be out maneuvered. If I'd built longer range lasers in the center, it would be much harder to break Andros. Unfortunately, I'd originally fortified the island with human enemies in mind. Those days seemed very distant now—almost absurd.

138

The walls shook and buckled. Everyone staggered in their suits.

"A direct hit," I said. "what's happening topside, Major Sarin?"

"The headquarters building is gone, sir. We'll have to dig out after this."

I nodded. I looked around at the walls, which now bulged in spots. The nanites weren't able to keep back the pressure from the surrounding earth as it pressed in on our bunker. I turned to Kwon.

"Bring your marines down to this level. We'll all be safer down here."

He clanked off and began shouting up the stairs. His platoon hurried down to his call and crowded into the command post around us.

"Just stay back, stay quiet and don't bump the table, marines," I told them.

They stood around awkwardly, trying to follow my instructions. When we were down to less than one hundred active guns in range, the Macro fleet began to drift northward. They had seventy of their ships still operating, plus that dreadnaught. That they were moving northward was good news for us personally, as it upped our odds of survival. They were no longer pulverizing our base. But it also meant the enemy knew they were winning and were moving on to the next stage: scraping off our defenses from the entire coastline.

"The hovertanks should be arriving soon, sir," Barrera reported.

"Glad I can still hear you," I said. "When they get here, order them to move out over the water and fire up at the southern edge of the Macro line. As they retreat, the tanks will focus all their fire on the hindmost cruiser and bring it down fast. They'll be tearing us up going north, and we'll follow along hitting them in the rear."

I could see the new green contacts zooming over the cross-island highway I'd built a few years back.

"Sir," Major Sarin said urgently. "General Kerr wants to know if *now* is the time."

I thought about it. I could certainly use some help. If NORAD unleashed a barrage of ICBMS, the missiles would be here in about ten minutes. But that would put the U. S., if not all Earth, into this fight again. I didn't want to commit them unless I had no choice.

"Tell him to standby, we've got this."

My staff exchanged worried glances. I ignored them.

When Barrera's hovercraft finally got within range of the Macro formation and began taking down one cruiser at a time, the enemy did not react at first. More cruisers went down. With each enemy loss, my staff grew more cheery. When the forty-third cruiser of the battle fell, they shouted in unison. Kwon grew overexcited and slapped the computer table. A long crack ran across it. Ballistic glass or not, he had managed to damage it when the entire Macro fleet had failed.

"Oh..." he said. "Sorry about that, Colonel."

"First Sergeant, take your men upstairs and begin digging us out of this bunker, please," I said, trying not to sound pissed-off.

"Yes, sir!" he said. He led his men clanking away and the room felt dramatically less claustrophobic.

It was shortly after that when the Macros finally broke. In a typical fashion, they made the move decisively. They powered up their engines in unison and withdrew, gliding back to the east from which they'd come.

The cheering was deafening now. I peered at the screen, tapping for different views. I stared at data, and something began to worry me. "Barrera, those hovertanks are getting out of position. Call them back to the north shore coverage zone."

The hovertank pilots, eager to bring down every cruiser they could, were pursuing at high speeds eastward over the ocean. My retrieval command was barely transmitted in time. The Macros paused and turned on their tormenters and unleashed a fury of cannon fire. A cluster of new small contacts appeared.

"Missiles!" I roared, mashing the command override button. I was talking directly to the hovertank commanders and everyone else in Star Force. "Switch all targeting to air-defense. Shoot down those missiles."

The green beams flickered out on the screen, then restarted. They began stabbing at these new targets. There was only a few seconds to do so. My ground-based laser turrets joined the defense. The missiles, each bearing a Macro technician as pilot, did their best to reach the hovertanks, but they were decimated. When there were only two left, one of them detonated, destroying the other. The shockwave rolled across the glowing blue water and smashed into my hovertanks, flipping them over and turning those that had followed the most eagerly into dead, twisted wreckage.

After the blast, the hovertanks with functional brainboxes slowly picked themselves up and limped back to Andros. I curse and muttered about crazy pilots in my helmet.

"Damage report, Barrera," I said.

"They knocked out twenty-odd hovertanks. I'm not sure as to the exact numbers, sir. In many cases the pilots were killed but the brainbox is still operating. In some cases, it was the reverse. But there is no doubt they hurt us."

"They drew us out of our defensive perimeter, just as we did to them. Damn it."

I sensed a light touch through my armor's feedback system. Sandra was close to me. "We won, Colonel," she said.

I rotated my helmet toward her. "Not yet, we haven't. We've repelled an assault, yes. But their fleet is still at least sixty percent effective. They can siege us now if they like and wait for reinforcements to attack again. We need every asset we have."

She nodded, her face falling. She looked back to the screen. I knew she had only been trying to cheer me up, but I wasn't in a cheerful mood right now. They'd almost taken us out in one rush. The worst thing was they'd just learned their missiles were still effective. If they used them in the next assault, we would be in bad shape.

Sandra frowned at the screen. "What are they doing now?"

"They're dropping something, Colonel," Major Sarin said. "Into the sea."

I turned back to the screen and peered at it. I opened my gloves to handle the screen more gently and ran my fingertips over the cracked glass. There they were, about twenty miles offshore, dropping huge objects into the water. The ocean fountained with each splashing impact. It looked as if their ships were laying eggs of some kind.

"Which ships are those?" I demanded. "Barrera, which ships are dropping objects into the water? Are they dropping bombs on the U. S. subs out there?"

"I don't think so, sir," Barrera replied. His voice scratched for a moment as the connection fuzzed, then came back. "The ships making the drop have been identified, sir. They're invasion ships, Colonel. All six have dropped a large object in that area."

"That's the trench," I said.

The region was known as the Tongue of the Ocean, a deep gash in the sea that separated Andros from New Providence. The hundred mile long region reached depths of six thousand feet.

"What the hell are they dropping?" Major Sarin said.

"Macros," I said.

"Invasion forces?"

It looked all too familiar. I recalled the first Macro ship that had made it past our little Nano ships years ago. They had dropped payloads on Argentina. In the end, they had destroyed an entire continent.

"Yes," I said, staring.

"I didn't know they could operate on the sea bottom," Sandra said.

"Neither did I."

Within a few hours, we knew the full truth. The enemy had not only dropped unknown large objects into the sea, these objects had vanished into the oceanic trench off our eastern shore and sunk to the very bottom. I could only imagine the activity going on down there on the deepest seabeds of the Caribbean. While their fleet hovered far above like watchful parents, perhaps they were setting up domes of force and factory complexes to produce the monstrous foot soldiers of the Macros. Hundred foot tall robots I'd had nightmares about for years.

There could no longer be any confusion about the enemy's intent. They'd tried a direct assault, but when their losses had grown too high, they'd broken off and shifted to Plan B. Like colonies of ants, they would build their invasion army and when they came again, we would face a combination of invasion and bombardment.

"We have to assume they've set up six factories on the bottom of the ocean," I told General Kerr. He was the lucky recipient of my first call since the withdrawal.

"What? What are you talking about, Riggs?"

The General was out of the loop as far as direct input from the battle was concerned. The Macros had blown down all his satellites in the region as they came in, methodically popping any orbital object in the local sky like light bulbs.

"Down in the trench, sir," I said. "The invasion ships dropped their payloads to the bottom of it."

"No, no, no, Riggs. You have to be mistaken. Macros are land animals."

"They don't need to breathe, sir. They've unloaded six factories onto the bottom of the trench and they probably intend to invade after they build up their forces."

"You listen to me, Riggs," General Kerr said. "You told me to hide my subs down there to keep them safe."

"Yeah. Not a good spot, as it turns out. The Macros have apparently decided that's also a good locale to hide their breeding equipment."

"Just like that, huh? Scratch one half of the U. S. nuclear sub fleet? Now I suppose you want me to withdraw them."

"I apologize sir, but that's not why I'm calling."

"What do you want, then?"

"You have a number of attack subs. I believe they are equipped with nuclear-tipped torpedoes—"

"Now, you just hold on a second—"

"I need them to seek out the enemy in the oceanic trench, General."

"That's suicide."

"If they get set up and begin churning out those big invasion machines, we'll be overrun."

"I can't order my subs in—even if they had nuclear torpedoes, which I'm not confirming or denying. I can't communicate with the subs when they are that deep. We'll have to wait until they come up to shallower depths and can receive VLF signals. Do you think the Macros know they are down there with them?"

I thought about it. "Probably not, sir. But I can't be sure as to their underwater sensory systems."

"What are *you* going to do, Riggs?" Kerr asked me after a pause.

"I think we're going to have to rebuild here first. The trouble is, when they do come, they will be coming up out of the sea. Laser fire doesn't penetrate more than a few yards into the ocean. They will be able to march in extremely close before they surface. We won't be able to engage them at a distance. Worse, the laser turrets on that entire coastal zone have been knocked out."

The more I thought about it, the more I realized we were screwed. The Macros were going to churn out troops on the bottom

144

of the sea—something I'd never realized they could do. They would use their fleet of cruisers to cover them from any kind of aerial assault. If we were going to go after their undersea base before they built a robot army and overran us, we would have to do it by walking on the seafloor, just as they were.

"Well," General Kerr said, sighing, "I'll work on getting the approval I need to use those subs again. You work on a way to get rid of those underwater factories. Lord, when the press gets hold of this there will be a panic in Miami. The entire population of the planet has been traumatized by the last invasion. Every continent fears a Macro dome building an army nearby like an anthill. They are going to go ape when they figure out what the machines are up to."

I was barely listening to Kerr. To me, his problems seemed petty in comparison to my own. I had six giant factories in the sea next to my base, each no doubt was already churning out workers to gather the required materials to build more and more Macros.

We broke off the discussion and I stressed and mumbled over the computer table until Kwon tapped me on the shoulder. Fortunately I was wearing armor, otherwise his metal-wrapped finger would have broken my collar bone. I turned to him, and nodded.

"What is it, First Sergeant?"

"We've done it, sir."

"Done what?" I snapped. I was tired and worried.

"We've dug ourselves out of this hole."

"Ah, good," I said.

I followed him up toward a glimmer of distant sunlight. Sandra trailed behind us. Together, the three of us stepped out into the ruins that had once been Fort Pierre.

"Those damned machines," I said.

"Our headquarters building is gone, Kyle," Sandra said. "Your new office, that awful orange carpet…all gone."

The building had indeed been leveled. Of all the buildings scattered here and there, it had withstood the harshest pounding. I supposed Macro thinking was behind it. They knew our leadership was posted here, so they'd tried to obliterate the area.

I looked around the place. Not much was left standing. The landing pits had even suffered a pounding. The only place I really cared about was the officer's mess, which was still partially intact. They had excellent food, and I was hungry.

"Hey look, Sandra," I said. "They nailed our bungalow, but on the bright side, they only took out half the restaurant."

"You can think of food *now*? What if they come back? What if they fire their missiles? Can you see them, out there in the sky over the ocean?"

I followed her uplifted finger and I *did* see them. It was strange to see so many ships in Earth's sky. Dark, arrowhead shapes hung over our earthly sea. The day was clear except for drifting smoke. There was a slight haze, but the ships were so large and numerous you could not mistake them for what they were.

I called to Barrera and asked him if he could manage the clean-up without me. He assured me his staff was already on top of the task. I believed him. There were emergency operations going on all over the island, of course. Crews were digging people out, fire truck sirens warbled in the distance and the medical people were looking haggard. But I'd learned a long time ago to take a moment to rest whenever it presented itself. Star Force could run itself for a few hours, I decided.

"How long do you think we have?" Sandra asked me suddenly.

I removed my helmet and looked at her. She had already taken hers off. Dark flowing hair ran over the top of her armor, catching on the bulging plates at her shoulders.

"What do you mean?" I asked her gently.

"Before they come out of that trench. Before they crawl up onto our island to wipe us out."

The cool beach breezes dried my sweat. The smoldering craters around us stank of burnt charcoal and dust. I hugged Sandra then, armor to armor. I think I surprised her, but she didn't resist. Our battle suits scraped and groaned slightly at the pressure.

"Don't worry," I said. "I plan to go down there and hit them first."

She studied my face. "I don't know why I'm surprised. I really shouldn't be."

I expected her to become angry and try to talk me out of it. But she didn't. Maybe she thought I was right, and it was the only thing to do. Or maybe she realized that I would do it anyway. In any case, I didn't bring it up again. We walked through the smoking mess that had hours ago been a tropical paradise. I was sad, rather like walking through the ashes of one's own home.

"Let's see if the officer's mess is still serving," I suggested.

She agreed and we headed toward the sagging doors. One wouldn't budge, having been folded down by the building when it leaned forward like an old man that's taken a hard blow. I forced it with my armored hands. The metal screeched and groaned as it came reluctantly open.

Inside, we found the officer's mess serviceable, if abandoned. Kwon and his team were in the area, digging people out of their bunkers. Most of the base personnel had survived. We had drinks until the kitchen people showed up. When they finally did, we were pretty well lit. With big smiles, we welcomed them to the facility, still wearing our battle armor.

The cooks gave us odd, sidelong glances. They looked away quickly when we returned their gaze. I didn't care. I hammered the table until it dented, and demanded a good meal. I didn't care what it was, as long as it was hot and tasted good.

After awhile, they came up with a shrimp dish they called *camarones salvajes*. It was a seafood plate full of wonderful flavors. Shrimp, marinated octopus, calamari and mussels, all mixed with black olives, roasted peppers and tomato. There was other stuff in there I couldn't identify, but it all tasted hot and good.

We polished off a bottle of wine, but I made sure I didn't reach the point of actual drunkenness. Sandra became loud and silly, and when we finally left the place, I think the staff was glad to see us go. I gave them a tip they wouldn't soon forget and my first thought was to lead my girl back to our bungalow. We headed that way, but soon were reminded our home wasn't in the best condition. It was demolished, smashed to sticks by a strike on a nearby building.

"Hmm," I said, realizing I wasn't going to get laid in this place anytime soon.

Sandra gave a deep sigh, but she didn't start crying. I think before our campaign against the Worms and the long journey home fighting against the Macros, she would have broken down. Now, she understood that things were just things. As long as the people you cared about were alive, crying wasn't worthwhile.

"I've got an idea," she said, then led me down to the sea.

It was getting dark now, but when we took off our battle suits and slipped into the waves, they were very warm. I looked off down the beach and saw a lot of dead sea creatures on the sand. All the hits in the water had killed thousands of fish. I turned her away from the washed up bodies.

"Why here?" I asked.

"Because those damned turrets can't see us now," she said. "I want to have some fun before you fix them all and they stare at me again."

I laughed, and as the darkness fell we enjoyed ourselves in the waves. The water still felt warmer than usual, almost hot, but I'd checked my Geiger counter before we went out there. It registered increased activity with a mild amount of clicking. It was nothing a couple of Star Force marines couldn't handle.

-23-

About thirty-six hours later, a fresh dawn broke over Andros. The radioactive clouds had dissipated, brought to Earth by a light drizzling rain. I stood in my battle suit alongside a good five thousand of my comrades. We were organized in tight units, because radio transmissions were going to be our biggest problem. I'd spent the last day and a half coming up with solutions.

The normal means of communications underwater consisted of either sonic signals—essentially shouting at one another with directed vibrations, or very low frequency radio. Of the two, VLF radio was much less workable. Conductive seawater was not a good medium for radio transmissions of any kind, but with long wavelengths and huge antennas it could be managed over distances of several hundred yards. Unfortunately, using low frequencies meant really *long* antennas—much longer than a man was tall.

We had the opposite problem with sound. It traveled too far and worked too well. A good loud noise under the ocean, such as a dolphin's clicking, carried quite a distance. Whale songs went the furthest, in some cases thousands of miles. I didn't know how sensitive the Macros were to underwater sounds, but I figured our clanking along in armor was going to be noisy enough.

In the end, we decided on a hybrid strategy. We would use sound only for longer range communications. After all, it worked pretty well for the whales. We used radio for close, whispered conversations between soldiers in the same unit.

I built a brainbox attached to a directional hydrophone it could manipulate and had a non-com in every unit carry one. It wasn't perfect, but it worked. The biggest problem with this sort of communication was the lack of security. If the Macros were listening, they would hear our command chatter. Accordingly, I ordered each team to maintain sonic silence until the battle began, barring some kind of disaster.

Every company had to operate independently under this model, due to isolation. We had suit radio, but that didn't work very well under the waves. A man's normal shouting voice on the beach had more range than our radios did at the bottom of the ocean. Separating into companies of one hundred marines, we each had a geographic location we were to get down to. We weren't sure where the enemy was in the trench, but we were going to have to find them on foot. It was a shotgun approach, but I didn't know what else to do. We'd tried getting aerial photos and using sonar, but hadn't seen much down there. Anyone who has searched deep water for a shipwreck can tell you it's easier to find a rock on the Moon than find an object at the bottom of the sea. Essentially, you had to go down there and look around.

"Kwon," I said, clanking out onto the beach, "let's move our team out."

"Moving out, sir!"

We weren't the first ones to enter the sea. I'd already sent twenty companies forward. I had them fly out over the waves first so they could move faster, but when the water got deep—which it did with alarming suddenness a about a mile offshore—they were to drop down directly, hugging the cliff and letting gravity do the trick. They sank like stones, or maybe like big steel bricks.

Soon, it was our turn to move out. We engaged our repellers and left the sandy beach behind. We leaned our bodies forward and increased our speed. The repellers pushed us forward and away from the water at the same time. Like a hundred strange little helicopters, we flew over the cresting whitecaps. As we sailed over the waves at around a hundred knots. Every marine left a white line of froth in the water due to the pushing of his repellers in the bright, Caribbean-blue surface.

"Is it okay to use radio while flying, sir?" Kwon asked me.

"Yes, as long as we don't overdo it and keep the power low on our transmissions. As I said in the briefing, the signals won't get down to the Macros through the seawater."

Kwon pointed overhead. "What about them?"

"The enemy fleet has withdrawn to higher orbit, I'm happy to report. They apparently don't want to sit close to the Earth's surface."

"Why have they pulled back?"

"Maybe they think we could nuke them in a surprise sucker-punch. I wish we had a hundred subs waiting to do just that, but we don't."

Kwon stopped asking questions. It was just as well, because we'd reached the end of the line. It was easy to see where the land-shelf ended from an aerial view. This close to it, I found it harder to tell. The water did look somewhat deeper blue. Below us was a cliff thousands of feet deep. I leaned back and halted my forward motion.

"Slow down, this is it," Kwon shouted, seeing my move.

The company clustered around, tipping their helmets awkwardly to look down in the water. "Let's drop," I said, and I switched off my repellers.

The water splashed around me and I sank with dramatic speed. Being accustomed to being much more buoyant, it was alarming to go down so fast. I felt like I was drowning. I watched as dark cliffs covered in crusty growths whirled past my faceplate. I looked up and saw a spiral of bubbles spinning away overhead toward the silvery surface. Below, the water was deep blue. As I continued to drop, the water above grew darker and the surface was no longer discernable. Below, the sea had turned an oily black.

I snapped on my suit lights. A dozen others did the same all around me. Their existence was a comfort.

Normally, a dive like this took many stages and an ever increasing level of pressure inside the suit which had to be built up carefully to avoid popping eardrums and other unpleasant things. Fortunately, I had a team of about a zillion nanites working internally to balance out my body. On the way back up however, I knew we would have to take it slower to avoid decompression sickness, nanites or no.

My suit hissed and creaked as the pressure increased. The battle suits performed remarkably well as one-man submarines. This was accidental, but I was still proud of the design. When I'd planned the systems, I'd been thinking of the rigors of open space with all its deadly dangers. One of them was great pressure, of course. I wanted these systems to function effectively on high gravity planets, worlds with high atmospheric pressures and wild variations in temperature and radiation. I'd considered undersea combat, but only as a remote possibility. I had had no inkling that these suits would see their first real combat test under Earth's own oceans.

"Any problems?" I signaled Kwon.

I heard a fuzzy, static-filled response. I cursed. I didn't know how far away he was, but I'd hoped we would be able to converse over more than a few yards distant. I was immediately tempted to use sonic communications, but sternly forbade myself. I had to follow my own orders just like everyone else.

It had been such a long, sliding fall I'd almost forgotten to look for the bottom. Looking was futile in any case, as there was nothing to see outside the shaft of my suit's chest lights other than more dark ocean.

A warning beeper sounded, and I barely managed to squeeze the hand control in my glove that started up my repellers in time. Boulders shot up on either side of me. I heard clanking and crashing as marines slammed their armored boots into them all around. The bottom came crunching into my boots with shocking speed.

"We're down," I said. "Activate repellers. Relay the warning."

In my helmet, I heard a dozen voices shouting to each other over the com-links. Many were indecipherable. I took a moment to examine the bottom of the cliffs. We'd done a lot of brainstorming about what the Macros intended to do down here. One theoretical plan we'd come up was the possibility of building digging machines and sending them to Andros Island via a network of tunnels. I hadn't found evidence of tunnels, however. I suspected they planned to march up out of the sea and onto the shoreline when they were ready.

I soon located Kwon. He was trying to pull a man out from between two closely-parked boulders. The marine had the green

152

suit-lights of a non-com. He seemed unhurt, but one big boot was stuck.

"Is everyone okay, First Sergeant?" I asked.

"No, sir," he said, grunting and heaving at the bounder on the right. It had leaned in and was covered in sharp thorny growths.

"Casualties?"

"One man I've found didn't make it. He's over there."

I turned to see a dark shape lying draped over more broken rocks. I turned back to the trapped man. The living are always more important than the dead, so I reached out to help.

I'd thought the bottom would be free of life, but maybe this had fallen from above recently. I joined him and the three of us working together managed to free the man's foot without ripping it off and killing him. Afterward, I moved over to the dead man. He was a private, his suit's red LEDs told me that. The lower half of the lights were out, however. I saw a gap in the suit and shook my head. It had split open at the waist, allowing the pressure of the mile-deep ocean inside. Had he tried to take it off? Or had the suit malfunctioned somehow?

I considered my own control systems. I thought I might have the answer. The suit had emergency buttons near my face inside the helmet. If I twisted my neck and brought down my chin hard, the emergency release would trigger. Maybe when he'd come down and jarringly struck the seafloor, this man had done exactly that by accident. I grimaced. A redesign was required.

"What happened to him?" Kwon asked, looming near.

Kwon made me startle. He reminded me of some huge, scary sea creature looming out of the dark water. I'd had to specially order his suit. The factory standard issue unit just hadn't fit right.

"My fault," I said. "I need to reprogram the suit units. In low pressure, the suits are built to prevent accidental opening. That way, this couldn't happen out in the vacuum of space. I hadn't considered that high pressure could be just as deadly."

"Ah," Kwon said. He promptly relayed a warning to the nearest marines, who were now gathering around.

A dozen red-lit men talked among themselves. No doubt they figured *Riggs' Pigs* were about to earn their reputation for insane losses once again. I allowed the chatter for now.

I opened the dead man's suit, attached an emergency line to his wrist and inflated the balloon. In seconds, he was shooting toward the surface. When he arrived, the balloon would begin beeping an emergency signal, and the body would be picked up. The system had been intended as a lifesaver, but it worked just as well to send corpses to the surface in a hurry.

"One down, ninety-nine to go," muttered one of the men.

"Belay that shit, marine!" Kwon barked, clanking into the midst of the men. "Was that you, Swenson? I'm going to check the logs when we get back."

"Sorry, First Sergeant."

I felt like telling Kwon to let it slide, but that wasn't the way discipline was maintained in my unit. I let Kwon do his job, so I could do mine. I ignored the entire affair and engaged my repellers. Moments later I had a fix on our gathering point and glided toward it. A throng of quiet marines followed me. We were already a few minutes behind schedule.

-24-

Due to the particulate matter floating around in any ocean and the powerful nature of our lasers, I didn't know how our weapons would perform in the undersea environment. Tests had shown our projectors were effective at short range, but there were many practical problems. Earth science had developed uses for lasers underwater, such as welding, since the nineteen-nineties. But our weapons were an order of magnitude more powerful.

The intense beams tended to heat up the cloudy water as they passed through it, causing steam bubbles to form, especially around the projector units themselves. This was problematic, as the bubbles obstructed the beam, reducing its striking power. The final result of these difficulties was that our weapons *did* work, but only over a short range and only for short bursts of duration. Over longer ranges or longer durations, their effectiveness dropped off dramatically.

Still, our lasers were the best weapons we had. I could have tried to design some kind of harpoon with an explosive charge, maybe, but I didn't have time. I didn't want to leave the Macros down here unmolested, festering at the bottom of our ocean. I didn't know exactly what their plans were, but I was certain I didn't want them to succeed.

We kept moving and reached our battalion gathering point unmolested. Three other companies were there, waiting. There were supposed to be a total of five, including us. I talked to the

155

captain of each company and determined they'd not met any resistance.

Several minutes went by. When the last company didn't show up, I became concerned. I ordered the rest of the men to follow me, backtracking along the route the fifth company should have taken from the cliffs. Kwon came up beside me as we glided over the seabed on a gentle decline that led ever deeper into the ocean trench.

"Uh, sir?" he asked.

I knew what was bothering him without asking. This looked like a detour that would delay our planned search pattern and put us out of position relative to the other battalions that were moving over the seabed looking for the Macros.

"We are down here to search for the Macros, First Sergeant," I told him. "One company is missing, that's evidence of Macro activity."

"Yes sir, but aren't their domes supposed to be further ahead?"

"No other units have reported in sonically," I told him. "They are all probing forward, but not finding anything. I believe there is something nearby, between us and the cliffs."

"But wouldn't the company have called in if they met the Macros?"

"Not if their communications man was killed fast enough."

Kwon made a troubled-sounding grunt. I kept pressing ahead. Spreading out on all sides of me were four companies of marines. If there was something out here, we were going to find it.

When we did, it came as a surprise. My first thought was: *the machines have been busy.*

They ambushed us. They were worker-type Macros, equipped with huge pinchers. A large number of them were drilling-types as well. As soon as I saw them, I knew we'd stumbled upon some kind of resource, probably a mine. That's why they were hard to see. They'd been in burrowed holes in the rocky bottom. Like a hundred moray eels, they popped up and attacked when we were right on top of them.

Pinchers clanked hard on battle armor and the leading men were sucked down into holes. I knew then how it had happened. Each company had been equipped with only one hydrophone, assigned to a non-com to lug around behind the captain. If those

156

men had been leading the company and all been pulled down into these black holes, they could have been torn apart down there in the dark before they could engage their equipment. That's why we hadn't heard a call for support.

Lasers flashed. My headset was full of chatter. I moved to the nearest opening where a corpsman had been dragged down, flailing. I dove into the hole and Kwon followed. We quickly found a large chamber underneath.

It took three Macros to kill one of my men—at least three of this relatively weak variety. Two held him locked in their pinchers while the third used drilling equipment to burn through the armor. Using a laser drill that could melt rock, the burrower opened up the marine's suit and once it lost its integrity it popped and the man was instantly killed by the intense pressure at this depth. We were about a mile deep, and the pressure here was over a hundred fifty times that felt while standing on the beach.

"Kill the drillers, kill the drillers! Relay that," I shouted over my suit radio with the strongest possible signal.

Kwon's twin beams were already blazing, striking the drilling Macro. I joined him.

"Use pulses!" I shouted. "No long burns, you'll cloud up the water."

Both of us fired in bursts, hammering at the driller. The two pincher-armed workers dropped the body of the marine they'd methodically killed and churned toward us. They crawled over the rocky interior of the chamber like steel lobsters.

We soon had disabled the drilling Macro. After that, there wasn't much they could do to us. We kept wrestling and firing at point-blank range, until they sagged down in bubbling ruins.

Working together and targeting the drilling machines, my four companies made fast work of the entire nest. That could not be said of Bravo Company, who'd run into the nest alone and had been annihilated.

"Looks like Bravo Company gave them hell, at least," Kwon said.

"Indeed they did," I said, trying not to grind my teeth.

There had been only about fifty of the machines active when we arrived. I counted my marine dead. Besides the company they'd first ambushed, they'd only managed to kill five men. Still, that was a hundred and five, total.

I gathered my survivors and prepared to move out. This took longer than I was accustomed to, as commands had to be relayed and people took time to do headcounts. I wondered if we should have all gone down as a mass force. The Macros had to know we were down here by now.

I decided it was time to use the hydrophone. Possibly, other units had run into nests like this one. If they hadn't, they needed to know about the possibility. We were looking for underwater Macro domes with factories inside, but as yet hadn't found one.

Every battalion was under orders to report a dome the moment they located it. The plan at that point was simple: we'd mass our strength and take it out. Unfortunately, if none of us had yet found a dome to attack, the plan was a failure.

At my call, a corporal came to me with his com unit floating behind him. It was about the size of an ice chest and was tethered to his waist with a silver line of nanites.

"Now, sir?"

"Yeah," I said. "Power this thing up and aim it at the closest gathering point."

He worked the controls, tapping at metal nubs and scratching his armor over beads of metal that moved under his rough touch. In order to make sure the com unit was durable, I'd built the shell entirely of constructive nanites. My marines were clumsy in their suits, especially underwater. We tended to dent equipment, but these systems naturally smoothed themselves out. Smart-metal made an excellent material for infantry equipment.

"Battalion One calling Battalion Three," I said. "Respond, please."

I waited for a time and made the request once every thirty seconds. After three repeats, I began to worry slightly, but then a voice came back. It was tinny and difficult to hear using this system.

"…here…" my earpiece squawked, after a period of crackling static.

"Battalion Three," I said, "calibrate your equipment, please."

Silence for another half-minute, then finally: "Is that better, Colonel?"

158

"Much. Who am I talking to, please?"

"Captain Sloan, sir," came the reply.

I smiled. He had been Warrant Officer Sloan, but after surviving two of my campaigns, I had decided to move him up. He'd shown more smarts than many of my Ivy League champions ever had.

"Sloan, good to hear your voice," I said. I quickly described the enemy nest we'd tangled with. After ordering him to relay the warning, I asked him if he'd made contact with the enemy.

"Just one machine, sir. We figured it was a foraging scout. We took it out and haven't seen any enemy response."

"You probably won't at this point of the invasion. The enemy is weak now, that's why we are coming after him. Like ants, they'll build workers first and—"

"Got it at the briefing, sir," Sloan said. "Sorry to interrupt, but I've received a call from Battalion Six. Mind if I listen to them?"

"Go right ahead, they might have something interesting to report."

I waited another minute or two. When Sloan came back, he sounded excited.

"They've got another entrance, sir. Just like the one you found, but larger. They are in action now."

Entrance? I thought. It took about three seconds—sometimes I'm slow. "Captain Sloan, where does the entrance lead?"

"Unknown, sir. Battalion Six reports strong resistance at a cave entrance of some kind. Sounds like what you encountered."

"Relay this news around the other battalions on the southern flank," I said. "I want everyone to know what we're facing. They are to relay back their status and try to maintain their position on the seafloor at their gathering points."

"I'm on it sir," Sloan said, "but it will take me a few minutes."

"Roger that. We'll do the same with the northern units. Riggs out."

I handed the set over to the non-com who was dragging it and had him relay my messages. I felt uneasy. I didn't like being down here at the bottom of the cold dark sea. I didn't know what was happening to my men. We could be losing this battle, winning it, or perhaps idly standing around, mostly ignored by the Macros.

"Kwon!" I roared.

"Colonel!"

"Take a squad down and investigate the corners of these tunnels. Find out if they go deeper. Do not enter unexplored tunnels, just report back to me. You got that?"

"On it, sir," Kwon said, bouncing away over the rocky bottom. He rounded up a team and headed down into the holes around us.

I rolled out a computer scroll—it was really like a tablet computer, but mounted on a plastic mat. It filled my faceplate with a blue-white glow. I flattened it on a boulder and looked over the scene. I was in Battalion One, in the center of the formation. There were ten battalions in all. Most of the others were off to the north and south, but several were directly ahead. They'd made the dive first, and had moved the farthest out into the underwater trench. If we were already in contact with the enemy at two points, there might be a pitched battle going in other spots. I now felt I'd screwed up in regards to the hydrophone equipment. One unit per company was not enough. If the unit was lost, the company would be out of contact for the duration. If the Macros caught on, they could target our hydrophones. We could then be divided and swallowed up one company at a time.

Taking a deep breath of stale air, I tried to think clearly. This place was oppressive—worse than space. The trouble was you couldn't *see* anything around you. At least in space, there wasn't much to obscure your view of the enemy. Out there, I'd always had a pretty good idea of what I was up against.

Kwon reported back several minutes later. "No tunnels sir. At least, we didn't see any. I think they really were mining here."

"Good going. Prepare the men to move out in three minutes. I'm not standing around here any longer than that."

"Excellent, Colonel," Kwon said.

I could tell he didn't like this place anymore than I did and I'd made his day by giving the order to move out. Moments later, Captain Sloan finally got back to me. By that time, I was ready to demote him.

"Colonel?"

"Riggs here."

"None of the other battalions have met the enemy, sir."

I felt immediately relieved.

"But Battalion Ten," he continued, "the one directly north of you, isn't responding. No one has been able to get into contact with them."

I didn't like the sound of that at all. *Five* companies lost? Or at least, unable to respond?

"Okay Sloan, your team and mine are the closest to Ten's position. We'll go investigate, double-time. I want all the other battalions to move to the large cave entrance Battalion Six located. We have a definite enemy contact there, and we have to keep the pressure up."

Very soon I was gliding through the dark waters again, going deeper still into the ocean. Occasionally, there was a clicking sound in my suit and a fresh trickle of cold seawater ran down to wet my toes. The nanites worked hard to weld the microscopic hole shut again, and all was well. I wondered just how deep these suits could go—how much pressure from the billions of gallons of water above they could take. Would men begin popping like eggs at a given depth? I'd never had the time to test them under these conditions.

But most of all, as I slid through the burbling quiet, I thought about the Macro factories and their protective domes. I'd expected to encounter them by now. Where were they?

-25-

We reached Battalion Ten's designated gathering spot before Captain Sloan's team did. We glided swiftly to the area, but everyone along the line slowed down warily as we drew near.

Something was desperately wrong. Instead of a flat area of seabed before us, a great *hole* presented itself. It was hard to tell at first what we were looking at. It resembled a cliff edge, similar to the one we'd dropped down to get here. The rim was ragged, as if it had broken away recently. Exposed sediment was darker than the bottom we'd been passing over, which consisted of sand intermixed with tumbled stones. When we reached the edge, I ordered a halt and everyone obeyed.

I gazed in both directions, seeing my men line up. Their suit lights could be identified at a hundred yards or more in the cloudy water. I could tell they formed a crescent.

"It's a pit," I said. "Kwon?"

"Right here, sir."

"Send a squad in each direction. Tell them to try to follow the edge of this formation all the way around. If they run into each other on the far side, they are to return. If they keep going for more than five minutes without finding anything, tell them to do an about-face and come back anyway."

Kwon found two non-coms in green-lit suits and sent them off to follow my orders. I waved the corporal with the communications unit forward and tried to contact Captain Sloan. He should be arriving very soon.

162

Before I could get the hydrophone working, Sloan arrived. He sailed along, looking for blue-lit officers until he found me. It was a relief to be able to communicate clearly with radio.

"What the hell is this, Colonel?" Sloan asked me as soon as he was in range.

"A big hole."

"Pardon me, but that's not helpful."

"Yeah, I think it didn't help Battalion Ten, either."

"You think they glided right off this cliff? Five hundred men?"

"No," I said. "I don't think the cliff was here when they arrived. This is the gathering spot they had staked out. They showed up on station, waited for orders, but something hit them before our transmission came in."

Sloan was quiet for a moment. "Something that big? So soon?"

"I don't think it was some kind of super-Macro. I think it was an explosion. The concussion could have knocked out their suit systems. Either that, or it was a whole lot of little Macros under the surface."

"What are we going to do about it, sir?"

It was my turn to hesitate. There was a big part of me that wanted to head over to that cave the majority of my force was assaulting. But I didn't like leaving marines behind without investigating. I also didn't like massing all my marines in a single spot on the ocean floor. Mostly, I wanted to know what had hit my men at this spot.

Before I'd made any kind of decision, the squads I'd sent off to circumnavigate the pit returned. They'd met up on the far side, as I had suspected they would. The hole was circular, and roughly a mile in diameter.

"We're going down," I told Sloan. "One company at a time. If a unit lives long enough to signal back the all-clear, the next company will step off this cliff."

"But sir—"

"Don't freak out, Sloan," I said. "I'll lead the first unit. You can wait up here. We'll step off the edge in one minute."

"I don't know what you are trying in imply," Sloan said. He sounded hurt.

Too bad, I thought. "You are a survivor, Sloan," I told him. "That's not the same as a coward. It's not a bad thing."

"Well, sir," Captain Sloan said. "I'd like the honor of leading the first team down."

I was surprised, but decided if he wanted to do it, he could have the job. I watched him line his men along the edge. A hundred of Star Force's finest. When they jumped, a small part of me knew that if they all died, I was going to feel badly. But I had to find out what was going on. If the Macros had somehow slaughtered five hundred of my men at the bottom of the sea, I wanted to at least know how they had done it.

I had a sudden thought as I watched Sloan marshal his marines. "Captain," I said over the command channel.

"Colonel?"

"Send them down one squad at a time. Weapons out."

He liked the idea and gave the orders. The first squad took the leap, then the second. Sloan stepped out with the third squad. I saw his blue suit among the numerous red-lit ones. I was able to pick him out for a long time as he fell deeper.

More squads went, but when the last ones were stepping off, there was a sudden commotion. A rush of bubbles came up from the hole. Then more bubbles. They were silver and there were way too many of them. Far from thinking them lovely, I saw those bubbles and knew his men were in trouble. The only way these suits should be able to release bubbles was when they ruptured.

I heard calls up the line, from suit-to-suit, man-to-man. They were passing up a message. When it got back up to us, it was a scream.

"Too deep! Release your pods!"

Every man had an emergency bubble to take them upward. Unfortunately, they found out that they didn't really work once you went down more than six thousand feet. They hadn't been designed for that depth. When the gas canister fired to fill the plastic bladder, it popped in most cases. A few men shot upward, dragged toward the distance surface by one wrist. When they passed us, they cut themselves free and glided to the rim of the hole.

Others came back up using their suit's repellers. It wasn't as fast, but it was more controlled. I counted the men as they came back up. We'd sent down about seventy, and we'd lost most of them.

164

I gazed down into the hole, frowning fiercely. Kwon came up beside me. He was unmistakable in his green-lit, oversized suit.

"Colonel Riggs?" he asked. "What happened?"

"The suits can't go down that far," I said. "They imploded. Like a sub that sinks to the bottom. Their suits ruptured and the nanites couldn't keep up. In short, they died."

"But how did this hole get here?"

"I suspect the Macros did it. They set off a big charge here under our marines. Maybe there was an underground chamber beneath the gathering spot for Battalion Ten. In any case, I think they collapsed the seabed, and the marines fell. They could have used their flight systems to get out of the trap, but I'm guessing their commander ordered them to take the drop, to see what was at the bottom. He must not have realized their suits would pop when they went too deep."

"But the lead men should have seen what was happening and flown out the way Sloan's men did."

"Maybe," I said. "Or maybe they all went down at more or less the same time and hit the kill zone together."

"Hey sir," Kwon said, pointing down over the rim. "Who's that?"

I looked down. I smiled slowly. A blue-lit suit was rising up toward us. I didn't know how he'd lived, but I knew who it had to be.

"That, my good man, is the unkillable Captain Sloan."

All along the line of leaning marines a cry went up as he kept coming. Every second he came slowly, but doggedly, closer.

"Maybe his suit is damaged," Kwon said. "One repeller might be out."

"Hey Sloan," I shouted. "Good to see you slip out of that one. I lost a bet with Kwon, because of you."

"You did?" Kwon asked, bewildered. He pointed downward again. "What's that thing?"

No one answered him, because we could all see it now. Sloan didn't have a problem with his suit—not exactly. He had all his repellers going full blast and had his gas-bubble out too. Unfortunately, he also had the upper half of a Macro latched onto his foot.

We aimed and lit up the tenacious monster. A mass of steam-bubbles rolled upward from every gun, and the robot was torn apart. Moments later, Captain Sloan drifted over to me and I took his hand and hauled him up over the rim.

"That was close," he said.

I nodded, impressed. "Closer than usual, even for you."

Kwon knelt and busied himself removing the last clamped-on Macro arm that dangled from Sloan's left leg.

"Did you build the officer's suits to the same specs, Colonel?"

I opened my mouth to say yes, but hesitated. I recalled leaving Sandra in charge of the duplication process. Could she have tampered with the design? Could she have altered it to keep me safe, knowing I would wear one of the officer's suits?

"I thought I did," I said.

"Well, everyone else's seemed to collapse when we got to certain depth," Sloan reported. "We got down there, and we could see bubbles coming up from the first squads. But I figured they were in trouble and ordered weapons at the ready. It was hard to see, sir."

"Go on."

"We were all expecting enemy at the bottom, and figured maybe they'd already gotten their first kills. But it wasn't like that. All of a sudden, the men around me were popping—shooting out bubbles and going radio silent. It took me a second to realize what was happening. I radioed back up, but you know how short our range is down here."

"How'd you get that lobster on your foot?" I asked.

"We'd about reached the bottom. The men who were still alive were being taken out. There were more marines down there already, sir. I must have seen fifty battle suits. It had to be Battalion Ten. The ones that survived the pressure died from a Macro ambush at the bottom."

I grunted. He sounded shook-up. I ordered a head count. He'd lost about forty more. In retrospect, it had been stupid to send the whole company down. But in these situations, it was so hard to tell what the right move was. If I'd ordered down a squad and they'd dropped into a mass of Macros, we would have lost them all and learned nothing. By going down in strength, I'd thought I was

166

offering my men protection. Unfortunately, the real enemy in this battle had been the depth of the ocean, and it had won the day.

"What are we going to do about the Macros down there?" Kwon asked me.

"Get out the grenades," I said.

We stood a man at three points around the rim with a small-yield tactical nuclear grenade. We set them for contact-detonation, and tossed them in. Then—we ran for it.

The shockwave rolled up from behind to smacked my marines in the ass. It sent us tumbling out of control through the water. I felt as if I'd been hit by a train. Fortunately, I'd ordered my troops to glide upward so only a few were smashed into the rocky seabed. After another headcount, we found we'd lost only two more men, both of them were men who'd jumped into the hole on Sloan's ill-fated adventure. I figured their suits had been damaged and couldn't handle the shockwave from the explosion, even though we should have reached a safe distance by then.

I reported my situation to the other battalions via the hydrophone. They were assaulting the cave entrance while we spent our time jumping in holes.

Things had gone badly on their front—worse than they had for my two battalions. The enemy had suckered them into narrow tunnels and ambushed my men. Outside on the open seafloor we had the advantage due to our superior numbers and firepower. Every macro that showed its nose outside the tunnels was burned by a hundred guns. But once we went into their warren of tunnels, we lost that advantage. There had been savage fighting down there, and we'd lost more men than they had lost machines.

When I arrived and saw the scene, I began kicking the butt of every officer I saw. But it didn't change the facts. These Macros weren't going to be driven out of their holes without a determined assault. I was certain the factories must be down there, so I prepared to do the impossible. I reorganized my marines into independent platoons. That was as big of a unit as could operate effectively in the tunnels. A platoon could all stay within radio distance of one another. A company could not when stretched out down the length of a tunnel.

I felt good about the situation. This next was strong and deeply dug-in, but it had to be protecting their factories. We'd scoured much of the seabed and this was the most strongly protected point.

I was about to order the final assault, expecting grim losses in trade for victory, when the oceans above darkened and very bad things began to come down toward us.

-26-

The Macros had called for air support. I can't say that I blamed them. They were in trouble. Every beachhead is at its weakest when it first hits enemy territory. Part of my basic plan had been to attack them before they could get organized, before their numbers could grow. With luck, I'd figured they would not be able to defend themselves.

We hadn't had that kind of luck, but we'd done them a lot of damage. The fighting was hard, but at that moment, I figured we were clearly on the winning team. Unfortunately, the Macros realized this before we could wipe out their main nest.

Everything changed when several wedge-shaped vessels the size of buildings dove into the oceans with us and glided through the water toward my massed formations. We were all in one place now—maybe that was what they'd been waiting for. They came down and came in close to fire their big belly turrets at us at point-blank range.

A spaceship really isn't all that different from a submarine in design. Both have to be self-contained and airtight. Both are designed to withstand extreme environments. I'd never seen the Macros fly a cruiser down into the oceans, but I'd never seen anything indicating they *couldn't* do it.

The second I realized what was coming for us, I ordered my men to scatter. My first thought was to swarm the cruisers one at a time and use our grenades to take them out. Maybe, I thought, this was an opportunity to take the enemy fleet out, to deal a devastating blow.

But then more of them kept diving down after us like greedy seabirds finding a nest teaming with thousands of hatchling turtles. I gave a general bug-out order to every commander and pulled my own rip-cord. With repellers on full and my gasbag dragging me up by the wrist, I shot up past the shark-like cruisers that swam near. Once we were above them, we were safe from their belly-turrets. The escaping last men dropped a barrage of grenades down like depth charges, but we couldn't see if they did much damage in the inky dark water below.

Once we broke the surface, we flew for the beaches at top speed. We had to get under the Andros Island's defensive umbrella as soon as possible. The cruisers didn't dare follow us to the surface and gun us down. They'd taken enough loss against Andros Island's stinging lasers. Over the intervening days, we'd rebuilt a large number of them, and we'd stationed most of the hovertanks on the beach as well to patch the gap in the island's defenses and to cover any retreat from the sea.

My marines reached the beaches with their tails between their legs, but most of us had lived to fight another day. I walked the shoreline, counting dead, wounded and missing. We were still eight-five percent effective. I wasn't sure exactly how much damage we'd done the enemy with our campaign, but I was fairly certain we couldn't knock them off the planet like that—not as long as they still rule the skies with their fleet.

Decompression sickness was a major issue for hundreds of my men. Our suits had the ability to function as mini-decompression systems, maintaining stable pressure inside. They operated the way a submarine allowed her crew to go up and down in the water without building up nitrogen in every man's blood. Unfortunately, a number of the suits had ruptured due to our speedy exit from the sea. We'd been down too deep and there were limits to what nanites could do and how fast they could do it.

Getting an idea, I decided to find out if those new-age pressure-chamber devices were still on the island. Ping, the purchasing agent in charge, had recently died. Unsurprisingly, she had never filled out the paperwork to return the machines. We broke them out of a surviving warehouse south of the main base and used our suit generators with gleaming lines of nanites to supply the required power. We had to be careful not to step on the nanites, as they were alive with voltage—essentially, they were bare wires. We ran the machines and they did their job. We set up an odd sort of triage in the middle of burnt trees and scorched sands, and it helped my marines. I thought I would have to praise Crow for accidentally having bought something useful.

I looked around me, and I took another kind of accounting. Most of my men had removed their helmets, allowing me to see their faces. Their expressions were grim. No one likes losing. Contrary to the popular adage, a loss does not make you stronger for the next fight, it makes you weaker. Morale is a critical factor in any fight for a human force. As a species, we can be talked into self-sacrifice, but we don't want to risk our lives when we believe it's all for nothing.

I looked out to the sea, where there were still floating bodies marked with puddles of bright dye. We'd sent our dead up to the world of sunlight that way, but now that we'd been chased out of ocean, it simply looked gruesome. No one had gotten to the dead yet, there were too many wounded and suffering from decompression sickness for them to be gathered any time soon.

The demoralization of my men got to me as I walked among them. I wondered how many of my men had quietly considered another obvious option: we could throw down our arms and abandon Andros. If we simply evacuated the island, the Macros might well march over it, find nothing of interest and declare themselves winners. Every human in Star Force could live on the rest of the planet. None of us had to again face the horrors that now brewed beneath the waves or above the clouds. Some of my men must have thought of this, and I knew the thought would turn into words in time, and then it would spread and invade the mind of every marine. Why fight if we could not win? Why not retreat, build-up and wait until the Macros grew tired of circling our world and went to pester some other trouble-spot in their empire?

I might have fallen prey to this kind of thinking if I'd not seen the Eden system myself. I imagined now that the herd peoples we called Centaurs had at some point been faced with a similar choice. Since the surface of their worlds were overrun by Macros, I had to assume they had negotiated to survive on their satellite habitats.

171

The Macros had encircled them, just as they did to us now. But the machines hadn't left. The enemy hadn't forgotten the Centaurs. They were patient beyond measure. What meaning did passing years have for a race of machines? They bided their time, and had already made attempts to bypass their arrangements with the defeated herds. They had used us for precisely such a purpose.

I could well imagine Earth enduring a similar fate, with the Macros bringing a third party of killers to root us out once and for all. They would never forget us. They would never retreat. They would never leave us alone.

My ruminations led me to an inescapable conclusion: we had to fight this battle, and we had to win it somehow. My men required a morale boost in order to stay effective. I thought for a minute or two, and came up with a plan to keep their minds in this fight. Something to give them hope. We would busy ourselves with fortifications. We would prepare for the inevitable Macro assault we all knew was coming with a fresh set of defenses.

A few hours later, I had my entire force off the beach and back inside the burnt-out husk that was our base. The clean up and rebuilding had begun here, mostly evidenced by tireless crawlers and fit marines who stacked debris into earthen mounds. It was often easier, given Nano technology, to shove aside the old and rebuild fresh structures. Corrugated steel and concrete was outdated and had been surpassed by newer construction materials.

To start with, I dumped out a foot-thick bead of constructive nanites just beyond where the old concrete wall had stood. For years now, whenever our Nano factories had an idle moment, they'd been instructed to produce constructive nanites. We had thousands of tons of them stashed around the islands. Now was the time, I calculated, to make use of this resource.

The nanite lines, without orders, looked like mounds of metallic sand granules. They shone almost like liquid mercury in the sun, but were more textured than mercury. Too small for the human eye to pick out individuals in the mix, it looked like a single mass of gelatinous metal. Adding to the eerie look of them, the nanite mounds tended to move of their own accord, shivering, bubbling and slowly stirring in circular eddies. I could not recall ever having seen so many nanites massed in a single place as I did today.

When the entirety of Fort Pierre was encircled with the silver snake of nanites, I knew I had shifted the conversation among my men. They stared in fascination, wondering and speculating what I had in mind. What new trick was the conjurer about to perform?

I avoided looking at them. I stayed intently focused on my efforts. But secretly, I allowed myself a grin in the dark interior of my helmet. I had piqued their interest. Now was the time to move things forward.

I instructed the entire nanite mass to put up a thin outer wall of metal. I sent crawlers forward with pallets of metals for the nanites to chew up and spit out. We served up thousands chunks of raw steel, aluminum, tin and copper. The nanites dug into the metals like a hot meal and soon the walls were rising, blotting out the picturesque view of the beach. I knew Sandra would complain about that part, but this was a military operation and we were at war. Defense had to come first.

When the outer wall was a good thirty feet high, it was a yellowy color due to the mixing alloys. I knew the nanites were part of the mix as well, so the wall would be self-repairing if the enemy should blow a hole in it. The structure was tall, but only about two inches thick.

Barrera was the first one to approach me as I worked on the walls. Kwon tagged along with him.

"Colonel?" Barrera asked.

"What is it?"

"Um, I can see you are busy sir. Maybe I should talk to you after you are...uh, done with this thing."

"Thing?" I asked, finally turning to look at him. "What does it look like to you, Barrera?"

"A wall sir."

"What's wrong with it?"

"Nothing, sir," he said.

I stared at him, knowing he had more to say. Barrera looked at the thin walls doubtfully. At his side, Kwon shuffled from foot to foot slowly. I waited for them to speak.

"It's just that—well, this is a very thin wall, Colonel," Barrera said at last.

"Ah," I said, "so that's it. Well, tell the men I'm not done yet."

173

"Okay, sir," Barrera said. He turned around sharply and left me to my work. Kwon stumped off after him. Both men were frowning.

I chuckled and decided it was time to call in the crawlers again. All the while I'd been building this thin, high wall the crawlers had been following their standard programming to mound up the smashed rubble into mini-mountains. Like tall, ugly anthills, slag-heaps were everywhere around the base.

I ordered the crawlers to turn their blades in a new direction. They were to push the mounds of earth and debris to the perimeter, mounding it up against the outer metal wall I'd put up.

Once I had the machines working to my satisfaction, I called up Barrera and ordered him to put the marines on shovel duty. It's hard to think about desertion and hopelessness while you're shoveling your ass off, especially if you're building something interesting and impressive. After another hour of work, the new walls were really taking shape. Looking at the wall, none of the men could doubt them now. The outer surface was inches thick of bright, reactive metal. Behind that was a mound of rubble ten feet thick at the top and forty feet thick at the bottom.

I walked the perimeter, making sure the walls stood a uniform forty feet in height. I had fresh barrels of nanites dumped over the mounds of rubble next. They covered the interior with a glaring metal skin of nanites and loose metals leeched from the debris. I nodded to myself appreciatively. The structure would serve fairly well as a defensive fortification against a ground attack.

The outside face of the walls was straight and sheer. The inside was slanted, as it was really metal covering mounds of dirt and trash. I began putting up the finishing touches, adding stairways and ramps to the top, and a crenulated line of battlements all along the parapet. I had marines set up heavy gun emplacements with clamshell turrets here and there then added automated lasers in-between all along the top of the wall.

As darkness fell, I burned massive arrays of lamps and kept the men working in shifts, allowing the exhausted to shower and rest. Barrera approached me at around midnight.

"Hello Colonel," he said, his mood was obviously brighter—but it was always hard to tell with Barrera.

"Hello," I grunted. My mood was beginning to sour as fatigue set in. Even with nanotized bodies, we all grew tired and needed to rest eventually.

"This is very impressive, sir."

"Glad you approve."

Barrera looked at me. "I never said I disapproved, sir."

"Oh come on," I said. "Admit it man, you thought I'd lost it when I first started building this thing."

Barrera gave me a ghostly smile. A rare expression for him. "Well, I'm more at ease now. I've got just three things I wish to ask you about."

"Name them."

"First, what if they come from above? Will this wall help against their fleet?"

"No, not really. But they aren't massing on the bottom of our oceans for a science experiment. They will come up and assault these walls, I'm sure of that."

"Very good sir. On to my second point: What if they come from below?"

I paused. He had me there. They *were* diggers, these mechanical monsters. I'd fought drilling Macros before in South America and they were clearly active under the sea.

"You make a good point there. I'll have to build underground defensive layers as we did on Helios against the Worms."

Barrera nodded. "Excellent idea, sir."

"And the third thing?"

He looked at me appraisingly. "When's the last time you had some sleep, sir?"

I felt a surge of irritation. I felt like slapping him just for saying the word *sleep*. But then, I realized I was exhausted. I'd fought a hard underwater campaign, then exited the sea just in time to begin a massive rebuilding effort. I sat down on the tracks of a deactivated crawler.

"Just sitting down feels good," I said. "You're right, Lieutenant-Colonel. Can you carry on while I get some rest?"

"It's as if you read my mind, sir."

I was too tired to laugh or even smile at him. I did shake his hand, however, and headed toward the sleeping tents we'd set up in the landing pits. A sound made by moving fabric caused me to stop and look behind me. There, in the blackness, I saw a familiar outline. It was Sandra. She was particularly disturbing at night, as she no longer seemed to require light to see by. I wondered if her eyes had been rebuilt with the ability to see in the infrared spectrum. I suspected that was the case, but I'd never asked her about it. We rarely talked about our special abilities—at least, not the freaky ones. It was a turn-off to notice how much our bodies had changed over time. We just went with it, and by silent mutual agreement, pretended we were the same normal human couple from years past.

"Did you put Barrera up to that?" I asked.

"He handled it well, didn't he?"

"Yeah," I said. "He did. He's more diplomatic than you are."

"More than either of us."

I nodded in agreement and fell onto a cot. Sandra fell into bed beside me. I wondered if she had been following me ever since I'd stepped out of the sea. I figured she probably had. I'd half-expected to run into her while underwater.

-27-

Being a commanding officer had its perks. One of them was being given a cot and a tent, even when such things were in short supply. Normally, after a base had been wiped out, I would have spent the night in my personal ship. But I'd given up the *Socorro* now for the good of the cause. She was behind the Moon, hiding from the Macros with the rest of the Fleet. The only good thing about that was Crow was hiding out in space with the rest of the Fleet, which meant I didn't have to listen to him. He only rarely sent a message out to us. Maybe he feared the Macros would home in on his signal and run down his comparatively small force of ships.

I woke up the next time the sun shone. It could have been morning, but it felt more like noon. The tropical heat was already in the tent with me, making my face stick to things. The inadequate pillow they'd given me was glued to my head with sweat. I knew enough not to complain, however. Most of my marines could only fantasize about a bed and a pillow. They were out shoveling already, finishing up the walls and the underground nanite-woven defenses I'd had them working on for over a day now.

I groaned and looked around blearily, but didn't get up. Sandra was gone, probably having become bored with waiting for me to wake up. I finally hauled myself up and put my feet on the floor.

When my feet touched the floor I triggered some kind of trap. At the time, I had no idea what was happening to me, but I felt a powerful shock running up through my body. I flopped back on the cot, and saw flashes of light in my head.

Something had gone off. At least, that was what the part of my mind that still operated told me. Something like a flashbulb, but with only the tiniest flare of bluish light. Whatever it was, I felt stunned.

I commanded my muscles to leap out of bed, but it didn't work out that way. Forcing myself to move, I rolled off my cot and slumped onto the floor on the other side of cot. My body wasn't obeying me yet.

What had hit me? I could only think it was an electrical shock of some kind. Something meant to stun me into submission. In my foggy mind, there were no happy reasons why someone would want to do this.

I heard words then: "That's it, *move, move, move!*"

The words came from strange throats—voices I didn't recognize. The words were spoken in low tones, louder than whispers but clearly not meant to be heard at a distance. I heard feet tapping and cloth swishing as unseen figures approached.

I managed to struggle up to all fours before they reached me. I reached for my pillow, which was still soaked with my sweat. My hand slid under the cloth and my fist closed around the hilt of a combat blade. Every second that passed brought greater strength and coordination to my limbs. I pulled out the blade and held it low as I slowly began to stand up.

Coincidentally, my assassins were armed with blades as well. The first one made a mistake. He grabbed my hair, yanking my head back and moving his blade to my throat. His knife never quite made it to my neck, however. I took his hand off for him, as my blade was ready and flicked a split-second faster than his did. A hand fell, still tightly gripping a combat knife like my own. I don't think the guy even knew what had happened at first. Maybe he was confused at the sudden lightness at the end of his treacherous wrist. He made two more sawing motions at my face. Blood gushed hotly onto my cheek.

He figured it out after that and began to howl and keen in shock. The other guy was smarter, unfortunately. Perhaps he'd grown wiser after seeing what happened to his buddy. He just stuck his knife in my back, nothing fancy about it. The blade bit deeply into my left kidney—wrecking it. The explosion of pain was a new kind of shock. Oddly, rather than stunning me, it seemed to bring me more fully awake.

I didn't have the time or agility to jump up and fight with him. Instead, I slashed at an ankle that was too close. He was stooping over me, and when his foot left his leg, he pitched forward onto my back. It was understandable, as he was now seriously off-balance.

Things became nasty after that. We were all injured. There was blood everywhere. I caught a glimpse of my pillow and saw it was no longer white except in patches. I knew I was getting weaker. I had several cuts—but I hadn't lost a limb or a major artery yet.

I looked at the two assassins. Their faces were pale, terrified. They were both Caucasian-looking men. They weren't wearing uniforms, so I knew they weren't my own marines. I was glad for that small comfort. To know I was dying at the hands of my own men, that would have made my last seconds more horrible.

Losing a limb each seemed to have taken some of the fight out of them. They weren't nanotized, either. I could tell that. Probably, that had been the reason they had tried to stun me first. It had almost worked, too. But now I was up on my knees, and I had a blade up between us. They were both watched the edge in shock.

The guy with the missing hand had figured out what was missing by now. He took up his blade again in his remaining hand and appeared to still be game. He was coming at me, making thrusting motions. Spittle and blood ran from his face. I wasn't sure where the blood in his mouth was from. Maybe he'd bitten his own tongue in the excitement.

The second guy was in worse shape. He was on his hands and knees. He held up his blade too, but more in a defensive posture.

I felt sick inside. My back was numb. They gotten at least two stab wounds in there after popping my kidney. I knew I was losing blood as fast as they were, and I was going to be passed out on the floor in a minute or two. That gave me the impetus to go for them. In this kind of fight, whoever passed out from hemorrhaging first lost the game.

"Come on, ladies," I said to them between gritted, blood-lined teeth. "Let's finish this."

My attitude didn't fill them with confidence. They hesitated for a moment with eyes staring in disbelief. It was their move, but as it turned out, they made the wrong one. They advanced toward me together.

Something blurred into the tent. A dark shape with thin, flashing limbs. Their heads flew from their necks a moment later. The two assassins didn't even seem to know what was happening. I don't even know if they saw death coming. The heads rolled on the floor, smeared in blood and sweat. Their eyes were still staring with that same expression of confusion, disbelief and uncertainty about what to do next.

"Hi honey," I said, "I think I overslept."

I went down onto all fours again. I couldn't even raise my eyes up to meet Sandra's. My knife slipped from my numbing fingers. I grabbed it up again, not letting it go.

Small hands grabbed me. Arms like bands of steel lifted me into the air and cradled me against her chest. Fabric tore and I felt it slide over me. She had run right through the nearest wall of the tent. A moment later, we were outside. The sun was brilliant, making me squint.

"You were right about assassins, by the way," I admitted.

"Don't you die on me, Kyle," she said angrily.

"I think I'm going to puke."

But I didn't puke. Instead, my head slumped against her chest. She ran with me, sprinting as only our kind could while carrying a comrade. She moved faster than I could have, I was certain of that. No Olympic sprinter in history could have beaten her. She carried me to the medical tents, I knew. To the place where brainbox doctors with skinny arms of black metal would do foul things to me.

Thinking of nanites just before I lost consciousness, I wonder where mine had gone. Usually by this time, I would have felt them tickling and crawling in their millions, working on my wound to seal it up faster than my biological systems could hope to do. But I didn't feel them. I barely felt anything at all.

I could still move my eyes, so I looked up at the sun. It was hot today, even for the tropics. My home star looked dimmer to me, however. The brightest light in the world was only a cold spark as my mind shut down.

* * *

When I woke up, Sandra was crouching on another medical table nearby. I could tell she was upsetting the nanite medical systems. Three arms of jet black whipped around her ankles. Occasionally, one of them probed at her body, touching her shapely thighs or tickling at her ankle. I knew they were trying to figure out why she was there, to discern if she was injured in some way. She slapped the three-fingered hands away as one might slap at the unwanted touch of an overly-affectionate pet.

"They want to fix you," I said to her, slurring my words slightly.

Sandra perked up and shifted on her haunches. I reflected how often she chose that kind of pose lately. Since the Microbes had changed her, she seemed to be comfortable in positions that would be unnatural to most humans. She liked to crouch rather than sit. And when she crouched, she liked to do it up on a high platform.

"You're alive," she said. I heard her sigh.

"Why do you perch on things like that?" I asked. I wasn't sure why I'd asked the question. Maybe I had some extra chemicals in my bloodstream that had loosened my tongue and allowed my mind to wander more than usual.

"I can move faster from this position," she said. "My legs are coiled under me, and I can spring into the air if I need to. When I come down, I'm running very fast." Then she smiled at me. "Besides, it feels good."

"Ah," I said, nodding painfully. "That's what I thought."

"You don't think I'm a weirdo, do you Kyle?" she asked suddenly.

Despite the drugs in my system and my heavy loss of blood, alarm bells went off in my mind. I knew I had to answer this question carefully. The problem was, it was hard to think. I needed to think of something clever to say, but I couldn't.

I squinted at her in concentration until she laughed.

"It wasn't that serious of a question," she said.

"I—I'm glad you're a weirdo," I said at last. "Otherwise, I'd be dead right now."

181

I was pretty sure it wasn't the right answer, but it was the best I could do. She pouted for a moment, but quickly recovered. I gauged my answer a near-failure. Probably, I'd been given extra points for my state of body and mind. I had enough brainpower left to try to change the subject.

"They hit me with something. A shock of some kind."

She nodded. "A metal plate. It looked like a nanite-made surface. Same kind of yellowy alloy. When your bare feet touched it, an electric shock was set off. It was a tiny EMP-blast, actually."

"Really?" I said, nodding slightly. I winced in pain and stopped nodding. I thought then about lifting the sheet over me and checking my wounds, but I didn't feel like it. Not yet.

"Yes, they knocked out over ninety-percent of the nanites in your system. They were normals, and must have thought you would be easy game without nanites."

What most people didn't realize was that once nanotized, my marines were changed internally forever. The nanites rebuilt us, and once that was done their task became one of maintenance and repair. We weren't stronger and faster because the nanites moved our limbs for us, they essentially upgraded our bodies and then served later as tiny surgeons to patch up any injuries we might sustain. Still, knocking them out and very nearly knocking me out had been a nice opening move.

My mind coalesced slowly, but steadily. I shook my head as I thought about the assassins and how they had looked at me. They had feared me. Even after they'd pulled their little trick, they had still feared me. "I don't think they thought I'd be weak. They were afraid of me."

"Maybe that's because you chopped off parts of them."

"They were afraid right from the start."

"What difference does it make?"

"It means they knew something about fighting one of us. They weren't experts at killing a Star Force marine, but they had a clue as to how to go about it. That increases the odds they had inside help."

"Oh, they definitely had help. How the hell else did they manage to rig-up a trap in our tent? Did you think of that?"

I looked at her. She was both lovely and deadly. She crouched there like a guardian angel—or a guardian gargoyle.

"Is there an investigation going on yet?" I asked.

Sandra nodded. "Barrera put himself in charge of it. He's going through the regular base staff to see what they know. These men came in from a ship, supposedly to seek a job here on the base. They were on the first supply boat from Miami after the Macros retreated over the ocean."

I tried to get up and Sandra blurred closer in immediate response. I looked down in surprise. Her hand was on my chest, and she was crouching over me on my medical table. Three whipping arms rose up, startled. They reached out tentatively and tapped at her calves. She ignored them.

"Don't get up yet," she said sweetly.

"You can't push me around like this when I'm wearing my battle suit," I grumbled.

"Well, you're not wearing it now. You are weak, Kyle. We gave you a fresh dose of nanites while you were out. But they have to learn your body and grow accustomed to it."

I thought about that. It was a strange thought. I felt a little bad that millions of tiny robots who'd been my friends, swimming in my body for years, had all died. I had new nanites now, but somehow it wasn't the same.

"I want to know who did this," I said.

"Don't worry," Sandra said, "I do too."

"Go get Barrera," I said. "I want to talk to him."

"I'll call him for you," she said. "But I'm not leaving you again."

She kissed me then. My lips were sore for some reason, but hers were soft and insistent. I enjoyed the kiss and the tingling burn she left on my lips when it was over.

-28-

With a fresh shot of nanites I began healing very fast. After two days, I was as good as new except for a few deep scars.

I examined myself in a mirror on a Tuesday morning. I tapped at raised, red seams of crusty flesh on my back where the skin hadn't quite regrown yet. The recovery had been nothing less than miraculous. I reflected upon how quickly we'd become accustomed to the miracles of the nanites.

If anything, these new nanites were working faster than the old ones. It made sense, as the nanites must cease working now and then. They might run out of power, or become damaged, or simply wear out. Over time, there would be fewer and fewer in a man's system to do the needed repair work. I was sure my men wouldn't be happy about it, but they should really have a booster-shot of fresh nanites every year or so. I thought I might have to institute a system of medical nanite replacement, where my marines would have to undergo an oil change, so to speak, periodically.

My body was functioning again. I was whole and strong, but my mind was unhappy. I couldn't get certain questions out of my head. Who was behind these two attacks, and why? Ping had tried it first with a sweet smile and a bomb. The second pair had been more direct and urgent. It seemed obvious my attackers had had some kind of internal help. How else could men fresh on the base have found my tent, set up a sophisticated trap within it and nearly murdered me all within a single day?

184

Barrera's investigation turned up very little. It was too bad Sandra had killed the pair so effectively, instead of capturing them. I couldn't blame her for that, however. I would have done the same if the situation had been reversed. We'd identified them as ex-members of the KCT—Dutch commandos. Their government claimed they were mercenaries now, and claimed they knew nothing about it. Strangely enough, I believed them. The Netherlands had no cause to go up against Star Force. It would be a senseless, suicidal move for them. Therefore, someone else had to be behind the attempt.

And that was the bad part. The worst thing the assassins did to me was make me doubt my own people. The injuries were healing much faster than the loss of trust. After the second attack I began going through a list of likely suspects in my mind over and over again. I couldn't help it.

Topping the list was General Kerr and his Pentagon crew. I'd asked them to hold back when the Macro battle fleet arrived. Maybe someone up there on the Potomac River didn't like that. The Americans had made a few plays to kill me in the past. I still recalled hugging Esmeralda, their failed assassin, as she died in my arms. She had been the first human I'd killed up close and personal. Prior to that, I'd shot a few enemy insurgents back during my brief tour of the Mideast, but they'd died a hundred yards away from me. Fighting to the death hand-to-hand with a woman wasn't the same.

Kerr and his crew had sent Esmeralda after me, and then they'd sent troops to Andros to take out Star Force the following year. Maybe these attacks were their latest attempts. The possibility could not be ignored.

Next on the list was fine, old Admiral Crow himself. Sure, he was off hiding in his ship behind the Moon right now, but that didn't give him an airtight alibi in my book. Hadn't we come to blows just days ago? There had been more than one fight between us that had become physical. The whole attempt seemed overly-sneaky for Crow, however. He tended to move on me very openly when he did it. He would lose his temper and take a swing at me—assassination through third parties had never been his style. He'd never worked through go-betweens, preferring to come at me man-to-man when the mood struck him. In a strange way, I respected that trait. Still, it was impossible to leave him off the list.

If it wasn't Kerr or Crow, the list became much longer and more disturbing. One of my own marines? Another party I'd yet to identify? One of my officers, seeing their chance to move up the ladder? It could be anyone in that case.

After I'd showered and dressed, I took a deep breath and headed toward the new headquarters building. I was still thinking about my mental list of suspects, and it wasn't getting any shorter.

The new headquarters building was much less imposing than it had been. Gone was Crow's four-story castle. Instead, the Star Force command center had been reborn as a single-story structure. It was flat and thickly-built with walls of nanite-coated rubble. Most of the structure was underground now in a deep, anthill-like bunker meant to defend us from another aerial bombardment. The building on the surface served primarily as a secure entrance.

I saw Sandra as I approached. She lifted a hand to wave at me. She was crouching on the low roof of the headquarters bunker, leaning over the entrance and scrutinizing everyone who passed through. She'd been worried about my safety before, and now she was absolutely paranoid.

As I walked through the doors, she hopped down and joined me, matching my measured step. We were going down to a staff meeting to review the state of our defenses. I figured the Macros would assault us within the next week. They would only wait long enough to mass up sufficient forces to overrun the island. Fortunately, we were preparing as well and had a few surprises in store for them.

Nanotized marines didn't really need elevators. Since they tended to break down under heavy bombardment, we didn't bother to build any. We walked down steep stairs that rang metallically as my foot touched down on every riser. Each set of steps ended in a long hallway, followed by another stairway. Behind me, Sandra watched everything except me. She watched the ceiling, the floor—even the walls themselves.

Sandra appraised every door that opened as we approached with intense suspicion. Often, when a staffer popped out into the corridor, he was startled when Sandra appeared in his face. Moving with uncanny speed, she placed her body between me and the stranger. The staffers never complained, however. They froze in place, eyes wide, until I passed and Sandra stepped away. They eyed her knives and her steely gaze. They knew how fast she could move, and they didn't want to end up with their heads bouncing on the metal floors of the corridor due to a misunderstanding. Freezing was the safest move.

As we walked, I kept thinking about the assassination and who was behind it. As annoying as it was, the situation had to be dealt with. Who could it be? In an attempt to make myself feel better I decided to mark down names I *did* trust. Sandra headed that short list, of course. She had a nightly opportunity to kill me, and if she had wanted the job done it would have happened long ago. Kwon was on the no-way list as well. He'd had just as many chances as Sandra over the years, and he was almost as protective of me as she was. Besides, he simply lacked the imagination to cook up a complex plot like the EMP blast I'd dealt with. There were a few loyal officers I trusted, such as Major Robinson. Unfortunately, they were all dead now.

Try as I might, I couldn't come up with more names I could absolutely count on. It was depressing. I could only think of two people I could trust with my life under any circumstances. I shook my head slightly and went back to the grim task of sorting out the list of suspects.

After Crow and Kerr, who else could it be? Barrera? Unlikely, but not impossible. He was second in command of the marines and would doubtlessly be chosen as my successor should I be taken out. He'd always supported me with unwavering efficiency, but his naturally cool exterior made him easy to suspect.

The next name my mind conjured up was Major Sarin. I knew she had developed an emotional attachment to me over the last year, which I had foolishly encouraged. I still thought of her as Jasmine in my mind, but didn't dare speak her first name out loud. Jasmine had been hurt emotionally—as well as physically—when Sandra had awakened from her coma and attacked her. Still, if jealousy was her motivation, wouldn't Jasmine be more likely to try to take out Sandra than me, if it came to that? Regardless, she just wasn't the type to try assassination anyway.

Who else was there? As I asked the question, the faces of a dozen other officers swam into my mind. They'd all lost friends,

187

limbs or loved ones. Maybe one of them figured that removing me from command would improve our world's odds of survival. Perhaps they were right. Moving on to humanity at large, I realized there were the thousands—no, *millions* of people who'd lost a loved one and might hold a grudge against me. They all had good cause to want me dead.

I heaved a sigh, which caused Sandra to flick her gaze toward me. Finding me healthy, her eyes slid away again to prowl our environment. I opened the door to the new conference room and stepped inside. Sandra followed close behind me, as always. She rarely left my side these days, taking her job as my bodyguard more seriously than ever before. I felt like some kind of nervous dictator. Would I soon be recruiting a look-alike version of Kyle Riggs to sleep in my bed? Would I be shuffling beds from night to night, never sleeping in the same place? I didn't want that kind of life, I had to get to the bottom of this. But I didn't really have time to investigate the latest assassination attempt properly. I had a war to run and a coming invasion to repel.

"Colonel," Barrera said the moment I walked in. "I'm glad you're here. We have a situation."

All thoughts of assassins evaporated. I kicked myself mentally for having dwelled on the subject for so long. Again, I'd let my enemies get the best of me by distracting me and making me mistrust my own people. In a way, it made me angrier than the injuries I'd sustained.

"What are they doing?" I asked. "Have they hit land yet?"

Barrera stared at me for a second then frowned. "Sir? No, sir, I mean we have a situation in space."

I opened my mouth and closed it again. I looked down at the newest big screen. This was a nice unit. I'd had it built with thicker glass this time on top of a solid base of nanite alloys. There were shock-absorbers under the base. This system was ready to ride out a heavy bombardment.

To my surprise, the images on the screen depicted the solar system rather than Andros Island. My heart sank as I scanned the screen. It must be a reinforcing fleet. I looked for distant red contacts, but didn't see any.

"Are they coming in with fresh Macros ships?" I asked.

"No, look at the outer rim. Look at the Tyche ring, sir."

Major Sarin helpfully rotated and zoomed the map so I could see the Oort cloud region in question up close. We had sensors out there now among the frozen comets and silent, orbital debris. There had once been a theory in astronomical circles that the Oort cloud harbored a hypothetical planet of significant mass. Unseen for decades despite our searching for it, we only knew that there was a strange gravity well out there that affected the behavior of the chunks of dirty ice we call comets. In the end, when we explored the region in recent years we discovered Tyche didn't exist. Instead, we found one of the enigmatic rings left behind by unknown ancients who were so technologically advanced they could build a system of instantaneous transport between star systems. The ring was closer in than Tyche had been thought to be, but still seemed to be affecting the orbital behavior of various Oort cloud objects. Although the planet had turned out to be mythical, we'd come to use the name Tyche for the Solar System's outlying ring.

I examined the big screen closely, as Barrera had suggested. I saw something and tapped at it with my finger. A yellowish contact. It had to be a ship, and it was speeding directly toward the Tyche ring.

"That's Marvin, isn't it?" I asked.

"Yes, sir. He came through the Venus ring after the Macro fleet was out of the way and has been quietly flying toward the far side of the Solar System on a wide, curved path. He's avoiding both the Macros and Earth."

I nodded. Marvin never liked combat. He was an explorer, not a fighter. But he managed to get himself into plenty of trouble despite his peaceful nature.

Then I noticed a set of small red contacts following Marvin. "The Macros fired on him?" I asked. "Those are missiles following him, right?"

"Yes, they did that while you were incapacitated. The missiles seem low on fuel. They are no longer gaining on him, and they are falling further behind. If I had to guess, I'd say they only have enough power left to make course adjustments and keep following him."

"So he's taking them out to the Tyche ring. The mines may well destroy them when he gets there. Do you think he's going to actually fly through the ring?"

"We were hoping you could tell us that, sir. He's not responding to our questions. He says things like: 'all neural chains are currently engaged' when we hail him."

I snorted. Marvin fed lines like that to people he didn't want to bother with. "If we try to talk to him, what's the delay at this distance?"

"Several hours, sir. He's pretty far out."

"Hmm… He's pretty close to the ring, too. If we transmit to him now, will he have time to get the message and respond before he enters the ring?"

Major Sarin brought up a spreadsheet on the screen in front of her and tapped at it with light, expert touches. She looked cute like that, and I couldn't help but think of her as Jasmine in my head. I stared at her, waiting for an answer. Jasmine leaned forward and her ponytail fell off her shoulder to hang around her neck attractively.

After about twenty seconds of staring, I became aware of Sandra, who was watching me closely. I didn't look at her. Instead, I opened up another screen and reviewed our force listings. Sandra's scrutiny lifted. I wanted to smile, but I didn't dare.

"He'll have time for one reply," Major Sarin said at last. "Given his acceleration rate and current velocity, before we can send him a second message, he'll be through the ring."

"Unless I can get him to change course now, before he goes zipping through the Tyche ring?"

Major Sarin nodded. "Right, sir."

"Open a channel. Let's see what that crazy robot has to say for himself."

I took a moment to consider my words. Although he was an AI entity, Marvin could be evasive and touchy. He was likely to take anything I said in the way he preferred to take it. I considered him to be even more self-centered than most humans. I could threaten him, but that might just be taken as a license to do whatever he wished. It was best to keep him tied to us as best I could.

As I composed my words in my head, I found myself wishing I'd never given him a spaceship body. That had been a mistake. If I

190

caught hold of him again, I'd strip his wings for good. Maybe he sensed that, and thus kept far out of my reach.

I knew most of my command staff had long since convicted him of treason, but the jury was still out on Marvin as far as I was concerned. He had proven himself to be a loyal friend on many occasions, but almost as often he'd given us a royal problem to solve. In the case of the Macros, he'd nearly dismantled our minefield, but at the same time had caused them to come through early and lose many ships which they might not have lost otherwise. The Macros were obviously out to destroy him now, and would never trust him again. I considered that a very positive development. Of all the trouble he could get into in the future, making friends with the enemy was no longer on the list.

I saw everyone else looking at me, frowning. Even Major Sarin looked like she smelled a big nanite-brained rat. I sympathized, and wondered if I'd been too forgiving with Marvin. Was I projecting a sense of friendship on an intelligent machine he didn't deserve? I knew that our close involvement on the return trip from Eden had somehow created a soft spot in my normally hard mind for Marvin. Was it because I had helped him survive and watched him grow and build himself, both mentally and physically? What would a psych officer say about that? I didn't think I wanted to know.

"Open channel," I said at last. "Marvin, this is Colonel Kyle Riggs. You are a part of Star Force, and I am your commanding officer. I want to thank you for your successful ruse played against the Macros. They were severely damaged by your action. By destroying Macro ships, you proved you are on the side of Star Force and the enemy of the Macros. They will never stop trying to destroy you now, while we will remain your loyal friends."

I stopped to take a breath, but lifted my hand to prevent Jasmine from sending the message prematurely. "We are aware of your current circumstances. The enemy missiles chasing you probably can't overtake you at this point if you keep running. We see that you are heading in the direction of Tyche ring. We'd prefer you stayed in the Solar System. We need your help against the Macro Fleet. Please respect our wishes in this regard. Riggs out."

"Send it?" Major Sarin asked.

"Yeah, send it."

"Kyle," Sandra said, "why didn't you order him to stop what he was doing? If he goes through that ring we don't know what he might do."

"Yeah," I said. "But if I did order him to do that and he disobeyed, we'd have lost our hold over him. He's not like a regular human soldier. He's a free spirit, so to speak."

Barrera shook his head.

"Would you like to add something, Lieutenant Colonel?" I asked him sharply.

"No, sir."

I could tell he disapproved. They all did. I figured they didn't understand Marvin the way I did. If he didn't obey orders, they wanted to destroy him. But he wasn't a recruit, or a normal robot. He was Marvin, and he was unique.

We planned our defenses while we waited for Marvin's response. It took all day and hours into the night to come back. By that time, I'd reviewed our defensive posture. Fort Pierre was much stronger than it had ever been. New laser turrets had sprung up by the hundreds. We had at least a thousand guns on the island now, and most of them were on the east coast facing the dark trench known as the Tongue of the Ocean.

I'd built new defensive fortifications in the center of the island as well. If they brought in their ships again, they'd have a harder time of it now. The Macros had been building as well, I knew. I knew their rate of production was phenomenal. And the next time they came, they would have ground support from the sea.

Finally Marvin's response came in. "Friend Riggs, I am so glad to learn of your continued survival. Upon my eventual return, I will accept the offered commission in the Star Force Fleet. Can you make me a captain, please? No matter what my rank may be, I will help Star Force defeat the Macros. I am exiting the system now to evade the enemy missiles, but I also have another purpose. Do not worry! I will not disappoint you. Marvin out."

My staff exchanged disgusted glances which I did my best to ignore. I didn't bother sending Marvin another message. He wouldn't get it before he left the star system. We all watched as he flew through the Tyche ring and vanished some time later. The enemy missiles winked out as well. Our mines had destroyed them, but ignored Marvin due to his friend-or-foe signaling system.

Marvin had ignored my request to stay in the Solar System. That fact made my jaws flex and ache the more I thought about it. If he did wander back to Earth someday and came within my reach again, I wondered what I would do.

I knew that at the very least, I would clip his wings. Right now, I was leaning toward blasting him out of space.

-29-

The Macros finally marched upon Andros Island on Saturday, at about eleven in the morning. I don't know what they had against Saturdays. I supposed they probably didn't even know it *was* Saturday, nor did they understand our uniquely human concept of naming days in cycles. But even if they had understood the tradition, I was sure they wouldn't care in the slightest. It felt wrong somehow to be killed by any enemy that didn't even know what day it was. Whatever the case, the battle was forever afterward called the Saturday Assault, and it was destined to be one of the worst days of my life.

Saturday started off well enough. I wasn't living in a tent anymore, and the island defenses looked stronger. The forest around the base was still a mess, however. Every third tree looked like it had been struck by lightning. But due to the miracles of Nano technology, we were able to rebuild our fortifications with startling speed. One of the keys had been my stockpiling of constructive nanites. Many of the laser turrets didn't need to be rebuilt from scratch. The nanites, when properly applied, were like duct tape. You could fix just about anything with them. We broke out barrel after barrel, and every second turret on the beach was repairable without the delivery of a new projector unit from the factories.

We went farther than that, of course. We built new systems. A key element of my reinforced defense of Andros took shape in the form of three central forts located along the spine of the island.

194

These were placed atop low hills that were no more than a hundred feet above sea level, but which in comparison to the rest of the island stood out as landmarks. With a little earth-moving and some nanite-alloy walls poured over the top of them, I soon had three strong-points bristling with new weaponry. The bright metal hemispheres resembled observatories with multiple telescopes poking out of their domes.

I'd realized I needed heavier guns immediately after our first engagement with the Macro fleet. No lesson had been drilled into my head more clearly that day. We had to outrange the enemy to keep them at bay. The new guns weren't difficult to produce. The design couldn't have been simpler. All I had to do was tell my factories to produce new ship guns at triple the normal size. The standard sensory systems and brainboxes served well enough. Then by hooking up a stack of several standard fusion generators big enough to power a ship, we were able to produce enough power to fire the weapons. We had some cooling problems at first, due to the greater size and power of the units, but some creative work-arounds took care of these details. The only real difficulty was producing mounts large enough to aim the huge guns and hold them on a precise target. In the end, I went for expediency here, too. I used standard ship's arms, the same systems our tugs and ships used to put the weapons in place. I reasoned that if the black, cable-like arms could lift and position the projectors during construction, they could continue to do so, like a man using two hands to hold and aim a rifle. The result was less than perfect, as the aiming had some bounce and secondary retargeting was required. Not being built for such precision, the big construction arms tended to move slowly and after shifting targets, they would waver for a moment before locking into place. Still, given the time constraints, it was the best I could do.

On Saturday morning I stood at the bottom of the hill of Fort Two, the central fort and the largest of the three. Barrera stood near me, and Sandra was even closer.

"That is the weirdest-looking thing you've ever built, Kyle," Sandra told me. "Except maybe for Marvin."

"Marvin designed himself, really," I replied.

Together we gazed up at the big projectors. The crews were testing them out, targeting and retargeting the Macro cruisers hanging over the eastern horizon. The black arms, the bright metal domes and the faintly golden projectors all functioned together smoothly enough, but they did appear bizarre to an observer.

"They look like a man with thin black arms," Barrera said, "aiming a golden pen or something."

I turned to Barrera with upraised eyebrows. "Such poetry!" I said. "Out of character, but well said, Lieutenant Colonel. Let's hope they can hit what they aim at."

"We should test fire them," Barrera said. "The brainboxes need to learn their new tasks."

I shook my head. "I'm not going to give the Macros a break. They seem to be on hold out there. I'm hoping they are waiting for a reinforcement fleet from the Venus ring. I hope they are going to wait out there for years. But I'm going to wait until all of these weird-looking forts are ready to fire. The moment they are, the brainboxes are going to get some on-the-job training."

The brainboxes were all taken out of knocked-out laser turrets, so they weren't going to start the battle as green systems. They were, however, unfamiliar with these ungainly guns. Hopefully the task of hitting large, nearly stationary ships wasn't too much for them. On a theoretical spreadsheet, these new weapons could punch through cloud-cover and atmosphere to a range of nearly fifty miles. They could reach all the way out into low orbit if they fired straight upward, as there was less atmosphere to get in the way the higher you went up. All that was based on computer simulations, of course. We didn't really know what they could do yet. But I wasn't going to test fire them in front of the Macros. I wanted to surprise the bastards.

My forts had started off as a plan to drive the Macro fleet back. By positioning themselves over the oceanic trench, they were preventing us from destroying their undersea bases. If we could outrange them, we could push them out of position. If we put them under heavy fire at a distance too great for them to return fire, they would be forced to either engage us, retreat, or be destroyed. I figured they would choose to engage, so I waited. I wanted all three forts functional first, then I would allow the brainbox gunners to begin taking potshots at the distant enemy fleet.

And so the Macro ships sat drifting in the sky to the east— sitting directly over the island of New Providence, in fact. I knew the Macro fleet was terrifying the inhabitants of the Bahaman capital, but I couldn't do anything about it. At least, not yet. Every day the islanders waited, holding their breath. The enemy could decide at any moment to annihilate them. Each day passed uneventfully, but the dark ships clouded the skies and left doom in the heart of anyone who gazed up at them.

The Saturday Assault did not begin with any action by the enemy fleet, however. The Macro ships floated up there, silent and nearly motionless. They resembled great, dark islands of metal, hanging in the skies.

The first report came to Barrera. His face turned more serious even than his usual norm, and his hand flew up to his ear piece. Sandra noticed first and touched my shoulder. I was still marveling at my big guns and the black metal arms that held them on target.

"Where are they?" Barrera said. His lips drew into a tight line. He turned around toward the east coast. He looked eastward, away from Fort Two. He took two steps and listened closely. "All three at once? ETA?"

I almost interrupted him, but held back. I could see Sandra wanted to do the same. It was a bad habit everyone had picked up. If any sort of news came in, everyone was tense and demanded to know what was said immediately. Underneath our calm exteriors, we were all edgy.

I thought of getting on the command channel and requesting the data they were feeding Barrera, but that would only slow things down by making them repeat themselves. Barrera was on duty as the commander of the daily ops. It was his shift, and I had to let him do his job.

Barrera finished his conversation and turned back to me soon enough. "Three groups sir. Hitting Fort Pierre, our production base and a barracks area in the northern sector of the island."

"Hitting us?" I stared out at the Macro ships, they were still motionless. The beaches were quiet. None of the laser turrets were targeting or firing at anything. No sirens were going off yet, at least not that I could hear.

"Where are they?" I demanded. "I don't see any enemy."

"They are below us, sir. They have been detected tunneling upward from channels they've dug under the island."

197

I looked at him for a second. "We don't have much in the way of cover down there. Only woven Nano-alloys."

"Exactly sir. Apparently, they surmised the same thing."

I stared out at the sea. They weren't going to come in, I could see that now. I'd been a fool. They were going to drill up under us from the sea itself, never giving all my turrets *anything* to fire upon. I understood the beauty of their plan in an instant, and understood that I'd fallen in the classic trap of mostly earthly generals. I'd planned to win the last fight, when the next fight was going to be fought differently.

I turned then and looked up at the big cannons.

"Do it Kyle," Sandra said, "don't let them guide us."

I wasn't sure if she was right or not. The guns weren't ready, and they weren't tested. "If we start this now," I said, "we'll be tipping our hand before we're ready."

"It doesn't matter," Sandra said. "They've already started it."

"I would have to agree with you," Barrera said to Sandra. He turned his dark, intense eyes to me. "They probably already know what these guns can do. They aren't exactly hidden up here, Colonel."

I nodded, and ran back to our flitter. It was a small, unarmed hovercraft. I grabbed up my headset and put it onto my head. I opened the command channel and ordered the three Forts to commence fire upon the enemy fleet. They might have forced our hands, but at least we would fire the first shot in this fight.

Barrera walked up behind me. "Where do you want me to make my stand, sir?" he asked.

"Take another flitter and go down to headquarters in Fort Pierre. Man the big board."

"Where are we going, Kyle?" Sandra asked.

"We're going to our production facilities. Their defenses are relatively weak there. We can't afford to lose our factories."

Sandra climbed into the small vehicle with me and moments later we were skimming over the treetops at two hundred knots. I held the throttle down and kept it pinned there. The wind screamed by, and Sandra's hair fluttered wildly. I waved at her until she reluctantly put on a helmet. At this speed, a stray insect could take out your eye, nanites or no.

Internally, my mind and stomach were in turmoil. It had all been an illusion. Historically, preparations for war on a quiet front often went like this. One only saw your own improving defenses, not the growing strength and dark plans of the enemy. When the attack finally did come, the defenders were often dismayed by what they faced.

In this case, I'd put all my defensive efforts into countering their fleet and stopping them on the beaches. I hadn't considered a deep assault, one in which the enemy tunneled under the soft sandy soil ten or more miles beyond the eastern shores. They had outmaneuvered me and were striking at the very heart of my territory. They were trying to take out my factories.

My mind was racing. I already considered two of the attacks to be feints. Even if they weren't, the only attack that really mattered was the deep thrust at my Nano factories. If they took out my production capability, they could keep mining and building under the sea, while every asset I lost was permanently gone. There would be no more fresh barrels of nanites to repair things. Only Crow's factories would remain, which I wasn't in direct control of, and which they might locate as well at any time. Once we were deprived of steady production, they could slowly siege my island. I would not be able to replace my losses, while they could produce an endless stream of Macro ground troops. They would win through attrition, and I wouldn't be able to do a thing about it.

-30-

When Sandra and I reached the production base, hidden deep within the western interior of Andros, we found the garrison consisted of only two companies. I'd ordered a third to move to reinforce the position, but I still felt that was thin. We just didn't have time to move our forces around at this point. The enemy were right under our feet and we didn't have Crow's ships to transport my men. Modified hovertanks were doing most of the work, puffed out to whale-size personnel-carrying form.

I didn't like seeing the hovertanks in that state, as big as buses with metal skins as thin as a soup can. They seemed so fragile when facing a serious enemy like the Macros. Branches could dent those ballooning skins when they were in that state, and any beam hit would punch right through and kill the marines inside. I made a mental note as I observed the transports: I needed heavier armor units in the future. I watched the hovertanks as they reconfigured themselves, folding down into a shark-like shape. Even in battle-configuration, they were easily knocked out. These hovertanks had the same design I'd come up with to repel U. S. forces from Andros, then used later for the Helios campaign against the Worms. They were really light tanks, not much better than a flying humvee with long range weaponry. When I had the time, I would have to come up with a new design for heavy armor. Something that could stand up to a Macro machine and take a punch or two.

I felt more confident when I saw my marines piling out of the light vehicles, however. These men in their battle suits were superb fighting systems. They were the most versatile element of my

200

forces. They'd managed to prove to me they could even be effective in an underwater battle. They could fight anywhere, including in space. I looked forward to seeing how they performed head-to-head against the Macro invaders on dry land.

We landed the flitter in the central region of the base, bypassing protocol. A dozen men in battle suits swarmed, exactly as they should. They rose up into the air and encircled the flitter with their weapons trained on both of us. Only after we'd landed and identified ourselves to their satisfaction did they relax. The biggest battle suit landed on the flitter's tail section and began complaining.

"Colonel? This is a breach of protocol, sir," Kwon said.

"Indeed it is, First Sergeant. My apologies."

"We would have been within our rules of engagement to bring down your aircraft, sir," Kwon continued.

I could tell he wasn't quite willing to let this one go. "The laser turrets would have fried me if I was a Macro, Kwon. Relax. The enemy is under our boots, not in the sky today."

"We don't know that, sir. Remember the recent attack upon your person? Not every enemy is a machine today."

I glanced at Kwon as I marched toward the officer's quarters, Sandra followed on my right side, while he followed on my left. Directly behind us, a squad of marines suspiciously poked around at the contents of our flitter, as if they thought we were robot mimics and the flitter contained a bomb of some kind. I chuckled.

"That's why your men are so jumpy. I think those assassins wanted to kill me, not all of Star Force."

"Why, sir?"

I shrugged. "Not everyone likes me, Kwon. I make a mistake now and then, and they blame me for the entire situation. They're all a bunch of armchair generals, enjoying the clarity of hindsight."

Kwon stopped asking questions. I was surprised he'd asked so many. Usually, he didn't sweat the small stuff. I'd placed him here at the factories to guard them, but hadn't really expected him to see much action. He knew the lay of the land, having fought here before. Now that the battle was on, I was glad to have him at my side again.

The base CO was a new guy, Captain Francisco Diaz. At least, he was new to me. He'd joined Star Force over a year ago, but I'd never really had the time to chat with him. I didn't have the time today, either.

Diaz was a chunky fellow, built wide and low to the ground. He wasn't fat—but he wasn't thin, either. He was bald on top except for a scrim of hair around the ears and had eyes like twin drops of black oil.

"Diaz, good to meet you," I said, thrusting out my hand.

He saluted first, then shook hands with me. He seemed somewhat surprised to see me. I supposed everyone on the base was.

"Good to meet you too, Colonel," he said.

"Time for a full report later—maybe," I said. "Right now, get your battle suit on, marine. We've got company coming."

Diaz stared at me with his liquid black eyes. "Uh, I had assumed you were going to ride this out at headquarters, Colonel."

I stared back. "Captain, I do believe I gave you an order."

Diaz jumped to attention. "Yes, sir," he said. He snapped off another salute and went right to the lockers. He pulled out the first suit he saw and began climbing into the legs.

"Help him, Kwon," I said. "Full helmet now, Diaz. I'm suiting up too. Sandra, help me into this contraption. You'll put on a lighter scout suit."

"I'm okay," she said.

I threw her a glare. "What is it with everyone ignoring my instructions today?"

Sandra shrugged. "We know the machines are down there, but they might take hours to dig up into the base. And we have Nano-alloy nets to prevent it."

"Is that right? Get in your damned suits, people. If you have to urinate, use the elimination systems or let it run down your leg. The nanites will drop it out of bottom of your boots eventually.

Kwon laughed at that. The other two seemed less amused. As we suited-up, two lieutenants wandered in. I ordered them into gear as well.

"Kyle," Sandra asked me quietly over a private channel as she helped me slide the helmet down over my nose. "Why the rush? We know where the enemy are. The Macros—"

"Have fooled us once already today. I'm not giving them a second break. Now, everyone come with me up to the observation deck."

On top of the officers' quarters, which doubled as the command post for the base, was an observation deck with thick railing that was perfect for a rifleman to fire over. I inspected it briefly, approving of the design.

"Is this fortification your work, Diaz?" I asked the captain as he clanked after me.

"Yes, colonel. I've been experimenting with programming and shaping constructive nanites."

"Good work. I need creative men. Take a look out eastward. Make sure your autoshades are on."

We all stood on the upper deck and stared to the east. I could see the nearest of the three central forts. From this distance, the black arms holding the projectors were too small to make out, but I could see the beam projectors aiming toward the distant ships. They hung over the eastern horizon, so large and black against the sky they could be seen easily with some adjustments to our helmet zoom controls.

Periodically, as we watched, the big guns flared. There wasn't much to see, a streak of burning atmosphere. A dimming of our helmets as the autoshades kicked in. Most of the dangerous light was in the infrared.

"Enough power is being released that those heavy weapons could damage our optic nerves even at this distance."

"I don't hear anything," Sandra said.

"You won't. Not at this range. They are beam weapons, not cannons firing shells. If you were close enough, you would hear a thunder-like effect as the atmosphere has holes punched through it."

We stared and suddenly, one of the ships dipped forward, as if it were hung by wires—and one of the wires had just broken. It slid downward then, nose first. Smoke trailed behind it. The ship fell until it vanished below the horizon.

Kwon hooted. "We got one, sir!"

"Where did it go down?" Captain Diaz asked.

"Either over New Providence, or into the sea itself," I said. "It's difficult to tell at this distance, even with the helmet zoomed

203

to max. Because of the curvature of the Earth, we can't see the endpoint of a crash landing."

"Why does it take so many hits to bring one down?" Kwon asked.

"Because they are at the very limits of our range. We can damage them, but it takes a lot of pounding to do so."

"What are they doing out there, Kyle?" Sandra asked. "Aren't they going to move? Are they going to let us just destroy their ships one at a time?"

"Unfortunately, I doubt they will," Captain Diaz answered her.

I rotated my helmet to look at him. "What do you think they will do, captain?"

He extended an armored arm. I followed his fingertip and zoomed in on the spot. There, engines were flaring. The ships in the farthest northern end of their formation were moving now. And they were coming toward us.

"Looks like they are going to pull back, sir," Diaz said.

"Good," I said, presenting a confident exterior that I didn't really feel. Out of their three options, this was the least helpful. If they'd stood there, we could have had fun blasting them. If they'd advanced and committed themselves, we would have known this was it, the final battle was on. Since they'd retreated, we could concentrate on their burrowing forces, but with the knowledge their fleet could change its course and get into the fight whenever they wished.

"Looks like we're driving them off, Colonel," Diaz said.

"Doesn't matter," I lied smoothly. "We're ready for them no matter what they do."

Unexpectedly, the building we were standing on shook. We all stumbled.

"What the hell was that?" Sandra asked.

We scanned the horizons, looking for a telltale pall of smoke rising up out of the surrounding forest. I didn't see anything. Another trembler hit, making the building rock and sway under us for a moment.

"Charges sir," Captain Diaz said suddenly. He was listening to his headset. "They are detonating charges under the base."

As the base C. O. he had plugged himself into the local tactical channel. I hadn't done so yet. I worked the setting in my helmet, and it connected almost instantly.

"They're in bunker eleven, sir!" I heard a voice say. It sounded young, high-pitched and terrified.

Suddenly, I got it. They weren't going to come up and attack the base directly. They were going to dig into the bunkers where each of the Nano factories were hidden and attack them individually. Using that approach, they could isolate our defensive forces.

"Damn it," I said aloud. I flipped the override and spoke right over Diaz. "This is Colonel Riggs. I want a squad deployed underground in every bunker with a factory unit in it. Report enemy contact immediately."

I keyed off my transmission and spoke to Kwon. "Get a platoon together. We'll play reserve support and rush down to every hotspot."

Kwon didn't ask any questions. He took a flying leap off the building, switching on the repellers in his boots. He sailed down into the center of the base and began bellowing orders at every marine in sight.

"Sir," Diaz said to me, looking alarmed. "That will leave us very thin up top. They could march right into the base."

"I don't think that's their intention," I told him. "Besides, another full company of reinforcements is due to arrive in— eighteen minutes."

Diaz began to say something else, but I was already flying after Kwon. I vaulted over the observation deck railing and sailed down into the center of the base. I didn't much care about Diaz's objections. I had to protect those factories. Human lives, this base—everything was secondary to that goal.

I sensed in Diaz a certain level of dismay at losing command of this base in the midst of what was probably his first real combat experience. I also sensed he would get over it eventually. And if he didn't…well, that was just too bad.

-31-

Kwon and I charged down an underground ramp toward bunker eleven. It wasn't hard to find. The men there were fighting hard. I could hear their grunts, screams and blazing weapons up ahead. When we got there, we were already too late. The last marine fell in the hallway at the bottom of the ramp. His lower half was missing, having been removed by a team of Macros. They were operating in pairs now, one with a heavy weapon on the head, the second with two lobster claw-looking mandibles. I wondered if that was an upgrade they'd come up with just to deal with our battle suits. If so, it was alarming. They were adapting faster than usual to our tactics.

The dead man didn't know he was dead yet, typical of my people. The upper half of his body fought on, gunning the robot that held him with one gun while the other weapon fired directly into the ceiling, hitting nothing. He was screaming and incoherent. Nanites were building a lower mesh to hold the last of his guts in, I knew, but I doubted he would live much longer. There were limits to what even my men could take.

Kwon and I knelt on the ramp and we concentrated our fire. More beams leapt out over our helmeted heads. At least ten beams caught the macro with the lobster claws and burned right through his armor in less than a second. He slumped down, releasing a gout of oily blue smoke that filled the cramped hallway. The men behind us hopped over our heads and pressed ahead. Kwon and I were right behind them.

The guy in the hallway was the last survivor. There had only been three guards down here, apparently. The other two had been expertly killed. Six more Macros were busy ripping my factory from its moorings. They'd cut through the Nano alloy flooring and a set of thick anchor bolts. The flooring flapped and squirmed where it had been cut open. Being smart-metal, it was upset at being out of contact with its fellow deck plates.

On the far wall was a gaping hole, large enough to allow two Macros abreast to walk through. That hole was way larger than it needed to be. I knew in a flash what the enemy plan was: they were trying to steal my machines.

Eighteen of us launched into close-quarters combat without hesitation. Kwon and I leapt together onto one of the cutter robots with the big laser on the head section. These were the type that cut our suits apart, while the lobsters held them down. Right now, it was busy tearing the factory unit free of the floor. We landed on it and slammed the flat of our weapon projectors against the enemy's joints. After years of study, we'd found certain weak points in the enemy armor. Usually, these were just below the joints where the machine's limbs attached to the central thorax. We put our weapons there and fired them, burning through the weak armor quickly. They had a team methodology for taking us out, and we had come up with our own approach.

The machine didn't appreciate our efforts. It made the mistake of trying to scrape off Kwon first. He was much tougher to dislodge than I was, I could have told it that. Kwon hung on, grunting as he took hammering blows from flailing legs that should have crumpled him, armor or no. I hung onto my side and kept burning.

As always when fighting in an enclosed space, our vision quickly blurred. Our helmets had to dim our vision in order to keep us from being blinded by the intense radiation. Soon, we had to depend on the flashes of light coming from our weapons to see anything at all. The smoke wasn't helping anything either.

The fight took less than two minutes to finish. We simply outweighed them in this case. Six Macros were no match for a platoon of my men in these new suits.

"Casualties?" I asked.

"Three in the room, one more out of my platoon, sir," Kwon reported.

"Your platoon? What happened to the commanding lieutenant?"

Kwon gestured toward a mess on the floor. The lieutenant had been the single casualty in the platoon.

"Damn," I said. "I'd had hopes for that man. He was young, but he had fire in his belly."

Kwon didn't answer. He was standing with most of the others near the hole the Macros had dug to get in here. I now figured I'd been a fool to put my factories down here in these bunkers. They would have been safer up topside inside their sheds. I shook my head, trying to erase the thought. What was done was done. I'd built my defenses to protect my assets against an aerial bombardment, and from the looks of the sky before I came down here, it looked like we might see an attack from above soon as well.

I looked around next for the half-man. He was dead already, bled out despite the best efforts of the nanites. If I'd had the Microbes that had saved Sandra, I would have dipped him into some of that goop and hoped for the best. But sadly, we didn't have much that could reconstruct half a body from scratch. Especially not in the midst of a pitched battle.

"All right," I said. "We have two choices. We can seal this up and let them have one factory, or we can stand here until they hit us again."

"There's a third option, sir," said a voice from behind me.

I turned to find Captain Diaz standing there. "What's that, Captain?"

He gestured toward the gaping hole in the wall ahead of us. "We can advance. We can go down there after them."

"Do you have any idea of what a Macro hole looks like from the inside, Captain?"

"Only from vids, sir. Ones taken by your suit, I believe."

I nodded. I had a habit of recording battlefield action for later training purposes. Most of my troops weren't equipped with cameras and recording brainboxes.

I turned toward the hole. A sifting runnel of sand ran down the walls and vanished into the blackness. I stepped over to the hole and looked downward. It seemed like a vertical shaft, about a hundred yards deep. I didn't like the look of it.

"There you are," Sandra said, appearing at the doorway to the bunker. She pushed through the debris and came to look down at my side.

A private channel request came beeping into my helmet. I winced. It was from Sandra. She was standing right there, but she wanted to talk helmet-to-helmet. I hesitated a second before opening it.

"You're thinking about going down this shit-hole, aren't you, Kyle?" she asked. She sounded furious.

"The thought had crossed my mind."

"You better give me a damned good reason right now, or I'll cut you out of that suit and embarrass you in front of everyone by dragging up back up into the sunlight."

"It's Diaz's idea, actually."

"That bastard. Let him go down, then."

I thought about it, then nodded. The point of this operation was to keep as many factories as possible. If I stayed with a fast-reaction central force, we could move and deploy wherever the enemy hit us. Still, going after them wasn't a bad idea. I needed to employ both tactics. Coming to a quick decision, I turned to face the captain.

"Permission granted, Diaz."

"Sir?"

I waved at the gaping hole. "Take this platoon and go down there. Cause havoc. With luck, you can disrupt their plans. If you live, I'll give you a medal or something."

"Uh, thanks sir," he said. He shouted orders and headed toward the hole.

I reached out and grabbed his armored shoulder. "Send scouts around every corner first," I told him. "And good luck, marine."

"Thank you, sir."

The platoon vanished down the hole less than a minute later. I kept Kwon and Sandra with me, and we trotted up the ramps. We were back in the sunlight again a few minutes later.

More bunkers were attacked soon thereafter. It became clear the enemy had no intention of attacking the base openly. They were only interested in the factories buried underneath it. We ended up fighting in seven more rooms full of Macros and thrumming factories. We repelled the enemy in every case. But in the last three fights, the enemy turned their fire upon the factory and destroyed it, even as we did our damnedest to take them out first. The change in tactics was alarming. If this continued all night long, there would be nothing left to defend.

In all that time, I didn't hear anything from Diaz. I'd begun to suspect the worst. It was an hour after he'd disappeared into that first hole that we learned the truth.

The insight came when the ground bucked up under the command post. This time, it wasn't just a little hiccup. The building heaved under our feet and the north wall sagged down, folding up on the ground under the weight of the observation deck and Kwon's big feet. I rolled out onto the ground in the middle of the base.

Out in the forest around us, hundreds of trees heeled over and fell like dying men. Puffs of dust and debris rolled out of every entrance to the underground bunker system.

Sandra strained and lifted my battle suit into a standing position. Together, we dug Kwon out of the rubble.

"What the hell was that?" Sandra demanded.

"Felt like one of ours," I said.

"Radiation signature matches, sir," Kwon said, checking his gauges. "It must have been Captain Diaz."

"He blew himself up?" Sandra asked.

"He blew the enemy up," I corrected her sharply. "I'm sure he dealt the Macros a fatal blow with his self-sacrifice."

I walked away from them. I wasn't sure Diaz had done any such thing, but it sounded good, and I would keep on saying it to anyone who asked me. I'd been down a few holes full of Macros myself, and there were plenty of reasons to blow yourself up in that situation. Who was I to say whether Diaz had made the right decision or not? I'd give him the benefit of the doubt, no matter what had really happened down there.

As it turned out, the enemy stopped coming after the explosion. As best we could tell by our mapping of the tunnels using sonic sensors on the surface, the enemy was either all dead from cave-ins or they'd retreated from the explosion. I suspected the explosion, which had been a low-yield atomic blast, had collapsed their tunnels for miles. I imagined the machines down there in the dark, squirming and grinding under the weight of a million tons of loose earth. The image brought a grim smile to my face. If Macros could suffer pain or feel loss in any form, I wished to heap it upon them.

Almost as clear a signal of our success was the change in the enemy behavior on other fronts. They'd come up outside the walls of Fort Pierre, which had a much thicker underground net of nanite threads to protect it. So far, they'd yet to hit the walls, but they were massing in the forests and our men had retreated inside the fort itself. What were they waiting for? I wasn't sure, and neither was anyone else.

Less than an hour later, however, we had our answer. Red contacts appeared on our boards marching up out of the sea. Hundreds of them. This wouldn't normally be alarming, except for one thing: their size. These weren't worker Macros.

It had been a long time since I'd run into their real ground-invasion hardware. These were hundred-foot tall invasion bots—monsters taller than the trees themselves. They had yet to surface, but they were marching underwater all along the entire eastern seaboard.

My scalp itched as I absorbed this news. Once again, I'd missed the bet. I'd built systems to repel an aerial attack and they'd used sappers to dig underneath me. I'd built walls around Fort Pierre to slow down a thousand car-sized, worker Macros, and now they were attacking with behemoths that could step over those walls without a qualm.

I wanted to rub my face and my hair, but I couldn't. My helmet prevented such relief, and I wasn't going to take it off now.

"What are we going to do now, Kyle?" Sandra asked me. "This fight is over, I think."

I looked around the base. I had to agree with her. I found the captain of the reinforcement company and briefed him quickly. He was the senior officer after me, so I gave him command of the garrison.

"Oh, and captain," I said as I boarded my flitter with Sandra beside me. Kwon was up front, piloting.

"Sir?"

"If the Macros break through again—don't chase them down their holes. Not unless you really want to know what's down there."

"Uh, no sir."

We lifted off and headed east.

"Where to, Colonel?" Kwon asked me.

"Head for the center fort," I said. "I want to know if we can target the beach with those big guns."

Kwon swung the aircraft around sickeningly. In seconds, we were skimming over the dark treetops. The palm fronds whipped and rattled as we whizzed past.

The Moon was a rising crescent that hung over the sea to the east, right behind the advancing enemy lines. The crescent was mirrored in the ocean below the Moon, forming a wavering silver reflection. I took a moment to stare at the ancient light of Earth's only natural satellite, marveling at its timeless beauty. I wondered how many human battles it had witnessed and how many more it was destined to observe before the last of us was snuffed out.

-32-

We headed to the central laser-battery fort, the biggest of the three. I'd ordered two companies of marines to support each of the forts and act as a garrison. I saw the men standing around in squads on the loose earth outside the fort. I was pleased they were all wearing our latest battle suits. Most of my men had them now.

Of the three red lines of tunneling Macros, one group had committed themselves at this point. The first line had apparently been digging the longest, and they'd come up to hit my production base. That failure had been costly for both sides, but I had to mark it down as a Macro victory. Although we'd beaten them back, they had damaged or destroyed nearly half my factories. My productions systems took around a month each to build and required many rare earths to construct. They would take much longer to replace than a thousand tunneling Macro troops.

The second line of Macros were trying to dig up into the heart of Fort Pierre, and thus bypass the walls and gun emplacements I'd built up to defend the base. So far, they had been unsuccessful. We'd put a lot of constructive nanites into that soil. They'd killed the local forests, but they'd also made it nearly impossible for the Macros to dig through. Forming tight nets of alloy cable in layer after layer beneath the base, the enemy wasn't having an easy time of it.

It was the third line of underground attack that worried me most. It hadn't yet committed itself and wasn't moving. I suspected it was a reserve force meant to come up upon a target of opportunity. The Macros waited down there in their tunnels, about a mile down underneath the central region of the island. That put them in easy striking distance of several key targets, including all three of my new laser batteries. None of the forts had underground defense systems. We simply hadn't had time to build them. Just getting the forts operational had taken every marine and crawler I had.

When Sandra, Kwon and I reached the central fort, we leapt out of the open canopy of the flitter and charged into the command post under the big guns. When the garrison CO asked if I expected trouble, I told him to set up listening sensors around the newly built laser batteries and to expect an assault from underground. He paled, then rushed to follow my orders.

The big guns mounted on the fort's dome angled downward to aim at the sea. They did not fire yet, however. The enemy had not yet shown themselves. Big screens had been rigged up all around the command post. Some monitored radar systems, others provided live vid feed from the beaches. Technicians were all around us, ignoring us and working their controls determinedly. We watched, transfixed as the battle took form. Red contacts showed on radar as formations of large Macro walking machines approached. Our laser turrets were strung out along the beaches. They waited for the approaching enemy and quivered in anticipation.

It was eerie. I knew those sands, I knew those rolling waves and those shifting palms. The enemy's plan was clear. They were marching up in trenches underwater, keeping themselves low and out of sight as long as they can. My laser turrets were right on the beach, easily within range. They tracked the underwater targets as they came closer.

"Why don't they fire, Kyle?" Sandra asked beside me.

"They can't do any damage yet," I said. "Lasers won't penetrate a cold, dark ocean. The waves make it even worse. Lots of sediment and foam. The beams wouldn't be effective for more than a few feet down. They have to wait until the Macros are in water that is too shallow to hide them."

"I get it," Kwon said. "Our turrets are smart. They will wait to blast them until they are in close."

"Not exactly," I said. "Our turrets are smart enough to know they can't do any damage, so they are waiting. I would say the

214

Macros are the smart ones this time. By coming under the cover of deep water they will be very close when the surface. They'll burn down our turrets at point-blank range."

"Look, they're stopping all along the line," Sandra said. She took a step toward the screens and pointed at the main radar display. She turned and looked at me. "They're waiting under there like spiders, aren't they? Waiting until all of them are into position, then they'll all rush us at once."

I nodded, and contacted Barrera. He answered almost immediately, despite what had to be an overwhelming number of details to worry about.

"Colonel?" he asked.

"I see about twenty of the big machines are poised to strike your position at Fort Pierre. I don't think you'll be able to hold."

"We'll be all right, sir."

"No, you won't. I'm going to back you up. Clear the area of all air traffic."

"Will do, sir."

I broke the connection. I called Crow next. I hadn't talked to him for a day or two, but I knew he was watching the battle unfold like everyone else. It took several minutes to get hold of him, but I finally did so.

"What's up, Riggs?"

"The end of the world," I said.

Crow laughed at that. "Always a drama fan, aren't you?"

"We can't hold this time, Admiral."

"Admiral, is it? You must want a big favor, right mate?"

"Yes. Bring your fleet down to cover the island."

"Suicide. You know that. I thought we'd talked this out by now."

I closed my eyes and gritted my teeth. I counted to three before going on, so I wouldn't curse and scream at him. I knew that wasn't the best way to get his cooperation.

"You still there, Riggs?"

"You don't have to engage them. Stay out of range. I need you to be ready to run interference."

"What if they fire missiles at us?"

"Then you've managed to distract them from Andros. That's a good thing."

215

Crow grumbled about being outnumbered and outgunned. I ignored most of it. I'd heard it all before.

"Why did you build all those ships in the first place if you meant to hide behind the Moon?" I demanded at last in exasperation.

"If I had four times as many ships as I have now, you wouldn't be asking that. You'd be cheering me on as I blasted the enemy out of the sky. As long as these ships survive, they are an asset. Blown up, they aren't worth a damn to you or me."

Crow had a good point, but I was desperate. I could see the Macros were not cooperating with any of my plans. They were coming at me methodically, and I wasn't winning any of the skirmishes so far. I could sense doom approaching, and I wanted every ounce of firepower I could get on the table to stop it.

"Fine," I said. "I'll set up a gun emplacement on top of your little secret base. It'll take potshots at enemy Macros until they come to investigate."

"You wouldn't do that. Those factories are our ace in the hole."

"This entire island is everything we have. We can't lose just half of it. If they overrun us, we're all dead anyway. Are you in this mess or not?"

More grumbling ensued, but after another few minutes he said he would come down and provide cover fire for us.

"But let me tell you straight," he said, "if they fire bloody missiles at us and we can't shoot them down, we're going to run again."

"Just get down here and support us."

He finally agreed and I broke the channel. I heaved a long sigh. Dealing with Crow was one of the worst things about my job. Having him hanging out behind the Moon had been like a vacation. I would have left him out there if I hadn't needed him so desperately.

"Colonel?" the fort CO called to me. "They are starting to stand up."

I frowned, not knowing at first what he meant. Then I saw the forward screens. The Macros had apparently come up as close to the beach as they could in a crouched position, moving like crabs with their legs bent. Now they stood up together, water gushing off their metal bodies. Our lasers flashed and their guns answered. The night was split apart with brilliant streaks of light. Our coastal turrets fired a dozen stabbing beams at once at the invasion Macros as they crawled up out of the sea. The enemy methodically returned fire. We watched the Macros as their legs churned the ocean below them. Explosive impact points flared and gushed vapor as intense beams touched cold, wet metal. They shrugged off the hits however, and did not stop advancing. They returned fire, frequently knocking out our small turrets with a few good hits.

Sandra stood directly under the main screen, staring up at it. "I know that cove," she said. "They'll wreck it."

I had to agree. I called to the fort CO. The captain turned to stare at me with wide eyes. I figured he wasn't excited about the order I was about to give him.

"Captain," I said. "Target the machines closest to Fort Pierre and burn them down."

Nodding an acknowledgement, he relayed my orders to his operators. The big guns wobbled as the black nanite arms that held them shifted slightly. I could hear them move out there, grinding metal against metal and making the entire building creak and groan. First one projector spoke, then more fired. Soon, the guns were going off rhythmically in a slow, repetitive pattern. Big lasers fired more slowly, as they took longer for the chemical gases to dissipate from the firing chamber. They also generated a lot more heat. Liquid nitrogen was puffed into the chambers after each shot, cooling the tanks before the next big gout of energy was released.

I was surprised to feel recoil from these guns. They were so large, and released so much energy that they actually rocked the installation when they went off. This made them slower as well, because the arms that aimed them had to stabilize and retarget the projectors slightly. Each shot burned for a duration of around five hundred milliseconds, then took about ten more seconds to reset and fire again. The effects were impressive, however.

"Wow," Sandra said. "Look at that, a hit!"

For all their ponderousness, the guns were effective. We watched as one of the big machines took a direct hit in the upper plating. Unlike the lighter fire of our coastal laser turrets, the fort's cannons didn't just gouge the armor of the big machines. Instead, they burned right through it. The stricken machine was at first shrouded in a plume of flaring light green vapor, but as it cleared, I saw it was badly damaged. Two of the six massive legs no longer operated. It was tipping and dragging its upper body through the surf. Like a wounded man, it struggled to make it to shore.

Another big beam struck the smoking invader. A secondary explosion inside finished it, and it crashed down on the beach. A whoop went up around the control room. It was our first kill.

I smiled tightly, but didn't share in the enthusiasm of those around me. It had taken nearly two minutes to bring down a single machine, and there were hundreds of them rising up all along the coastline now. My coastal turrets were almost ineffective, and once the enemy machines reached the land, they would be harder for the big cannons to hit as they crashed through the forests.

Now that my central forts had demonstrated their long-range firepower, I knew the enemy would want to destroy them. Despite that, I had decided to commit them. I did not regret the decision. After all, what was the point of a military asset if you were too scared to use it?

I watched as the battle unfolded before us. My neck ached from tension, but I didn't dare try to massage it while wearing my battle suit. The gloves would probably rip my skin off.

-33-

I barely had time to sip some coffee and shake the armored gloves of a few smiling technicians before the Macros made their next move. The third group of tunneling Macros was active again. They'd gotten a message and had selected a target. Splitting into three groups, their numbers swelled on our monitoring screens. They had apparently been reinforced by survivors of the assault on my production base. En masse, they were digging upward.

We calculated where they would come out. The math wasn't too difficult. Being centrally located, the fort I stood within was going to be visited first. After that, the other two forts would each be assaulted.

"Bring your garrison troops inside," I ordered the fort CO.

The captain relayed the order without hesitation or argument. I liked this man more every minute. I checked his nametag for the first time. Captain Flynn, it said. I watched him work with nervous speed. I could deal with a man who didn't know what he was doing, as long as he was aware of his deficiency and willing to learn. It was the rookie idiots with big ideas of their own that bothered me the most.

The command post was roomy, and there were sleeping quarters for twelve, but two hundred marines simply couldn't fit inside the space. I thought about it. I didn't want them to stand around outside on the fresh earth. When the Macros dug up to assault us, they were going to suck them down under the ground and grind them up in dusty holes.

219

"Sir," Kwon said, understanding my dilemma. "I'll take a platoon up on to the roof of the dome. We'll keep out of the way of the big guns, of course."

I nodded slowly. "Up," I said. "Yeah, that's it. Commander, get these men back out of here. Leave a platoon inside. Spread the rest in the trees outside. We can fly, so put them up there. When the enemy dig their way into the open, we'll jump down on them."

Eyes wider than ever, Captain Flynn relayed my order. Battle suits clanked back out of the building. I could hear men complaining and speculating on the intelligence of their leaders. I didn't blame them. Smiling, I had Sandra help me put my helmet back on.

We returned to the big screen and watched the damage we were doing to the enemy Macros. They reached the tree line, but were missing seven machines by that time. Other groups were unmolested, unfortunately. Up and down the coast most of the machines reached the safety of the shore, blowing up our automated turrets and smashing their way into the cover of the trees. But where my fort concentrated its firepower, they melted. That was in a cove not far south of Fort Pierre. It was the nearest landing point of the enemy to our main base. We gave them hell, and they couldn't even fire back. We were out of range for the guns mounted on their backs.

In the trees around and inside Fort Pierre I had placed about a thousand marines. Most of the island was vacant, of course. It was over two thousand square miles of wilderness and there were only about ten thousand marines on the island. I hadn't been given the time to rebuild my forces before the Macros had begun their assault. Some had questioned why I didn't bring down more recruits from Miami, but it would have been pointless. Without battle suits, nanites and most critically, proper training, they would not have been able to fight these monsters.

I'd fought them myself on several occasions, learning the hard way how to bring down one of these big machines in the South American campaign. The knowledge had cost us thousands and thousands of lives. One of the biggest lessons I'd learned was how ineffective normal earth troops were against them. It was like sending men with bolt action rifles against entrenched machine guns—the butcher's bill had been incredible and the enemy machines had been unfazed.

Another possible defensive move had been used in South America, but we'd avoided it thus far: nuclear mines. We didn't have endless miles of ground here on Andros. I could have killed a few machines that way, but nuclear weapons are relatively risky when used in close-quarters. Perhaps I'd been naive, thinking I could win without using every asset, but that was still unknown. What I did know is that fighting in a radioactive cloud would be a hardship that would reduce the effectiveness of my men much more than it would the Macros.

When the tunnels began to open up around the base, they did so with surprising coordination. I had ordered the men in the command post to ignore the enemy unless they were right there in the room with them. They were to keep firing salvo after salvo at the easiest big invader—it was the job of the marine garrison to stop any assaults from smaller machines below us. Still, when it comes right down to it, such orders can be difficult to follow. I had to give Flynn and his crew credit, they really tried. But when the report came in the enemy had dug up into the mess hall and firing broke out under our feet, it was hard to keep staring straight ahead.

I sent Kwon down, and the disturbance subsided for a minute or so. Then the floor bucked up of its own accord. The big screens died, losing power, and some screamed: "The generators!"

I didn't hesitate, and neither did Kwon. If the damned machines cut off our generators, the big guns would stop firing. Mission accomplished for the enemy.

I called in two more platoons out of the trees. Apparently, the enemy weren't going for that route yet. Charging down the ramps, we half-ran and half-flew to generator room. Four Macro workers were in there. One had committed suicide by using his big lobster claws to cut into the central feed leading to the base. He'd been electrocuted, but I was certain he'd earned whatever award Macros had in their database for a successful self-sacrifice.

Twenty-one of us went down there, including Sandra with her flashing twin carbon knives. Nineteen of us walked out unaided, but the machines had been destroyed. I posted a squad with orders to call for backup the second they saw anything suspicious and sealed the tunnel with nanites.

221

We headed back to the command post. There was a kind of new commotion going on up there. When we reached the screens and they flickered into life again as power was restored, I saw what it was. The mounds of fresh earth all around the fort were frothing with flashing metal mandibles. The enemy didn't come out of just one hole, or four holes, they came up in dozens of spots at the same time. Without orders, my men in the trees fired down on them. The machines boiled up onto the surface like ants, taking hits as they did so. Those that survived their first critical seconds in the open returned fire with heavy beamers of their own.

I turned to Flynn. "Keep firing these big guns until you don't see any more machines downslope, Captain."

Flynn nodded. His mouth was a grim line. I could tell he wasn't afraid anymore. He was determined.

I left him and ordered the marines outside to come down out of the trees and meet the enemy on the ground. They were too exposed up there. A ferocious firefight began on mostly open ground. I headed up to the main entrance. Sandra was ahead of me, while Kwon led a squad of men in my wake.

We pressed out onto the field and engaged every Macro we saw. Within ten minutes of hard fighting, I knew we weren't going to be able to kill them all. There were just too many flowing up out of those holes. Kwon tapped my helmet as I sited on a Macro stalking a man who was injured and crawling for safety. I fired repeatedly until the Macro stopped moving.

Kwon thumped his glove on my helmet again.

"What is it, Sergeant?" I snapped, looking at him.

He extended a metal-covered index finger and pointed upward. I followed the gesture. I saw them then, the big guns. They were hanging down loosely. The arms no longer held them up, because they no longer were powered. To me the arms and the guns looked like giant riflemen, dead at their posts.

I looked back at Kwon. "We're pulling out. We've lost this one."

Kwon nodded. He did not seem surprised or upset. He shouted orders and soon flocks of flying marines took flight. I reached out and slipped my arm around Sandra's waist. She struggled for a second, then realized who I was and gave me a quizzical look. I didn't have time to explain matters to her, the Macros were closing in as my men left around us.

I lifted off, carrying her under my arm. She didn't weigh much, compared to the suit itself. I tilted my body forward at a forty-five degree angle. It felt as if I was falling over the land and about to pitch forward onto my faceplate at any second.

We zoomed over the Macros, dropping frag grenades down open holes as we went. These parting gifts were received with an ant-like frenzy of activity.

Behind us, explosions boomed. I crashed through pine branches and palm fronds, heading for Fort Pierre at top speed. I couldn't see Kwon, but I figured he could take care of himself. He always did.

-34-

When I brought a hundred and fifty marines cruising out of the trees into Fort Pierre, I saw a lot of scorch marks, but the walls were still largely intact. We were challenged as we came down in the landing pits and I identified myself and my unit. I handed the wounded off to medical teams and the able-bodied were sent to the walls. Sandra and I headed for the headquarters bunker, where I knew Lieutenant Colonel Barrera and Major Sarin were managing the battle. Kwon stumped along behind us.

When we reached the entrance, I turned to Kwon. "Why don't you see if you can help out on the walls?" I suggested.

Kwon stepped from one size-eighteen foot the other twice before answering. "I'd rather follow you, sir," he said.

I narrowed my eyes. It had to be the assassination thing. He and Sandra had both been like glue on my shoe since then. I sighed and told him to take a break and get some food inside the bunker. This seemed to mollify him.

I turned to Sandra next.

"Don't even try to get rid of me," she said.

I nodded. Knowing when you're beaten is a critical attribute for any commander. I turned away and headed down to the command center. Sandra followed close behind. I didn't make my play until we passed the mess hall.

"Getting something to eat sounds pretty good to me. Aren't you hungry?"

"Yeah," she said warily.

"Well, get in line and bring us both down a tray. We're going to be watching this fight all night long. Bring coffee, too."

Making an unhappy sound, she finally relented. We were only one level from the bottom floor, where the command center was located. What could happen?

I walked down the final ramp, feeling somewhat relieved. It was nice to be on my own for a minute or two, without any concerned citizens hovering over me. I walked into the command center and stepped up to the big central screen. Things had improved down here. Unlike the command center I'd co-opted from Crow, things were no longer built for style and magnificence. It was all about functionality under fire. Every wall was reinforced smart-metal. There were large screens on three of the surrounding walls, depicting different areas of the battle, which was in a lull right now.

The big machines had all chosen spots and parked themselves here and there. Lowering their hulls down to touch the ground in thickly forested regions, our guns couldn't reach them. Crow's ships might well spark a new phase when they arrived, but they hadn't returned yet. They were taking the long way around Earth, to avoid the Macro fleet. They were going to come into orbit from the west and park themselves over Andros without ever offering a clear target to the enemy—or at least, that was the plan.

The subterranean assaults had ended for now. They'd managed to knock out all three of my central forts, but then the ant-like worker machines had gone back down into their deep tunnels. This did nothing to make me feel better. If anything, this lull was disturbing. The Macros were obviously planning something nasty—but what was it?

I was surprised to see the only member of my command staff present was Major Sarin. There was also a guard in the room—standard procedure during an attack. When I walked in, Jasmine flicked her gaze to me, held it there a second, then looked back down at her command table. She was busy counting enemy positions and coming up with force ratings as to their effectiveness. I saw the lowest measurement was over the Macro group close to Fort Pierre. They were down to a thirty-eight percent effectiveness rating, according to her calculations. The other enemy invasion groups were in the nineties.

"They are waiting for something, aren't they sir?" she asked me.

I looked at the screens. "Clearly, the next phase of their assault plan has not yet begun."

She kept tapping at the screen. I realized this was a rare moment. Jasmine and I were *never* alone together. Sandra or someone else was always present. I knew Sandra liked it that way. But it had never given me the opportunity to air a few thoughts that never seemed to stop bouncing around in my head. I'd never had any kind of closure with Jasmine. I'd kissed her that once, and had felt a rush of interest growing in both of us. But Sandra had slammed a lid down on all that nonsense, and had kept a close watch ever since. I didn't mind that, having chosen to remain faithful to her. Some things, however, had been left unsaid.

I turned suddenly to the single guard in the room. "Staff Sergeant," I said. "How long have you been on duty down here?"

"Uh, around fifteen hours, sir."

"I want you to report to your commander and request a replacement. You belong in a bunk or on the walls. Your pick."

"Thank you, sir," he said. Surprised and elated, he clanked away down the hall before I could change my mind.

There was a brief moment of silence between Jasmine and I after he'd left. She had followed the Staff Sergeant with her dark, pretty eyes, then glanced at me in surprise when he was gone. I didn't say anything. I was doing this for her benefit, to see if she wanted to speak up.

"Why did you do that?" she asked finally.

"The man looked like he needed a break."

Jasmine shook her head. "You shouldn't…what do you want from me?"

I stared at her. She met my eyes for a few seconds, then dropped them.

"I wanted to know if you had anything you wanted to say. We've never gotten the chance to talk."

She sucked in a breath, let it out slowly, then did it again. I could tell she was hunting for the right words.

"Speak up," I said. "Someone is bound to walk in here soon."

Jasmine glared at me. I knew immediately I'd said the wrong thing. When it came to women, I rarely did anything right.

226

"Colonel Riggs," she began.

"You used to call me Kyle."

She shook her head. "Colonel Riggs," she said emphatically. "All of that is in the past. I don't want to discuss any of it. Mistakes were made. Let's leave it at that."

"Okay."

"But why did you kiss me?"

"Because I wanted to, Jasmine."

She made an exasperated sound. "But that's over now, right?"

"Yes," I said with a firmness I didn't entirely feel. Right then, I wondered why I was having this conversation. I could tell it wasn't healing any wounds. It was probably opening them up again. I thought about it, and I realized I'd created this moment on purpose. Maybe it wasn't Jasmine who needed a chance to talk.

"She's changed," I said suddenly.

Jasmine looked at me—for the first time, she really looked at me.

"She's not entirely human anymore," I said. "It's hard to adjust."

"You and I aren't normal either. The nanites have rebuilt us into something new. We are like a new species. Haven't you felt it when you are around normal people? They fear us. We seem strange to them."

I was surprised by her words. For Major Sarin, this was a veritable speech. I wondered if she'd tried to have a relationship outside of Star Force. Maybe she'd tried to have a normal human boyfriend, and he'd been creeped out by the fact she could snap his spine at any moment if she had chosen to do so.

"Sandra has moved further out on the scale of humanity. She died, and was brought back as something new."

"That upsets you?"

"How could it not?"

Jasmine walked around the table suddenly and gave me a light stroke, running her fingers over my head and through my hair. I stood there, not knowing what else to do. She kissed my cheek, and then retreated with light, quick steps. She was a slight woman, I realized. Thinner and an inch or so shorter than Sandra. I gazed after her fixedly. I felt a pang of longing. My heart accelerated in my chest.

I opened my mouth, about to say something stupid. Something along the lines of: 'I *do* have feelings for you.' But Jasmine spoke up suddenly, intensely.

"Why did you do it?" she demanded.

I looked at her, baffled. She'd been the one to come over and kiss me. This time, it was all her fault. I hadn't so much as twitched.

"Do what?"

She caught my eye and flicked her gaze toward the entrance. She looked back at me and gave me a tiny nod. Suddenly, I knew what she meant. Someone was out in the corridor, listening.

I felt a new sensation. I wouldn't call it *fear*, exactly, although both our lives might well be in danger. Maybe *guilt* was closer. I felt as if I'd been caught with one gloved fist firmly planted in the forbidden cookie jar. I studied the screen between us, but didn't see anything. Was it Sandra in the hallway? How much had she heard? How was I going to talk myself out of this one?

"You know what I'm talking about, sir," Jasmine continued. "Why did you promote Barrera over me? I went out there to the stars for nearly a year with you, Colonel. I think I deserve an explanation."

I tried to think. I wasn't quite sure if Jasmine was bringing up this new point as a cover, or if she really wanted to know the answer. I suspected it was a little of both.

"Major Sarin," I said. "You did well on the Helios Campaign. But my second in command needs some direct experience in combat. Not just operational experience. You didn't have that, while Barrera did."

"I shot at a few Worms and Macros, sir."

"I know you did. But there's more to it than that. Barrera has shown more initiative. You are an excellent supporting officer. But it has been my opinion, since you've asked, that you have not yet shown the same leadership qualities he has."

Jasmine looked positively pissed now. I reflected that it was a good thing she hadn't asked about the promotion first. I would never have gotten a caressing touch out of her if she'd heard this earlier.

"I accept your judgment, but I don't agree with it, Colonel."

"Good," I said.

She glanced at me in annoyance and irritation. I smiled at her. At that moment, Sandra decided to walk in.

"Ah, finally," I said. "Coffee?"

Sandra looked at me frostily. She didn't hand me the tray. Instead, she slid it over the table toward me. I caught the tray with one hand and the coffee cup with the other before they both slid off onto the floor.

"That looks good," Jasmine said. "I'll think I'll go get dinner, with your permission, sir."

"By all means," I said.

As she left the room, I tried hard not to stare after her. She had a nice walk, almost as good as Sandra's. It was different—less overt, but still sexy.

Sandra was in my face faster than the doughnut and coffee I was trying to eat.

"Thanks for coffee," I said.

"If I find out you two were making out while I went to get your dinner, I'm going to kill you both."

I managed to look surprised. "Come on," I said. "You're with me every second of the day."

"I heard your heartbeat, Kyle. I heard hers, too. You were both excited about something. I think it was each other."

"Well, there was one thing."

Sandra stiffened. She crushed her coffee cup in her hand, creating an instant fountain of hot, brown liquid. She cursed and threw it on the floor, where the nanites dutifully cleaned it up.

"She didn't like me promoting Barrera over her," I said.

Sandra took a deep breath. "I heard that part. But you two were already worked up about something."

"Take a look at the boards. We're in the midst of a battle. A lot of good people have died out there today. Don't the Macros scare you?"

She looked at me suspiciously, then flicked her eyes down to the boards. Macros contacts were everywhere. Motionless red circles glowed in clumps all over the island.

"Yes, they do scare me," she admitted. "What the hell are they waiting for?"

"Some element of their plan isn't quite ready yet. When everything is in place, they'll move decisively."

229

"You changed the subject," she said, giving me a hard stare.

"I answered a question."

Suddenly, she melted. She kissed me fiercely, and I responded, enjoying myself.

When the kiss was over, I reflected I'd narrowly escaped a very bad scene. I'd only spoken with Jasmine to clear the air, but things had nearly gotten out of control. I told myself I had been a fool to flirt with Jasmine. Sandra was the real deal.

Sandra came at me again. We kissed even harder. A small fear nagged at me as we made out. I grew afraid she would smell Jasmine's touch on me somehow.

But she didn't.

-35-

The machines made their next move shortly after dawn. I doubt they planned it for that time, that's just when their final tunnels breached and Macro diggers swarmed out of their holes. They had brought all their underground units to encircle Fort Pierre. Since they weren't able to dig through our underground defenses, they came up outside the walls and rushed us from every side.

The big machines began to move then, standing up from their dormant states and forming groups of their own. They marched forward, all surging toward Fort Pierre. I nodded to myself, blinking sleep from my eyes. Typical Macro behavior. They often waited for a crucial tipping point, then slammed everything against a critical juncture. Unfortunately, in this case the juncture was the base I was standing in.

We'd had some forewarning this was their plan. The underground movements showed they were massing more troops under us all the time. They had already knocked out our heavy weapons, weakening us against the big machines.

I had my helmet off. Barrera and Sandra leaned over the table with me. Everyone had dark circles around their eyes. I'd learned the delicate art of scratching my cheek with battle gloves on, and employed it now. I winced as a few hairs of stubble were caught and yanked out. But I was successful. No skin had been removed, and the itch had been vanquished.

"Barrera," I said, "what do you think we should do in this situation?"

He shrugged and eyed the boards speculatively. "Fight on the walls. That's why we built them."

"Can we hold the walls against the tunnelers?"

"Probably."

"And when the big machines come racing up behind them, what then?"

He shook his head. "I don't know. They'll step right over the walls. We'll be overrun."

"Major, have you ever been underneath an invasion Macro with all sixteen of its belly turrets spraying fire down onto your troops?"

Barrera shook his head. "No, sir."

He was looking at me now, warily. The others followed his lead. They all stared at me. They knew I had an idea in my head, and that I was bringing them around to making the same conclusion I had. I could tell from their expressions they doubted they would like my conclusion.

"No, you have not," I said. "None of you have. I can tell you, it is an unpleasant experience, one you will never forget should you be so lucky as to survive. We can't sit here and wait for them to hit the walls. Not all of us. We have to go on the offensive. Small units will hunt the big machines in the deep forest."

"Small units?" Barrera asked.

"In the *forest*, sir?" Major Sarin asked. "Why?"

"Small groups are harder to focus on and wipe out. If they try, we will have succeeded in distracting them and keeping them off the main base. We'll meet them out in the forest because I don't want to set off even a small nuclear device inside these walls. And that is how we are going to have to stop them, people—by going nuclear."

Out of nowhere, Kwon clanked up to my side. He banged his hands together with an ear-punishing ring of metal striking metal. "When do we fly, Colonel?"

I saw the excitement in his eyes and I had to smile. Everyone else in the room looked faintly sick at the prospect of combat with giant robots, but not Kwon. He had signed up with Star Force to kill machines. He never tired of it.

"We'll send out half the garrison. That should leave you with more than a thousand marines to man this base. Don't lose it, Lieutenant-Colonel."

"I'd like to command one of those units, Colonel," Major Sarin said.

I looked at her in surprise. "Have you trained with the new battle suits?" I asked.

Her lips drew tight. "No, sir. I haven't had time. I've been on ops since—"

"I know," I said. "I put you on ops. But I wouldn't send you out in any case, Major. No one is more critical to this operation than you are, and I need you right here running this command screen."

I watched Jasmine's face. She wasn't happy, but she wasn't going to say anything. I could practically hear her thoughts. She was angry I'd told her she needed command experience, then denied her the chance to get it when the opportunity arose.

I caught Sandra glaring at the two of us and frowned. I could tell she was becoming jealous again. If we didn't all die in the next twenty-four hours, I planned to assign one of these two women to a new base on the Moon.

"Is there any reason why you have to go personally, Colonel?" Sandra asked me, speaking up for the first time.

"Kwon and I have taken down more of these machines than most. At last count, only five hundred of our Star Force marines are veterans of the South American campaign. If you are thinking of my personal safety—don't bother. This base, even this bunker, will not be any safer than the forest. Possibly, it is a deathtrap."

Sandra backed off, and everyone looked grim as my words sank in.

"Colonel," Barrera said, "as your second in command, I've seriously considered your plan. I think you are making the right decision."

If anyone else had said it, that man might have been called a kiss-ass. But everyone here knew Barrera didn't kiss anyone's butt, not even mine. The decision was made without further debate and within three minutes I had my helmet on and was jogging up toward the surface. Kwon clanged ahead while Sandra ran lightly behind me.

Sandra sent me a private message, helmet-to-helmet. I opened the channel.

"Did you ever think, Kyle, that Barrera might be the one behind the assassinations?"

"No," I lied. To tell her *yes*, I had thought such a thing, might unnecessarily threaten the life of my second in command.

"Well, you should. Maybe he thinks your idea is crazy. Maybe he wants you to go out and get yourself killed."

She snapped off the channel after that, and I briefly thought about her concerns. I couldn't think of anything to do about them at the moment, so I dropped those worries from my mind. Assassins were small matters in comparison to the robots we were now going to engage. That was one detail where I'd bent the truth. By any sane measure, it was safer to stay in the fort. I would have ordered Sandra to stay behind if I'd thought I could get away with it.

We gathered a team of men, bringing along Captain Sloan as the company CO. Kwon shouted most of the orders, seemingly giving them before I had time to pass them down. He was an excellent non-com, the kind that had a mental link to his officer. Again I thought I should promote him to lieutenant, but I knew he wouldn't feel completely comfortable in that role. More importantly, he didn't want it. Kwon wasn't interested in rank. He was interested in killing machines. From his viewpoint, today was going to be a dream come true.

We flew low, only a foot or so off the ground. Single-file, we glided through the forest. Only Sandra was on her feet, as disinterested as she usually was in wearing a heavy battle suit. She could run as fast as we could fly between the trees, so it wasn't a problem. Sloan led the point squad while Kwon, Sandra and I accompanied the second squad of the three. We wended our way northwest, then swung back to the east, hoping to hit the Macros' right flank. We could tell we were getting close when the bird sounds cut out. Soon thereafter even the insects fell silent, saving their humming and buzzing for a safer day.

My helmet radio squawked, and excited words from the lead squad spilled out. There was no need for elaboration; we'd obviously made contact with the enemy. A series of rapid cracking sounds approached as a dozen trees were shocked by powerful impacts. The sounds were distant at first, then swooped closer and closer. I could see treetops ahead, bending forward as if they'd been battered by a passing giant. In a way, that was exactly what occurred.

The first squad engaged the monster with flashing laser fire. Trees smoked and burned. The crashing legs of steel, visible only in flashes up ahead, slowed and turned with a loud mechanical whirring sound.

Following our simple, but precisely-timed plan, my group didn't charge ahead underneath the enemy as the first squad did. We took up what cover there was and fired our beamers up at the monster that darkened the forest like a passing cloud.

The machine looked bigger than I remembered. Those six churning legs were each as massive as a dozen tree trunks and formed of scarred, dull metal. Atop the towering, swinging legs was the vast body. Like a crab's carapace, it was curved, but unlike any natural beast it bore sixteen belly-turrets to deal with irritants such as ourselves. The turrets blazed, sending ripples of blinding flashes down at my troops.

Sloan and his squad had what was easily the least enviable job of the unit. They were to get underneath the machine and dodge the legs and turrets. They were to fire and attract attention, but it didn't really matter if they hit anything. The important part for them was to keep moving. The enemy turrets took nearly a second to lock onto a man and pour down streams of deadly fire. If you kept moving, you were much harder to hit.

It was our job, standing back with the second and third squads, to bring down the machine. My plan was to do so by focusing fire on the legs and ignoring the belly turrets. If the machine was flat on the ground, the turrets were useless anyway.

"Target is right-center leg, the one caught up on that big pine. Fire on my mark...*mark!*" I shouted.

My two squads had two heavy beamers each, one in each arm. Nearly forty streaks of energy flashed out to slice into the thick metal. First, a gush of vapor and plasma erupted from the leg. Dozens of lines were being cut into a single spot, a single massive joint. The metal soon turned orange and curled, opening up with curving lines as our lasers sliced into the outer hull. After a second, we cut the beams.

I squinted through the smoke and saw the machine was limping on that one leg, but it wasn't down yet. I saw it catch one of Sloan's troops with three turrets at once. Two others swung in our direction and raked our tree cover with suppressing fire. Men ducked and cursed all around me. Some returned fire, aiming at the turrets.

"Stay on target!" I roared.

I heard Kwon echo my command. He cuffed two helmets and strode around the crouched men as if the enemy Macro couldn't hit him on a bet.

"Right-center again, fire!" I shouted.

The beams leapt out—more ragged than before, but still on target. The machine buckled and tipped down. One leg was useless. It couldn't walk with that leg, but it could still use it as a club. Flailing, it caught another of Sloan's squad and smashed him into the earth like a hammer driving a nail.

I called a new target. We repeated the procedure until three legs were incapacitated. This was when things became dangerous. The machine still had big weaponry on its back. Since it was tilting as its far set of legs struggled to stand up again, the weapons on its back were directed toward us. I gave the order to disperse as rockets and anti-air lasers ripped up the landscape around us. Each squad ran in the opposite direction, circling around to come to the other side of the machine.

"Let's finish it, sir," Kwon said, breathing hard.

I looked at him, understanding his eagerness. It had been a very long time since we'd killed one of these big Macros. To us, these would always be the real enemy, the kind of machines we had nightmares about.

"We're sticking to the plan, First Sergeant."

"What if it doesn't work?"

"Then we've screwed up. Set the charges."

We laid our four mines—it was more than necessary, but we wanted to be sure. They had proximity fuses with timers. Once another metallic object of sufficient mass came near, the timer would begin ticking. We set it for one minute. It was a guess, really. Hopefully, it would do the job.

As we glided away from the scene of our raid, we could hear more crashing, more snapping tree trunks. The first machine had called its brethren for aid.

"What if they repair it?" Captain Sloan asked me. "I don't want to think I lost three men for nothing."

"In the South American campaign, we lost a hundred to every machine we knocked out, and that was only after we figured out how to do it right," I told him.

"We could have at least disarmed it, sir," Sloan complained.

"If we had, the Macros wouldn't bother to come help."

"Proximity fuse is reporting, sir," Kwon said. "It's been triggered."

"Fly everyone!" I roared. "Thirty more seconds, then hit the deck. Look for a depression in the ground to hide in. Watch the trees, if they come down on you, you will be crushed, armor or no."

Men scattered, whizzing ahead through the trees. I watched a man hit his helmet on a low branch and go into a spin. He flopped on the ground, senseless. There was a dent in his helmet. The smart-metal helmet uncreased itself as I watched, but the damage had been done. The equipment was better at taking laser-fire than hard blows from solid objects.

Cursing, I grabbed the red-lit private by the leg and dragged him another hundred yards through the forest before I threw myself down beside Sandra. She'd found a hole to crouch in. I climbed over her body, realizing for the first time her nanite suit wasn't really adequate to the kind of shockwave we were about to experience.

"Stay under me," I said, and tried to cover her with the hard shell of my metal armor. She grunted at the weight, but didn't complain. I pulled the limp private after me, not sure if he was dead or alive. In either case, he would serve to keep my girl breathing.

A blinding flash of light swelled up behind me. I didn't look. I didn't have time to take a breath.

The shockwave hit then, and the forest went down all around me like matchsticks. I lost consciousness, and when I reawakened, the world looked different.

237

-36-

I struggled to my feet, screaming "KWON!" in my helmet. I knew I was screaming, but I couldn't hear anything except a loud ringing sound. I kept at it anyway. "KWON!"

I checked Sandra first. She was squirming, which had to be a good sign. I tried to help her to her feet, but she slapped me away, wanting to stay down. I let her. I wasn't sure how hurt she was, but if she wanted to stay lying there, she could.

I staggered in a circle. Ash was up to my ankles. Most of the trees nearby were down, and most of the trunks were on fire. I walked around in a world of white smoke and debris. Dead men were scattered here and there. The next time I shouted, "KWON!" I could hear my own voice.

Apparently, the First Sergeant could too. He stumped up, dragging an ankle that was obviously broken. It twisted away from his body at an odd angle, doubtlessly held in place by the stiffness of his boot.

"What is it, Colonel?" Kwon asked.

"What is it?" I echoed his words in disbelief. "Look around us, what do you think I'm upset about?"

"Yes, sir. I see causalities, sir."

"Causalities, right. Did something go wrong, here?"

"The blast was too big, sir."

I clapped him on the shoulder with a gloved hand. The sound of metal on metal clanked and rasped.

238

"Exactly, First Sergeant," I said. "You did it again, didn't you?"

"Sir?"

"You left the grenades on default. I specifically instructed you to set the devices to their lowest yield setting."

"No, sir," Kwon said.

"No?"

"I did not, sir. I set them for low yield. I double-checked, sir."

I stared at Kwon for a second. "You're sure?"

"Absolutely, sir. After that time we nearly died on the Macro cruiser, I always double-check settings."

I didn't know what to make of it. I tried to clear my thoughts, but it was difficult under the circumstances.

"Okay," I said, "we'll figure out what went wrong later. Get all the men together. Gather the wounded and the dead too, even if we have to drag them out of here. Let's move to a safe position."

We ended up using fallen saplings covered in charcoal as stretchers. We dragged, limped and drifted out of the forest. I was thinking hard as we retreated. The blast had been much too big. Instead of less than a kiloton, I estimated the yield at closer to ten times what it was supposed to be. Possibly even Hiroshima-level. The enemy had been decimated, but so had we. I could only hope there hadn't been any other teams operating in the forest near us at the time. If another platoon had been caught even closer to the blast, they had probably been wiped out.

How could it have happened? Only three possibilities came to mind. Either Kwon was an idiot and had set the yield to high by accident—a possibility I was willing to entertain—or a device had malfunctioned. The third possible scenario was the one that concerned me the most, however. What if it had been sabotage? What if the devices had been tampered with, either after Kwon had set them or before we'd come out here? That was the thought that would not leave my mind, and it haunted me as we escaped the burning trees.

When we got to the open zone around Fort Pierre, we came up behind thousands of smaller Macros attacking the walls. The free-fire zone around the fort had long ago been cleared of trees to create a field without cover for enemy attackers. There were so many beam flashes going off our autoshades dimmed to near blackout. It seemed like every marine we had was up on that wall, blazing away with both his arm-mounted projectors. Larger cannons were mounted at the corners as well, and they fired in pulsing sprays of light. With so many beam projectors flashing, our autoshades made it difficult to see. The sunlight overhead was too dim to penetrate the gloom of our helmets. It was like witnessing combat in a room full of strobe lights.

"Switch helmets to wireframe perception mode," I ordered.

One of the newest improvements I'd made to our equipment load-out was a new sensory system for the HUD. Instead of using direct visual input, a brainbox interrupted the signal and transformed the data from pickups into a three-D environment. Enemies were red wireframes, while friendlies were outlined in green. Neutral equipment and unknowns appeared as blue or yellow, respectively. The system took a little getting used to, but it was a lot better than getting a headache from constantly shifting brightness levels. Before, intense firefights had often resembled wild lightning storms from the point of view of a marine in the middle of it.

We formed up at the tree line and shot a few lingering Macros in the back. They were mostly focused on attacking our walls. I didn't call for an open assault yet, however. There were just too few of us and too many of the enemy. Kwon counted less than twenty effectives left in our unit.

"Do we attack, sir?" Kwon asked me doubtfully.

Captain Sloan came up beside us and threw himself down. We were all lying in the dirt behind the enemy lines. "Suicide, sir."

"I agree," I said. I wanted to get into the fort, but I didn't want to die right off. "If we hit them enough to make them turn on us. They'll do it with overwhelming force and annihilate us, or at least chase us off."

"Do you think they know we are here, sir?"

"Oh, hell yeah," I said. "They've got cameras at both ends, same as we do. They knew even before we smoked their snipers back here."

"In that case, why did we get this close?" Sandra asked from above me.

I looked up and saw her form crouching in a mangrove tree. I was amused to see the HUD system had her marked down as yellow—the brainbox was not completely sure if she was friend or foe.

"Because I understand Macro Command," I said. "They like to do things in an all-or-nothing fashion. Pecking at them lightly isn't enough to make them break their plans and turn on us. But if we push things, they will."

"So," Sloan added, "we're safe as long as we don't hit them hard."

I glanced at him in irritation. "We are marines. We're not here to be safe."

"I just meant—"

"Excuse me, Colonel," Kwon interrupted. "Could we try to fly right over them?"

"If we all want to die," Sandra said unhelpfully.

"I'm not sure," I said, "but I think that is pushing their decision to ignore us too far, First Sergeant. Right now, they are going all-out to breach the fort walls. But if we look like we are joining the defenders, we'll almost certainly come under fire."

No one had a snappy comeback for that statement. For a few moments, we watched the battle rage. Men on the walls fired with discipline, popping up for a moment, beaming down on a single machine for a fraction of a second and usually disabling it. A dozen Macros were left kicking and thrashing in the dirt all along the bottom of the wall. Frequently, small EMP grenades and explosives were tossed down into the throng as well. Every time one of my men showed himself, however, he instantly came under heavy fire. A dozen beams slashed this armor. Each marine hit in such a fashion invariably was crisscrossed with glowing burns and shrouded in smoke from the vaporized metals. Usually, the men survived due to the effectiveness of the new armor. I knew they were under orders to fire, then quickly duck back down behind the scarred walls. When they were behind cover, another marine on repair-duty would spray fresh constructives over the damaged area, effectively filling in the burning holes in the damaged helmet and breastplate.

Things didn't always work out the way they were supposed to, however. As I watched, men were occasionally caught by too many enemy beams at once. Sometimes, this was their own fault as they kept their fire going for too long before ducking back behind cover. I understood the temptation. If you exposed yourself for half a second, you might not seriously damage your target. If you dared to go longer—more than a full second—you were much more likely to kill a machine outright, but you might be taken out in return.

"We can't just sit here, Colonel," Kwon said. "We have to get into this fight somehow."

I didn't answer right away. I felt the same emotions he did. Watching fellow marines struggle just a few hundred yards away while sitting idle was torment. Fortunately, a solution pushed up through the trees behind us less than a minute later.

I figured the machine had been hit by our blast, or a blast from one of the other platoons on hunter-killer duty. One side of it was scorched black and dented in spots. The gigantic machine was damaged and missing one of its thick walking legs, but it was still able to move faster than a man could run. It shouldered its way among the trees and loomed over us. The tree Sandra was in went over and down with a resounding crash. I saw her spring out of it to safety, like a cat leaping from danger.

My men engaged it without orders, which was fine with me. Being well-trained and somewhat experienced in dealing with the big machines, they tripled up on each of the flashing anti-personnel turrets that sprayed us with raking fire. My men in their new battle suits had several advantages over previous marine units that had met such enemies. We had approximately double the firepower, greater mobility and superior armor. Still, we were taking casualties. Within thirty seconds, we'd taken out six of the sixteen turrets but were down to seventeen effectives. I gritted my teeth as the enemy beam turrets focused in on our dead and wounded and hosed them with merciless fire. Incapacitated men were burned to slag. The Macros hadn't updated their software much in the area of identifying active threats versus disabled ones. They liked to be sure.

There was one more critical power our troops now had that they'd never been able to employ before. I decided to use it now.

"Fly *up*," I shouted on the unit override. "Get up on top of this tin can. We'll knock out its big gun, and it won't be able to touch us."

The men liked my idea. They lifted off in every direction. Sandra couldn't fly, but she was still one of the first ones to reach the top. Using her two knives like a pair of mountain-climbers ice-axes, she sprang up the nearest massive leg. She was up to the top faster than one of the local monkeys could reach the top of a palm tree.

Up top, the enemy had two weapons systems to deal with. There was a heavy beam projector and a flechette-style anti-air battery. Neither was effective against a team of armored infantry at very close range. We disabled the systems and the Macro couldn't touch us.

"That was great, Colonel," Kwon said, breathing hard. He clanked up to me, his boots heavily stomping on the metal skin of the Macro's back. He'd turned on his magnetics to keep a firm footing. I ordered the rest of the men to do the same.

"What are we going to do now?" Kwon asked me.

"Just wait a second. We'll see if this Macro figures it out."

"Figures out what?"

I didn't have to answer him. The monster proceeded to do exactly what I'd hoped it would. Calculating that it could not effectively remove us, it decided to ignore us and moved on to the next target of opportunity. It strode toward the walls of Fort Pierre and stepped right over them. There, it could use its belly-turrets on a target-rich environment.

"What now, sir?" shouted Captain Sloan.

"The free ride is over," I told him. "Now, we kill it."

I threw myself over the side and glided down to join the base defenders. In a massive blaze of firepower, we tore the huge machine apart.

-37-

When the enemy had taken losses of approximately thirty percent of their assaulting force, they suddenly withdrew into the trees. I knew it was only temporary. Speculating as to why they had withdrawn, one man's interpretation was as good as another's. Perhaps they'd reached a preset loss-limit. I doubted that one, as they were taking out a strongpoint and had to expect heavy losses to begin with. The only other conclusion was they had to regroup and rejoin with supporting forces. I put my money on that possibility, and it later turned out to be correct.

When the enemy pulled back, Sandra was at my side and full of questions.

"I heard from the men that the nuke was set too high," she said.

"Yes. Somehow, one of the grenades must have malfunctioned."

"I thought maybe it was because you put four bombs down, not just one."

"We put down four in case they were detected by the Macros. I wanted to be sure they couldn't all be knocked out before one went off. The first that detonated should have destroyed all the others."

Sandra narrowed her eyes. I could tell there were wheels turning up there.

"So either all four malfunctioned," she said, "or it was a twenty-five percent chance the bad one happened to go off first."

"Something like that. Time to head to the bunker and check on the overall situation."

"Not so fast," she said. "How often does Nano tech equipment fail on you, Kyle?"

"Uh, not very often."

"Nearly never. How many of the other hunter-killer teams reported this kind of trouble with their grenades?"

"I'm not sure."

"Try none. I checked with ops."

"What are you getting at? I can tell you have an idea in your head and you are working up to it."

Sandra looked at me oddly. I could see her intense expression through her faceplate, but she tried to sound calm. "Nothing," she said. "I need to go take care of a few things now. I'll see you at the bunker."

She sprinted off, and I looked after her in concern. I knew her pretty well by now, and her odd behavior caused alarm bells to go off in my mind. I frowned, wondering at her attitude. She'd clearly reasoned out that someone must have tampered with the grenades, just as I had. But what did she plan to do about it?

The more I thought about her demeanor, the less I liked it. I recalled when she'd brought in Ping like a cat's kill dropped on a doorstep. She had that predatory attitude right now.

I reached the door of the bunker and hesitated before entering. I'd half-expected to find Sandra doing her gargoyle routine on the roof, but she wasn't there.

I cursed and turned toward the officers' barracks. Sandra had headed in that direction.

"What's wrong, sir?" Kwon asked me.

"I don't know…" I said, "and I don't like not knowing."

"Are we going down now?"

"No," I said. I turned and headed toward the barracks. I thought I had an inkling of what was going on. Maybe Sandra had reasoned out there had been sabotage. Maybe she believed she knew who was behind it. The last time she'd had such a suspicion, she'd been right, and Ping had died.

I saw a commotion up ahead. Was that laser-fire? I began to run. Kwon chased after me. I jumped into the air and glided over the ground. The scorched sand and ashes swirled and rippled below me as I flew at top speed toward the disturbance.

I saw two lieutenants running out of the officer's mess.

"What's going on in there?"

"Some kind of a duel, sir. They ordered us out."

I threw open the door and walked inside. I supposed when I saw the scene, I shouldn't have been surprised, but somehow I was. Sandra was there, standing on a mess hall table. In the farthest corner was Major Sarin. She had a beam pistol in her hand. Both wore light nanite armor. Sandra had two knives out, and she had assumed an easy, relaxed pose.

Sunlight streamed in from several holes behind and above her. The holes were bigger than bullet holes, about the size a small beam weapon would make punching through nanite alloy.

Sandra glanced at me as I walked in.

"What the hell is going on?" I roared at them. "Both of you lower your weapons. It's against Star Force code to fight amongst yourselves in the face of the enemy."

"But she *is* the enemy, Kyle," Sandra said.

"What?"

"You know what happened out there. Someone tampered with those grenades. It had to be someone inside Star Force, who would have had access. An officer with technical knowledge."

I looked at Jasmine. Her faceplate had cleared enough to allow me to see her eyes. Her sides were heaving and she kept her eyes and her weapon trained on Sandra. Both women watched the other. Sandra was much faster, but she couldn't outrun a laser beam. As long as Jasmine kept her at a distance, she would be safe. Apparently, that was her intent.

Could Sandra be right? Someone had to be doing this, possibly someone who high-up in my command structure. First, there had been Ping, the infiltrator. Who had let her in? Then the two assassins who'd tried to fry and gut me in my tent. The last straw was the sabotaged grenade.

I knew Sandra was becoming increasingly paranoid, but she had a point, someone was behind all this and Major Sarin had the means and the motivation. Could Jasmine be that upset with me and Star Force?

"She nearly killed us all, Kyle," Sandra said. "Don't protect her just because you think she's cute."

"Jasmine, is there any truth to all this?" I asked.

Jasmine's attention flicked to me, I could see the hurt in her eyes. Unfortunately, that was all the distraction Sandra needed. She flashed across the room, snatched the pistol out of Jasmine's hand and placed one of her knives against the smaller woman's throat.

I took two steps forward. "Hold on now, Sandra. We'll get to the truth. Let's do this by the book."

The two women were nose-to-nose, glaring at each other.

"Since when did you ever do anything by the book?" Sandra asked. "Screw the book. I'm going to cut her head off and mount it on the wall over our bed for you to look at whenever you like."

"Look down," Jasmine told Sandra.

We all did, we couldn't help it. Sandra had removed Jasmine's pistol, tossed it away and pinned one of Jasmine's weaker wrists to the wall. But the other hand was still free, however. Jasmine had drawn her combat knife and held it poised at Sandra's tight belly. It was aimed upward. One quick thrust, and it would be driven into the heart. Nanotized marine reaction times being what they were, I suspected both women would die in an instant if either made the final move. I wasn't sure if we could patch them up afterward or not.

"Uh-oh," Kwon said unhelpfully.

"Stay here at the door," I told him. "Don't let anyone else inside. We're going to settle this."

Sandra looked surprised by Jasmine's move, but not frightened. By their expressions, I thought neither of them was afraid. Instead, both women appeared to be intensely pissed-off. I drew a breath and let it slowly out. I knew I was partly responsible for all this. I'd been unprofessional, and I'd caused strife among my staff. Probably, this was why most generals didn't have their spouses in the command post with them. Hell, in the old days they didn't even let women crew ships because people in close quarters for long periods tended to get funny ideas.

"This is all my fault, ladies," I said. "Can we possibly disarm and sit around a table to discuss it?"

"It's not just about you and your cheating, Kyle," Sandra said. "She nearly killed us. She's a traitor to Star Force."

"You're a psychotic killer, and you aren't even human anymore," Jasmine retorted.

I winced. Things weren't winding down. I got to within ten feet of them, and stopped. I put my arms up, palms forward, hands empty.

"Whoa," I said. "Let's take things down a notch or two."

"You can't keep us both," Sandra told me. "I want you to choose. The loser dies—now."

"Um," I said, "that's not reasonable."

"You have a thing for her, admit it."

"Sandra, there was one moment—after you'd been in a coma for a long time. It was wrong, I've admitted that."

"Don't bullshit me. You were making out with her in the command post yesterday. I'm not an idiot."

"Oh no," Kwon said in a quiet, groaning voice behind me.

"We were *not* making out," I insisted. "We were having a moment of closure. At least, that's what I would call it."

Both women glanced at me with questioning expressions.

"That's what you thought?" Jasmine asked.

"Yeah," I said. "That's what I wanted. I wanted everything to go back to how it was before I screwed it all up. Back on the ship, you two had become friends again, I thought. What happened to that?"

"She changed her mind," Sandra said. "Women do that, you know. She made another move on you, and then maybe she realized you weren't going to give her a chance. So, she decided to dump you—permanently."

"Come on," I said. "Major Sarin is a professional. She isn't so petty as to kill me just because she felt spurned."

Sandra gave her head a tiny shake and made a tsking noise. "You don't really believe that, do you?"

Jasmine remained quiet and continued glaring. Her attitude was beginning to concern me. I wondered if Sandra was right. If she really was innocent, why wasn't she saying so?

"What do you have to say, Jasmine?" I asked.

"I'm too upset to talk right now," she said.

Great, I thought. "Come on, we're all friends and comrades. We've fought over a thousand lightyears of space together. Tell us what you have to say. Sandra, pull back that knife so she can think."

Slowly, ever so slowly, the two women backed away from one another. When they were a foot apart, everyone felt better. They were still glowering at each other like two cats in a sealed trashcan, however.

"Did you let infiltrators onto the island?" I asked her.

"Am I really being interrogated here, sir? Your girlfriend has assaulted me. Maybe she did it."

"Just answer the questions, Jasmine," I said. "That's an order."

In the face of a direct order, she deflated somewhat. I knew that wouldn't work with Sandra, but Jasmine had more respect for our chain of command.

"I did not allow any unauthorized personnel to do anything," she said.

"Did you help the assassins that entered my tent in any way? Did you know who they were? Have you had any past associations with any of them?"

"No, no and no."

"What about our nuclear grenades? Did you tamper with them or adjust their settings?"

Jasmine frowned, looking honestly puzzled now. "What happened?"

"Just answer the question!" Sandra shouted at her.

"No, I didn't tamper with anything!" she shouted back. "I spend all day on duty on the command screens."

I looked at Sandra questioningly. She made a frustrated growling sound. She stepped back, sheathed her weapon and crossed her arms under her breasts.

"Well?" I asked.

"No change in her pulse—her heart beats like a little bird anyway. No other autonomic shifts I can detect. As far as I can tell, she's telling the truth. But she still loves you."

"Excellent," I said, clapping my armored hands together loudly. I decided it was time to put the best face on this I possibly could and move on. Both women looked at me in cold displeasure. I ignored their expressions and smiled broadly.

"Now that the matter is settled, we can move on to dealing with several thousand robots I've noticed roaming around our territory. You two don't mind doing your jobs, do you? Wonderful. In the future, I want to see a little less paranoia toward my senior staff,

Sandra. And Major Sarin, please state your innocence more immediately and keep your personal feelings out of my command post. Actually, that goes for both of you. If either one of you wants to fall in love with the First Sergeant over there, that's fine with me, but I don't want to hear about it while I'm trying to handle combat ops."

Kwon looked alarmed and shook his head vigorously at my suggestion.

No one looked happy after my little speech except for me, and I was faking it. But the scene did quietly break up. We all walked outside and headed for the command bunker. Sandra fell in step beside me. Jasmine and Kwon lagged behind.

"If it wasn't that little snake, then who tried to kill us with that nuke?" Sandra asked me. "Someone must have done it. You know that."

"I'll figure it out. Don't worry."

"You always say stuff like that."

"Okay," I said, stopping and facing her. "Then *you* do it. I want *you* to figure out who is behind the security breaches. That's your job for the next few days. You know it wasn't Jasmine, so check out everyone else."

Sandra looked surprised. "Okay," she said after a few moments thought. "I will find the truth."

Kwon and Major Sarin had walked up behind us and stood there, looking wary. Perhaps they expected another outburst.

"Kwon, you stay with Colonel Riggs," Sandra said. "Go everywhere he does. If he orders you away, sneak back when he isn't looking."

"Um," he said, looking at me.

I nodded slightly.

"Okay," Kwon said brightly. He seemed happy about the assignment.

Sandra nodded too, satisfied with the idea of Kwon performing bodyguard duty again. She turned and left us then, heading toward the ramparts at a shocking pace. Each step took her ten or twenty feet over the ground. To Sandra, Earth's gravity must have felt like the Moon.

Crawlers and teams of marines were working all around the fort, shoring up the walls. Sandra disappeared among a knot of marines working on the fortifications. I had no idea what was in her head at that moment, but I pitied whoever was next on her suspect list.

I reached the headquarters building and passed inside the entrance. The nanites recognized my touch and dilated an opening in what appeared to be a smooth metal surface. I stepped through into the building. Kwon and Jasmine were recognized and allowed inside as well. Before I reached the first ramp heading down to the bunkers, I heard a familiar voice in my ear.

"They are coming again, marines," Barrera said.

I'd joined the base defense channel, and since Barrera was running ops, I could hear him like everyone else. I wanted to ask him what they had with them, but before I could transmit over the command channel, he answered my question.

"Looks like they are rolling up new supporters. The big machines that survived our hunter-killer platoons have surrounded Fort Pierre. They've suffered over fifty-percent losses, but they are still a viable force."

I grinned in my helmet at that news. My marines, armed with nuclear grenades, had done more damage than I'd dared to hope for. Still, half an army of giant machines would be powerful in a single mass.

"All the Macros, big and small, will be hitting us shortly," Barrera's voice continued in an announcer's monotone. "In addition, the enemy fleet has decided to advance into range of our position. They are flying cautiously over the ocean toward us from the east. They'll be in range within—three minutes."

I made a sound that was somewhere between a sigh and a grunt. That was it—the end of the game. We couldn't face the Macro workers, the big invasion machines, *and* their fleet. The heavy laser forts I'd built to drive back the enemy fleet had all been knocked out.

Fort Pierre was about to fall. After that, Andros Island was doomed.

-38-

Running through the bunker, I took flight when I reached each ramp downward. Marines threw themselves out of the way as we passed. Alarms were sounding, and I could hear tramping boots on the bunker's metal floors as marines were mustered from their brief respites. It was time for battle again, and I knew already this was going to be the big one.

The command center glowed with the soft blue light of a dozen screens. Standing in the center of it all was Lieutenant Colonel Barrera. He had a grim look on his face, but there was nothing unusual about that.

"How long do we have?" I asked him as I stepped up to his side.

Behind me, Kwon took up a post at the door. Barrera didn't look at me. He continued to gaze at the screens instead. Hundreds of red contacts slowly closed upon our position from every angle.

"Not long, sir," he said. "Not long at all."

I knew what he meant. We were about to be overrun, and we both knew it. Now was the time to pull in the last cards I had. There would be no retreat from here other than sweet death.

"Major Sarin," I said, "get Admiral Crow on the command channel."

A moment later, she made the connection.

"Colonel Riggs," Crow said. "I thought you might be calling me soon. Let me say before you make any requests, I'm not in a suicidal mood today. I suggest you pull out right now. Have your men abandon the island to the west. Let the robots fight this one, Kyle. Your automated laser turrets against their ships and walkers."

"That's unacceptable," I said.

"Don't make any rash judgments, Kyle."

"I'm not."

"You can't expect me to wade into this fight with my last hundred ships. I'm all Earth has left."

"I don't want you to fight over Andros."

"You don't?" Crow asked. "What's in that twisted mind of yours, then?"

"Move your ships over the U. S. mainland. Position them over Florida."

"What the hell for?"

"You'll see. Will you do it?"

Crow hesitated. I knew he was calculating how fast he could run if the Macro fleet turned and charged after him. I'd already made those calculations. He could easily escape.

"All right, but this better not be some kind of trick."

"It is, and you'd better hope that it works. Riggs out."

Barrera finally turned to look at me when the conversation ended. He raised his eyebrows and stared. I didn't feel like explaining things right then, so I ignored him.

"Major Sarin," I said, "connect me to General Kerr in NORAD please."

Barrera gave a small nod. Was that a smile? Perhaps he'd figured out what I was going to attempt. After another thirty seconds, Kerr was on the line.

"It's been a few days of hard fighting, Colonel," he said. "I want to say from all of us, that we've been impressed up here. Everyone knows you did your best."

"Thank you, General."

"Are you calling to tell us you're pulling out, or to tell us what to inscribe on your tombstones? I've got money on this one, Riggs. Think hard."

I smiled grimly. "Neither, General. We are neither quitting nor dying today. But I do need your help, sir."

"Ah, option three! I'll have you know I just won an easy hundred bucks."

"Is your cooperation required for you to cash in?"

"Unfortunately, no. I'm equally sad to report our subs are out of position to fire upon the enemy. It would be suicide to do so, anyway."

"That's not what I wanted, sir."

"What then?"

"I need ICBMs, sir. A lot of them. Every ship-killer you've got. But I only want them coming from the U. S. Tell the others to hold back."

"The Macros won't fall for that this time. And we're watching your fleet, which is massing over our airspace now. We aren't excited about the idea of Star Force 'punishing' us the way you did to the Chinese a while back."

"I'm sure you're not, sir. But that is not my intent. My intent is to win this battle, not slip out of it."

"I don't know, Riggs. We've wargamed this out six ways from Sunday. I don't think Star Force has a prayer."

"Are you reneging on our deal, sir?"

"Riggs—"

"Why the hell did you build all those ship-killers anyway? Are you going to hang flowers on them? Fire on the enemy. That's all I'm asking, sir. Take it to the President."

I heard a sigh. "All right Riggs, give me a minute."

The connection broke.

We watched tensely as the enemy began assaulting the walls. The first wave consisted of smaller machines, the ones that had crawled up out of the tunnels that now riddled Andros Island. Behind them the surviving big machines, hung back. I realized they were waiting for their fleet to support them. They were taking no more chances.

Out over the ocean the Macro fleet formed up and became a line three layers deep. They began firing their big cannons down on us. We didn't have much left to fire back with. The coastal turrets on the eastern side of the island had been pretty much wiped out. The three central forts with their big lasers had all been knocked out and we hadn't had time to repair them. The laser turrets on the island's western flank were out of range. I still had one more card left, however.

"Barrera, commit the hovertanks," I ordered.

254

"How many of them, sir?"

"All of them. Hit the enemy's northern flank."

"Is that wise, sir? We'll have nothing left to cover a withdrawal."

I looked at him. He stared back for a second and then relayed my orders. Was that a tiny shake of the head? The man had his doubts, I could tell. I was used to that, however. I stepped closer to the screens and watched the battle rage in the form of a thousand multi-colored contacts.

"Look up north, Colonel," Major Sarin said.

I switched my gaze to another screen which showed the entire hemisphere. A cloud of yellow contacts had appeared out over the American Midwest.

"Mark those as friendly," I snapped.

"Are we sure of that?"

I laughed bitterly. "Those weapons are coming out of the missile silos around South Dakota. If they are coming for us— we're screwed anyway."

Major Sarin tapped at the screens. The missile contacts changed to a bright green. They moved with alarming speed down toward us. I knew right away these were new missiles, with new technology. Old ICBMs would have taken a good seven minutes to reach the Caribbean. These new birds would be here in less than four. I nodded to myself, glad to see the rest of the world had been staying up nights trying to build better weapons.

The Macro Fleet was pounding us now, all along the coast. I could feel the ground shudder and tremble with impacts under my smart-metal boots.

"Helmets on, everyone," I said. "If this bunker sustains a direct hit, we'll need full armor."

The ship-killer missiles reached Florida and passed among the hundred or so contacts that represented Star Force's Fleet. The missiles began coming down from their sub-orbital flight then, making their intentions obvious. Finally, the enemy fleet took notice. They slowly wheeled their formation to face this new threat. Their dreadnaught moved forward to defend their cruisers. The bombardment of the base slackened, but did not let up entirely.

Major Sarin gasped. My eyes snapped up. Hundreds of new red contacts had appeared on the boards. I stepped toward the screens, swallowing.

"They've unleashed a heavy barrage," Barrera said, his tone maddeningly calm.

"How many?" I snapped.

"Over forty …forty-five…fifty…"

More and more missiles poured out. Every cruiser fired several. I knew they'd kept half their missiles in reserve at the very least. Possibly, they had been building more aboard their ships. I didn't know if they had the capability to rearm, but I had to assume they did.

"They've stopped firing, sir. About sixty birds in total. All standard Macro design."

I opened my mouth to tell Jasmine to contact Crow, but he beat me to it.

"Admiral Crow sir," she said.

"Open the connection," I said.

"Riggs? What the hell is this? How did you get the entire planet to fire on me at once?"

"The missiles are not intended for your ships, Jack."

"I'm sorry, I'm pulling out. We can't take the risk."

"Hold your position, Jack, damn it!" I shouted. "Raise up out of the atmosphere if you feel like it. You'll see, the missiles won't track after you. Just hang there and shoot down everything the Macros fired. That's all I'm asking."

Crow cursed at me. I was some kind of cross between a pig's ass and a wallaby, as best I could make out. "All right, but this had better not be a trick."

I breathed deeply again as the Star Force ships held firm. They did lift up higher, and when the Macro missiles passed by they fired thousands of pulsing beams down into them.

I caught Barrera nodding. "Very good move, sir. How did you know where the Macros would aim their missiles?"

"They are literal-minded, even for machines. They'll try to take out the missile bases first. Florida is right on the flight-path between the two locations. Crow's Fleet is too weak to hit the Macros head-on, but they can still thin the missile barrage. I had been hoping they would fire fewer missiles."

256

"On the good side," Barrera said, "that means they have less missiles to fire at us. But on the negative, you've just brought the U. S. and possibly all of Earth into this war. I thought we weren't going to do that, Colonel."

We exchanged glances. "I had hoped it could be avoided," I said.

Barrera continued to stare at me. "Did you always intend to risk all of humanity in this struggle?"

"If necessary. I'd rather die free than live as a slave."

Barrera was scowling now. I could tell he didn't like my position. Who knew, maybe he was right. But I didn't think so. I'd been inside the ships of these monsters. I understood them better than most. They weren't going to stop coming until we were all dead or enslaved. And they would only tolerate us as slaves as long as were useful to them. This war was about extinction, and if we didn't fight now, I didn't think we would become stronger over time. Historically, species, tribes, nations and the like that were pushed to the brink and defeated rarely saw their revenge later on.

"Fleet is stopping the Macro missiles, sir," Major Sarin said with relief.

We all looked up at the screen expectantly. The red slivers of color that represented the enemy missiles over the coast of Florida were indeed being burned down, one after another. Suddenly, however, a flash appeared on the coast. I frowned.

"Was that…?"

"A hit, sir," Major Sarin said, her voice catching in her throat.

We all watched in stunned silence. Another flash went off, then another.

"Riggs, this is Crow," the ceiling said.

I was almost too stunned to respond. "Miami is gone, Admiral," I managed to say a moment later without losing control of my emotions or my voice.

"I know. I'm sorry about that, mate. The missiles must have realized that they weren't going to get through. They are dropping on the coast. I'm moving further south now to prevent that."

I nodded, and watched as Fleet did advance, shooting down the last missiles. Before it was over, four had hit alternate targets. Boca Raton, Fort Lauderdale and Miami—they were all glowing white spots on our screens. Casualty estimates flashed up on the screen. They were in seven digits. I gritted my teeth and avoided looking at them.

"Regrettable, right sir?" Barrera asked.

I glanced at him sharply, feeling an urge to smash my fist into his helmet. I resisted the feeling, but was surprised I'd felt it at all. I could not recall ever having felt that way about Barrera before. I supposed it was just the emotions of the moment.

I turned back to the boards. "Professionalism, Lieutenant Colonel," I said. "The U. S. ship-killers are about to make their strike."

The flock of green contacts finally slammed home. The big dreadnaught had glided forward to meet them, and beams flashed from its back, expertly taking out missiles with each lash of invisible heat. Still, the surviving missiles rolled in. The Macros broke formation, scattering. Missiles homed, burning their engines up until the last second.

We held our breath until the first one flared white. Then more went off.

"Eight kills, sir," Major Sarin said.

I couldn't even hear her over the cheering that came from the hallway. Most of it came from higher up in the bunker, where marines were watching summary screens. To my surprise, I realized Kwon and I were cheering too. Even the taciturn Barrera gave a hoarse shout.

"Why don't they fire their missiles at us?" Barrera asked. "I've been expecting that all along."

"We took out their entire barrage last time. They went for a hammer-blow, a single strike to take out the whole island, and they lost everything they put into it. Macros don't mind losses if goals are met, but they don't like to repeat serious mistakes. I suspect they've marked us as 'un-nukeable' in their database."

"But they've wiped out our laser defenses."

"I also think they like to hold their missiles in reserve. Or maybe they came in with their magazines half-empty. Let's just hope they don't change their minds now."

"Their dreadnaught has been hit, sir," Jasmine continued. "It survived the strike, however. They've lost a total of thirteen cruisers."

258

I didn't know if the U. S. had used all their missiles, but I suspected they probably had. They'd fired over two hundred birds and taken out about a quarter of the enemy fleet. It was a good hit, but possibly not enough to save Andros.

"Sir," Major Sarin said. I glanced at her and she directed my attention toward another screen. A new flock of yellowish contacts had appeared over Great Britain.

"What the hell?" I asked of no one in particular.

"There are seventy-six missiles in this barrage, sir," Major Sarin said. "They are roughly of the same design as the U. S. missiles."

"Huh," I said. "I didn't think the Brits had it in them. Apparently, they've decided to join this war. Maybe they think it's now or never. Change those missile contacts to green, Major, and relay a request to Crow. Have him move his ships to interpose themselves between the Macro fleet and Britain, in case the Macros decide to respond with a barrage of their own."

"Admiral Crow has agreed to your request. Fleet is moving away from their position over Florida."

Contacts slid this way and that on the boards. The battle remained fluid. Slowly, the enemy fleet organized and turned back toward Andros. Their dreadnaught moved separately, out to sea. It clearly meant to meet the barrage from Britain and halt as many of the missiles as possible. I scanned the map until my eyes landed on our hovertank reserves, which had nearly joined the battle. Up until now, I'd kept them on the western half of the island where they could not be hit easily. Soon however, they would be under fire.

"They still have too many ships bearing down on us," I said. "Order the hovertanks to chase the dreadnaught on the eastern side of their formation. If they can, they should attack out on the water, where they have a clear field of fire against it."

Barrera looked at me as if I was insane. "They'll be out of range of all our defensive fire. They'll be annihilated, sir."

"Not before they take down that dreadnaught."

"The dreadnaught?"

"The key to the enemy forces now is that dreadnaught. Without it, they can't shoot down Earth's ship-killer missiles. Without the dreadnaught, we'll be able to destroy their fleet. If they lose their

259

fleet, they won't commit their big invasion machines against us, and Fort Pierre will not fall."

Barrera shook his head in bafflement. I ignored him and relayed the order to the hovertank commander myself. I watched as they slid slowly over the sea to chase the enemy dreadnaught. I knew they didn't have much of a chance to survive against more than forty cruisers, but if they could just take down the enemy's big ship, the rest of the ships would be exposed to our side's missiles.

Sandra came into the room then. She had a predatory tension to her. My eyes flashed to Jasmine, who had seen her as well. Jasmine reached for her sidearm and drew it.

Sandra scanned the room once, her eyes sliding past Jasmine and I. She spotted Barrera, and leaped over the battle computer with a single bound. Her knife was in her hand, gleaming.

I was surprised, and barely had time to take a step forward before she grabbed Barrera by the neck and pushed a knife into his breastplate. Barrera was wearing a battle suit. He clamped her wrist with an armored glove and struggled with her. The knife made a horrible scratching sound, the screeching of metal cutting metal. Blood, nanites and sparks flew everywhere.

I reached the struggling pair and tried to pull Sandra off him— her strength was shocking. Even with an exoskeleton to help me, I had a hard time pulling her off Barrera. A beam went off, burning a hole in the ceiling. Barrera had fired one of his arm-mounted weapons.

"It was *him*, Kyle!" Sandra said, her voice rasping in her throat. "It was him all along."

-39-

Kwon and I managed to get Sandra and Barrera separated before anyone died. Of the two, Sandra was the harder to control. She was like a shark with a mouthful of blood—she wanted more. And there was blood everywhere, all of it Barrera's as far as I could tell. One of her knives had managed to get through his armor and score an inch-deep puncture wound.

"Tell me what the hell is going on, but do it fast," I said.

"He's the one," Sandra said. "He's the assassin, the mole, the *traitor*. I checked the armory. He went in there and did an *inspection* on the grenades before we left to hunt the big machines. He was especially interested in our team's weapons."

While Sandra explained herself, I continually glanced over my shoulder toward the big screens that hung above us. The missiles from England were about a third of the way across the Atlantic. Our hovertanks were gliding out over the waves now, positioning themselves to hit the enemy fleet, which had not yet taken notice of them. Once they started firing of course, they would get plenty of attention. I had to wonder if it would have killed anyone if Sandra had waited until this battle was over before making her accusations. She had never been good at waiting.

I looked at Barrera. His eyes were slits and his mouth was a straight line. That could have meant he was pissed off or just needed to cough. It all looked the same on Barrera.

"Lieutenant Colonel, are these accusations true?" I asked him.

He nodded once, slowly. This surprised me. I'd expected a list of denials and counter accusations. Instead, he admitted it right up front. I didn't quite know what to do next.

As I thought about it, my heart sank. We'd really found the traitor, and the answer was the worst possible one on the list. I didn't want it to be Barrera. I didn't want to lose him—to execute him. But I had no choice now.

"Why the hell did you do it?" I asked with feeling.

"Permission to speak plainly, Colonel," he said.

I snorted. The man had tried to kill me on at least three occasions, but still wanted to follow protocol. A disciplined marine to the last.

"By all means," I said. "I can see why you might want to get me out of the way to gain command. But do you realize I lost fourteen marines out there due solely to your sabotage?"

Barrera shook Kwon's heavy hands off. I nodded to Kwon, who let him go but watched him with intensity. Barrera walked to the computer table and tapped the map. Florida zoomed in and we saw the southern coast was still glowing with fires and plumes of white smoke. The upper atmosphere was filling slowly with fallout. The numbers there had updated to a new total.

"Two point seven million now, sir," Barrera said. "You've managed to lose millions more lives than I did with my sabotage attempt. Who do you think should be court-martialed?"

I felt a heavy pang of guilt. I'd managed not to think about Miami much up until now. In the middle of battle, a veteran didn't dwell on the dead. If you did, you were much more likely to join them.

"As I recall, the Macros killed those people, not me."

"No feelings about it at all, sir?"

"Of course I'm sick about it. But there will be time for grief later."

"I put to you Colonel, that you are undisciplined and unprofessional. You have been placed in a position beyond your capacities. You have overseen the deaths of many millions of humans, and possibly billions of other living creatures. South America is a wasteland. China will not recover for the better part of the next century. Every continent has lost major cities. Abroad, the Centaurs, Worms, Microbes and who knows what others have

262

all lost countless members of their species. We haven't formed a coherent coalition with any of them. We proceed from month to month, day to day in a random haphazard series of events, driven by your spur of the moment decisions."

I felt pain as his words rained down on me. "Sure, there have been losses," I said. "We are fighting a war unlike any in the history of our species. This isn't some organized parade-ground exercise. Losses are high, but we are still standing. We are not on our knees."

"But we are not winning, Colonel. We are losing ground. The last straw for me was when you restarted this war with an enemy we can't beat. I thought of the millions you'd consigned to death, and decided to take action—to take command."

I nodded, understanding perfectly. It was not entirely out of character. He'd never spoken about his feelings, he'd just taken action when he'd quietly decided to do so. It was so hard to tell what this man was thinking. Even now, he was as grim-faced and calm as ever.

"Millions have died," I said, "and I can't promise millions more will not follow them. I don't think freedom comes cheaply. Have you ever heard the expression 'when one man dies it is a tragedy, when millions die it is a statistic'?"

Barrera snorted at me. "Yes sir, but do you realize you are quoting Joseph Stalin?"

"Uh," I said, squinting. "Yes, right. But the point I'm trying to make is that the individual counts. I'd rather fight and die free than live as a slave. The Macros do not intend to allow us to survive. They intend to kill us all in time."

"But why do not have to make that decision today?"

"You shouldn't listen to this bullshit, Colonel," Kwon said suddenly.

I turned to Kwon. "I understand how you feel, First Sergeant. But if one of my senior staff turns on me, I at least have to know why."

"Let us evacuate to the mainland, sue for peace and work on our defenses," Barrera said.

I shook my head. "I've seen what peace with the Macros looks like. They will not allow us to build up, nor even to survive in the long term. They would demand the destruction of all threatening technology on Earth."

Barrera stared at me. "It's all about your ego, isn't it, sir? It's all about you."

I stared back. "I believe as did Frederick the Great of Prussia. He was a mini-napoleon in his time. He said most generals were inherently timid, but that a brave leader who was competent would always beat them. You have to be willing to take risks to win at the game of war."

"This is not a game, Colonel. Real lives are being lost out there. Your risks and mistakes have cost us too much."

"There is some truth to what you say," I said. "But no one else was there—only me. No one else was in the position to make these decisions. Right or wrong, they had to be made."

"I accept that, Colonel," Barrera said. "But I just don't think you are the best man for the job."

"And so we come down to it. I am forced to order your imprisonment, court-martial and eventual execution."

"I understand, sir," Barrera said.

I could see by his eyes that he did. I could also see that he was troubled. He looked back to the screens where the next phase of the battle was unfolding. Kwon moved forward to restrain Barrera, but I waved him back. He shadowed the disgraced Lieutenant Colonel's every move.

"Colonel," Major Sarin said quietly. "Our tanks are engaging the enemy now."

I flicked my eyes quickly back to the overhead screens. The hovertanks were firing now. They were all hitting the big dreadnaught, just as I'd ordered. The enemy fleet was beginning to respond, to turn on them. The British missiles were only a few minutes from impacting. They'd reached the apogee of their flight and were now coming back down into the atmosphere.

The enemy cruisers took notice of our hovertanks after their first dozen strikes against their protective dreadnaught. Forty-odd cannons swiveled to fire down upon the smaller craft that scooted around over the waves below them.

The dreadnaught had been damaged earlier, when it had been hit by the U. S. missiles. But it was huge, and I wasn't sure if my tanks with their relatively light guns could bring it down.

"Two hovercraft have been hit, Colonel," Major Sarin reported. "...six hit...seven."

"Keep them on target. Take out the dreadnaught's forward point-defense pods as primary targets. Secondarily, take out the enemy engines."

The battle raged. The British missiles were less than a minute away. Everyone's eyes were locked on the screen. Only Major Sarin tapped at the screen. The rest of us watched fixedly.

"We've lost forty percent of our hovertanks," Major Sarin said, somehow keeping her voice even. "Due to losses, command has switched from Major Feng to Lieutenant Koslov. The new commander is requesting an order for an orderly withdrawal."

"What have we done to that dreadnaught?" I asked.

"One of the four defensive pods is knocked out, two more damaged. Of six identified engine ports, three are damaged. Other hits have been scored all over the hull, but it is not known if this damage has reduced the enemy vessel's effectiveness."

I glanced at Barrera. I could tell he'd pull back the hovertanks. I tried not to let that fact alter my judgment in any way. It was more difficult than usual. Part of me wanted to show him how these things were done—but the rest of me wanted to save the tanks and their crews to prove I wasn't a wild-eyed madman.

I took a deep breath. No! I thought. I had to think clearly about victory. Barrera didn't matter. I looked back to the screens and thought hard. If we took down that ship, the ship-killer missiles would do great damage to the fleet and probably save Star Force. Perhaps that was self-serving, but really we represented the majority of Earth's defensive capacity. Most importantly, we had the only known versions of Nano factories on the planet. If they wiped those out, the rest of Earth would be reliant on centuries-behind technology and wouldn't stand a chance against the Macros. They wouldn't be able to build a single ship that could stand up to the machines.

"Order Lieutenant Koslov to continue the attack until his unit is down to ten percent effectiveness."

Major Sarin hesitated, glancing at me. Our eyes met, and then she looked back down and relayed the orders. Both of us knew we'd just consigned those brave men to death.

Barrera let out an audible sigh. I knew how he felt, but I couldn't worry about that now. The hovertanks were the last asset I had in the region that could take out that big ship. I could request that Fleet assault the dreadnaught, but even if Crow did listen to me, I didn't want to make that move. I wanted my fleet of ships to survive until the end of this. I would much rather lose the hovertanks than lose my ships. Such was the harsh calculus of war.

"Sir!" Major Sarin shouted, pointing toward a screen depicting the enemy fleet in close-up.

The big dreadnaught was in trouble. Something inside it was burning. I heard a surge of excitement from upstairs. Marines in battle suits stomped their boots. I watched, drawing back my lips from my teeth in a tense grimace.

The big ship reared up and began to climb. It was increasing its altitude. Was it dodging the British missiles, having calculated it couldn't shoot them all down? I could see now the missiles were converging on it. At least half the incoming contacts were headed just for that one ship.

It rose up and up, higher than the highest clouds. As forty miles up, it was well beyond the reach of my hovertanks.

"Order Koslov to scatter and retreat," I said.

We watched as a few missiles got close and set themselves off with suicidal spherical explosions in the high atmosphere.

"Get Crow on the command channel," I ordered.

"Riggs, we're on station here, but the Macros don't seem to be firing at England just now. Lucky pommies."

Pommies? I wondered, but didn't have time to ask about Aussie slang just now. "Crow, hit that big ship. Don't let it get away. It's limping now, leaving its protective cruisers. Finish it off."

"You know, mate, I'm going to do this one for you. I think you're beginning to understand how to use a force like ours. We're light cavalry, see? We're mostly good for running down the peasants after they break."

Crow began another of his nasty laughs, but I cut him off.

Barrera watched the battle in interest. I stared at him for a moment, wondering what I should do. We didn't have laws in place yet—martial punishments for crimes. But attempted

266

assassination of one's commanding officer? Tradition was pretty clear on that one.

Barrera finally noticed me eyeing him. He turned and faced me. "May I make a final request, sir?"

"What's that?"

"I'd like to man the turret on the eastern wall when the machines hit us again."

"We've abandoned that wall. Every defensive position has been evacuated."

"Exactly, sir."

I thought about it. The marines would watch my second in command go down in a blaze of glory. It would be better for morale than putting him up in front of a firing squad.

Finally, I nodded to him. "Good luck, Barrera."

"Good luck, sir."

We shook hands. As he headed for the door, I turned to Kwon and Sandra, who both looked skeptical.

"You two make sure he gets there."

"Will do, sir," Kwon said.

-40-

The second battle for Earth didn't end the way I'd expected. Barrera made a fine last stand, but that part didn't really surprise me. He wasn't exactly a dishonorable man, he was someone who was so dedicated to the cause he'd decided to take matters into his own hands. In some ways, I could understand that. I'd made similar decisions against the U. S. government in the past. I wondered to myself how I would react if I had been playing second banana to someone I disagreed with all these years. Someone like Crow, perhaps. Maybe I would have gotten ideas, over time. After watching my C. O. make mistakes that killed off millions, I could imagine deciding the time had come to act. I might even have become fed up enough to move against my commander.

I hadn't excused Barrera, but I had allowed him to choose his own form of execution. He died on the walls inside a beam turret that had already been knocked out several times over the preceding days. The nanites had rebuilt it after every assault, because they could repair a turret clamshell much faster than the twisted fleshy part inside. After we'd had to scrape the remains of several marines from the eastern turret, the one that faced the sea and the big bombarding cruisers, we'd abandoned the eastern wall entirely. Manning that wall was quick, messy suicide.

We'd all expected Barrera to be taken out by a cruiser cannon, but it didn't turn out that way. The enemy fleet in fact did not participate in the last of the battle for Andros Island. Crow had seen to that, along with the brave pilots of nearly two hundred hovertanks and several barrages of ship-killing missiles. Once the enemy dreadnaught broke and ran, the battle went our way. Crow chased the dreadnaught, burning the wounded ship with hundreds of stinging laser cannons. Our Fleet swarmed the mighty vessel, taking out its defensive armament first, then beginning the lengthy process of disemboweling the ship one system at a time. I thought about ordering marines to fly in to attack, but in the end didn't bother. Why risk losing men in the final blossoming explosion?

Macro Command seemed to realize their control of the skies had been broken. Without the dreadnaught to protect them from our missiles, they were doomed. The last forty-one cruisers nosed upward and their engines flared blue. They left Earth behind. Another salvo of missiles followed the ships, dozens of them closing in from dozens of directions. The missiles never caught up with the ships, but they did give them a nice send-off and prevented them from changing their minds.

Marveling at the number of missiles the militaries of Earth had fired, I had to hand it to Kerr and the rest, they'd distributed what technology they could. Perhaps it had been the example the Chinese set years ago that convinced their governments. They had managed to bring down one of the invaders on that occasion. Since nothing else they could build had ever proven effective, they dumped their budgets into long range ship-killers with low-yield tactical nukes aboard. Preventing the proliferation of nuclear missile technology was no longer an issue amongst the rulers of Old Earth. Survival of the species was all any government cared about now. Lines on maps meant little when entire continents were being off-handedly erased from those same maps by alien invaders. I recalled reading that President Reagan had once said the world would only unite in peace if invaded by aliens. Perhaps, in the end, he had been proven correct.

Back on Andros, our problems weren't over with. Far from it. The enemy machines, now that their fleet support was gone, had nothing to lose. They rose up en masse, big and small, to storm our battered walls.

There, ready to meet them, sat Lieutenant Colonel Barrera in his clamshell turret. The same turret that had been destroyed three times over the last few days. He fired and fired, quickly killing a dozen of the smaller machines. When a big one finally showed up—an invasion monster severely damaged by my hunter-killer platoons—it came from the sea, dragging two useless legs behind it. Barrera engaged it immediately as it crested above the waves, firing for a third leg. With less than four, it couldn't hope to get over our walls and thus would be effectively out of the fight. Sensing the danger, the enemy Macro engaged him in return. Hot metal melted on both sides until the clamshell was burnt black, but still Barrera kept pouring laser fire into the enemy's last vulnerable leg on the left side. The leg went down at last, and the Macro listed to one side, sinking back to the sea with a hissing plume of steam.

Immobile now, but still armed, the big machine relentlessly pounded upon Barrera's turret until the projector shattered and the turret itself was reduced to glowing slag. My marines glided out into the surf and used a few low-yield grenades to finish the machine, but it had done its work. Barrera had been executed.

The battle raged on for hours, but became one-sided when Crow's fleet returned and sat above the base, stabbing beams down into the enemy machines. With my marines working grenades and arm-mounted projectors and a hundred ships darkening the skies, the Macros were finally outgunned. Lieutenant Koslov rolled in with the surviving hovertanks, providing us a mobile strong point. In the end, he did a slow rotation around the base, clearing out the last of the struggling enemy.

The death toll was grim on our side as well. We'd lost more than a thousand marines on foot, battle suits or no. Hundreds more had died in turrets, hovertanks and even a few aboard our spacecraft. But for all of that, my weary men gave a ragged cheer when victory was declared. We were exhausted, but successful.

* * *

I woke up hours after the battle had ended. I startled awake, and felt disoriented. In my dreams, fresh assassins stalked me. Silver-eyed men that were half-Macro and half-human. I shook my head, unclamped my helmet and gulped cool air.

I was stretched across three chairs in the mess hall on the third floor of the command bunker. There was wet sand, blood and bits of crumbling nanite metals all over the floor. Many of the wounded had been brought here, as it was relatively safe. Now that the battle was over, they recuperated in the dimly lit chamber, sipping drinks and watching the clean up on the wall-screens.

I turned my head around slowly. It was good to know all these men were loyal. I smiled slightly. That was the best gift Barrera had given me personally. By confessing his guilt and taking the honorable way out, he'd left me assured for now that I wasn't being hunted—at least not by anything human.

Sandra walked up to me and crouched to kiss me.

"Morning," I said.

"It's two a. m."

"Close enough," I said, struggling into a sitting position. I groaned as I did so.

Sandra pushed me back down, gently but firmly. I suddenly realized why I was here. I'd been injured in the fighting. I could tell by the burning sensation in my abdomen.

I let her push me down again and forced myself to relax.

"Can you buy me a drink?" I asked.

She put something up to my lips, and I slurped on a straw. I'd been hoping for alcohol, but I was disappointed. It was syrupy and yellow-green, but at least it was ice-cold.

I struggled to get up again. This time, I made it into a sitting position. "Help me get up," I said.

"No."

"I'll just use my suit and fly down there."

Sandra made a face. She heaved and I was quickly lifted into a standing position. I made my way stiffly down to the command post. Major Sarin was there, looking concerned.

"Sir, you shouldn't be—" she began.

I waved away her words. "Save it," I said. "Sandra's already tried to get me to lie down. I've done too much of that already."

I checked the screens. I didn't like what I saw. The Macro ships had not retreated to Venus, as I'd hoped. Instead, they were lingering in high orbit, over a hundred thousand miles out. Doubtlessly, they believed Earth's ship-killer missiles could not reach them there. And they were right. None of the ICBMs I was aware of were capable of reaching escape velocity and leaving Earth's orbit.

"Where's Fleet?" I asked.

"Grounded, sir. They are down on Andros with us, effecting repairs."

I mumbled something about chicken admirals and tried to think. As long as these cruisers were still in the system we weren't out of danger yet. I shifted my attention to the Tongue of the Ocean, the undersea playground our Macro friends had decided to turn into a breeding ground. I frowned as I saw several green contacts moving around down there.

"What are those?"

"Subs, sir," Jasmine said. "They've been nuking the seabed. They found the enemy factories. Apparently, their domes don't work properly that far down underwater. U. S. British, French and Russian subs have destroyed their production capacity."

I made an appreciative, low whistle. "That's very thoughtful of them. They must have been building up sub support in the area while we fought the Macros. Makes sense. They were effective against the early missile barrage."

"Either that," Sandra said, "or they've always been out there, lurking around, waiting for a weak moment on our part."

I looked at her. "Waiting for a good moment to slip onto Andros and grab our factories?"

"Exactly."

I nodded slowly. I didn't like her theory, but it was a realistic one. In any case, I was happy to have the help. It was quite a change, not having to do everything to defend Earth. Star Force had needed help this time, and the governments of Earth had backed us up. I wouldn't forget that. In a way, it healed over some of the wounds from their earlier attempts to take us out of the picture.

I returned my attention to the higher ground. We appeared to be mopping up on Earth, but we did not yet rule the entire Solar System. I stared at the enemy cruisers. They could not be allowed to sit out there, to fester.

"Get Admiral Crow on the line," I ordered.

Eventually, I got him to answer my calls. He sounded like he'd been sleeping. Somehow, this pissed me off. Sure, it was two a. m., and he'd doubtlessly been awake for many hours. But it seemed wrong that he'd be taking a break now while our home space was still full of enemy ships.

"Crow? Get to your ship, man. Get all your crews to their ships. I'll be sending along marines to board all of them, too. The freshest men I have."

"Uh…what are you on about, Riggs?"

"What do you think I'm on about?" I demanded. "We've got forty-one Macro cruisers hanging out there, no doubt waiting for reinforcements to come and support them so they can start the next assault. We have the advantage now, and I mean to press it home. We're flying out there and chasing them out of our system."

"Don't you ever take a break, mate?"

"No."

-41-

In the end, we didn't mount the pursuit until the next day. By then, I was yawning and getting tired of Crow's complaints.

"There's no real need for this, Kyle. We've driven them off. Let's build up everything we can and chase them when we've got two hundred ships. We'll take lower losses that way."

"And if enemy reinforcements show up at Venus?" I asked.

"We'll launch the minute that happens. I promise you."

I thought about it. There was some logic to Crow's caution, but I didn't like it. We needed to get out there and put our minefield back into place to stop the next invading force. Next time, they wouldn't conveniently go for Andros Island. They'd come at Earth without any reservations.

We were having an early breakfast, and dawn hadn't yet broken over the ocean outside. Crow was having a stack of overly-syrupy waffles while I stirred my fork in an omelet packed with big Caribbean shrimp.

"We can't afford to wait, Crow," I told him.

"I'll have another squadron of nine destroyers out in a week or so, mate. At least wait for that."

"Right now, the cruisers can't do much against our fleet. Those cannons are showy, but they can be dodged. They're really only good for planetary bombardment. Our lasers outrange them and we're more maneuverable, too."

"They've still got missiles left," Crow argued. "We've calculated the numbers carefully over here at Fleet—yes, we can do sums. We figure they've kept around four hundred missiles in reserve. That's enough to do a lot of damage to my light ships."

I grimaced. Crow was right on this point. Four hundred missiles were enough to wipe out our entire force. We couldn't shoot down that many coming at us all at once.

"Very unlikely," I said. "If you count a standard allotment of sixteen missiles on each ship and they'd fired only half, you'd be right. But they've fired more than half of them. Besides, if they had so many in their magazines, why haven't they used them up until now?"

"Did you think they might have been waiting for this very situation, Kyle?" Crow asked me intently. "They know the missiles are their only real ship-to-ship weapon. Once they fire the last ones, they are helpless."

I nodded, he had me there. Looking back on their behavior, they'd fired their weapons in percentages. The first barrage was around half our estimated total. The secondary barrages had been much smaller. From what I could tell now, they probably had one to two hundred shots left. Enough to be a serious threat to our fleet.

I shook my head after mulling for a while. "Good arguments," I said. "But we still need to kick them out of the system. I can't start rebuilding our space defenses until they do. Their next fleet could roll right in and finish us any day."

Crow looked stubborn. His red cheeks bulged and his heavy brows knitted together as he chewed his breakfast. I could tell at a glance he was going to argue for the rest of the morning. It was time to throw him a bone.

"Admiral, I've got another concern you can help me with," I said.

Crow immediately narrowed his eyes in suspicion. He knew by now that if I called him 'admiral' I was buttering him up for something.

"What's that?" he asked.

"Only about half our factories at the main production base survived the invasion. I've been quite impressed by your hidden production facility under that pond up north. Do you think you could choose two quiet spots on the island, split up our factories into thirds and place them in equally well-hidden locations? I want access to all of them, of course. You'll have the same. But I really

275

think your system is superior. Rather than putting them all into an armed camp, hide them. If the enemy have no idea what to hit, they probably won't find any of them."

Crow smiled proudly and puffed up a bit as my words of praise for his skullduggery sunk in. "Glad you see the strategic benefit of my careful planning, Riggs," he said.

"We'll still keep the fortified production facility, but it will be empty."

"Ah, I like it. Two levels of deception. Keep them guessing."

"Exactly," I said, leaning over the table toward him and using my hands for emphasis. I could see I'd captured him by talking about one of his natural obsessions. Hiding valuables underground had been a favorite pastime of pirates throughout history. "We've got to get right on this one. In the long run, the factories are our most valuable asset. Everything else can be replaced quickly. We have to hide them now, before more Macros show up and hit us again."

Crow looked upset at the concept of fresh Macro forces arriving. I could tell he'd been thinking along the lines of most of Star Force. The general belief was that we'd won the round. That we'd earned a breather. But I knew differently. The enemy was still out there in strength. They might show up with two hundred more ships any day. We didn't have time to sit around.

"Problem though, mate," Crow said thoughtfully. "What about the Macros out there right now? They are monitoring us, watching us closely. Won't they see and record our digging? If they know where these new bases are, what's the bloody point of building them?"

"Hmm," I said, as if he'd come up with a concern I hadn't already considered. "I'll tell you what: I'll take care of that."

"You'll do what? Ah, hold on!"

"No, *you* hold on. I'll take the fleet out and push them from our system. You bury our factories where they'll never be found. Both jobs have to be done before they come at us again."

Crow sucked air through his teeth. He flashed me a dark look. I knew he suspected he'd been finessed, and he had, but he was having a hard time refuting my logic. The key to the whole thing was I'd given him an excuse to stay on Earth. He didn't want to lose command of his fleet, but he didn't want to die, either. If he

276

had a critical job to do on Earth, he could let me take the fleet into battle without looking like a coward. Even better, he wouldn't be risking his own skin.

"All right," he said at last. "I'm agreeing to this with reservations, mind you. And I will not appreciate it if you go up there and get my carefully built-up fleet blown out of the sky, mate."

I smiled at him. "Believe me Admiral, I don't want to lose a single ship."

"But you will," he grumbled.

I couldn't argue with him there. The odds were grim. I had a few tactical ideas, but I wasn't sure they would work out. What I was sure of was I couldn't wait around for the Macros to make the next move. We finally had the initiative, and I planned to force them to react to *me* for once.

In the end, he agreed to my plan. I had the keys to the fleet, and I had a smile on my face. As I headed straight for the landing pits, Sandra appeared at my side. She'd been gone for a while, I didn't ask why.

"Don't you want to know where I've been?" she asked.

"Um, sure."

She frowned at me for a long second. "You are the most frustrating man."

"But that's a good thing, right?"

"No."

"Just tell me where you've been and why you are upset."

She sighed. "I've been talking to Jasmine."

I stopped walking. We'd reached landing pit five. I had been on my way to number seventeen, but I paused to give Sandra a hard look.

"Is Jasmine—okay?" I asked her.

Sandra flapped her hands at me and pursed her lips as if my question was insulting. "Of course she is. I went there to apologize."

I nodded slowly, keeping all hints of shock off my face. "Ah," I said. I didn't say anything else, as I wasn't sure it was safe to do so.

"I told her I was wrong about her," Sandra went on. "She might have had feelings for you, but she wasn't trying to kill us. She was loyal. I was the fool."

"Really?" I asked. I allowed mild surprise to creep upon my face now, but kept my voice neutral. When the topic of Jasmine came up, I instinctively knew anything I said might be misinterpreted. I therefore let Sandra do all the talking.

"Yes, I should have found out about Barrera sooner," she said. "It's my job to protect you. My jealousy blinded me to any suspects other than Jasmine. It wasn't fair to her, and it was dangerous for you. I failed."

"Not in the end. In the end, you got your man. Jasmine was on my list of suspects too, and I'd have placed her higher than Barrera."

She looked at me quizzically. "Really?"

"Yes. Did you think you were the only one trying to figure it out?"

"I thought you didn't care."

I laughed and we started walking again, passing more landing pits. "Even I care when assassins jump me."

"Where are we going?" Sandra asked.

I stopped walking. We'd reached landing pit seventeen. I pointed to the sleek destroyer that waited there, being loaded with marines in battle suits and ordinance. Sandra followed my finger and her face fell.

"You're going out there, aren't you?" she asked. She sounded depressed and lost.

"Yeah. This is Captain Miklos' ship. He's a good man. I've flown with him before. We'll be fine."

"Yes, Miklos," Sandra said. She eyed the ship the way one might eye a giant shark in a tank. "He was the one that flew you up to talk to the Macros."

"Exactly. I'll be fine while flying with him."

She looked at me intently. She reached out a hand and clamped it onto my arm. "Kyle, I don't want you to go up there today."

"I'll be fine," I chuckled. I wiggled my arm slightly, but she held on. "Miklos and his crew are experienced fliers."

278

She shook her head. "You can't fool me. You're not going up there to fly around and shoot some lasers at the enemy. You're going to jump out of the ship and do crazy things."

"I can't take you with me this time," I told her gently. I tried to pluck her hand off my arm. It didn't budge. Her fingers were like the steel cables of a three-fingered nanite hand.

"I don't want to go with you. I want you to stay home."

I sighed. How many marines had a conversation like this with his woman? I understood her feelings, but I had to go. I hugged her, and it was the right move. After a long time, she finally melted against me. Her flesh no longer felt like a piece of metal, but like the shapely young woman she was.

"How long until you leave me?" she whispered.

"We'll be loaded and flying in five hours. Less, maybe."

"That's long enough."

"For what? Oh...."

She led me to a private place amongst the tents, rubble and newly erected buildings. It was amazing how fast Star Force could rebuild after a battle. A big part of the magic was the smart metal and the nanites, of course. They rebuilt structures by themselves, often without any instructions from us. Left to their own devices, nanites tended to return to their last remembered configuration. When the wounds were too great, however, they had left holes in the smart metal, gaps that couldn't be troweled over without the addition of fresh barrels of nanites. The walls in particular had suffered. There were big gaping holes here and there in the outer barrier and on top of the ramparts. Wet earth, blackened by scorching heat, showed through the silvery planes of metal here and there.

Sandra and I made love between two new buildings. One of them contained a generator, and the fusion process hummed loudly enough to provide a little cover noise. Still, I suspected that passersby might have heard something. If they did, none of them were rude enough to poke their noses into our hideaway and discover us.

We could have gone back to our new quarters, or found an empty room deep inside the headquarters bunker. But she had led me here, and I didn't object. I had to wonder if she had found this place while lurking around the base. She did a lot of lurking.

I enjoyed her soft skin the most. The blue sky above was second. Making love in daylight under a clear sky was always invigorating. She was almost desperate in her love-making. She often behaved this way when I was leaving her, possibly for the last time.

I enjoyed every second of it.

-42-

When I boarded *Barbarossa*, I was in an excellent mood. Captain Miklos' destroyer still had the gleaming interior of a freshly built ship. The walls and particularly the floor of any smart-metal hull were impossible to stain, but crews invariably added their own furnishings over time and that made them more homey. Barbarossa looked like it had been built yesterday, as the crew had had no time to settle in.

The crew greeted me with cautious enthusiasm. They had emerged from the recent battles with the Macros unscathed. As a Star Force marine, I felt slightly jealous of these Fleet people. They had no appreciation for the grim combat my men had endured in the dirt, ashes and blood that was the battle for Andros from our perspective. I took solace in the knowledge that they were going to be encountering the Macros much more closely in the near future.

Captain Miklos' crew was the same as I'd left it days earlier. The gunner still appeared to be the most nervous of the lot, while the helmsman barely made eye-contact. Miklos himself seemed honored I'd requested to fly with him again. I sincerely hoped he wouldn't be disappointed by the end of our journey.

Kwon loaded sixteen grunts on after me. I stood in the bridge, watching them take their jump seats in the troop pod located directly below the bridge section, in the belly of the lower deck. Right behind the marines were the engines, and right below them was empty space. The floor was designed to flash open, just as the nanite floors had done to me and my kids years ago when I first encountered the Nanos. I followed the men into the troop pod and gave them a short pep talk. I told them this was really the sweet spot in the ship. If anything went wrong, they would die instantly—a blessing in the grim environment of space. No one wanted to hang around out there waiting to suffocate or burn up when their personal orbit decayed.

When I was finished, only Kwon seemed to be cheered up. The rest gave me a 'hooah', but I sensed their morale wasn't a hundred and ten percent. I chalked it up to a general need for a break we weren't going to get. These men needed a few weeks of R&R, but as far as I was concerned, that was going to have to wait until there wasn't an enemy robot within a lightyear of Earth.

I returned to the bridge and took my seat behind Captain Miklos. The crewmen glanced at me now and then, but looked away quickly when I returned the scrutiny. I wondered as we lifted off if they were still thinking about the time I'd taken over their ship and threatened to shoot their captain. To me, that was all water under the bridge. We were all in this together, and we would live or die as a team today.

When the mass of ships had risen up and gathered in a loose formation about a hundred miles above Andros, I ordered the fleet to swing around the planet once to gather momentum, and also to possibly throw off the Macros as to our intent.

"We'll get up to just over escape velocity," I told the captains on a joint channel, "then slingshot ourselves toward high orbit. With any luck, we'll catch them sitting there and have a good combat-pass before they know what hit them."

The kind of combat I intended would be enhanced by a stationary or slow-moving enemy. Getting in close to the Macros was going to be difficult with their massed firepower and unknown supplies of missiles. Getting in close was a requirement for my attack plan, which consisted of harassing the enemy ships with laser fire while covering the real assault, which would consist of around a thousand marines swarming the cruisers like tiny individual spacecraft. Once in close enough, my marines in their powered battle suits could maneuver to the enemy and hurl nuclear grenades at the hulls. If necessary, they could invade surviving

282

ships and destroy the Macro crews in detail. In my fantasies, some of the enemy craft might even be captured.

Before we'd made half of our initial orbit, however, my hopes were thrown out the window.

"Colonel?" Captain Miklos asked. "I'm getting reports, sir—yes, the enemy fleet is getting underway."

"Shit," I said. I slammed my fist down on the command chair. The metal shell of the chair was much thinner than my armored battle suit, and it gave way under the blow. I irritably yanked my fist out of the dent it had formed. Over the next minute or so, the smart metal rebuilt the armrest. Nanites were nothing if not dutiful.

I glared at the forward metallic-relief screens and occasionally eyed the normal computer-driven flat screen in front of my chair. They were definitely moving. They'd not been fooled in the slightest. I had to give these machines credit, they could do their math. They'd projected my likely trajectory. Each ounce of thrust that sped us toward them committed us to a shrinking array of objectives. The faster we went, the more easily they could predict where we were headed. Under no illusions, the Macros had reacted immediately rather than sitting and waiting to see just how we were going to hit them.

"Which way are they going?" I asked.

"Not conclusive yet, sir—but it looks like they are *not* heading toward us."

I looked at the helmsman in surprise. "Is that from your math? Let's see it on the boards. Project the likely enemy path on the screen."

"Yes, sir."

Soon I had my answer. The enemy were swinging around the Moon and out of the system. The odds were already eighty percent and ticking higher as they continued accelerating.

I frowned at the screen. "Zoom out," I said. "Continue the projection to its likely destination."

This took a few seconds. I squirmed in my command chair, waiting uncomfortably. Visions of an easy surprise victory were fast evaporating. I'd hoped the enemy didn't understand how dangerous my ships were. The key was my force of ship-storming marines, of course. We'd used similar boarding tactics against four macro cruisers recently, but since none of the enemy had survived, I'd hoped this fleet wouldn't suspect our intentions.

When the projections solidified I was even more surprised. "Are you kidding me? Why are they flying out there?"

The projected flight path of the enemy fleet didn't lead toward us. It didn't lead out toward Venus, either. I'd expected them to follow one of these two routes—either to attack us, or to retreat out of the system. But instead, the enemy was in full flight to the outer system.

"Show me what's out there," I said.

"It looks like they are heading for Jupiter," Captain Miklos said.

I shook my head, eying the path with growing concern. "No. They are heading for the Tyche ring. They are going to head to Alpha Centauri, then maybe Helios. Hell, who knows? They might be planning to knock out the Centaurs once and for all, since they failed against us."

Captain Miklos brightened considerably. So did the rest of his crew, as the curve of the enemy projected path continued to solidify and possibilities narrowed.

"You're right, Colonel," Miklos said. "They are heading for the Oort cloud ring. They are going to run right out of the system. We've run them off without a fight."

"Let's keep them running," I said. "Lay in a new course to follow the enemy fleet."

Captain Miklos looked startled. "Sir, might I suggest—"

"No," I said.

"But we've already achieved our mission. We could return to Earth orbit now, secure in the knowledge they are exiting the system. Perhaps they don't even know about our secondary minefield out there. Why not let the mines do their work?"

"Fortunately, I'm in command of this expedition," I said. "Follow them."

Without further argument, Miklos flew his ship after the Macros. A hundred other vessels glided silently through space after us.

I could tell Miklos was pissed off. I was too, but not at him. I wanted to crush the enemy ships while I had them at a disadvantage. For all I knew, they were moving to meet up with another task force. Together with reinforcements the Macros could easily take out my fleet. They knew that, and so did I. As it was now, the odds didn't lean very far in my favor.

The worst part of it was not knowing the enemy mindset. Were they running because they were uncertain about their success? Or because we'd become too expensive in terms of materials to defeat? Or did they have some kind of cold trick waiting for me farther out in space? I just didn't know, and not knowing ate at any commander.

We flew on for hours. Slowly, we were gaining on the enemy. We ran the numbers, and double-checked them. Our smaller ships were faster than their cruisers. We were going to catch them before they could reach the ring and fly through it.

"Maybe we should slow down, sir," Captain Miklos suggested.

I gave him a disgusted look.

"No, no, sir. I don't say this out of cowardice. I'm simply suggesting we let the enemy hit the minefield at the Tyche ring at full speed before we get into range to finish off their damaged ships."

I nodded. "A reasonable suggestion," I said. "Yes, the more I think about it, the more I like it. Helmsman, ease-off to three-quarters velocity and relay the command to the rest of the fleet. We'll hang back just a little and hope they don't know what they're running into."

The chase went on for two solid days. When the Macros finally reached the Tyche ring, they did something unexpected. They fired a barrage of missiles.

"Missiles launched!" shouted the weapons officer.

"Count?"

"About twenty, sir. Make that thirty."

"Scatter the fleet," I ordered.

"Second barrage sir, pulsed thirty seconds after the first."

"One mile between ships," I said. "Globular formation, relay and execute. How long do we have before they hit us?"

"No estimate yet, sir. But at this distance, we'll have less than half an hour."

I watched the screens tensely, as did every commander in the fleet. The battle monitors slowly filled with a crowded mass of tiny red contacts. The contacts finally moved a pixel, and I raised my eyebrows in surprise. The two clouds of missiles were not moving toward us.

"They didn't fire at us?"

"No sir," the weapons officer replied. "They seem to have fired—at the ring, sir."

I stared at the screens and frowned. I couldn't find any fault with the information I was receiving.

"They know about the mines," Captain Miklos said. His voice sounded dead and distant. I surmised he'd been hoping for an easy end to this.

"Yes," I agreed, reviewing the data. The enemy was laying down a blast pattern directly in front of their advancing ships. They intended to destroy the mines we had floating in a tight cluster around the Tyche ring. Either that, or they meant to blow up the ring itself.

In either case, I was less than happy.

"Increase our speed," I ordered. "Push the engines up to one hundred percent, and tighten up our formation again."

"Is that wise, sir?"

I looked at Miklos. I wanted to ask him what had happened to the bravado I'd witnessed in him the last time I'd been aboard his vessel. Perhaps that was the answer right there. We'd had some close calls last time I'd flown with him. Maybe he'd had time to think about his mortality and realize how close we'd come to destruction on that occasion. Or perhaps, he'd had a few bad moments serving under Crow when they'd chased down and taken out the dreadnaught. Fleet had lost some good crews that day. In any case, he'd become overly-cautious. It was a common enough problem among my new officers.

"We're going after them, Captain. Give the damned order."

He did so without further comment. I thought his face was slightly red over his beard. Perhaps he felt a little embarrassed by his hints that we should slow down. If that was the case, I was glad. The first step toward real bravery was to admit you were afraid of the enemy.

God knew this enemy was worthy of our fears.

-43-

The first barrage exploded just short of the ring, punching a hole in the minefield we had waiting for them in front of the opening. The second barrage charged through that pall of vapor and vanished. Presumably, those missiles exploded on the far side of the ring to destroy the twin minefield we had placed in the Alpha Centauri system. Macro Command had learned a thing or two about our tactics, and responded accordingly.

I now felt sure this was one of the reasons they'd managed their missile supplies so closely. They knew they needed the missiles to destroy our minefields, if nothing else. It was enough to make me grind my teeth in frustration. These Macro ships weren't dying. They were slipping away, and I knew that the further they got from Earth the greater the temptation would be to let them go, to allow them to leave us and slip away into the vast dark of space. The problem with that was they could return at any time, with fresh ships and fresh ideas on how to defeat us.

"Colonel," Captain Miklos said. "If we are going to slow down, or change course, we need to do it now."

I didn't look at him. I sighed instead. Things were not going as planned.

"Sir?" Miklos prompted. "Any orders? Or are we just going to blast right through after them?"

"I should have maintained my velocity."

"What?"

"I made a mistake," I said. I didn't add *by listening to you*, but I was thinking it. "I should have caught them before they reached the ring and engaged them. Now, they've made it through the ring first. They could be laying mines in front of us on the far side."

Miklos looked alarmed. He nodded, acknowledging the possibility. "They could be," he agreed. "Or maybe they will hit the brakes, wait for us to zoom through, and fire every missile they have left into our faces."

I nodded slowly, but gave no orders.

"Decelerate, Colonel," Miklos said urgently. "We'll pull up to the ring and send through a few scouting ships. When we know the situation on the far side, we can fly after them safely—if that is the best course."

I drummed armored fingers on the command chair. Metal struck metal in a repeating pattern, making a rhythmic, ringing sound. The helmsman turned and frowned at me in irritation. I ignored him. The drumming helped me think.

"No," I said at last. I stopped drumming, and watched the helmsman relax in visible relief.

"Helmsman, reduce speed by ten percent. Relay that to the fleet. Tighten up the formation more. We'll fly through in a column."

"Fly through, sir?" Captain Miklos asked nervously. "I thought we—"

"You thought wrong, Captain. I know the Macros. I know how they think. If they want to ambush us, they'll do it by firing a barrage in our faces. They'll do it by timing us, so we can't get out of the way. Slowing down by ten percent will make us hit the ring several minutes late. Their missiles, if they fire any, will come through the ring to hit us at our last projected speed and course. If we don't see them show up, there aren't going to be any."

Miklos flopped back into his chair in defeat. He relayed the orders without further complaint. Did he think himself a doomed man with a mad commander? It was quite possible he was right on both counts.

"Let me explain myself, Captain," I said. "I know we are taking a risk, but the enemy can't be allowed to escape us if at all possible. This force of cruisers knows our tactics. They may well do a great deal of damage to our biotic friends in the Helios and

288

Eden systems. Almost as importantly, we have to press home the advantage we have now. I don't want to fight these ships again as part of a larger force at a later date. I don't want them to rearm, form up with another dreadnaught, or even report home. I want to knock them out while they are weak. I want to get the most we can out of this victory."

"We've driven them from our home system," Captain Miklos said reasonably. "Isn't that enough?"

"No. It really isn't. We need more. We need to hurt them, and we must take risks to do so. We are the underdogs in this war, Captain. Don't ever doubt it. Possibly, the entire affair is hopeless. What if they have thousands of systems and millions of ships? Perhaps we are fleas on a T-Rex."

"What's the point then, in that case?"

I shrugged. "We don't know the truth. But I'm pretty sure they are stronger than we are, far stronger. In order to have a chance, we have to get lucky. You get lucky by going for opportunities when they present themselves. I think the destruction of this enemy task force is just such an opportunity. I've read every book I can find on strategy lately—including the writings of many historical figures on the subject, from Caesar, to Napoleon, to Sun Tzu. We must turn this marginal victory into a decisive one. Not only to hurt the enemy's fleet, but to worry them. The Macros are conservative, and they like to attack with overwhelming force. They might not attack again for years after this beating, convinced we are stronger than we really are."

"All right sir," Miklos said thoughtfully. "I understand your reasoning. But at some point we'll have to give up on killing them all if they keep escaping us. How far from Earth are you willing to go? Once we leave the system, we won't be able to tell what's happening behind us. More Macros could come back through the Venus ring and we wouldn't know we were needed back home."

"Hmm," I said, thinking it over. He had a good point. I quickly came up with a partial solution. "How about this? We'll leave a small ship behind at the ring. Their job will be to dash back and forth through it, every few hours. They can relay messages and scan both systems. If we do that at every ring we pass through, it won't cost us many ships, and will put us within a few days transmission time from several systems away."

He nodded appreciatively. "A pony express system?"

"Something like that," I said, smiling.

"They said you were inventive."

"They told me you were a hard-ass."

We both laughed and turned our attention back to the screen. We had just about reached the ring. The time came and passed when the enemy missiles should have showered through, trying to hit us in the face. I had just begun to smile, figuring I had Miklos on this one, when a mass of contacts did appear.

"Evasive action, sir?" the helmsman asked, his voice cracking.

"How many are there?"

"Sixteen, sir."

"Decelerate! Shoot them down!"

My hundred-odd ships all began firing at once. This time, we were playing the part of the Macro vanguard, leading the way at the head of a column of ships into the unknown. Beams slashed out from hundreds of projectors. The missiles popped one after another, but two got through. There were no direct hits, but the explosions buffeted our destroyer when they went off nearby. I could see by the boards we'd lost at least one small ship—and then everything on the screens vanished and reset.

"We're going through the ring, sir!"

"I feel it."

I hadn't even had time to assess fleet damage. We'd have to figure that out on the far side of the ring. As always it sent a thrill through my body like an electric shock to know I was traveling across lightyears of space in an instant. When we came out on the other side of the ring, however, we got the biggest surprise of the voyage.

"Enemy ships sir!" the helmsman all but screamed.

I scanned the screens in irritation. Of course there were enemy ships. What did the young officer think we had been chasing?

But then I saw the panels shift and shimmer. The new system leapt into life. The three stars were there, Alpha, Beta and the distant, dim red dwarf known as Proxima Centauri. None of this was surprising. What did shock me were the number of enemy ships that quickly populated the scene. There were somewhere around two hundred of them, plus clouds of what could only be debris—fragments of destroyed spacecraft.

"What the hell?" I asked no one. My mind leapt to a dozen conclusions, none of them good.

"The Macros must have known they had supporters out here," Captain Miklos said. "They weren't running from us, they were luring us into a trap."

"Trap?" I asked. "There are a lot of blown-up ships here."

"Maybe our mines took some of them out as they passed through."

None of it made sense to me. Things looked bad, but I refused to panic.

"Are we under fire?"

"No sir, no reports of incoming fire. Our ships have locked on the nearest alien vessels—they are quite small, sir."

"Hold your fire," I ordered the gunner. "Relay that, helmsman."

"But sir—"

"Show me the configuration of the new ships," I demanded. "What are we facing?"

"They are considerably smaller than any Macro ships we've ever encountered."

"Put one up on the damned screen," I told him. "Give me a close-up."

The new enemy ships finally came into sight. There was a large wing of them moving after the Macro Cruisers. They looked vaguely like the old NASA shuttlecrafts to me, but a bit larger. They had stubby wings and a pointed snout. They were clearly designed for atmospheric travel as well as voyaging in space.

I squinted at the vessels. The lines were unmistakable.

"That's a Worm ship!" I shouted. I whooped for joy, and the crew looked at me as if I were mad. "Show me more, what are they doing?"

Data poured in and the reports were *good*. All good. The Worms had nearly two hundred vessels. They were all small, but they were pursuing the fleeing Macro cruisers and firing on them. I shook my head in amazement. They'd been busy. I had to admit, of all the people's I'd met in space so far, these creatures impressed me the most. They'd never even considered surrender or peace agreements. They simply fought the Macros and they'd died in their millions, but the moment they'd been given a breather they were back at it, putting up an offensive fleet rather than focusing purely on defense and rebuilding their lost cities. If anything, they were even tougher than we were.

Fortunately, I had had the foresight to transfer translation neural patterns from Marvin for all known species into every brainbox in the fleet. Our ships could talk to these aliens. But I knew from experience such translations were not that simple. The symbolic pictographs of the Worms and the idiomatic poetry of the Centaurs were challenging mediums, even after you had established a means of communication.

The Worms were particularly challenging to communicate with. They used images to communicate remotely and sculptures to communicate in person. They were tactile, rather than audio or optical in their conversations. When using radio communications, they'd fortunately developed a simplified set of pictographic symbols to express ideas. They weren't words, exactly, but rather images that conveyed concepts. When combined together, they communicated meaning. It was rather like having a pen pal who only understood Egyptian hieroglyphs.

"Barbarossa," I said, addressing the ship directly. "I need to open up a channel to the Worm ships."

"Clarification required: *Worm ship*. Please define."

"Scan the nearby vessels. Many of the smaller ships are not Star Force ships, nor do they meet the definition known as Macro cruisers. These ships are known to us as Worm ships."

"Definition complete. Associations established."

"Good," I said pausing for a moment to think. "We need to transmit something to them. Access your data on translations of English into Worm pictographs."

"A one-to-one translation of human speech into Worm pictographs is not possible. It is suggested—"

"Yeah, yeah," I said, interrupting in annoyance. "Believe me, I know all about it. I need the pictograph for hunting together— some kind of fat, sliced-grub thing. Send that along with the images for machine and destruction."

Captain Miklos looked at me with a bloodless face. We were in the domain of new aliens, and I sensed this crew felt out of their depth. Well, that was just too bad. You had to pick things up quickly in space—either that, or you died.

292

"Symbol group selected," *Barbarossa* said. "Transmitting."

"Let me know when you get a response from them."

There were perhaps thirty long seconds to wait. During that time, much of my fleet had flown through the ring after me. They came in two or three abreast and advanced quickly after us. We were not yet in firing range. I squirmed in my chair, and my armor *squinked* as I did so, the cringe-worthy sound of metal rasping against metal.

"Incoming repeating message from Worm ships: grub, machine, destruction."

"Good," I said in relief. "Accelerate to full speed, helmsman. Relay to the fleet, we are going to chase down those Macros and engage them. No one is to fire upon a Worm ship without authorization. Maybe with luck, we can catch some or all of the Macros before they reach the far side of this system."

I wanted to get into the fight, but it was going to take some time. We'd slowed down before plunging through the ring, and that delay had cost us a lot of momentum. Even with our faster ships, we'd have to accelerate hard for days to catch up and join the running battle.

Captain Miklos leaned toward me and eyed my screen. "What the heck do those symbols mean, Colonel?"

"The grub means hunting, a team interaction. The machine symbol clearly refers to the Macros. Destruction indicates we are going to destroy the machines. The Worms communicate differently than we do. Did you attend the officer's briefing on alien cultures?"

"Yes, of course, sir," Miklos said, leaning back into his own chair. "But it isn't every day you meet a new alien species."

"Well, get used to it," I told him.

We pursued, watching the two groups of aliens fight it out ahead of us. We were all heading toward the next ring, which linked the Alpha Centauri system to Aldebaran system, the home system of the Worms. Frequently, the Worms made passes at the Macros, harassing and skirmishing with the larger ships. I grinned broadly. Having allies made the universe a brighter place.

It took time for our sensors to figure out everything we were looking at in a new system after crossing through a ring. The distances were immense, and some of the ships presented little or no radar signature. They were only visible when they fired weapons and could thus be counted optically by our sensors and the brainboxes connected to them. After an hour, we had hard numbers. The Worms had started with two hundred and seven ships when we'd entered the system. The Macros had started out with forty-one cruisers. At this point, the Macros were down to thirty-four ships, while the Worms had a hundred and seventy-nine ships left.

Calculating the loss ratios, I realized the Worms were only barely on the winning side thus far. The Macro cannons were taking their toll each time the Worms drove in close to hit them in a sweeping pass. On two occasions as we watched, the Macros fired two barrages of eight missiles. In each case, a few Worm ships were caught and destroyed by the missiles. The Macros were clearly holding back their firepower, and the enemy cruisers only fired their last weapons when they were too badly damaged to keep up with the rest of the pack.

The tactics of the Worms were effective and impressive. They would make a strafing pass, firing at a particular cruiser at the rear of the formation. Targeting the engines, they sought to damage and slow the vessel. When a doomed cruiser lagged behind the protective cover of its fellow it fired its last salvo at its tormentors. Immediately afterward, the cruiser would be set upon by the Worm ships. Like a cloud of swarming piranha, the Worm ships tore the straggler apart.

The Worm weapons were unlike anything I'd ever seen. They appeared to be particle-beam systems. Gushes of hard radiation flared lavender as we watched from afar. The guns seemed effective, but the beams moved at less than the speed of light and didn't have anywhere near the range that our lasers had. Still, after witnessing their power, I was impressed. If a Worm ship got in close to one of our laser vessels, I had no doubt their ship would win the duel. That was the trick, though—they had to get in close. We calculated their effective range at about twenty percent of the distance our own weapons could reach.

"Just like back home on their homeworld," I remarked to Captain Miklos. "The Worms like short-ranged, hard-hitting weapons. If we showed them a sawed-off shotgun, I bet they'd heartily approve of the design."

294

Captain Miklos nodded, staring intently at the screens. "The Worms are taking serious losses. Are they always this—vicious?"

"Pretty much, yeah," I said. "But remember, they have good reasons. This fleet is heading away from Earth, but its flying *toward* their system. They are fighting to defend Helios, not just to help us out."

"Ah, right. This is fascinating, sir. Do you ever wonder how many civilizations there are out there? How many races like the Worms or abominations like the Macros might exist?"

"All the time, Captain. All the time."

"Sirs," the gunner interrupted. "There's a new unknown contact out there."

"Why didn't you pick it up until now?" I snapped.

"The ship has been hanging low, below the plane of the ecliptic," the gunner explained. "It hasn't been firing or using visible thrusters. It's been shadowing all the other ships. I only just picked it up now."

"Great, a fourth player at this party," I grumbled. I didn't like this news at all. We had this battle in hand. In time, the enemy would be taken apart ship by ship. Once we were able to join in the battle, we'd speed up the process. The enemy would either have to turn and make a last stand like a wounded bear brought down by a pack of wolves, or they would be torn apart bit by bit. Any new elements to the equation were not welcome.

It was several minutes before the brainbox interpreting the data gave us input on the ship's configuration.

"Uh, it looks like one of ours, sir," the gunner told me in surprise. "Either that, or it's an odd Nano-ship design."

I leaned forward. "Put a close-up on my screens."

The gunner deftly tapped at his boards and my screen lit up with an odd wireframe image in yellow. Green was for known friendlies, red for enemy, blue for structures and yellow for unknowns. Barbarossa's brainbox didn't know how to classify this vessel any more than I did. I looked at the lines of it, puzzled. It had curves in the center, in a pattern similar to our own vessels. But it had a large number of oddments hanging off it—almost like they'd been tacked on. Metal struts, parabolic dishes, chunks of metal that appeared to have no obvious purpose.

"What's all that crap hanging on it?" Captain Miklos asked. "Is it a junkyard hauler?"

I smiled suddenly.

"Sort of," I said. "He probably picked up a load of broken pieces from the debris we just flew through. He wouldn't be able to help himself. Chunks blasted off Worm ships—those would be especially enticing."

"What?" Miklos asked, looking at me as if I were mad.

"It's Marvin," I explained. "It has to be."

-44-

"That crazy robot couldn't resist a pile of alien junk if it meant his own doom," I explained to the bemused captain. "He caught the curiosity gene somehow when he was born. He's got it bad. Maybe it was passed down by the Nanos who formed his original nanite brain."

"*Born*, sir? He's a machine, isn't he?"

"Yeah, you're right. Maybe born is the wrong word. His creation was an accident, to be sure. But couldn't that be said of most of us?"

Captain Miklos gave me a strange, sidelong glance. I ignored him and smiled at the yellow wireframe sketch of Marvin. In a strange way, I was glad to see he'd survived this long. Here he was, cruising around the Alpha Centauri system picking up more junk. He was part genius and part homeless guy with a shopping cart.

"Let's contact him and see what he has to say for himself," I said. "Barbarossa, open a channel to the unknown ship. Its designation is *Marvin*. You can use standard English when communicating. Transmit my voice without interpretation."

"Channel request sent...request accepted..." the ship said. After a few more moments, it spoke again. "Channel open."

"Marvin, you mechanical weasel," I said. "This is your daddy, Kyle Riggs."

"Hello, Colonel Riggs," Marvin said politely. "Are you here to destroy my being?"

"Uh—no Marvin," I said. "We're here to destroy the Macros you're shadowing."

"I'm glad to hear that, Colonel."

"Why do you think we're here to shoot you? Have you been a bad robot?"

"By no means. But I'd calculated a small probability that Star Force was displeased by some of my actions in the recent past."

"I am annoyed with you for helping take out our mines at Venus," I said. "But let's talk seriously, Marvin. You realize the Macros will never do anything other than try to destroy you upon detection from now on, right?"

"Yes—unless some other arrangement was made to their satisfaction."

I frowned at that. Once again, I thought to myself I had to figure out a way to clip his wings.

"What do you know about the Worm fleet?" I asked. "Did the Worms set up an ambush here at the ring and wait for the Macros to come through?"

"Yes."

"And how did you talk them out of blasting you?"

"I told them about the approaching Macro fleet."

I frowned at the walls of *Barbarossa* from which Marvin's voice emanated. "Did I get that right? Did you talk the Worms into setting up their ambush?"

"Well, I told them the Macro fleet was coming to their system. They were quite pleased at the prospect of attacking it."

I laughed. "I bet they were. Good going, Marvin. Maybe I didn't screw up by letting you loose in the first place."

"I'm glad you feel that way, Colonel Riggs."

I glanced over at Captain Miklos. He looked doubtful. He probably thought I should lure Marvin into weapons range and blow him away. I had to admit, that was the safest move. He'd done several odd things and right now I was willing to total them all up as a positive for Star Force, but that could change at any time. I couldn't let him run around loose forever. I didn't have an easy way to get him back into my grasp, however.

"Hey Marvin," I said, "would you mind easing off your engines a little and flying back here to join my fleet?"

He didn't answer that one right away. I could tell the neural chains in that brainbox of his were recursing deeply, looking for danger. I could almost hear him thinking *what's his angle?*

"Why would you suggest that, Colonel Riggs?"

There it was—he didn't trust me. It was sad, in a way. I tried to come up with a snappy reply. I didn't want to take a long time to respond. Marvin was smart, and he knew it took us longer to come up with plausible deceptions than it took to tell the truth.

"Actually, I'd like to examine some of the junk you have all over your ship, if you don't mind," I said. "We really need to study both Worm and Macro technologies more closely. So far, we've never captured a Macro ship and brought it back to Earth in one piece. That is doubly true of Worm technology. We know very little about it. We've never even seen one of their spacecraft or their particle weapons up close. Do you have anything like that in your little collection?"

Another hesitation. If he'd been in the room with me, I'd bet he'd be staring at me with at least three of his four cameras. I had his full attention now—or as close to his full attention as any human could warrant.

"I do have samples of Worm technology. In fact, most of my current specimens are scraps of Worm ships. They are quite different, you know. They are more like humans than Macros, being biotics, but they are more—wild, you might say. If that description makes any sense to you. Their technological devices are constructed individually, they are works of art rather than mass-manufactured duplicates."

"Having met them in battle up-close and personal, that makes perfect sense to me. They do seem to fashion their warrior harnesses and kits in a custom fashion. I didn't realize this trait extended to their ship designs."

"Oh, but it does!" Marvin said. He blathered on for a while, telling me how the Worms managed to build various elements of their electronics and drive systems. Even their circuit boards were individually fabricated, being assembled on a substrate of vomitous resin rather than fiberglass.

I knew as I listened that I had him. I waved for the helmsman's attention.

"Range?" I asked quietly.

"He's slowing and gently gliding back toward us," the helmsman said.

I smiled, pleased. Without directly agreeing to anything, Marvin was drifting closer. I got the feeling he was glad to have someone to talk to. Space was a lonely place for a solitary intellect.

Captain Miklos caught my eye and gave me a knowing nod. I was sure he figured we'd lock our lasers on Marvin and blast him the second we could. I hadn't made my decision on that point. The robot was a wild card, but he had yet to do us any real harm.

Marvin and I continued talking for a time, back and forth. Now and then, I checked the ranges, which the helmsman had helpfully relayed to my screen. I was somewhat disturbed when I realized we would reach the Macro fleet before Marvin was within range. He was slowing and drifting toward us at a very gentle rate. He'd only given his course and speed a nudge in our direction. We would be in a firefight with the Macros before he was in our grasp. At that point, we'd probably have bigger things to worry about. Clearly, Marvin's trust was not yet absolute.

I had options, of course. I could change our fleet's trajectory slightly and bring us together faster. That would slow us down in our pursuit of the Macro fleet, however. Hmm. Maybe that was exactly what Marvin wanted. Maybe he was testing us, to see if we were really here to catch him or to catch the Macros. I nodded to myself, feeling a growing certainty I was being tested. Marvin had managed to stay alive in the face of the Macros, Star Force and the Worms. If he was anything, he was adept at survival.

After we broke off our little chat, Captain Miklos turned to me, smiling grimly. "That was masterfully done, Colonel," he said. "I'd underestimated your capacity to deal with these aliens. I can see it must be done with care and subtlety. We'll be in range of the rogue robot after we are engaged with the Macros, but we can always spare a few beams for him."

I snorted. "No," I said. "He won't let us get into range. He's only testing us."

Miklos frowned, uncertain.

"Just watch," I told him.

More hours passed. The Macro fleet had lost three more vessels. The Worms had lost a dozen ships in the same time. The Worms seemed to be running out of steam. They were still making

300

passes at the enemy, but with less of their characteristic vigor. I figured they'd realized we would catch up soon and they should wait to hit hard when we were all together.

The ring that led to Helios loomed near over the next hour. As they drew close, the Macros again fired salvoes of missiles to eliminate any mines they may meet as they passed through the ring. I watched the tiny pinpoints of light flare then quickly fade as nuclear fires cleansed the volume of space in front of the ring. The ships began filing through after that.

The first to vanish were the Macro ships. The Worms followed, then Marvin. We glided up in silence. Every crewmember stared tensely. What was on the other side? The last time we'd jumped, we'd met with the happy surprise of a Worm fleet and enemy wreckage. This time, the surprise might be played upon us.

I glanced at Captain Miklos. He gripped his command chair tightly. His face was staring at the forward wall, squinting as if he expected a painful surprise.

I couldn't see any way we could know what was ahead, and neither did he. Whining about it wasn't going to help either. We sat in our chairs tensely, waiting for the stab of the needle.

We jumped.

-45-

The star known to Earthlings as Aldebaran was a red giant about sixty-five lightyears from our world. From the point of view of Earth it was in the Taurus constellation and lined up with the belt of Orion. The star was truly *huge*, its diameter being forty-four times that of our sun. There were a few crispy planets circling the ancient, monstrous star. Only the planet Helios was in a position to support life. It was a heavy-gravity planet with sunken seas and towering Worm cities that stood like termite mounds here and there on the hot surface.

Nothing shocking occurred as we flew through the ring. The only surprising thing was the behavior of the Worm ships. They were falling farther behind the Macros and veering off slightly—moving above the plane of the ecliptic for the Aldebaran system. I studied them, frowning.

"What are they up to?" Captain Miklos asked, becoming nervous. "Their ships are no longer in range of the Macros. They've broken off."

"They probably decided to hit them again when we catch up. Maybe they finally realized we can't go any faster than we are currently traveling. A bit of math will predict the intersect of this fleet and the Macros. Speaking of that, when will we catch them, helmsman?"

"Just short of the next ring, sir," he said, working his computer.

"Excellent. I didn't want to have to wait until we reached the next system to fight them. I'd like to see Eden again, but every jump we make is nerve-wracking at this speed."

"It bothers me too, sir," Captain Miklos said. "But I'm not used to spreading my atoms over lightyears via alien technology. You've done it a number of times. Is there some special danger I should be aware of?"

I chuckled. "Using a little imagination, the dangers are countless."

"Sir?"

I took a deep breath. "Think about it, captain. What if the ring on the far side malfunctions, or simply isn't there? Worse, we've see these rings switch on and off. There's even some evidence to indicate they can be reset to go to a different destination. What if we came out in the atmosphere of a planet? The rings on Venus and the one on Helios both are inside the gaseous envelop of a world which connects to a point in space."

Miklos stared at me. He shook his head. "We'd be smashed like ants, sir. At this speed, hitting an atmosphere would be like hitting a wall of granite."

"Exactly," I said. "Now you know why I'm nervous. I don't expect a problem, but I can imagine plenty of them."

Miklos sat back in his chair and looked disturbed. I shook my head. He shouldn't have asked me.

Many hours passed. We were gaining on the Macros, but only slightly. To make matters worse, they seemed to be more capable of managing curving course changes. As the next ring wasn't perfectly lined up with the entry point into the Aldebaran system, we had to turn our ships toward the next ring. Since we were already moving at high speed, we had to fight our own inertia. We would still catch up with the enemy before they escaped the Worm system, but it was going to be a close thing.

I didn't like cutting things closely. I didn't like the prospect of failing to catch them and having to fly into the unknown yet again at these speeds. We couldn't afford to slow down, or they would lose us. We couldn't veer off and miss the next ring either, as that would only leave us with the long process of braking, turning around and going back through it. The maneuver would take us a day or so at least, depending on how cautiously we moved. No, we were committed and I hated it. I much preferred to keep an enemy guessing. An enemy that knew what you were going to do many long hours ahead of time had plenty of opportunities to screw you over.

Marvin now flew between us and the Macros. He'd slid through the ring, but had managed to stay out of range of every gun in all three fleets. I could hardly blame him. Slowly, he was drifting closer to us. But he wasn't going to let himself come into laser range. We'd plotted his flight path. At no point did it enter the globe on my screen that represented our possible range of fire.

As there was nothing better to do, I headed back into the troop pod and played games on rolled-up screens with the marines. Kwon and I had a drink or two—the man never entered battle without a body-warm flask of something on him. When I grew tired I headed back to the bridge to sleep in my command chair with Captain Miklos and his crew.

I noticed how the marines and flight crew didn't really mix. I thought about urging them to sit down together, but decided against it. We were about to get into a death fight with more cruisers than we'd ever dealt with before. If these men didn't want to cozy up with one another, that was their business.

I fell asleep for an entire shift in my chair. I probably couldn't have done it without the help of Kwon's rotgut. When I woke up, I saw Miklos' face near mine. He was tapping on my visor.

My armored hand reached up and batted away his hand. I saw him wince in pain. When a battle-suited hand slapped you, it hurt.

"Sorry," Captain Miklos said, withdrawing out of my face.

"Me too," I said, groaning and stretching. "What's up?"

"There's an incoming message, sir."

"From who?"

"The Worms. They are repeating a message over and over."

Frowning, I pulled up the symbol set on my computer. The first one was the grub-thing which I'd seen before. It meant buddy or hunting-partner. The next one was an image of something big and round. The last one was some kind of odd organ. If I had to guess, it might have been an eyeball. But that was only a guess.

"What the hell are these things?" I asked no one in particular. I needed a hot shower, my brain was slightly fuzzy.

"Barbarossa has no clue," Miklos said.

"I thought these ships could speak Worm."

"They know everything we've recorded from past transactions. But the last two of these symbols are new to us, and the ships."

"How long until we reach the enemy line?" I asked.

"A little under two hours."

I shook my head. "That's cutting it close. You should have awakened me sooner."

Miklos and the helmsman exchanged glances and shrugged. I heaved myself to a standing position and made irritated noises. I headed for the elimination chamber and struggled to get my helmet off. I gulped coffee and thought about a shower. There wasn't really enough time.

"Barbarossa," I shouted. "Forward that message to Marvin. Request a translation."

"Message sent," said the ship.

"Sirs?" the helmsman spoke up suddenly. "The Macros are changing formation."

I stumbled out the elimination chamber and climbed back into my crash seat. I shook my head to clear it. "What the hell are they doing?"

No one answered. As we watched, the enemy fleet spread out, seemingly in every direction. Ships went, up, down and sideways. They were slowing, too.

"We have them!" I said. "They have decided not to dare another ring. They are going to turn and fight. We've run them up the proverbial tree, gentlemen."

Miklos didn't answer. He looked less convinced of victory and more worried than I was.

"Full deceleration," the helmsman said. "Scattered pattern. Could they be running into something?"

I frowned at him, then addressed the ship. "Any answer from Marvin yet, Barbarossa?"

"Incoming now."

I heard Marvin's voice next. "Symbol translations vary. The first one indicates a hunting party or comradery."

"I know that."

"The second symbol is the image of their sun, the red giant known to humans as Aldebaran."

"Okay, what does it mean?"

"It means many things. Life, heat, danger. It depends on context."

"Wonderful. What about the last one?"

"That is an image of a Worm organ. Specifically, the optical organ located in the anterior portion of Worm physiology."

"Huh," I said, trying to puzzle that one out. Hunting-partner, sun, eyeball.... No wonder *Barbarossa* had no clue. "What does it all mean in this context, Marvin?"

"I could only guess."

"Then guess!"

"Since we are close to combat, I would assume the sun means danger. I would also hazard that the eyeball means either watchfulness, or a forward perspective."

I suddenly had it. "Are you telling me the Worms are saying, 'Friends, danger ahead?'"

"Yes," Marvin said. "That would summarize the concepts nicely."

"Well," Miklos said. "The enemy *are* directly ahead of us. And they are turning to fight now."

"Yeah, but they sent this even before the Macros started turning around."

"Colonel," the helmsman said. "There's something else. The Macros—one of them just blew up, sir."

"Why?"

"Nuclear explosive, low-yield. They probably hit a mine."

I stared at him for a long second, thinking.

"Mines," I said. "The Worms put a mine field out here in the middle of open space, on the likely path between the two rings. That way, the enemy couldn't just blow them up the way they've been doing with tightly placed fields right in front of the rings."

"Two more explosions. One more Macro destroyed, another damaged."

"New message incoming from the Worms, sir."

Worried, I examined the new symbol-set on the screen. The first and second symbols were the same. The last one, however, was a full-sized worm warrior.

"Tell me what this is, Marvin."

"Friend, danger, and the raging worm warrior," Marvin mused. "In this case, I think they are marveling at our bravery. It is a compliment, sir."

"Our bravery? Why the hell are the complimenting us now?"

Captain Miklos made a strangled sound, then turned to me with a white face. "We must be *in it*, sir. The minefield."

I nodded. That had to be it. "Hit the brakes!" I shouted. "Turn us around for full thrust deceleration. Helmsman, give me numbers. How long until we are within effective range?"

"Less than ten minutes sir. They are ahead of us on the deceleration curve. In fact, we are going to plow right into them, even while braking at full power."

I struggled with my helmet. I clanked back to the troop pods. The door melted away and a platoon of startled marines looked at me. No one was buttoned up, not even Kwon.

"This is it, marines!" I roared. "Suit-up tight, double-time. Check your gear and say your prayers. We've got about ten minutes to live."

-46-

Barbarossa began firing her lasers automatically when we reached effective range. By then, two of our destroyers and four smaller ships had eaten a mine. The only consolation was that the enemy had lost three more cruisers.

I noted with chagrin that the Worm ships remained unscathed. No doubt they had a friend-or-foe recognition system which prevented the mines from detonating against their hulls. Bitterly, I watched my ships vanish one after another in puffs of white brilliance. No wonder they thought we were brave. They'd warned us about the danger, but we'd plowed ahead, determined to battle the machines in the midst of a widespread low-density minefield. I supposed I could have asked them for the code and the signal frequency of their mine-recognition system, but it would have taken days. We could barely communicate at this point, and no doubt they were as puzzled by our symbol translations as we were theirs. Transferring technical information was out of the question. There simply wasn't time.

The enemy were down to less than thirty cruisers when we came within range of their cannons. At that point, the Macros pulled an unexpected move. They trained their guns on *Barbarossa* and poured fire into my destroyer.

As closely as I could figure, they must have caught our radio signals and listened in. They clearly knew *Barbarossa* was the command ship, the one sending out orders to the others. Either that, or it was blind luck when Macro Command picked my ship to

308

concentrate upon. I don't believe in that kind of luck, so as our ship took a hammering, I cursed wildly in my helmet. Our communications were too open, our encoding weak.

I didn't get much time for cursing or thinking of any kind. The ship's hull couldn't take this kind of punishment. The first burst of fire ripped the roof off overhead. My only thought was it was a good thing we didn't get hit low. They would have knocked out my marines in the troop pod, which hung in the belly of the ship.

"Eject!" I screamed over the ship's com system. "All hands eject!"

The ship went into a spin. *Barbarossa* was already dead, her brainbox must have been hit. I could tell by the behavior of the smart-metal walls. They didn't bother to twist and reform themselves into smooth shapes. They stayed frozen like splattered solder. I could see star moving by laterally outside, indicating we were in a slow spin.

The helmsman was dead at his post. Something had punched through his relatively thin Fleet suit, probably a piece of shrapnel from the ship's hull. Captain Miklos shot out of the opening in the roof however, and I followed. When we were outside the dead ship, I saw flashes nearby.

"Keep moving! Head directly away from the ship!"

The Macros were still pouring fire at the crippled *Barbarossa*. I grabbed Miklos, as his suit didn't have propulsion power on its own, and I dragged him with my boot repellers at full power. We zoomed away from the ship laterally until we were at a safe distance. The ship blossomed into a flare of brilliance behind us that made my autoshades black out momentarily.

"Kwon, did you make it out?"

"Yes, sir," Kwon's signal came to me. His voice was clear and strong.

I smiled, looking around. A dark shape blotted out part of Aldebaran. Silhouetted by the massive blazing orange sphere, Kwon looked small, but he was relatively close to me. I was unsurprised. He seemed to have an extra sense useful only when it came to finding me when we were under fire.

I joined the platoon local circuit, and I could hear Kwon shouting in my helmet. He was working to gather the rest of the men to our position. We were soon flying in a loose formation in the general direction the rest of the fleet was headed.

I let him do his work and had a look around. We couldn't really see the other ships, they were out there in the darkness, close in astronomical terms, but too distant to make out with the human eye. Occasionally, we saw flares and flashes as ships died to either mines or enemy fire. Most of any space battle was like that, they were generally cold silent affairs. The void felt empty even in the midst of a passing fleet.

"How many got out, First Sergeant?" I asked.

"Fourteen sir—including us."

I nodded, pleased. Really, for having just bailed out of a dead destroyer, we'd beaten the odds.

"Who have you got there, sir?" Kwon asked me.

"Captain Miklos."

"Is he dead?"

I looked down at the figure in my grasp. I had his suit bunched up in my armored fist, holding him by the scruff of the neck. He was limp. I gave him a gentle shake. His body flopped like a rag doll in the mouth of a terrier.

"Captain? Are you alive in there?" I asked.

I got no response.

"Hmm," I said, "I don't think his suit has lost integrity. He'd be frozen stiff if it had. Maybe he lost consciousness somewhere along the way."

"Very good, sir," Kwon said. "What are your orders?"

"Keep flying. We need to turn feet first and start braking hard."

Kwon relayed those instructions and I ordered a radio blackout except for short-range unit communications. I decided I wasn't going to attempt to command the whole Fleet now, they were on their own. The Macros were gunning for me, and I might as well let them think I was dead.

"I think I've got good predictive numbers on the locations of the nearest enemy cruisers. If they haven't changed course much, we can intersect them at about a half-degree sunward from here."

We adjusted our trajectory and kept braking. The key difficulty was going to be our relative speeds. The Macros had been slowing down a lot. I hoped we could slow down even faster, matching their speeds. If we were going too fast when we hit the cruiser line, we would crash into them at killing velocity, or shoot right past. If we slowed down too much, we wouldn't reach them. It was a difficult set of calculations, but I had an officers' suit on, which had a superior brainbox. Still, I was worried. I needed better intel on the enemy fleet. We'd left our vessel so early in the battle, we couldn't expect to be perfectly on target.

With about one minute to go before the two fleets were scheduled to clash and fly through one another, I decided to chance a call on an open circuit.

"Marvin," I called. "Do you recognize my voice? Don't use my name, just say yes or no."

The response came several long seconds later. "Yes."

"Please use binary to upload the coordinates, relative course and velocity of the nearest enemy vessel."

The signal came in a moment later. I relayed it to my surviving marines. I tapped the green accept destination button virtually with my armored finger in space. I couldn't even see my hand in the blackness, but feedback in the suit allowed me to feel as if I was tapping at the virtual screen displayed on my HUD.

I was lurched around sickeningly as my suit's autopilot engaged. We had been heading in what was decidedly the wrong direction. In fact, as I swung around and began to accelerate in our direction of travel, I realized we'd been braking too long. The enemy was still ahead of us. I wasn't sure how far.

We flew on into the night, squinting ahead. Then I saw it, a pitch-black Macro cruiser. There were no running lights, as the machines didn't believe in safety. The ship looked bigger up close, something like a medium-sized office building in space. I knew we were coming toward the front of it, as we'd have been able to see the blue glow of the engines if we'd come up from behind.

"There," I said to Kwon, pointing. "How many grenades do we have?"

"An even dozen, sir."

Normally, it took as many as ten hits to ensure a cruiser was destroyed. They were very tough vessels.

"Throw all of them and break off," I ordered.

The operation went almost perfectly. We only lost a single man who had some kind of control malfunction at the last moment. I was never sure why, but he drifted too close to the final explosion and was vaporized with the Macro ship.

I didn't dare communicate with my fleet, but I could read the situation fairly well. The three fleets seemed to be locked in combat, neither side retreating. They'd matched speeds and now sat in space, taking one another out one at a time. The Worm ships seemed particularly effective, flying in erratic, swooping patterns around the enemy ships and slashing them with their particle beams. I hoped they wouldn't notice us and take a potshot.

A few minutes, we followed Marvin's second set of coordinates. We let our suits do the maneuvering and approached a second cruiser, which was locked in a fight with two Worm ships that swung around it like moths circling a lantern. The problem was, we were out of grenades and our arm-mounted beamers were never going to cut through that thick hull.

"The missile ports are opening up," I shouted. "Let's go for it."

Kwon relayed the order. A dozen shadows joined us as we tightened our formation, all intent on a single goal. A Macro missile flared brightly as we reached the port. I realized in an instant the cruiser was firing, probably at the Worms that circled the ship. It launched with a gush of hot vapor, and I could see the Macro technician driving the missile as it left its rack.

Macro missiles were not configured the same way ours were. They did not have to be as aerodynamic, as they were normally used in space. They were really small, suicidal spaceships. The pilot was just another machine, a crewmember bent on his own self-destruction.

I'd seen a missile like this up-close in the ground at Andros, where we'd tried to defuse it. Then it had been half-buried in the earth, however, and badly damaged. The nose section of the missile was the warhead, in the form of a metal cone. The midsection held the Macro pilot, enclosed in a framework of metal tubing. Behind him was the engine with its flaring plume of hot exhaust. The entire thing was a strange sight.

I thought, for just an instant, that the machine saw me as well. Then it was gone in the vastness of space, on a one-way journey to strike down one of our ships.

"Get inside the port, full throttle!" I ordered.

I saw men all around me surge forward in response to my order. I joined them.

The missile port closed as we slipped inside. Not all of us made it. One man had lost a leg, two more were trapped outside, thumping on the hull.

"What now, sir?" Kwon said, breathing hard.

We were cramped in the missile magazine. All around us was machinery and two more missiles. Fortunately, no other Macro technicians had loaded themselves into the last two spots.

Moments after we entered the port, we were rocked and tossed about by an explosion outside—very close. I imagined the missile had found one of the Worm ships or gotten close enough and detonated itself. The men we'd left outside stopped sending us signals, and I figured we would never find any remains.

"Disable these missiles," I ordered. "I don't want them taking out any more friendly ships."

"And after that?"

I sucked in a lungful of stale, suit air. "After that, we take this ship."

-47-

The fighting went hard, and we almost lost. We never made it to the engine room, the key to taking over any Macro ship. Kwon and I were down to five effectives, having left our wounded and dying in a quiet corner of the ship on the lower decks. Honestly, I thought we were dead. Any moment, I expected the Macro marines to find us and finish us off, or for our own fleet to blast the ship into fragments, unaware they'd killed their own commander.

In the end, help came from an unexpected source. Reflecting back on the situation, it was the only help that could have come.

A monstrous entity of shambling metal slithered down the passages, showering sparks as it came. I knew from experience most of the sparks were from the bare metal wires it touched as it passed by. Macro crews tended not to bother insulating their power wires. The monster itself was constructed of seemingly random articles of metal. The hind legs that pushed it forward had the grasshopper-like, spring-loaded anatomy of a Macro worker. But the head section and the torso was an open framework of steel tubing. What identified the creature to me, were the three whipping black arms that sprouted from the thorax region and which the thing used to drag its body forward along the passage.

"What the nine hells is that, sir?" Kwon asked me in a whisper.

I stared at it for a second, then turned to Kwon, grinning inside my helmet. "That's Marvin. Hold your fire, everyone!"

The marines did as they were told, but they weren't happy about it. They kept their weapons trained upon the approaching abomination, ready to blast it the moment it made a false move.

"Hello, Colonel Riggs," it said. The voice seemed very strange, being so civilized while emanating from such a frightening source.

"Where's the rest of you, Marvin?" I asked.

"Outside on the hull. I found a long burn-through scar on the dorsal side of the ship. The Worms must have done it."

"Yeah," I said, leaning back against the wall of the ship. "I assume Star Force has taken the rest of the ship?"

"No, I'm afraid not."

"Uh, why are you here then?"

"To warn you that this ship is scheduled for demolition. It's still active, and your replacement commander is systematically destroying all the vessels that didn't escape."

There were a string of things I didn't like about Marvin's statement. I fixated on the main point, however, which involved our survival.

"Why didn't you tell them I was aboard this ship?"

"Because the Macros are listening in to our communications. I didn't want the enemy to target you, sir."

"Oh yeah," I said. I had to agree with his logic. During our conflicts with the Macros since our rebellion, they'd taken pains to pinpoint my position and they seemed to be gunning for me. I heaved myself upright and my marines did the same. There were a number of groans.

"All right," I said. "How do we get out of here?"

"Follow me, sir."

We did so, picking up our survivors on the way. Fortunately, we were able to clamp them onto the back of Marvin's strange body. As he humped and sparked his way through the ship, our wounded flopped about on his back. Those that were able to do so, complained bitterly.

We found the rip in the hull Marvin had spoken of. It was a tight squeeze for him, but was easily managed by my marines. We were soon floating free in space.

"Are there any more active Macro cruisers in the area?"

"No sir, but several of them haven't been knocked out yet."

"Who is running fleet ops then?"

315

"Commodore Decker."

I winced. He was one of Crow's hand-picked favorites. The man was old guard British navy, with little in the way of imagination. He was competent, if annoying.

"Commodore Decker?" I called on an open channel. "This is Colonel Riggs, please respond."

The response didn't come for another minute or so. I began to become annoyed. "Commodore Decker, I repeat, this is—"

"Riggs? Where have you been hiding, man?"

"Inside the belly of a Macro cruiser."

"Humph. Glad to hear you made it."

"Let's connect on a private channel, Decker."

"I'm in the middle of Fleet ops now, so I'm afraid I can't chit-chat, Riggs."

"Private channel, please."

A few moments later, I had my private chat with him. He didn't want to give up ops, having assumed command when *Barbarossa* was hit and he'd figured I'd been lost. I couldn't blame him for that, but I didn't want these disabled Macro ships destroyed. After a short argument, he recognized my authority as mission commander and I resumed command. My surviving marines were taken aboard a second destroyer where they suffered the probing ministrations of the ship's medical room. Fortunately, I'd escaped serious injury. I avoided the skinny black arms of the medical nanites as well and let my own personal nanites repair my body. The process would be slower, but I would stay more lucid. For command, that was a necessity.

I managed to cancel all efforts to destroy the crippled enemy ships. We left the hulks floating in space and headed for the ring to Eden, through which the last handful of enemy ships had escaped. I was angry with Commodore Decker for not pressing ahead and stopping them, but the damage had been done. On the positive side, I had to admit he'd done a fair job of mopping up and managing a bad situation. We'd won the battle due to our superior numbers and the weakness of the Macro fleet after it had hit the Worm minefield first.

That thought brought me around to the Worms, who were still following us. They were down to seventy-three ships, while we had only forty effectives. I was glad to see half the Star Force destroyers had survived the engagement. I wanted to have something left to return to Crow when I went home.

We rolled through the Eden ring at a relatively cautious pace. No one knew what we'd meet on the far side, but I wasn't comfortable with allowing even a fraction of the enemy to escape if I could help it. If nothing else, they were carrying away copious amounts of intelligence about our strength and tactics.

On the far side, we were greeted with no explosions, enemy fleets or the like. Instead, I was treated again with the vista of Eden. A yellow star sat in the center, burning with unusual stability. A tightly-held ring of hot planets hugged the star's waist. Mid-system a band of six lovely, inhabitable worlds orbited at a stately pace. Farther out was the lone gas giant and beyond that were several far-flung, frozen rocks.

It took us a few minutes, but the sensory data soon came in. The enemy cruisers were retreating away toward the opposite side of the system. I had to wonder if there was another ring out there among the outlying ice-worlds. There didn't seem to be any other destination that made sense in that direction.

We posted a sentry ship at the ring and pursued the enemy. I relayed news of our battle through the sentry, knowing it would eventually get back to Earth via the chain of ships I'd left at each ring. Even at the speed of light, the radio waves would take several days to reach Star Force back on Andros Island, but at least Sandra and the rest of our homeworld would know the fleet had been victorious and had ground the enemy down to almost nothing.

A tense moment came when our sensor-data began to paint the picture from the rest of the Eden system. I knew there were enemy Macro ships here, orbiting the habitable worlds. At least there had been when I'd left the Centaurs to their fate.

I restlessly watched the screens as the brainboxes located enemy ships and Centaur satellites. Eventually, large Macro machines were spotted roaming the surfaces of various planets. The ships were what mattered to me most. I was relieved when the facts were displayed on the forward walls. There were only six cruisers garrisoning the system, the same number I'd seen when I'd last visited here.

A broad smile spread across my features. They were not going to be able to face us. We were too many, too strong. Besides that, they'd been beaten several times in a row by this fleet, and their instinct would be to run, and to keep running until they had the power to turn and destroy us once and for all.

As that thought crossed my mind, my smile diminished. If they truly were fleeing to the next ring—to yet another star system I'd never seen, what might be waiting for me there? For all I knew, the next system held their local nexus in the region. A vast armada could be nearby, and I had no way of knowing the truth.

Commodore Decker hailed me. I answered the call on a direct channel.

"I say we turn around," he said without preamble.

"No," I replied firmly. "I will not abandon the Centaurs a second time. I made a commitment to these people the last time I was here. We will press ahead."

I heard him mumble something, but could not make out the words. The channel with the Commodore closed suddenly. Information regarding the status of the Centaurs began to flow soon thereafter. They had two fewer satellites than they had possessed when we'd last visited. A grim development for a people who seemed to be on the edge, and who were precariously situated with their entire known population located in vulnerable satellite habitats. I wondered how many of them had died, and how the Macros had engineered their demise.

"Incoming alien message, Colonel," Marvin said into my helmet suddenly.

"What is it, Marvin?"

"It's the Centaurs, sir."

"Open a channel, I wish to speak to them."

"The message isn't for you, sir. It's for me."

"What?"

"I—I don't understand. I believe I'm—I'm experiencing an update, sir. I'm about to restart, sorry."

"What?" I shouted the question. Concern ran through me. *An update?* I thought of all the times software had spuriously updated itself on my home computer. Marvin's mind would be destroyed.

"Jam that signal," I ordered. "Helmsman, you are in charge of communications. Jam the alien signal coming from the Centaurs."

"Uh, yes sir," the helmsman said, he began speaking urgently with the destroyer's brainbox. Soon a powerful signal was sent out into space around us.

I ordered the crew to direct cameras toward Marvin, who was following us in his junkyard ship. An image came onto the screen that filled me with worry. Marvin was drifting. His engines had stopped. He was lifeless.

We slowed long enough for a long ship's arm to reach out and latch onto him. I felt the loss deeply. Somehow, I'd lost another friend. Oddly, I felt it more than I did most deaths, as this one was a unique intellect. And partly, I suspected, because I had helped create Marvin, to make him what he was.

How could I feel attached to this bizarre robot? I wasn't sure, but I did feel something. I was left staring at the screen in grief.

-48-

Marvin didn't show any signs of life for the next several minutes. As each moment passed, my hopes faded. I was reminded of the day my children had died at the cold steel hands of a ship like the one we flew within now. Marvin's mind had been stilled by an automated, thoughtless subsystem.

Quite possibly, the Centaurs hadn't ordered the download of a blank intellect into his brainbox. When we'd last left Eden, they'd been in the act of transmitting the contents of a powerful brainbox to give us information about other species and the like. The operation had been suspended when we'd left the system before the download was complete. That partial mind of Marvin's had made him what he was, had given him his unique personality.

I imagined the original download had been queued since we'd left the region by some server on their side. Months had passed, but the moment their server detected Marvin's return, it had decided to finish what it had started. He seemed to have no choice or defense against the erasure of his mind. I supposed any piece of software set up to accept automated updates would be in the same situation.

I sighed.

"Sir, the Centaurs are attempting to communicate."

"Keep jamming them."

"But sir, this could be seen as a diplomatic breach."

I stared at the young lieutenant. "I don't care. Continue jamming."

The helmsman turned away. He appeared huffy about it. I truly didn't care what he thought. I watched the screen with Marvin being dragged behind us. As I watched, an oddment of metal peeled away and was lost in space behind us. He was beginning to disintegrate—or at least his collection of junk was.

After about five minutes, I heard a weak signal in my helmet. "Restart complete."

"Marvin?"

"Backup restoring. Please wait...."

Breathing through my teeth, I waited. I felt like a father hovering outside an operating room.

Finally, Marvin's voice came through again. "Colonel Riggs?" he asked. "What happened? I appear to have malfunctioned. Am I being towed or am I a prisoner?"

I laughed. "You are being towed," I assured him. "You—sort of fainted."

I explained the download the Centaur brainboxes were trying to make to him and the automatic nature of such things. I could tell while conversing with him his mind was undamaged. I supposed the system worked in a similar fashion to an earthly computer system when doing an update—it didn't erase the old software until the new code was completely downloaded and ready to install. My jamming had caused it to retry for a while, then give up and call it a failure. The update operation had timed out, and then reloaded the backup, meaning Marvin's original mind. Marvin's mind had been restored.

"Originally, your software was interrupted while being downloaded from their computers," I told him. "I think that's why you've always been so inquisitive. You are always looking for the missing part."

"Perhaps the download should be allowed to continue," he said. "I'd like to know more of my origins."

"I don't think it will work that way, buddy. You are what you are *because* the download was incomplete. If it is allowed to finish, you'll be different. I would suspect your memories will be erased as well."

"How awful. Are these Centaur creatures barbarians?"

"I don't think so. They don't understand you and your unique mind. The computers that originally copied you to our systems know the job was never finished. They are only trying to complete what they started."

"I see, and you interrupted the process?"

"Yes."

"Why, Colonel Riggs? I've been so much trouble for you."

"Yeah," I admitted. "But you've been a friend as well. I'll tell you what, Marvin. If you will give up your flying body, I'll protect your mind from this transmission."

Marvin hesitated. "Give up my body?"

"Not entirely, just the space propulsion systems. I'd like to have you aboard as a regular member of Star Force. Maybe you could assume a humanoid shape, so you fit into our environments more naturally."

At this point, the helmsman swiveled in his chair and stared at me. His expression clearly indicated he thought I was stark, raving mad. I gave him an irritable frown, and then ignored him.

"I will accept," Marvin said after a time, "if I'm allowed to study the specimens I've found."

"That seems reasonable. I just want you to be ground-based, not a spaceship anymore, Marvin."

"I understand, Colonel Riggs."

I suspected that he truly did.

* * *

The following days brought significant changes to our tactical situation and presented us with new choices. We followed the Macro cruisers toward the outer planets. At a certain key point, each of the enemy cruisers that circled the six habitable worlds on guard duty suddenly left orbit. At perfectly matching speeds, they accelerated to join the fleet we were chasing after.

I'd managed to talk to the herd peoples of Eden and get them to turn off Marvin's download. They did so without an argument, telling me the sky was bountiful and the winds would forever ruffle my fur. Something like that. I was sure to them, they were paying me the highest of compliments for coming back and driving the Macros out of their system.

I anxiously watched this development with my command staff. But according to all our calculations, they were all targeting the same remote point, the spot which we suspected contained a second hidden ring in the Eden system. I realized thoughtfully that every system we'd visited thus far had at least two rings. The Aldebaran system had three, including the small one on Helios. Even the blue giant, which we believed to be the star Bellatrix, must have had more than one ring. How else had the Macros appeared at our Venus ring with over a hundred ships? I'd gone through the Venus ring personally and seen the blue giant system on the other side. I hadn't found another ring, but I'd only been there a short time. I was certain, however, there had not been over a hundred enemy cruisers in the system.

All logic pointed toward the conclusion the Macros were abandoning Eden. They were badly outnumbered against our fleet and the Worm fleet combined. I decided to continue pressing onward, to drive the machines as far as I could. Not everyone in my command staff agreed with this decision.

The very first relayed message I received from Earth was from Crow. It was impossible via our system to have a real conversation. All we could do was transmit a recording of our voices over the vast distances, in each case relayed via the ships I'd posted for this very duty at each of the rings. Each ship caught the message, flew through the ring to the next system in the chain and relayed the message to the next ship waiting at the next ring. Even at the speed of light, the distance between the rings required hours of transmission time to cross each star system. When I finally did get something from Crow, it was about two days old. I played it privately in my helmet while sitting in a command chair in the destroyer.

"Riggs? This is Admiral Jack Crow, the supreme commander of all Star Force Fleet operations…"

I suppressed the urge to roll my eyes, but kept listening.

"…I've received and reviewed Commodore Decker's report concerning your engagements with the enemy. I want to say right off mate, I'm impressed. I'm not sure how you made friends with those slimy Worm bastards, but I guess it turned out for the best. You've managed to drive the Macros from two systems, and as I understand it now, you are pushing across a third system.

"But Riggs, I want to caution you. There is no way you can continue your string of victories forever. You are the conquering hero now, but you must halt your rampage and consolidate our gains. We've conquered four systems now, including our own. That should be enough. We can't even defend them all, and I don't want you to keep fighting until you lose all my ships and leave Earth defenseless. Crow out."

I frowned fiercely, not liking the message. I didn't bother to listen to it a second time. I deleted it in fact, purging it from my system. I sat there, thinking hard. The crew around me tossed me frequent glances, but I maintained my stony silence. I had a decision to make.

Crow had a point. I knew in some ways he was right. Logically, I couldn't go on forever. If I jumped again through the next ring, none of us knew what we would encounter. A hundred more cruisers, or a million more mines could be waiting for us. It could be the end of our fleet.

The other side of the argument was the one I couldn't get out of my head. I wanted to destroy every Macro I'd encountered. I didn't want any of them to escape. After a string of victories, I found myself wanting more. I realized I'd begun to have fantasies of ending this war right now, of pushing the enemy to the ends of the universe and destroying them all.

A beeping began in my helmet. I glanced at the readout. It was Commodore Decker. I let out a growling breath. I knew without a doubt he had received a message from Crow as well. At this point, the system worked like email with voice attachments. There was no central control, no easy way to find out what anyone else with an account was hearing. I had dark thoughts as the beeping continued. Perhaps in future updates, this system should become more centralized and controlled.

I opened the channel at last. "What is it, Commodore?"

"Riggs? Why are we still following the enemy?"

"Because I plan to destroy every Macro I see, Decker. That is my mission."

There was a pause. "Have you gotten any messages, Colonel?"

"From who?"

"From Star Force."

I closed my eyes and bit back a stream of curses. Crow *had* sent him a message. From the sound of it, he'd told Decker what he was telling me, that we should cease and desist.

"I heard what Crow had to say, Decker," I told him. "I was not impressed."

"Colonel," Decker began, but then his voice shifted. He paused, as if uncertain. "I understand, Riggs. I understand how you feel, and how you think. We have them on the run. The enemy that had eluded us for so long."

I opened my eyes. "Yes. Yes, that's it exactly. I've got them, and I don't want to let them get away now."

"You are an excellent tactician, Riggs," Decker continued. "But this is a strategic decision. You need to elevate your thinking. Contemplate the bigger picture, that's all I ask. Commodore Decker out."

I did think about it. It was impossible not to. We'd chased the Macros out of our home system, and pushed them back from three more. Was that enough? Was it time now to lick our wounds, to rebuild and plan our next move? It would be a great waste to lose these systems. What if the Centaurs could help us by building their own fleet, given the time? We could work on better communications with the Worms, and let them rebuild as well. Star Force was no longer in this alone. We were leading a coalition of sorts.

"Sir?" the helmsman asked a half hour later. "We are coming to a decision point. Are we going to head straight on toward the ring or are we going to start decelerating? If we don't start braking now, we'll overshoot the target area even if we turn around and apply full power."

I grunted unhappily. Every eye in the cabin sought mine, then looked away.

"Keep going," I said at last. "We'll chase these machines out of the Eden system. I don't want them to have a moment of peace. I don't want them to even think they've escaped us."

Glum and determined, the crew turned back to their boards and relayed my instructions. We flew onward. A few hours later, the enemy fleet formed a tight formation and disappeared through the ring. It was at that very moment a message came in from the Worm ships. I contacted Marvin, who came to the bridge.

Marvin had given himself yet another makeover. I forced a smile when I saw him. He was truly horrifying to look upon now, all wires and struts and random pieces of equipment. He had somehow formed himself into a hulking humanoid shape however, as I'd suggested. The most disconcerting thing about him was the whipping arms. There were seven of them, all of varied lengths. He moved via these snake-like independent tentacles, slithering over the hull of the ship. At any given point, four of the tentacles reached out and grasped walls and chair backs around him, presumably for support. The entire ungainly mess didn't look very well balanced. A dozen camera eyes poked out of his body-mass at odd points such as the lower knee-joints and two from one shoulder. Every camera simultaneously moved and tracked something different.

The overall effect was very disconcerting for a human observer. The helmsman made an odd whooping sound, as if he'd swallowed his own tongue, when the robot loomed near. I had to admit, Marvin was a monstrosity. Wisps of vapor escaped his misshapen body when he moved, and I could tell he was still freezing-cold from the depths of space. I felt him chill the air as he passed by my chair.

"Welcome aboard, Marvin," I said as warmly as I could. I wanted him to feel at home. I figured I could help him edit himself later.

"Thank you, Colonel Riggs," Marvin said in cheery fashion. "Is something wrong with your helmsman?"

"He appears to have eaten too much for lunch," I said.

A few cameras studied the helmsman, who withered under the scrutiny. A tentacle snapped out toward him, and the helmsman flinched. But the skinny little black arm only grabbed the back of his chair and steadied Marvin's central mass.

"I apologize if my appearance is intimidating," he said to the squirming lieutenant.

"Marvin, I need you translate a new message from the Worms," I told him.

"Certainly, Colonel."

I relayed the message to him. It consisted of four symbols. The first two consisted of the grub and the raging Worm warrior. I got that much of it. They were telling us we were friends and brave. I confirmed this with Marvin, and he agreed with my interpretation. The third was an image of a full-bodied Worm, but not in battle gear. The fourth was of an odd, finger-like structure.

"The third symbol is that used to refer to all Worms, not just warriors," Marvin explained. "It means 'the people'."

"And the second?"

"That is an image representing their home mounds."

"Hmm," I said thoughtfully. "They are talking about home and civilians? Is that it?"

"Yes."

I puzzled the message for a minute or so, but then the Worms made their meaning clear. They began braking hard. Soon, we were plunging alone toward the next ring where the Macros had vanished.

"Sir?" asked the helmsman. "What now?"

I sat in my command chair and stared into space—literally. It was decision time.

-49-

In the end, I ordered the fleet to power-slide to a halt. We all did a one-eighty, and poured on engine power, braking as hard as we could. Even so, we didn't manage to stop completely before we slid past the newly-discovered ring. We didn't go through it, although the temptation to explore was great.

I didn't know what was on the other side of this ring, and I dearly wished to send a scout through to find out—but I didn't quite dare. The Macros were machines, and machines had software that worked on triggers. Each action I took risked a reaction. There could be a hundred more ships on the far side. They would come through to attack us eventually, but they might wait a year or so before doing it. If I dared to peep beyond the next ring, I might cause an avalanche that would lose everything we'd gained.

No, I decided. If I was going to halt the advance, the halt would be complete. We had to consolidate our gains, and our new allies needed help. There were still mining machines in this system, walking monsters that needed to be sought out and destroyed one my one.

The ring hung over an icy world that was thick with nickel, iron, water and ammonia. There were cyrovolcanoes on the surface, structures that fountained frozen methane, ice crystals and the like when other bodies swung near. The tidal forces caused the planetary interior to heat up inside and shoot thawing liquids up onto the surface where they quickly refroze.

The planet was beautiful in its own cold fashion. It was dark out here so far from the yellow sun which burned brightly in the distance. The system's yellow star did not deliver enough heat to warm this snowball of a world. After we'd come to a halt and begun to slowly turn around, reversing our course and heading home, I got an idea. I had finally had time to really think things through by then.

What occupied my mind more than anything else was the need to hold onto our gains. How could I take what I'd learned in this phase of the war, and apply it to assure victory in the future? After some hard thinking, I came to a conclusion: we'd won the battle with the combination of minefields and our heavy fortifications on Andros. They'd been forced to come through at a certain tight point—the rings—and we'd broken much of their fleet with mines because we knew *where* they had to pass by. The rest of their fleet and their armies had been destroyed by the island itself, fortified as it was with lasers and the like. In that case we'd smashed them against our strongest defensive point. The enemy had helpfully come against our strength, beating their heads against a rock. Unfortunately, fortifying Andros Island further wouldn't win the next battle. I didn't think they could be talked into attacking only that single spot on Earth again.

The trick then, I thought, was to put something like Andros Island out near the rings themselves. The reason Andros had managed to stop a hundred ships was because it wasn't a ship, but an island, a brick of land bristling with weaponry. I decided we needed a platform like that in *space*. A huge structure we could drag out into place or build on the spot. It would have to be *big*, and it would have to put all its power into weapons.

The key problem with ships was the fact it took more power to run engines than it did to run weapons. Most of every ship's power went to the engines, and the guns were therefore comparatively small. But, if I could build a static defensive platform, I could mass heavy weaponry on it and blow away enemy ships as they wriggled through the rings a few at a time. A fort placed in range of a ring would be able to concentrate its fire, outgunning each ship as it came through. That was the key, the enemy would be blind easy to ambush, and they couldn't all come through at once. If I could generate enough firepower to blow away one ship at a

329

time every few seconds, they could throw a thousand ships into an attack and lose them all. And, knowing the Macros, they might just do that.

Minefields weren't going to cut it, and I couldn't station the fleet at every ring forever. We had to build a fortification. Something...*huge*.

I smiled to myself. Possibly, I had the tail of an idea that could win this war—not just another battle.

The End

More Books by B. V. Larson:

STAR FORCE SERIES
Swarm
Extinction
Rebellion
Conquest
Battle Station

IMPERIUM SERIES
Mech Zero: The Dominant
Mech 1: The Parent
Mech 2: The Savant
Mech 3: The Empress

Other Books by B. V. Larson
Technomancer
Velocity
Shifting

Visit BVLarson.com for more information.

Made in the USA
Monee, IL
21 May 2020